INDIAN RIVER CO MAIN LIBRARY

3 2901 00 87 3899

W9-AVB-831

300,000,000

Indian River County Main Library
1600 21st Street
Vero Beach, FL 32960

Also by Blake Butler

FICTION

Sky Saw

There Is No Year

Scorch Atlas

Ever

NONFICTION

Nothing: A Portrait of Insomnia

300,000,000

BLAKE BUTLER

HARPER ● PERENNIAL

NEW YORK ● LONDON ● TORONTO ● SYDNEY ● NEW DELHI ● AUCKLAND

"The Part About Darrel" is for Molly Brodak

HARPER PERENNIAL

THREE HUNDRED MILLION. Copyright © 2014 by Blake Butler. All rights reserved. Printed in the United States of America. No part of this book may be used or reproduced in any manner whatsoever without written permission except in the case of brief quotations embodied in critical articles and reviews. For information address HarperCollins Publishers, 195 Broadway, New York, NY 10007.

HarperCollins books may be purchased for educational, business, or sales promotional use. For information please e-mail the Special Markets Department at SPsales@harpercollins.com.

FIRST EDITION

Designed by Kris Tobiassen of Matchbook Digital

Library of Congress Cataloging-in-Publication Data is available upon request.

ISBN 978-0-06-227185-3

14 15 16 17 18 OV/RRD 10 9 8 7 6 5 4 3 2 1

3 2901 00587 3899

Every hundred feet the world changes.

—ROBERTO BOLAÑO, *2666*

CONTENTS

ONE *THE PART ABOUT GRAVEY*

This word occurs because of god. In our year here god is not a being but a system, composed in dehydrated fugue. Under terror–sleep alive we hear it heaving in and out from the long bruises on our communal eternal corpse, consuming memory. The wrecking flesh of Him surrounds, holds us laced together every hour, over-flowing and wide open, permeable to inverse, which no identity survives. As god is love, so is god not love. Same as I could kill you any minute, I could become you, and you wouldn't even feel the shift. Only when there's no one left to alter, all well beyond any ending or beginning, can actuality commence.

E. N. FLOOD: *This text was transcribed from a white notebook found at the foot of the stairs in the room beneath the home at address* ▮▮▮▮▮▮▮▮▮▮▮▮▮▮*. The original handwriting has been confirmed as that of the home's owner, Gretch Nathaniel Gravey, a forty-five-year-old Caucasian male, who, at the time of this writing, is being held without bond by the State for an as yet undetermined number of charges of murder in the first degree, as evidenced by the mass of human remains found occupying the same aforementioned basement. It is believed that other victims may exist outside the home, though the total tally and identities of even presently known victims remain uncertain due to the severity of their disfigurement and the intermingling of flesh. Gravey, beyond this document, stands mute.*

He who brought me brightest in the image of the human toward god was a series of shapes I knew as Darrel, though quickly I would come to see that's not his name. His name had squirmed as any word, appearing burned into the pages of the unholy books composed alone in pens and tongues by men before we were we, beneath a sky propped up with our lunchmeat flab asleep and praying. Each syllable in how anyone would say his name would deform itself depending on whose mouth was being used, and so the name could lace within all language. His name appeared inside all ageless rails of light, invoked malformed in the mouths of all as corporations, entertainments, narcotics, art. But with my human mouth I called him Darrel, after the son I'd never have. I lived with Darrel in the black house for more than thirteen billion years before I ever had a body, years in which the flood of ideas we would erect from incubated and formed blood inside our brains. The ground beneath the dirt of our whole future pressed against everything we wanted, became so thin with all the scraping of the nails and all the one-day-buried no ones and all the nothing waking up in our new bodies in the night, that what was left of the foundation underneath us was something so clear and timeless and deranged we couldn't feel it, and so wanted it again then even more, and in that wanting wanted every inch of now to produce further lengths to lust for, new skin to seethe inside of. I mean we began again like night again like night again every time we spoke or saw or felt anything. We were not us as we became us but someone else inside of someone else already all once again enslaved to live again as if we never had or known we could. Who we were from that point forward and what we did to all other bodies, to those hours and those men and women and people, was not us but someone we'd met long ago and wed and loved and killed, and buried over and again each time retaining less until there was nothing left to hump, and since then had wholly disremembered in a wish for preservation of daily sanity beyond where now the color of every mind appeared nightly inside my fleshless rest, wielding the knives of all my coming days repeating, and wearing skin made of all mirrors showing anyone but me, the silence of our deleted adoration so grown out all over our reflected faces and down our backs and up our asses we never even had to open our lids or mouth again to let the shape of night fill up our minds.

FLOOD: *Whether Gravey is using this opening disorientation voice as a way of disclaiming his own actions I am unsure. He seems sometimes to be speaking directly to the reader, while at other times at you or through you or around you; perhaps, forgive me, inside you. Frequently one gets the sense of several of these modes in play at once. There are as well perhaps still other modes I've yet to consider, though I hope that in my exploration of his words I can begin to draw out what lies underneath. Unfortunately, my transcription here removes the context of Gretch Gravey's particularly mangled/child-eyed/dogshit handwriting, which even after just minutes of staring at gives me a fever.*

Having already lived forever now beyond flesh like anybody, I knew I needed actual hands. I needed something I could touch myself with, and so touch others, link their lives. I took the body of a child first, that creature of the widest open brand of devotion. This kid was only one among the millions, arbitrary and impractical as any object is in its design; it could have been you, and maybe was you. Is you now. Like any other costume, then, inside the child's flesh, I had to absorb his human past; what itching infernal plagues and future lust he was wound up by, all the countless forms of bliss and hell crammed in a person even so young. My presence in him rapidly aged him. A week died with his every wet dream, false skies in all fantasies. Years he felt were, to me, only more wallpaper, phlegm in a baby. The more he grew the more I was him and always had been, and likewise his whole frame of orchestration, every fissure. Quickly he was large enough to want to touch others, to fuck others. Through the full child I began then to see in the eyes of others the asphyxiating spectrums they carried, the hues of their assgrabbery. It was easy to want the spectrums for my own; more color and more color's color. Inside the child I began to seek out ways in the world I would be granted access to everything not yet public—I began making friends, using prisms and medication and excess giggling as gifts I believed I enjoyed giving. I took part in pornography and vacations. Though more and more, these weren't enough. No matter which media I perused or substances I ingested or buttons I pushed or hole I inherited, I knew there was something always just beyond my contour, a veil shuddering and vast with the glimmer of mortality all through my gums and tongue continuously, hypercolor with internal wounds of aging. The more I knew I wanted more, the slower time dragged, the more impossible any actual future became as chained to mine. I needed someone less entirely alive than some teen to spread my mechanisms—someone whose brain was already halfway gore, a totem in the house of the human plague that had taken of our spirit so completely, over and over, they could not even feel me making a costume of their organs, their ideas. While on TV I watched the ruin of man go on half-assed in the hands of hilarious dicklickers, I held my place and waited for my promise to reveal the kernel of its cyst, the teething hole through which our becoming could bloat to burst its human frottage.

FLOOD: *Boxes of photographs of a recurring child were discovered in a hidden compartment under Gravey's bed. It was unclear at first if they were evidence of a particular victim, or mementos of his own childhood. The photos seem too recently developed, of contemporary technologies, but the look of the dress and architecture in the photos seem much older. The child doesn't look much like Gravey, and yet neither does he exactly not look like him when in the dark. As it stands, we have yet to find a body living or deceased who seems a right fit for the child, and none of the other boys in the house remembers anyone like him coming among them. In the photos, the child seems happy, even pleasant, though, oddly, in none of the pictures are his eyes open.*

I met Darrel cuz of Gravey. I met Gravey cuz of Josh, and Josh cuz where I went to school there was a breakspot in the fence and during our time between lunch and nothing they would let us out into the yard and we could go out there and wait till no one saw us and slip back through the fence to this long trail that Josh promised went to somewhere awesome and I believed him because I thought the most of all that Josh had ever said. It might have even been true I loved Josh in my soft life then, but I could not admit it to me because he was boy and I was boy; still the rat-make of his hair and how it fell along his shoulders in the yards and other hours not around us would appear when I felt nothing alone in my flesh too, and from his hair inside me I saw his shoulders and could imagine what would be connected just to those, and from there soon in the night I'd be inside him and could be him even and when I was him I put my hands into his (my) pants and with my (his) hands I spread me open and made me go on and even up till now that might be the biggest feeling I have made. Each of us was filled with semen; we wore the worry scars around our holes. There was so much music all those nights each night I died and still was there. And yet, I knew Josh was not my future body. He was too real to me, too much a man. I might have would have wished to enter eternity through Josh instead of Gravey but Josh just liked knives and money and getting messed up, which is why even that afternoon he took me from the school through the mudyard to the house where we met Gravey, who gave us drugs for taking off our shirts and socks and pants and sometimes something else. I knew the instant I saw Gravey I would become him, and he would fill me, and in our collision, god would bend. Gravey didn't try to fuck us mostly, he just did seeing and some fingers in our hair, the heavy breathing, but it was enough to leave him in me ever still, in a different way from Josh, in a way I could never learn to love. His eyes had dartboards in them and some gravel. He was very, very old. While he jacked off we inhaled gases and sometimes too we ate some pills or smoked the earth. Any I ate did big upon me: I was open. I could see then in each a new manner of operating color: how it was true that I had lived seven lives before mine started, like a pet, and how each life inside the life inside the one before it held seven more lives inside it too, though inside no life could I recall the resin of those before. It was the seventh life that made us humans, gave us the symbols through which we could believe we were only ever here and now. This in this as Gravey told us while we splayed before him on the floor in black of smoke-seas that seemed to rise invisible around him. Maybe Gravey did do more things while we were like that, to our bodies. Some hours for days I could not see at all, could not feel the color in me beyond what paper feels like rubbing in my palms.

FLOOD: *Like any of those mentioned by name in this proceeding, including the amorphously rendered "Darrel," no Josh has been identified or come forward. Though we have apprehended numerous suspects believed to be involved with the occurrences at* ███████████████ *during the period of* ███████████ *, the actual number of those involved, like the number of victims, remains in question. It is also as yet unclear to what extent, if at all, any parties who have claimed to live in the house with Gravey were active in his crimes; though some claim compliance and even pleasure, there has been no evidence implicating anyone but Gravey in the physical activity of murder. Many of the stories do not line up. Most of the boys do not acknowledge each other. Some seem to have suffered extreme emotional damage, not to mention what was done to their flesh.*

The space I lay in when I stayed at Gravey's had real mirrors on the walls and ceiling. There were so many of me in there underneath that and beside that I could not see me in the middle of us where I was: a throne of self made of my bone and flesh repeated. Asleep I'd hold so still and never move a second. I thought about asking Gravey some nights if I could come and live there when my father locked me out of the house as he often would for wearing black and speaking in voices that weren't mine, but the question hung inside me plane-sized. I felt devout to nowhere. I slept in the tall grass beside the shed full of old tools when I could not find a way to force my way in through Dad's locks. My father loved being alive: he was a photographer; he understood the human body, and machines; he had all these ways he meant to work inside the math of human ash to build from the deforming light of our great cities an empire of celebrated image memorized forever; models and actors; the living and the dead. He did not care how many other kinds of media there were inside this life already competing for the cash sold on corners and packed onto plastic. Soon anyway he fell too into wreck of air of America like anybody would; I could not spare him; I didn't want to. He was not really my father any more than where your eyes hit this silent sentence, the same way my mother mattered only long enough to push me out, then there was always this hidden air between us. From outside Gravey's house at night alone through the beams of the house freckled with ancient aging I could still hear what went on inside: walls not walls but idols. Could hear Josh and some of the other kids we went to school with who had come too to be around Him laughing or saying something in pig latin or whatever or eating angel dust up through their eyes and sometimes there'd be louder noises from the machines that made the house live so much you couldn't hear anybody else above the churning of the cooling of our bodies off and modems barfing back and forth at one another. Once inside the house again I remembered to try not to listen to the sound of the machines so long as all those others so I would be smarter when I got older and less hurt inside for certain whiles about the way things went on without me in the daily organism, though as that went on too I began to feel too I wasn't changing and anyway the effect of our inbred-from-Adam-and-Eve origins were beginning more and more to make effect in all of us. Some days inside the house the days inside the house went on so long and still the digits on the machines' clocks would not blink; I could feel inside me, as the time stayed like that sometimes for some great lengths, the old National Anthem squirting through my organs into the surrounding furniture and glass, sucked out of my teeth and face in all its daily iterations of ads and silent thinking and holy money, into the house where then the house would chew it up; soon each time the house would kill the Anthem into a silence longer than all my cells lined up one after another in a queue inside my wanting and that silence was the new Anthem and that was warm. As long as day went on in this way I could sleep there right inside my posture without feeling any older, weaker, guilty. Eventually I would always wake up back inside the mirror room; there I could see myself standing beside me and this was very beautiful, and I remembered my body, what it wanted me to bring it. Being with my me's long teeth made me less timid around the larger, higher boys and among the general community of people. One night I remember now I said some dark words to my father through a ham radio I found underneath my bed, its countless knobs marked with foreign symbols: this speaking through the wire would be the last tongues the we of me and Dad did to one another in America. I knew my dad's destruction need not be by my own hand, as had my mother's giving birth; there were so many other people past the mirrors; there was He in each of them, and so in his spirit each as much the father and mother of any other person ever as mine, and I too was their parent and always had been. In further time the room alone became my room; I did not have to ask, though often I might share the space with one or several others of us, which in the dark all looked like more of me. Some nights like these I would wake up and could not force my arms to move at all again for all the others we'd packed in. I'd find there hung above me so many of me I could no longer see the mirrors at all, and therefore the walls beneath them. Sometimes all I saw were all my eyes, through which I often found I felt if I could bring myself to press my own eye against my eye again, I could see far beyond this space, down a long glass into somewhere very gone and going further under each time my own sight inside me buckled into black, because it is not time to speak of that yet.

ADAM A., age 17: "I uh didn't know about Gravey's parents. Or like I didn't meet them. Sometimes he said he kept his mother in a glass cage in his brain and fed her money. He would have me pet him on the skull. He was exceptionally affectionate.

He was nice to be with, even if he was always really fucked up it seemed like though I never saw him eat pills or snort or smoke or whatever. I don't know why he's talking like he's not him, though he was always going on about how we were all made of the same person, or soon we would be, which is why we had to kill them, all of them. I do know there was no one else that was allowed to sleep in the mirror room with him, before the other rooms got mirrors anyway, because that was Gravey's room, though sometimes he'd let you go in there with him and whatever, though like of course when he was done you had to get out. I don't remember ever seeing anybody staying the whole night in there but maybe I just didn't ever see it. Sometimes he like would go in the room and lock it and not come out for a long time and that was fine because we knew where he kept some of his shit and there was always more there even though I don't think I saw him leave the house. Like any family, I only know as much as anyone would show me."

Everyone young that I could remember having been around before in rooms outside the house inside that false year, we hung out where Gravey lived without seeming beginning and without end. It came to be our days and evenings, small countless hours slipped under sweat and what the hell. I was still working up the ways within me I could find a way out of this body and into the next one, and I still had no idea, beyond how when my arms or face would go to sleep before my brain I'd feel this shaking, this speaking in me, like something fumbling through my cells. During this era, Gravey wore his white hair like a robe a lot, wrapped around his fangled body with the weird bruises at his softer points such as his calves and pits and chin, as the networking womb inside him widened. He never said a word. If he had any of what was going on between us, he smeared it in him with more smoke. Around him I felt older faster. I began to come around as who I was more. I put a picture of my dad I'd burnt the paper mouth off of with a blunt butt underneath my special mattress, which, when I was not there, other kids would use to be me too. Sometimes someone might come and stand above or lie beside me in the long haze of anywhere around us. I did not stop them. I did not feel nothing. Some nights the house would shake like a bead inside a baby rattle in another home. Other nights it felt as if there were no floors, and everyone kept just falling at the same rate through the same air with the lights out and the moths collecting on the eaves. We were not aging. In Gravey's house surrounded we listened to his recording of himself or someone else playing the drums: long looping thud of arrhythmic kick and floor tom stuttered like shitty pasta. Other tapes were only loops of long whats of muffling and chime beat, which reminded me of electronics being pulled apart by time. Gravey in the sound would turn to stone. His face hated itself. In some other era he, I think, Gravey, had been attractive; now he seemed unto himself alone, destroyed, a body walking around in the light of what he'd needed and not gotten like anybody else, waiting for something to blot him out or at least say his name. The growing kids who came around to be around Gravey daily rotated through a central corridor of spines, or I was unlearning how to recognize who. Me and Josh were the smaller of the standards. Some nights I knew no one's face. In my head I would refer to them by something wrong about them with their bodies, like Eternal Shithead or the Wolf Who Bleats Ash or simply You. Soon even that would fall away inside another kind of speech. Their faces would become mounds of hell and skin all run together in all our memories at once, even just seconds after having seen. No one knew me either. Often we boys each named and nameless all ended up faceup on the floor all bone, as the pills Gravey began to get from someone out there on the earth would make your body feel like it'd turned inside itself to stone too and shit upon you so hard that what our blood really awaited soon awoke.

PETER S., age 15: "The most people I ever saw come over at once was like five. Mostly Gravey didn't like a lot of people in the house until he started whatever. Everybody around school was talking about wanting to go to Gravey's since they could get fucked up there, to the point that I think he started being scared that someone was going to find out he was hanging out with all those kids and like what so he told us to shut the fuck up. All the music he ever played us that he had made when he was our age or whatever really sucked."

Then oh hey yeah one night at Gravey's we, I mean us people, guys or whoever, we were floating inside the house again like ever and the bubbles in my brain became a phone. I picked up the phone inside my skull and heard someone at the far end screaming in a slow striation, syllables splashing at my face. As I learned to listen harder I could make out little bits of what it was, and though the language wasn't mine quite, I learned to separate the sound that up till then had been my name inside me. The name no longer sounded like my name. Other guys inside the house around me not inside the phone were also screaming around the sound of the screaming coming through me in the phone, though these bodies were screaming at each other, swimming limbs and prodding sockets. The walls rammed in around me seemed higher than they had been before right now. The phone cord curled in my head meat made dizzy music with my blood in fury. I couldn't hear the voice. I couldn't hear Him; I heard me capitalize that pronoun in my aorta. I went in the mirror closet and closed the door with me there swimming in black fabric with the lights off. It smelled like going to the dentist. My hands were nothing. Inside it I could hear. This was the first time I heard Darrel. I heard Darrel tell me his name was Darrel. The mirror room closed around me closer even then. I knew right away he did not need me but I needed him. I could no longer find the door. Why Darrel, I said, what is a Darrel, why not another name, and I felt the receiver holes press through the back side of my skull, making little stirrups for the Listening. The syllables were curls, clenching licelike in my shape. Darrel said some of the things he had already said again. He gave his location in the house in a part of the house I had never been in and did not believe was in the house at all. Darrel told me he had lived inside the house as long as houses had been around and even longer than that. Then Darrel told me to kill Gravey. Darrel said I would understand why later maybe I had to do this and it didn't matter if I did or didn't, because by the time anybody else who could do anything to stop me knew about it it would be over and done with most exactly unremembered and this was the nature of the disembodiment of passion. Darrel's forehead was so large, and the tongue inside it whorled; I could hear him right beside me in seven voices all the same voice everlasting. Through the script I heard the wail of home trying also to come into the room and stop the word and be between us, slurring my sternum: I heard Josh laughing, Gravey laughing, someone someone someone someone else. How will I kill Gravey, I asked Darrel, in my inside-voice, and now inside the phone inside me Darrel too began to laugh throughout the house's hidden laughter saved like the maker's breath inside a stick of butter. Darrel's brand of laughing made me go goo-juiced and feel weirdo; it combed my hair and I was clean. Darrel said then that I would kill Gravey over time. He said that he would help me with this part, because we were married. He said I was married unto him; in the black book of years and sermons we had been written. He said once Gravey was dead we would begin. He said I was to enter Gravey once I had killed him and wear the body like our body and then the next phase could occur. He said we had time because time was coming and uncoming, because all of this had already happened and was happening right now, and would happen again in the near future. He said don't you remember. He slammed the phone down in my head; it shattered hard straight through my neck into my lungs into my belly, making red sleeves on my reams of vision, which when I shook my head still stayed. There with the voice still there inside me after, my teeth felt colder than my jaw and I was laughing in the sound of Darrel's laughing like I had always been and always would again all through my chest filled with the slowlight and I knew what I would be and then I instantly forgot. I felt along the closet for the knob and felt a wet thing surrounded by dark hair. In the dark I could not see my arms or anyone. This was our new daylight.

FLOOD: *I'm not surprised to find Gravey claiming here to have been, in so many words, psychically taken over by a child, who, again, I'm not sure if I believe is the same person. He very often acts like a hybrid of a thirteen- and sixty-year-old, spastic then tired, immature then graven. He will often revert to baby talk, even in midsentence, and often he switches between voices as if he's playing ventriloquist dummy on himself. It is clear now at least that the child at least some part of Gravey remembered being at some point and the burnout he is presently are at this point in the narrative becoming mixed, at least as far as Gravey's highly damaged point of view. As far as the identity of "Darrel," I don't know. Though Gravey will often respond to almost any name you call him, as if it is his name, anytime I mention Darrel, Gravey will gnash his teeth and squeal, in such a way that I can't tell if he enjoys it or despises it or both.*

I waited in the red. My cheeks wore weirder. I didn't believe the words I'd heard me say into me in the name of Darrel, corkscrewed with flat beer the ringing woke in me and which I drank. The house seemed rather tilted. I laughed too, though I could not feel a center from which the color of my sound came. I kept looking up toward the ceiling to see where Darrel might be through the floor as he had mentioned, but the house was ranch-style. The roof was diamond-eyed. The only stairwell in the whole space went to a stormroom someone had filled up with a bunch of wire and a white chunk of marble big as two of me. Someone said Gravey had been planning to carve a replica of someone famous out of the substance, though who they said the person was was someone I'd never heard of, which seemed not famous, and made in my mind the substance anyone at all. Anyone forever and unending. All over all earth. In the red I held my head inside me and the phone in me was silent. I was spinning. The bumps along my arm began to rise, form clusters. Some came where a watch would be if I would wear a watch but I do not believe in time; one large cushy pustule opened near the center of my skull meat, hidden underneath my hair; also a bulge on the foreskin of my penis, on the bottom side, so that while peeing it could not be seen; one last trio of ridges on the inside of my upper lip like a keyboard. These all rose out of me within eight hours of the first phone call; some became foamy and met my hunger. I tried to corner Josh and give unto him some witness, though he was already so gooey and socially negligible by this point in our lives he just smiled and smiled, taking no part. I nudged him with my boot and said goodbye, for while I knew I'd see him later, I no longer felt him in me anywhere I'd felt anyone I'd known before this hour right now. He was the last one. It was arbitrary. The red was all mine now.

FLOOD: *Gravey's Escherian perception of the architecture of his home and space surrounding is apparent by now: his house does not indeed have a stairwell (as far as we have uncovered), nor do many of the other physical elements or objects mentioned later actually appear. Perhaps some have been removed or destroyed.*

Perhaps there are multiple locations he is confabulating into one, much like the contours of his mind. At the same time, having spent dozens of hours in the house by now looking for answers as to the nature of this whole machine of events, certain of Gravey's enunciations have in some subtle way in me seemed to ring true: as if there is something more about the spatial dimension of the building and what would come to wake inside it than one might gather simply looking. I can't fully explain it as yet.

I did not kill Gravey with my hands. That is, my hands did not touch Gravey in the making of the leaving of the body of his blood, nor did I aim a knife or pistol or other tool in his direction, nor did I say a word into his head that caused an orchestral damning damage. How Gravey died was something came into his life. I mean the next time I saw him after my instructions he was wearing black earrings and a blue shirt with a circle in the center of his chest. I think it was supposed to be a tour tee of a band he'd loved or wished he had. He was stooping. His hair was shorter on his head and longer on his face. Whereas before he'd never really talked except in wrinkles now he would not stop it with his mouth. He'd make a little barking sound. He'd sniff the wallpaper and pull it off in the kitchen to reveal the white behind it. He brought down a whole strip and wrapped a mask around his head. You could hear him talking inside the paper but the paper caught the language. He, as a conduit, was already being diminished. I needed nothing but to believe. I watched him from inside me as he banged his skull on the stove and turned the stove on and was laughing in the seven voices, the sound inside which I could not then remember the name of the neighborhood of where my father had had his house. I couldn't remember my father's name or the dog he'd bought me when I was four and it had bit me on the cheek some but we'd still kept him and I still slept with him in my room. All the photographs of things I'd done before now were somewhere outside Gravey's house. Anything could go in just a single stroke of the eye against a portion of a building or a person in the long night around us. In knowing that, the house became not Gravey's house but so much my body's, I could smell it in my blood. This house needs to be painted, I heard Darrel say and now I was communicating with him not by the phone but in between my teeth and where my gloves would have been had I been wearing gloves. I understood. I went outside. Outside, in the mash surrounding the house with cash and unending television, by breathing in I gathered up the night. I felt it rummage in me, having traveled long for miles around the air of us in circuits everlasting. My skin around me did a slither; then I was sweat-logged, emptied of me. I used my arms to spread upon the eaves and locks and windows a shade more sky than nothing and less sky than what I already struggled to remember about the way the overhead had always seemed before: so dark despite the pins and orbs pretending to lend dimension to what otherwise went on no deeper than any body full of blood. Under the new moon my pores were so smooth. They gave the light back to the evening where the moon refused to take its turn as I spread upon the house our mortal color. I got less tired the more I worked. When I was the most not tired I could be, beyond my body, that was what I came to know as love.

JOHN R., age 18: "I don't know what the fuck he was thinking painting the house like that with all what was happening and going to happen. It was like he wanted to be stopped before he started, or like he had to have it so raw in the face of everybody if he was going to do it. He really wanted to die. I knew right then I should have left them. I couldn't leave."

Name withheld: "The black house was always black. It has always been black like any house and the painting placed upon it was only in the dimension meant to bring it right like any house should be. We would have painted every house on the street if we could have had that much to make for. Would have painted the houses on other streets and the streets and fucking Arnold Schwarzenegger and your fucking face you pig bitch ass fuck American fuck."

The longer Gravey walked inside the house shaped in the black mass pigment the older he got faster. The skin around his ankles sagged in ways as if made melting. His arms could not reach to touch even the persons of our congregation who had allowed him to do the touching without the help of chemicals or need. He took to standing in the kitchen by the knife rack and leaning forward, eliciting shadows. He saw himself in windows and feared his disappearance. The less of him in him there was allowed me further open. Any minute I began to feel empty or dismissive of our fate, the phone rang in my blood again and rang until I pressed my palms flat against my lap or face and swore to my prior self that there was nothing undesigned about us coming, nothing I had power to remold. Other times the ringing would not happen and I'd just be blown up with such high shriek in all the air it was like every phone in America invoked at once, though no one else inside the house there seemed to hear. Somehow that pulling off of power made me horny and I would forget to rest. The night was lifting from the night. I needed not to not think. I used another phone outside the phone inside me to call my dad now still at the birth location to speak his death wish but it was already underway and always had been, disguised in stomach cancer and insomnia. His answering machine was still me age six saying hello hello hello hello hello hello hello hello. My present mouth moved to match the words, slowly unlatching itself from repetition into unforeseen syllables. I heard the future me in me explain some things about the old me to the old me on the tape directly, for someone else to bury, my blue-brained memory meat so divorced from anything that mattered: days not even days as I'd lived them but mnemonic home video of someone else's shit-parade. Each word I said came out of me and left me without that word forever so that I could have new space to fill with how the future sounded. When I'd finished what I meant to say, I stayed on the phone until the machine ran out of tape, miming our silence, and my old house hung up on me and there I was now.

The next day Gravey was not there, or at least not Gravey as I had understood him. There was a slim window of excess time I spent between our transference. Our bodies now were both the same, like a shitting doll with several accessory skins you could force onto it. The quickening difference left in my memory a gap opened between who I'd been in my false youth and the present sack of meat I called my ongoing complexion. I'd spent my last night in the child awake inside the mirror chamber, pressed against it flat and laughing, waiting for Darrel to turn my hand into a saw or give me hope. The must of the room's lining and my dreams of human leather and fire cities in the closet fill the skin around my eyes with birthing pimples. I had to pick me clean for hours. I came out of the dark covered in fuzz and walked into the kitchen with the itch risen and re-sounding, ready to take him alive by my own hands as had been commanded by Darrel in my blood for him and us brightly colliding and in the kitchen where he was most days most often he was not. I didn't know that, no sooner had I made the decision to really kill him, he was me. He had always been me and always would be, just like for each new victim that I took I was always them also. The skin of every slipping minute passing as my human brain rattled to catch up to my condition sealed me deeper in our flesh, a vessel desperate for itself. In the needle den, no Gravey. No Gravey in the yard or in the drum rooms or rolled inside the closet where when I slept I dreamed of horses' blood, though here were seven boys there passed out in no shirts and white jeans with the word FLAGELLUM stitched along the seam of their bellies and their hair done up like people meant to be wished upon, another band. I hated when fucking shitty bands slept in the fucking shitty house because I could hear the fucking shitty music coming out of their fucking shitty face holes and their fingers, though I could not remember in the night before there having heard them making any fucking shitty noise. I closed them in the room and locked the door. Today was Saturday or Wednesday in October or July. It was 1981 like it was 1440 like it was last month when you were born. Like it was 2667. My arms inside me kept on reaching after my own life. Gravey wasn't in the yards. He wasn't in the bunker where the shit went or any of the bifurcated rooms the house had made where it had learned to pull apart. I called his name saying just nothing. It was way way back behind my brain. I was way way back behind my eyes' eyes in there with it wrapping gifts of undying adulation and absolute mirage.

FLOOD: *Time also seems to be a problem for Gravey's sense of person, which is not surprising considering he dresses like a mixture of the '80s and the '60s and the '40s and the dead. His bouquet could as well be considered a mash of many generations. Either way, we've apparently reached the point in the concurrent story where Gravey can attempt a plea, though there hasn't been a single detective or attorney who's spoken to him and not come out saying the whole thing is an act, that he is aware of every inch of him, and not only is he aware of where he is, he's just ahead.*

In the hallway bathroom I ran into another body, someone I knew I'd seen before, though now he looked like he'd aged a hundred months. He was busy flossing blood out of his teeth and chewing. Where is Gravey? I said, saying it seven times before it came out of my mouth. The other body looked at the me inside the mirror with his red gums gushing. His pupils looked like some pixels. Nice, he said. I feel you. He had a circle tattooed on his nose. I looked at him looking at me in the mirror and then I looked at me and back at him. Some of his mouthblood had flecked out on the flat reflections of us like confetti, a little party. Shut up with shit, I said. I'm after Gravey, I have a word to give him, have you seen him. The mirror bending. We watching we watching we watch we. Yeah, I see you, dude, the guy said, doubled. His many eyes drew slightly lighter. I felt much more tired now than before I'd ever gone to sleep at all.

CHARLES, age 15: "I remember coming in one night and seeing Gravey standing with his back against the wall of the room and looking with his eyes so big at everyone like he'd never seen not only any of us but any person ever. He wouldn't let anybody come within a few feet without swinging with his nails. He took some of my skin off, I remember, and then he started like licking at it, chewing it really hard and shit. It freaked me out then but later I would realize what gratitude was required of such honor. Whoever in him died to bring the making was the first of many necessary deaths, for which I am still praying to be given mine."

In the midst of my becoming, the mirrors from my bedroom spread over the floors. They became affixed too to the ceiling and the framework of the walls along the places where we would walk most first and then the lesser places, patch by patch and row on column. Where we got the mirrors from was anybody. The thing about a mirror is they always act the same, no matter how much the price or who had been in them previously or for how long hurting what meat or touching what where with what hand. My own reflection in the mirrors began changing. My hair grew out on my hands. Like Gravey, I began stooping, and I began to answer to his name, slick from the boys' mouths, toward who I now felt erotically charged. Some of the boys were women, though I felt nothing for those, and so learned to no longer know the difference. I tried to smile a lot and say not much of anything, in Gravey's manner, and when I said a thing at last it would be immediately done, as long as I had cash or pills to place on open palms, which I always did. The fortune poured out of my pockets or my fingers. It came and came like kin. In time the mirrors appeared procured from any nearby space with doors that opened; from dressing rooms and washrooms and display rooms we took the ones over the beds, long ones set in the backs of doors or thumb-sized ones inside lockets, all of them someone else's, wholly used. Soon there was no inch about the house that did not hold me seeing, and all the others. When someone walked, you heard it splinter. The blood was gorgeous, a temporary replicating gift. I rose.

FLOOD: A theory: Child-Gravey and Adult-Gravey have apparently at this point, as a narrator, become fused, a process tempered by Spirit-Gravey (AKA Darrel) (AKA, I think, perhaps, Gravey's idea of God? The future of god?) (who I might suggest is only Gravey too, or at least an idea in his mind, though I would not be surprised by the emergence of an actual OTHER Darrel, who for all we know, to Gravey's way of thinking, could be absolutely anybody ever in history and time). Quite a bit of me believes, too, that the Child-Gravey is actually just Gravey at a much earlier age, a kid who once was normal and natural and grew up into the animal Adult-Gravey, in mediation of which Adult-Gravey bisects and distorts, in an apparently conscious fashion, the time of for his own psychological purposes. Though I am also open to the idea that there was a kid, someone outside Gravey, who came to Gravey's house, and whom Gravey took to so completely that he truly believes they became one. As for whether this would have been one of the kids who lived in the house with Gravey over the many years he occupied the house, or another kid he killed or did away with on his own, what is real seems almost impossible to decipher by now.

It was hard in the first hours under Darrel to figure out how to make the voice come out of my lungs the way the blood in those lungs meant to barf the syllables rejected from the vocabularies of common man. Gravey had not spoken so well in so long and I newly here inside him burned like burning books searching for the locks to keyless ways. I had to breathe way hard deep inside me like I was to be going under water; then I would close my eyes and listen hard, and through the phone over the rolling of the water I could hear the things we meant to verbalize in bone. What came out of my mouth was different from what the flesh in me was screaming. I could feel the mirrors in me spurting ash all over all my other organs, black on black. I watched me tell the boys to gather around me and put their fingers on my head and let more words come out of me and into them so they could speak when I was not speaking which would be mostly. They listened to what I was saying without me listening to what I was saying. I don't know why they did that except there was something wrong with all their eyes, screwed up as if with the meat of past lives raining through them continuously. They looked at me as if I too was the mirror, and their mother, and their lover, which I was. I was our fingers and our rings. With my new mouth inside the common shaking I changed all the boys' names to Darrel. I spoke from all my holes: "There has been a long world in this world before us, a long world in this world the world has hid on the same air where we awake. The problem is is we believe this world cannot be touched. We see each word all as a different word, imagining we're actually here somewhere inside us in our speaking, faking muscle out of blood. The seed has leaked into our homes and flakes and cables. It has wrapped around our minds, and stirred in the gloss an internal fantasia, inside which we will go on eternally in fear: knitted to the Sod of Nothing. The night collapsing underneath itself. Leaving a hole where we were bigger than our time. What happens between the hour of the light returning to us and the rest of where we are today inside this Eating is every body in America must die, must be killed at once and all together at our own hands. This will be where we begin to become." My holes closed up then. The house was older. The boys were older. I was fine. The mirrors in the room encased us, held the day out. I threw up water, and we drank.

SAL, age 20: "He was very easy to believe in. Even if you didn't want to hear it and were coming to get fucked up he would go on and on for so long in all these ways and he would give you shit if you said otherwise and after a while it was like, Yeah that sounds good, and no one else was saying anything else to us except in obviously fucking stupid ways before outside the house so like we just started saying the things too. I was going along at first kind of making fun I think in my vast private retardation seeing how everyone I had known before had failed me like they do and yet as I kept saying and hearing and saying and hearing the words showed up in my sleep and in my lungs and stuff without me even having to do it. It felt really good. Even if you didn't think about it at all Gravey would do the speaking for you anyway in response. He would like make all these different voices come out of him and he would look at you and he had your voice and he could say things for you, and that was powerful. So you would let him. And then it just became this thing. It's hard to explain. It doesn't matter. The faster as well that it happened it happened faster and better and more and more, and just like that it was days passed and we all looked the same. We will forever. Even if he killed my parents and he made me wish I was somewhere else I still believe that."

FLOOD: *This section contains Gravey's first reference to* Sod, *which as far as I can make out is what he believed would be created in the wake of his murders, a kind of palace of bodies through which the total spirit and history of his idea of God could be arrived at. When I have asked him directly what the city of Sod is, he just sits and looks straight on at me as if I'm part of the wall.*

At night I played my drums. They would make anger. I would tell the boys to go to sleep and they would do that and then I'd go and sit behind the snare and raise the sticks. I might hover a whole hour or seven of them waiting for the scourge to roll up through my gut along my arms and make me shudder with the tremor of the phones and bodies turning yellow and the melting pyramids of every market in the ash of what overturning deathblow awaited all. I beat the shit out of the skins. In the drumming there was further music, which was also Darrel, and was war like all days. I had a job to do. I had this house now, and this body inside the house through which I could force others into service of it in the same way I'd changed me. I could not remember now what my body had looked like before Gravey, but when I looked down I saw nothing anyway. I mean I was not there: no teeth, no chest, no cock. I touched myself for days and never came. I let the drums into me as my purer fornication. I was a flesh virgin when I came into the house and I would be still mentally when eventually again by our negation we all died, and in the meantime, in the smallest room this mirrored black house could bear to bear, I lived inside the language. I was snowing like a crematorium on fire in the stem of August all throughout me. My mouth unlearned to dictate my ideas, which gave them precedence. When I was not playing the drums, the tapes would play what had already been played back louder and different from how I just had. I had an intercom installed, wired speakers in the bed frames and the kitchen and in the inches of the lamps, so that anyone could always hear. The hours lengthened. Each night for food we ordered steaks. There would not be no meat inside the house for any minute and there would not be food not of the flesh. Some of the boys had been confabulated into other ideas, and for this they had to learn. It did not take them long; in starvation, they might even bite into their arm and drink and laugh a little. We learned to see sound. I had FLAGEL-LUM change their name to Darrel, too; they set their set up in the den, in the room behind the room that held my drum sets, facing away. They believed in me at first as I was Gravey, then they began to believe in something else, the flesh of me in me surrounded in the body of Our Man. The players had to practice very hard to play a single lick about the music of what Darrel wanted from them. The new songs I had written for their music could be performed only in unnatural light. We began with neon panels, then to blacklights, then to candles; then we were there inside the blackness. The words the singer of the band sang were all one word. The word was Darrel. The songs were one note. The note was Darrel. They did not argue even once.

JOSEPH A., age 21: "I played bass in Flagellum before he made us change it. I was pissed at first because that was my name that I'd made up and I thought it sounded cool and weird, like sperm and like getting beat up and shit. Then this old hippie who likes just awful hippie shit comes in and starts telling us what to do, that the only way we'll get famous is if he helps us, if we do exactly as he says. We were all like uhhh what could you possibly do about anything besides being a burnout but we didn't have any other place to practice and it was mostly his gear anyway so we just played along to make him happy. At least that's how it started. We never planned to actually do the change, or do any of his songs. But then something in them started making sense. We started playing his shit more and more not just to please him but because it just kept going. Our hands were playing. Our mouths were open. Pretty soon we forgot all those other songs we'd worked so hard on."

FLOOD: *Tapes marked with the name "Darrel" found in the house contain no sound.*

At times there were bits of me before me-as-me that still occurred. While the boys ate or played or slept or burned a fire I might go into the first, locked mirrored room and lie down and hold still in the shape of nowhere. My prior self, the child in me, occurred again at slow moments: the grind of our shared cells against the house began to learn how there were layers to the world, layers to those layers. All of us were in all of these walls the present day touched, I knew; in every mother. Any way you drove or flew or typed a word or made a claim, our history was in all of those. Don't think you weren't there with me in the small locked room while noise through walls jostled my false flesh and made me warm and I ejaculated virgin semen into the mattress and made it swim alive. Each time I came I felt the future of the world becoming changed around me. The children I would never have of them, my creamy daughters, sons, spilled dead for the passing of the day tricked in the friction of my palms. Through this, too, Darrel entered. Darrel fluttered in my cavities. Soon I did not even have to hear the phone inside me ringing to feel him right there in my wires, on my buttons, calling home. Then just as quickly as I entered inside the house I began seeing on the mirrors all these movies I had not seen played on the flesh inside my head. What the movies were were operations. They had only partially survived themselves. Some I could still remember from before in darkened rooms bent by a slow strobe, but here in remembrance slightly off. Like in that one I'd watched once with my mother on the floor of our first apartment, where the machine kills men in outer space by turning against them; instead of that world ending with a tunnel of long color and a white room and a baby large as many earths, in this version it just drove itself straight into the sun and filled the night with so much screaming that the sky around the sun filled with milk. Another movie I remembered, where all these frogs rained out of the sky and brought the characters together, ended instead with the frogs continuing to rain and piling up and up on all the buildings and the people until there was nothing left to film or breathe except the frogs. Instead of in my mind me remembering how once I had remembered my mother making me a grilled cheese and some ham squares and putting me to bed, now here I was in this man's body and I could not even think of anything before the day I'd heard Darrel murmuring my heart. I knew the alterations in the movies meant that I would die before I became the age that people die at in this era, that I was an altar, not a person, but that was also soon to change, and also did not really matter, because when I died there would be finally a novel night, as in this nothing we are nothing, and in the nothing in the nothing we have all the days to come. I knew I must obliterate the films, record over them in every memory, to make space for the virtual flesh, to dream the blood of our god in total being. Every image must be fused, each death brought open wide into the same sod of His body, all private histories carried into language outside continuum. This was beyond any future, every future. Before Darrel had appeared in me I was no one and it does not matter and all is coming and you already know my mom is dead or will be and you know my father is nobody either and is dead or will be. Darrel at least through me is capable of showing love to the boys inside the house where light is made the widest. Darrel shows me how to stroke their heads though they are taller and older than me and can do more drugs and love me more than I love them since Darrel was so smart as to put me in the body of a person who gave everybody drugs. Everybody loves drugs even if they do not love drugs like my mother claimed to never, instead they love the lord because the lord is drugs really, and even if when I die I see the lord and he is a man standing above me in a white shroud pouring blood from palm to palm, and if I say to him before Him that I believe he is a man who came to walk among us and a man who always was, what I mean is that I think he is drugs. I want all of this inside my life. It takes the place of Passed Days, which were doing me no good to begin with as had I not come to Darrel I would have either failed or finished school; I would have left the school out of one hole or another and gone to work for Dad with his machines; I would have learned by him to love air too like you did and to be machines and fuck machines and live machines and eat and drink and want through every day and still have nothing real and die. I would have ended up before god having nothing.

FLOOD: *This quasi-sentimental bit about his mother and his father (apparently once again presented in the lurking residue of Gravey's identification as a child) seems to imply, if not a human side about Gravey, at least one capable of some semblance of reminiscence and pining, the likes of which I've seen no evidence of in person. Efforts to locate Gravey's parents at their homeplace have proved fruitless, and we have found no evidence of communication with Gravey among their suddenly seemingly* *abandoned belongings, nor any photographs of Gravey as an adult or a child. Likewise any other family or social relation beyond those who claim to have lived with him inside the Black House, though again no evidence of outsider involvement has been confirmed. I take all signs of desperation or emotion in his speaking as further elements of ploy, reinforced by the creeping feeling I get even just being in the same building as him that he is only ever looking for any number of entryways into my or anybody's mind.*

Some nights there were so many boys there I could not see beyond the walls of all their limbs. Boys heard the word I said and took it from me and went into the night and came back with more boys. While the mirrors and the low light and the songs of Darrel throttled through the backbone of the home, the boys would fold themselves over and over in the new flesh shared between us. The rising color in their output made me shriek more in my deathwish, thereby causing my vision and my body to sometimes split again, though this time in a way I slowly realized I could organize. I could see myself from there inside myself storming room to room in removed slo-mo, speaking in a language no longer ours or mine into the heads that floated past my face. The others of me did exactly what I wanted while I continued only sitting. I rarely suffered any pain. If I ran into a pane, it did not hurt and would not shatter unless I told it. Beyond the windows where the night curled I could see how in the sky the stars were going deaf, pocked out by something far behind them seeing. The world was full of others I could be. All the houses stacked like teeth around our lives holding the sleeping people. I needed all of them. Like god's own faith in god. The boys came and ate meat off my chest. They sucked until the pressure wrote out gorges through their heads, though which then I could place my destroyed treble. Their moaning made a roof against the night, covering the aspirations of our bodies against those who would never understand, the winking worship service trapped only ever in their own lives. They were out there putting their hands and mouths all over anything they wanted. How could we breathe now when there were even more alive now on the earth than had ever lived and now were dead. This was a balance that needed correction. The dead's number, I said, in Darrel's name, must soon rise. When we were born, I went on, in Darrel's name, the sky had been all written opaque with our speech, cut with a great yellow-font-on-melon shaping the Zodiac. The light of a dead star is not something to fuck around with, and yet all these people go and go. I said a lot more I can't remember beyond the necessity of massacre, the becoming out-of-world. To make my point clear I made the new boy with the long black hair go and look behind the clock hung in the room where most of the most recent people had been circle jerking in their sleep. At my command, Black Lock Darrel went and got the clock and pressed it to my hands. On the back side of the clock's face the flat black of the coming sky reflected. I heard my forehead bend in on my brain a bit. I hit Black Lock Darrel in the mouth with the whole clock's head and then again against the floor with my own head, then both my fists into his two cheeks, then the clock again. This was my first violence in this body. My boy's face bled long with the smell of gracious pussy. I felt his blood tell me to Begin, while Black Lock Darrel, weeping, kissed my hands with his long tongue. I heard him tell me Please, Amazing, Yes, Again. All I could hear then was applause.

JOHN R.: "There really were a ridiculous number of people coming around already. I don't know where they came from or how they knew, but some nights there would be like several dozen guys all just standing around to wait to hear Darrel talk. There were girls too but Darrel made Gravey make us say that they were boys. Once you saw him once you wanted to see him again, so like it just kept getting bigger like that, and Gravey was very quickly losing anything about the way he'd been before to all the speaking. I can remember the smell in the room that first night when he killed the first boy right in front of us. It was like take all of the perfumes they sell at one of those department stores in those long glass cases and spray it all into the room together. There was even some kind of color about it. You couldn't not breathe it all up in, and I have to say that once I'd smelled a little I wanted to smell more. I tried to not want that but the voice was all up in me."

Name withheld: "Man no there were never that many people. Especially once dude started getting weirder and not giving drugs unless you'd listen to him less people were coming. Yeah he was talking to himself a lot and shit and thought the mirrors were alive but some nights it was just he and some nights I was him myself because I loved him so hard. I mean, I did this. No I really did. It was me. Please kill me."

The band practiced long hours on our absence. They recorded new takes every night, where each take sounded like the old one but with new void in it, as I grew stronger. We were multiplying, every one of us, all overflowing with ripe brain beatbox. The endless angles of the mirrors made each chest become seven. Boys invited friend boys to the house and fed them what they'd come for and then they too would go on and take the sound to other houses. Some of the people were animals and family pets. I couldn't tell the difference between a dude and an aardvark. They were all Americans. I wasn't even never speaking any longer, but now so continuously you couldn't tell it from nothing. My outgrown silence went on in the brains of two boys I'd asked to extricate their lungs on plates for me to coat with gel and wear as a ball gag. I'd sewn their lips shut. Their bodies worshipped outlet malls like anyone alive. In this new year I could already shrink down if I wanted, I remembered, and witness anybody's most unfortunate fantasy. I was so busy and there were all those people out there and all these hours wired. I had to name two more boys to do my doll play for me and count my money and make up lyrics for my songs so that they then could be deleted and adhered to what the drums inside my wombs were doing. Today was our best day yet already: I had been saying this each day all through the year, and I would say it here tomorrow and the days before and when again it came into me the same thing again regardless and still every hour it held true. The worming word within me was wanting out even more now knowing exits in the day again begun again cut from the mother and she was only anyone. There were millions more, and just one sky. Under that dumb sky there, through the window in the kitchen where I'd cut into the mirror to remind it who was who, I watched the yard becoming spraytanned to match the shores of flesh the older gods had loved. Each new day that came and went forever gave the ground around us a riper shade. I began to wrap my wrists with wire. I heard Darrel in my knees, teaching me to kneel without actual motion. I heard him in the pistons of the car cold in our driveway, the keys to which I'd swallowed in my sleep. I set the car on fire by thinking of it only in one light in one way, like a promise. I heard the gas tank explode through the wall. Then the yard too was on fire.

Then the windows and the roof, though it did not destroy our house as it could not destroy our house. It made us stronger and stunk like rubber. It added new black layers to paint I'd painted in my last days, bringing such heat down on the house that boys were fainting in droves, all sweating eons. My own sweat rained inside the home. It rained for forty days and forty nights, each new day finding more new gloss-unfolding persons arrived to become drenched and sewn into the fold. I had to touch each arriving body on the center of the forehead to hear what was in there before they could be pronounced removed from their past life, given over to the invocation. The band was really bending up the air. Their songs were changing even inside the derivation, though what they played stayed the same each night. Our cold machines captured the image and the sound, erasing what had been previously recorded by anyone ever. Each night behind our closed eyes the fire raged again. I loved each of the new boys in his own way, and I said so. I told him each what I believed about us for us and would give to him with all of me each time I could get my body going good and in the best ways. I taught them how precisely to explode and still exist.

People from films began to appear inside the house beyond their replications. Their images were struggling to preserve the tradition of entertainment against my anti-comedy. From films I could remember and not remember I saw bodies I had seen on cartridges and in small apartments or rented warehouses and false velvet-lined screening booths at length materialize in piggish light and go on walking around the house in suits or without clothing. Their tattoos would reflect in the mirrors and try to remind my skeleton how I had lived among them as a witness, fondled their blowholes in my dreams. Men with necklaces made of a gold so false it made another light inside the light bend over. Men with no testicles and huge breasts. These were images my human mind had been trying to hide from my own spirit. I had to learn to shake them out, to kill the image of them as carried in me the same I would kill everybody else. One night I saw a man I'd seen at least in seven strong productions sit down behind my drum set and try to play with perfect limb independence. I punched him in the throat. He fell on the floor and coughed up language. He threatened me by god. He was worth billions and still as easily a phantom I could transmute through. I laughed at the word of his god splayed against me in my house of mirrors. I licked my thumb and pressed him dead in the fontanel. Though he continued to walk thereafter he was no one there again. His career went to commercials, then to appearing in newspapers catching men's room promises and ruin. In each new image he now looked exactly like me, as he had always, though only in his mental death did I see how. I couldn't even remember who he was in any other name from that point forward. It was so simple then to repeat this process against every other media, and with each my size grew more. Time grew shorter in between all of my people. It had been two days inside my mind since I was me last, though now I was more me than I was then. In the human air that moved in dog years we were older now already and so many of us had planned to grow fat only in the face. The boys in the house that I called boys had never been boys at all inside their lives, and were now even less boys and more just mobile walls around us bloating inward at the same rate, making the nearby houses horny with their friction. America had needs they did not know they had and we would show them how to know. We stacked more mirrors on top of the mirrors. The rooms got smaller. Something in me bent and I fell sick. We took the mirrors down but I still could then hear Darrel only under a trough of greater trembling that grew thicker the more I wished it out. I felt the curling in me trying to uncurl more where I uncurled it. I heard the dogs where their eggs had lain and my blood crushed them but this took power. We needed to begin to begin before this sickness thickened. There were so many possible mistakes. I asked Darrel what to do and in the throbvoice, in time in silence with the band, he told me that to begin I'd need to tell the boys to bring to us inside the mirror house a newer mother, made in my mother's name to be renamed as Him, amen.

A. F. F., age 18: "He said it didn't matter what she looked like as long as she was American and everyday. He said all of them were mothers and all of them were His. He said we'd know, or if we didn't know we would be led to her by just doing whatever. I didn't want to do it but several of the others were so incensed and ready by now to do almost anything Darrel asked that he didn't have to ask more than once. Mostly it was the new ones. I was recognizing less and less the faces of the people around me each day when I woke up. Yeah, some might have been famous before but no one gave a shit about legends. It was all changing way too fast. I tried to leave that night after he started talking about the woman. I went right out the front door. No one tried to stop me. I walked and walked and the further I walked from the house the harder it was to breathe. I mean about like halfway down the block I was gasping and turning blue in the face, like I was in outer space. I went back and felt fine. The next day when a small group of us got ready to go and find the woman to take off the street I put my clothes on the same way and I got up and went without saying anything. I had no trouble breathing at all. In fact I couldn't stop laughing."

No. Not amen yet. I didn't want to. Behind my lids inside the mirrored room my mother's head wore the bruises of where I'd lived. The blood poured from her eyes through slim cylinders in curlicue over the back side of her skull and out around her ears forming a helmet. Her breath condensed on no clear surface. She wanted to keep me. The face she was had become deformed from the gears and brakes and where she'd screamed into them trying to stop the cells coming apart, where she'd sang the song she'd sang at me in smallest hours trying to reverse in me the urge the blood of me had made. Though she was all these other mothers also. Where had I been, she asked; when would I come home; why was I fraught in this wishless virus while in all the other houses the babies grew into their own versions of the women and the men, deserving life. I knew her image was not memory, not even desire, but my own native resistance to simple faith. That I cared so much for anyone ever invigorated my ability to want more for everything surrounding all. Through the floor I felt the many floors: other layers to the house where other rooms were with others stacked in deep refraction, none of which I could reach. There would need to be another way to descend into the inevitability. These rooms, too, would lead beneath America into the other houses in the night. If I could find my way into the center of the mirrored house of our human network I could access any home for all it was, then we could replicate our kill. The bodies of the boys were the beginning. I could smell the teeth inside their balls having sex lessons with themselves. More would soon commence to fill His motion's promise. Through the walls I heard the band not playing and it was louder still than all. My mother's head spun around above me and showed me the face she'd always hid behind her head throughout my years beside her, one shaped like mine exactly. And yet my face was only one of several thousand faces that she'd carried in the corridors of eggs and sperm she lived with, from which I had been selected like an emotion on the way out. These were my people; cells in my best image; my negation and deletion. In seeing them, I named them, and they began to spurt. She leaned with her whole life to kiss me. I was awake again and so was Darrel, the most awake we'd ever been. I walked through the kitchen over the piles of sleeping or prone pleased bodies to pretend I could see out through the mirror over the window to the flat backyard. In the yard the flies had not arrived, but they were coming. I could not hear them because I wanted their cock so bad that I became them.

Name withheld: "I was confused about it and I didn't know about it and I didn't want to and I knew that I should leave and I knew that it was wrong and I wanted to stop them and I thought I could try to stop them and I wanted to and I was going to and then I didn't and then I didn't and was going to leave and tell someone and didn't and and and and. It could go on like that forever. Then one night Gravey saw me standing in the hall. He saw the weird light in my face and how I was frightened and the color in me and he took me by the hands and squeezed until I thought my skin was going to pop and he said, *A human's screaming is eternal music*, and he punched me in the face so hard I didn't fall but always from that point forward felt like I was falling and my body was the hole and Gravey was the space the hole was wrapped around forever and I would never land and never stop. All else after that was so easy, and totally awesome."

The first mother the boys brought to me wore blue slacks and a neck brace. They'd found her in the same school area I had come from though I could not remember then; even just the name of the school crusted a white foam against the inner tube of my spirit, then disappeared. Her head's lips were painted purple. She had white shoes turned darker by the mud. I asked her her name. She said a word of breathing. She did not appear upset. No, I said, your name is Darrel. She looked at me not with her eyes. A small ridge of fatter flesh pounded electric above her eyebrow, pulsing out a beat I would use to write the bass line to a song that did not exist. I told the boys to take the mother in the bathroom and clean the disease from her hands to prepare the entrance. I had them fill her mouth with pills and gave her water. I blessed the water in her mouth and watched some of it work down the chamber laid in her neck on through her chest. Some spat back up on her yellow shirt and formed a pattern. I locked her in the smallest mirrored room and told the Darrels to take turns waking her organs. Through the walls for hours after you could hear her squealing at the roof, the rafters of the house rising from what the boys or her together made unmade. I waited in great patience raw with itching. Then when Darrel said we'd broke the lip of her private ocean inside her, I pulled the boys away and let her lie. An unnamed range of time required passage. At night, locked in alone, she lip-synched words to a song again I would not write, but would hear forever in my head rendered in bumps naming the word all there among her while in my own body I made paste till I was ready and I could feel in me the blooming moons. In the false silence of the house encasing darkness alone I entered the locked room after all the others had gone down where I could no longer feel them. I found the girl's body on the bed with mouth wide open in a neon light from a glowing Timex. The watch's face said the time in zeroes: never set, or reset since entering the house, or struck by current, or any of the hidden ways time is deformed. Her head faced away from where I stood, its reflection corroborated in the mirror parallel, and again at oblong angle from above and below on either end. The folds of her in such light formed a town: a mass of others smoothed into her in snowbanks of pale skin. I moved to flatten myself beside her. I flanked her central image with the mirror to cause twins. Up close I could see me better in the mirror. I seemed ugly. The hair curled from my lengths of extra face. Black rouge where I had applied none. Cysts surrounded both my eyes in tiny white pills, all of them cursing. My age today contained the number nine. The boys were watching through the walls. I don't know who all inside the house was asleep, or where they slept when they were sleeping. I brought myself to tower above the female figure. I felt her skeleton under my erection. I made her trace a square across her forehead. I called her Darrel. She didn't answer. I called her Joyce. I called her Margaret and Dallas. I called her any name of any woman I could remember. With each name I felt new cysts rise in my brain, working hard to tunnel fast to join my appearance. I brought my meat into her vision. She was already pretty messy. Her hip bone cut into my own with every thrust. Darrel, I said. Say it, Darrel. All of us Darrel, all in all. I let the light back in the room. The way the light fell this time showed me the girl's face from a different space in my own head. Her head had my old head about it. It had the lips and chin I'd worn into the house. From there, the cheeks and lashes matched my mother's, same as mine. Along her back the girl was smooth like paper ready for writing. I came up to see into her eyes. Her eyes were open in the room seeing beneath me up into my seeing. I saw me seeing me trying to see something else. I tried to hide the light inside my hand again but it found ways out between my fingers and glowed bright warm through my palm, despite the absence of stigmata. Yet. The shape of where the girl had been began to try to rise up from her. I was smiling in her. My own head began to overflow with pixels. I had always wanted to kill me. The closer her face came, the more of me there was. Our mouths gave laughter to the darkness. I think we kissed, my first taste that I'd remember of someone else's open mouth. It tasted like my sleep had always tasted when I woke up in my skin again. If there was anything about the old me I must remember it was that. I let the form with my face put its tongue inside my head. I used my hands graced with the light to bring the other skull as near to mine as it could manage, tongue to teeth, and ate. From there forward I could not stop shitting.

CHARLES: "The sssssssssssscreaming that night lasted forty-seven billion yearssssss. It came out of every inch of every persssssssson in the housssssssssssse but the houssssssssssssssssssssse itself was still. Even right now it is in the wallsssssssssssssssssss and all over your face."

FLOOD: *Attempts to discern which among the many bodies believed undone by Gravey was the first have been pretty much absolutely impossible, given the nature of their undoing. Regardless, his intimation here of the practice of consuming flesh of the victim immediately after their undoing is indicative of his procedure across the board. In these early acts, his tendency would be toward consuming sections of the face of the victim (cheeks, jowls, cartilage, tongue), as if to place his mark on them in the most visible and personally associative sense; later, this habit will increase, and eventually disregard any seeming order to what is consumed, as his desire to "absorb the person wholly, all persons wholly, unto one body" becomes more central.*

I stood up from the mirror bed and flexed my mind inside the musics. Blood helicopters chopped across my slim cerebrum like fresh diamonds, rings in screaming on small hands coming awake inside my linings, each after its own way to reach beyond me. New light like ham bumped from my ducts and spilled against the floor gross for the worlds of corpses that purred in orbs beneath the floor. They'd wolfed up years of fake food in one hour in my gray space. Worms covered the house's slim north wall to defend again against whatever light infected from a false national conscience. Birds had laid ancestors in our pipes. I smoked some of the girl's hair out of a paper bong and ate the ashes. I loved the way she tasted like a soon-to-be-famous set of stab wounds: two to the head, five to the neck, and sixteen to the back. My bedroom's hall was painted gold. There had not been a hall there that I remembered any day before the day before. Gold was how I would forget anything about this set of hours; tomorrow I would need another. Through the hall I found my way back into the house another way entirely and so the house began again. The boys were there and they were still boys and they were growing. Some had acquired such enormous stomachs. In their lard something was promised. I sent three of the biggest to go blow kisses in the attic to consecrate some space where we could keep the coming breed of mothers. Having had one I needed every, and even more than that.

The beginning had begun and it was going and it was going fast and wanted more than what it had and more than what it wanted to want. I felt a continuous strumming connected in the fiber of my men. Our need made need need need. I shaved the hair off of my body so I could glide and do my best. I felt the rising hammer in my pudge where what I'd eaten all those years there sat upon me waiting to be fed what it had asked for every inch and hour in the theaters and the poll booths and the gas stations and the groceries and the houses of the other people who had let me down and those who had not meant to let us down, the same. It all welled up so fast between my heart and hands, in Darrel, in me, I could not hold it, so it flowed into the boys, and even then I had to teach myself to masturbate again by imagining the high mounds of our cities and the founts or mountains being lifted up and let to fall in fissure and land smashed into the earth. Through the window as far along the land I looked I saw more and more dirt, the bead of all the days surrounding going on in all ways and yet at the same time so hopelessly foreshortened and unexpanding it seemed to end right down the street. The dimensions had no dimensions and no dreamlife. The house was getting fuller faster yet, filling up with all our holes. Each hole could be the only one that led to what it led to. As they burst open, the earth spun. The distance between our house and the homes beside us seemed continuously to grow. I could see the lesions of the huddle of our neighbors spread like Pangaea in reverse to a new perimeter thereon, the bitchbrick of their sad fortresses unspasmatic as if right beside me. I could not keep still my aching meat teeth wanting more, a sweltering writhing so centered around nothing real despite the wars and wishing and the money and the motherfuckers and the cancer and what had I done all these hours until just right this second. Everything at once seemed so tired I could hardly hold my hands inside my hands, still colored in the blood of our first mother. I was grinding with impossible fury. The house asked questions. I went and set my drums on fire. I heard me call the boys in to surround me in the room to watch work burn and learn its tenor. It licked the walls and drums and left only the metal rims. The plastic stunk and got them high as fuck and then they like me were warm. We stomped the carpet clean. I gathered the ashes with a shovel and a blade. So all this black now. So our womb. I yelled over my yelling for the boys to go into the mirror room and bring the mother to me. Her body drug along the grooves between one mirror and another. I spread the ashes on the remainder of where I'd loved her, her posture firm, already of no smell. I tapped two boys to wrap her in a U.S.A. flag. The blue part went around her head so she could see the stars. Someone made a joke about a burrito and I punched him in the heart until he was no longer asthmatic. These were the stars we'd lived under as long as we'd been allowed to, wet with performance. The stars were screaming. The blue could no longer exist. I told the boys to lay with me now to listen near against the girl and learn the prattle of her linings through the American colors. I told them this would be the song they had to play to make the skyhole inside us all together want to be fucked and in reverse unleash upon our earth our worship, the heart of whom is not a kind of music at all but an itch that swallows one's whole shape. Now I was the one screaming, with all the stars live in my shafts. I reached into my pockets and pulled out the teeth I'd removed from the girl's head shaped like my mother's and showed them to everybody. These are Darrel's teeth, I said. Darrel no longer requires food to make his flesh. We are his mouths; he is our house. I put the girl's teeth shaped like my mother's teeth into my own mouth and on her teeth I chewed until I heard my own teeth in my head breaking and I swallowed and I smiled. My blood ran down my chin, my own blood, Darrel's. I heard the floors beneath us multiply, and underneath them old doors open. All of us were watched, I heard me shrieking, by each of us again, and so inside us. I leaned to let my streaming blood pour onto the flag around the girl. Some time went on in this time. I squeezed blood from me. I was pouring black of night from every inch of me that'd ever healed. I felt one of the other Darrels touch my elbow. Where I looked to see him he had split his body sevenfold, alike in each way. He said my old name in a slow voice. I threw his hand off my arm. I reached up with my own arm there between us and wiped my blood (our blood) flat on his flesh. There before the many other boys I made him touch his face and taste the silk of how we'd lived. The boy was crying, so we were crying. Others stood silent, so we were that. Do you love me, I asked anybody. They didn't have to answer. I knew they did. The house did. And the shells. The light today inside us loved me. The me inside the flag did. Inside the flag I heard the sperm of anybody sent inside our new god swimming for some flesh to set up shape in and teach its frame to truly eat.

A. F. F.: "Even when he was talking about it and we brought the girl back and all that I don't think many of us really believed he was going to do anything really serious like that. I mean yeah I know kidnapping is fucked up and I knew he'd been doing things to her, but like killing someone is really beyond what I thought. Which sounds stupid because he'd been talking about it all this time and I'd already been involved with the clearly messed up shit going on but man there was something about the way he'd tell it that made it seem okay, or at least important, or even not real or something. But seeing what he'd done to that girl's body and the way about his face when he showed us and how he just seemed to not even care that he himself was bleeding or what he'd done and how some of the other guys in the house were all about it and like fiendish for the ideas he was spouting out in all these other languages and shit, I don't know. It was becoming hard to tell who was who in there anymore, but from this point forward shit really started changing, and the people around the house were different. And yeah, I didn't leave. I let me do whatever also and went along and I listened until sometimes I couldn't even tell where I was anymore and sometimes it was just the brightest bright."

From outside the house the house was changing color in correlation to the earth. What it reflected in the grade of black paint became inverted. The roof had freckles that seemed mile-deep. Through the rasp of cavity the house hid from the backyard I could hear the boys inside us again at my order making my music again ring out between the rings of skyward foam and long along between the houses shaking glass. At certain windows even so far off along the stretch of city I felt families gathered pressed to bedroom walls inside their sleep wishing to walk into the next day's sunlight and be burned. America, I felt, was changing under Darrel. Many times inside that first night there would be a city of gold when I closed my eyes, but there would not be any life inside it. There would be a tree that bore the fruit we would need to eat to be there. Each instant it changed kind. There would be places where water came up to the lip of the ground when I wasn't looking and then it would go down again and we could not reach the water. It would come up again and come down again. There was a series of seven eternal shapes, burned in my vision on the face of all things: CIRCLE SQUARE HEXAGON STAR TRIANGLE DIAMOND RING. Each of these had appeared to me throughout my life emblazoned onto objects. They had formed the contours of the maps we used to find our way between the seas of people believing we were ending up somewhere we had not been. They defied all history. They rang and burned inside my brain, inert weapons allowing no ability beyond the fact of their creation. They had no eyes and no dimension. All else around them must be burnt, reduced to sand and dust, no water. Inside the house I knew a desert must begin. There must be a focus around which all the land could sink and pull the air down, and so after it, all other houses, cities, space. But to begin a desert you must have silence. You must remove the water from the mud. This means light. In each room of the house there must be so much light that there is no house at all. So much light that from the air outside the house surrounding the presence of America would be gored, stripped, and reversed of all its wet. With my mind inside my mind I sent all the boys not in the band to buy our new skin of electronic lamps and television. We began to fill the house with falsely burning objects. Light between mirrors. Light inside me. I felt the Wrath of Darrel strengthen with each added filament: his godmilk spurting through my vessels swimming and piling weight on and glorifying. His voice refracted in the pillow of the summoned light and held me hard. I looked down at my arms: the short arms I had seen once when I looked down trying to see me and seeing only part, the arms I'd come into the house with. I could not remember ever after going out, or how it might have smelled there, without the boys to need me, without the coming bodies of the mothers. My old arms on me again were black as charcoal, burnt and buried underground. In fear I touched me and I watched my old me chafe off on my hands.

FLOOD: At the time of his arrest, there were some 240+ working light fixtures on the property, lamps and fixtures of all size and kind, many of them plugged into the walls as well as several extra generators. How the house didn't burn up like a wig I have no idea. Absolutely blinding.

Under the same hour as we'd done apart the first flesh I sent the boys back out into the air to bring more mothers to the house. Some others of the boys were sent instead or as well to bring more bulbs for those that had blown out where everybody at the same time was trying to see. In the mirror in the rooms of light the air was making movies inside itself like Magic Eye. Bulbs would shatter in the lamps and the TVs. The faces of the people exploded from out of nowhere covered in glistening gunk and begging me to have sex with them; I was not attracted to them because they weren't aging. I was aging for them instead of the sex. I would reach biblical age in my dreamlife before there was no longer anyone remaining. With my black camera I caught as much shit as I could of every errant waking fantasy the boys enacted onto anything that made a sound, and burned it into pixels to be learned, onto tapes spanning the history of the nation's audiovisual entertainment. Each film drowned the next one out; I erased each entertainment one by one. With each deletion, time and space grew closer. In the mirror, while I waited for whatever else, I watched me watch me watch. I wanted to make love to me but I couldn't find the hole, so instead I pressed my head so hard against the glass I could not see me but the black inside me in which were written all these sentences, congregating in black battalions to replace my thinking with static blocks. I tried to write the words down on my hands with pencil or with reeds inside my mind to get them out but my arms would not stay still enough to get unshaken signal and my meat kept growing back over. Inside the house hungry for more mothers I found it hard to walk or think or want or know or ask or see beyond whatever walked just right there inches at my vision. Outside, the sun outside the house scraped against the house all hours for what it knew we grew and incubated. This was wearisome, like aging twice. It made the scraping appear again also mirrored in me welling over with such blood the films blurred. I did not want to masturbate again and yet my balls screamed between my legs and my shaft stood up doing stand up, the oldest jokes I'd ever heard. The mouth of the head would sometimes speak in Darrel's voice and beg and beg me. The corridors of Darrel were turning and unfurling. On every finger, Darrel's rings, ripped from planets falling into orbit of our bone.

Name withheld: "We made films of everyone we killed. We copied over the movies in every home's collection with the evidence of their ending. Their VHS death providing the death of cinema itself. As soon as you copied over, like, *Gone with the Wind*, it was also copied over in all the copies of it ever sold. It was fucking awesome. The cameras clung to our hands and tried to love us as creators. The majority of the films did not need to be filmed by us directly, as they had already always existed in the brains and layers of the mnemonic American mush. The tapes would fill the bloodstream of our future, and in it we would bathe and wake and so dissolve."

FLOOD: *The films, like the audiotapes, taken from the house of Gravey have as yet all appeared all blank, though the number of these films is significant, and the tapes appear to have been regularly played (the media inside them slightly battered, sometimes broken). Investigations into what content might be hidden among the archive is in process.*

"There is a public demand to kill. This was all simple negotiation. Millions of women will take only a few weeks more; the rest must automatically collapse. They will become absorbed. The few remaining bodies should be of use to a consecrating fuckfest for whoever's got a dong still in this country, male or female. With complete automation of our disease and old age we will mark the beginning of an emotional morality. There will be celebration on the face of every final breath. There will be no wake. We're not god because what god is does not end. The silence must expand between notes until there is no awareness. I call on you to stop. Death is all over. I'm glad it is. Peace in their lives a million times. If you knew what was ahead of you, you'd rest. Because what are people but the peddlers of we and all we're doing is I don't care."

CHARLES, age 15: "As his voice started to get raw he began whipping his hands around in front of him like I guess it was supposed to be sign language. After that he traced the words in some dark liquid along his arms and chest and face. I knew I understood, and had been waiting in my life to find these words presented, opened, burned onto my mind."

The second and third mothers the boys brought to me were much older than the first. They were sisters and had made babies before with other men. I could see where on their arms they had been bruised by the boys in handling from wherever they had come. I did not want to know the origin because here we were now. The smell of meat was flooding from their pores. I could hardly look at them, I was shaking so hard, with all the ascendancy inside me that they triggered. He who gives must give and give. This is the nature of the music. I told the boys to leave me now. I told them to all go in the band room and hold their instruments against their chests and think about what in them should not exist. On the floor inside the mirror room the women wept. Their gift was not at all like silence. For my pleasure I wept too. The wet upon my wide face sizzled and spattered in the mirrors and evaporated into flavor. I matched the women note for note resounding while their brownish nipples shook and shook. There was milk inside them. There were eggs inside them. There was a space inside them. They were mine. Ours. Today. I moved inside the room hearing my mother's inhale brushed in every inch of how my own meat fit together waiting to be made larger. I reached my arms to touch the twins both on their heads. We made a leaking tripod. Our fluids needed killing too. I took their tears up on my hands and licked them off me and could taste the aspiration of their young years becoming gifted in my blood, endless gifts of hell and semen I'd take for mine in contribution to my work. This had been a long time coming, in all those books and movies, and masturbation fantasy and bloodlust and laughter and church and days unwound in rooms with those we'd loved. Which was now too. I loved these mothers. Where I licked the skin burned and left a bruise in the shape of someone turning off a lamp inside a hive. The light around us mattered. It mattered even more I touched their heads again. I drew a hexagon in light. Each place I touched turned wet around my flesh unto the air and therefore inside made them drier. Their clothes had been remaindered. They wore stuffing they had pulled out of the bed to hide their naked. Tufts marring their nipples and obscuring the marks the boys had left where they were kissing on their way home to bring the mothers to me or where they had or had not found their way in. I hated to think of the men before me in these women's lives, and the women in their lives, and the women in my lives, and the men in my lives. I was kind of spinning in the minute. I touched the women harder. I wished my blood into their chests through my celebrity. I could see the way they felt it as their eyes grew open and they stopped sobbing. They were warm against me. I felt they wanted in me too, and so instead I brought them on and in and in into my body, inch by inch, face first. My coming birthday would be bluer. The newest New Year's would have no color ever again.

FLOOD: *The bodies of a pair of twins we believe to be those referred to here were located buried among the primary mass grave that would be created in the room beneath the house (frequently referred to as "the mirror room"). The flesh surrounding both victims' features (cheeks, nose, forehead, eyelids) had been stripped in large part from the bone; as well, various small incisions of flesh from the chests, backs, thighs, and forearms of both females. The cutting is crude, and will remain so as Gravey's ritual consumption of his victims' bodies becomes more and more important in his procedure. Many future bodies will be rendered unrecognizable.*

The bodies of the women. They came apart like women. They came apart like men. The bodies of the bodies. They came apart. In the mirrors there we were. We were not there. We were not us. I turned around and closed the room. I heard the house expanding. I was inside it. I was expanding too. I heard the boys. Heard them coming back in from our night in the cloak of the long ongoing vault of ash that rains. Have you seen me in rain. I know you have. I know you. I went out to see the boys with both my hands. My mouth was full and I was talking. I said the words the second and third mother made me say. They said to close the door. The boys were holding new lamps. I took the lamps out of their hands and broke them on the ground. I told them to move against me. I told them there were more wives. Mothers. Wives. There were other men. I told them to bring the bodies to me so we could write the word that closed the window on the house for good and opened new windows in the floor. Their eyes were pyramids. They stretched beside me. I think one said another's name not in the name. I grabbed him by the throat and made him spit into my hands on my chest. I made him spit till he was ugly. Till he was not a body made of him. I will wear him, and he will be me, I told another, whose eyes were rubbing at my head. I grabbed him by the throat too and bit with teeth that taste of women still and tasted in his self's skin a new history he would remember when he woke up some day. We. I would wake him up when when made when. The house was gold. I looked and saw where for both our twin mothers too late I'd made twin husbands of my friends of selves, my mashing hours. The other boys before me bowed. Their knees were purple like a machete in the mouth of a horse I'd loved and kissed and cannot remember now but for how one day he'd simply disappeared into my blood.

You. You taking my words from me. I wish that I could find and lie beside you in the room where you have been preparing for this sentence your whole life, so that as you take it in I could press my scourging dick against your forehead, correct a red impression on the center of the skin between your eyes so that those who pass you hereon will know you've taken part of something from which now there is no exit. What you've seen is rendered in our common leather. I am written in you, and erased. I wish you'd lay this book facedown on your lap now and think about your life while there is light still. I know you won't.

FLOOD: *The morning after I read this section, I woke up with the book against my chest. I found I'd copied all the words above exactly onto the cover of my Bible, which I've begun keeping near me when working with Gravey's pages. The handwriting looked like mine when I was a child more than it does now. The ink was all over my hands and face. I was clenching the pen so tightly even in my sleep that my nails had cut into the palm of my left hand, freeing the blood.*

The house began to fill. While the boys made boys between them, even more were mooring in. You could not throb a foot forward in the mess without connecting to another shoulder or coupling session. The house moaned for more house to move the house through, and the moaning moaned more for more mothers to make the house stay warmer than our machines, and the blood roared to match the need the incubating house had kept hidden long enough to turn invisible to the bored. The rising stink of all us becoming combined was never enough and made the boys even more horny to expand. The sea of heads the horizon promised yet to come were crispy, reproducing in my mind as we made mush from every love our house collected. I caught a little pinch of each boy's private pleasure expressions and witched the air around their butts so that without me they could not fantasize on their own time and they would never jerk off right again. Their come should only wake them up for fire, so that they might appear inside themselves at last. Some boys I sent to carry knives and fires into small businesses and get the cash and bring it back to us and to bring meat back to us. That money I spent on mold, crushed into the form of blue pills I had more of the boys sell in the streets or feed into me and them from them to me by lips. Light, more light. We were training in the system. We swallowed glass or lengths of rope and wore them. My slow bone boys. I watched from inside me and overhead while work among us warm was done. I told the sadder ones to take themselves into museums and put their limbs through masterworks. I told them scrape a Kandinsky with their teeth. Lay some semen on a Johns. I felt the claw marks on my insides where Richter and Ruscha and Twombly and Warhol and whoever forever had been burned and buried in no future for their crimes. Fuck art. A fist could take the face out of the pigment, a newer, longer, death. These boys had sickles in their eyes already They had lived long enough under developmental law. They would not come back but they would not need to. Their minds began with where the gash woke and hallelujah and amen with strokes larger than an eternity of media.

BILL L., age 14: "There are no museums in this city."

I watched from inside me and overhead while work among us warm was done. Our heat protected us. There was a ring around our house that made it look like anybody's. Detectives with silver badges would see no air and turn away. Their bones would melt inside their hands if they came nearer. No matter how many of the boys slipped away or did themselves in, in fear of really knowing, the house held more still. Every eye led back to ours. All of the rooms were one connected, though the boys slept in the belief that they were not aging, gifted with the basked blood and the elegance into which I had enslaved them. We were growing our own film inside the house now, from the cells shucked off of foreheads or from the backs of knees. Each scene provided its own nourishment to make the next one. I did not consume water or eat beyond the victims' bodies or the sprouts that grew up from their remainders in the locked room under the house. Sometimes I wore a headdress of their skin and sometimes gowns like a desperate princess. The smell of human leather made me erect, and I'd pinch the meatus till it disappeared into the future, for anyone to ride then. I needed every hour of me now for every mother. The boys shot my semen for me in the meantime, from our shared veins. They'd fuck anything that slept. Any flat surface. The house was coming open.

A. F. F.: "Yeah, a couple cops came sometime soon after the second set of girls. I don't think the officers knew necessarily about what was going on but there'd been complaints about the black paint and the noise that would go on and on around the house, and the rising grasses, and man, just looking at the house, you knew. I went in the hall closet and hid and listened. I heard no talking. About an hour passed and nothing happened. I came back out slow and saw Gravey lying on the floor faceup with his mouth open. I thought he was dead but then I could see that he was laughing though no sound was coming out."

Inside sleep I placed my own head on the machine of movies we had made or we had wished for in time recorded. As they played, they lost their color, turned monochrome and shaking without horizontal hold. From the inside looking out the days of us were in perpetual fast forward. Our song was on so many stations on the earth already and always had been, slid between the shit. Inside the muffled light of the house when I awoke again I'd have the boys come gather at a speaker each and pray in the leopard language of distortion and human vocals as gasping passage, to destroy this music, these head colds passed as hope. The paper cones vibrated with the nothing so hard, in certain frames it split my teeth; inside each tooth another field unfolding into seven where light I'd need when sundials had no one left to speak to could wait hidden. Where on the transmit span our song had not appeared yet, the other songs that came through hissed head colds into everyone we weren't. You could hear the bodies with their wires and beef chortle feeding each other right in plainclothes and getting paid to do it. The dance palaces of black luck collapsing in no rhythm as boys and ladies rubbed themselves ready for us to want them even childless. By now none of the boys had pistons left inside them to even laugh at what so much marketable prophecy had done to all their friends, the people they had been once. I listened to them fry against the light. I loved to hear them splitting down the middle, becoming many different people, more of us. The way a body loses the self it is in the instant of the self recognizing the leaving of the self had never been more clear as in the hour of us doing absolutely nothing in between doing the worst things we could think of in America, where more air begat more air. Meanwhile, I let these boys have love. I let them taste upon me the prior mothers by the cells their bodies passed not making children yet this month, and then the cells that held within them as the making of me hard and wide inside them tried to take hold, which did not matter, as the cage was closing even still. Even in these grips of our deleted songwork, and the cower and the pinch, my boys could not itch the trigger in their blood against me and my desire to make them walk upon the earth and raise the dead. I could feel the living thoughts of every person ever vibrating in my boner, and only worse the longer they were allowed to carry on being entirely themselves. There was, for one, the house beside our house, right next door, which could be any house in America for all you know. This house, the first of many, of all of them, wore the color of the days I had not lived, days I could have lived if I were anybody else. I watched these neighbors with my mind. I could catch them in my mirrors. I stayed in one position with my fingers at my throat over a significant stretch of evenings, aiming eyes into the eye of me and memorizing where they had been already so I would know what I was going to do. I was doing all these other things at the same time too like drawing maps and baking cakes and buying stock and thinking of the day.

The best thing about planning to kill everybody in America is you can begin with anybody in America. We'd been becoming all our lives. Always our fathers had dementia whose fathers had had dementia and made our fathers with our fathers' mothers loved our fathers and saw our fathers meet our mothers in transitory ecstasy and our mothers loved our fathers and made us in their image so that we too would do fuck and make more also. To have a mind now requires one to forget so hard even inside the perpetual familial forgetting that it now took so little crime for no crime to be distinct from all the rest, even a crime as fine as everybody in America at last at once dying, which is why it had to happen and is why I felt I had been given hands. Each object created in our image prior was a gun aimed at our forehead. Each word a hair on the finger that pulled the trigger. Each song baked into our heads so small to make room for the bigger song the band beat the shit out of with the instruments in the rooms around me, as I hawked up the liquid in which our arms and legs would be coated so that we could begin to leak the killing procedure into the cities in infestation, using every person's arms instead of just the boys' and mine. It would not take long to wake in where it already had been implanted. The faith that people have in people would be the very skin of the bag in which we buried our husks inside the bags of flesh we walk around in before the sun and wind and residue of all that speaking at last found us all in our eternal lack of motion there together, giving firm horizon to all this memory language and videotape, from off which we refract back into the refraction from which we'd come, beyond the edge of all possible communication, beyond reproduction.

R. A., age 22: "Something about the cream of the breath when words came out of Gravey made you want to make them happen, made you believe that what he said was really god. I never really believed in god before but if there was a god I thought it should feel like what I felt seeing the life come out of people. It was a power. We were making something of the earth's presence. All everybody seems to want is to feel consumed with something and surrounded by something and this did that to me more than any else I'd had before. So yeah, I did whatever Darrel said but it was what I wanted too."

And so we went unto the neighbors. The crash of night again rose shielding light against the sky for us to walk beneath unseen into the community with arms raised and faces washed. There were more of us than I could count between the mirrors, though as we surged out from the windows I realized there were less. It didn't matter. From the light our cords contained returning to the evening made my eyes hulk in every head. Around the house a whitewash gored over the yard in the husk of moths that came to feather at the warmth our home birthed by all the flesh and homebirth. No one could see shit besides what hadn't happened yet. Each of the boys carried long knives, which I had them select from the set of flatware in my heart according to their height: the shortest self carried the longest blade and so on unto there, where at the middle there had been the most medium of people, and the steak knife. I'd slit this middle child's throat for being average, which seemed too real. His common blood spread on the tile and would be repackaged into little vials I would have the boys take and release into random containers of organic juice in aisles across our minor cities. For my own part I carried the weapon of my silence where the wet inside me would not end. The animals and instruments we'd lived in and believed in by memory alone and worn as skin outside our skin unfurled a silent canopy above our heads as we paraded quiet into all that old United air. I walked hid at the center of our swarm toward the neighbors singing nothing, keeping Darrel's common brain poised in the Eye of our parade as words furled between us each to etch our presence totally common, beyond what the flanks of any municipal alarm might feel. The air I'd supplied in the boys' minds could blow straight a dead bolt on our imaginary war. This was not hyperbole. We were the neighbors, however many miles away. The street we held our heads to was everyone's. Their wish lived in my fingers as I pointed our way toward where was love. The current now-becoming-now was finally actually at last the instant it had always been meaning to act like.

SAL: "We didn't even have to kill the family next door to kill them. They would be dead the next morning regardless, only now they'd not be having breakfast. The radios played Gravey dictating the moves we made on the FM band so everyone could follow on at home, though to them it sounded like Madonna."

Name withheld: "I was involved. I was not involved. Both are the same. That's no more of a confession than pulling your car up in the drive-thru at Arby's and ordering just enough to fill you up in your imagination. There's no need for threatening me about getting to go home for saying any different than I have already, a thousand times over, since I was born. I'm a fire. My body is my helmet. Bleat."

We used our knives to cut the wires down around the neighbor's house. I ate some of the wire into my mind and felt it bake there, unto dissolution. It had a taste of smolder, its knotted innards fused and twined. The image of the hours burst into the house, laughing at us all forever at the seam of Exit Sky. What words those inches had accrued in shitting information back and forth between the people. I could taste where in the wire the neighbor mother's speech and seeing, all her wishes her best guesses, had already been rummaged through her coilings hot and hard so many times she hardly had an imagination left. I could taste the remainder of the days of pregnancy about her where the babies had come out. Each of the babies had their own films in them like mine and yours, some of which the father in transcription of flash and mangy memory had tried to store as homemade media on versions of hard drives of the house's machines before he was removed; the wire had eaten most of that too, by my order, encrypting its data into mental zits. It made the house's body glow under no moon, feeding a beacon for us to flood forth toward as a beginning with which we could begin to make this home into more of ours. I heard the paint murmuring inside me, baking organs I could spoot into the gaps for insulation, the singing crease. The lawn beneath my body as I walked with arms down turned to velvet Astroturf. The dirt beneath the lawn turned to a putty you could use to seal a tunnel cut through brick. The night sealed us inside it. Insects in its shitstorm murmured words the mother would have one day said had we not come, while in my blood the words she'd say instead became my torso. I had been carrying this moment's creation in the curls of my black sacs for thirty-four years and a tight collection of horrifying months. Each hour I could not be here in the moment of the passing moment was a death I lived through and would never have again. The boys did not understand this, I knew, and did not need to. They had their own words and hours to carry thick, to lie down inside of without crying on the softest nights knowing what would come for them among some end. They were only partially eternal. They were not yet their own death, so could go on now into any other. As we crossed the lawn of our new victim toward the coming house I made our gang sign with my shoulder at the moon, the throat of

Darrel, which could never be destroyed, no matter how much blood was hurtled through it, or what food the raining meat would ruin. The windows of the house our house descending in our vision above the neighbor house reflected nothing back at nothing. We did not appear in the smear, as we had had our own masks made of our faces and wore them now no longer left as masks but accusations of our heads. I could smell America warm for mating, like what else is new. Somewhere nearby men were carving ice into beautiful ideas. The glint of our knives against the window gleam made steam rise, become the planets. We encircled the house kissing the tips of blades. It made a hole around where we would enter. Through the rim of the house I could hear the fourth mother in preparation, rubbing her fingers, breathing the last gas her cells required to make her body's shape and smell into how it would be when it became. There had to be the exact amount of her left in her and the exact amount left out. The minute had been decided. I led the song in singing as the throat of the moon disappeared behind itself and gave us grace, opened up our pure eternal vision, and in we come.

FLOOD: *Indeed, no evidence in the homes of Gravey's victims demonstrated their penetration. No apparent damage to the sealing or the locks, as if the rooms did not separate their interiors from their exteriors. In cases where the homeowners had alarm systems or watch dogs, etc., the alarms were not reported tripped, nor were unusual activities reported by surviving neighbors, suggesting that Gravey's methods for entry were unusual, perhaps verbally or otherwise coerced.*

We did not need the breath of keys or codes to slit the windows or the doors to allow our entrance. They already believed in us as much as anything could ever, without the necessity of will. All walls are permeable by simply wishing back against them hard enough to stir inside it the wish to be parted. Like this me and the boys came through the brick of any home, and found there the same objects of belonging, like a library full of shit. Once in, the boys at once dispersed into the house in shafts of their own need, bleating their organs on the peace. The gristle of their mind clung to keep their innards from wanting so hard they burst out through their holes as they overturned the furniture and air, sniffing for the remainders of historical calamity we could fuse to right now. Our shapeless song began to splay and flub out of the holes the ceiling owned, turning sudden sense of present tense of coming killing into the night of what had always been the past. The fourth mother had yet to emerge. She had not completed her un-knowable, unmanageable mother preparation in skin and nails and hair in the bedroom of her last night with her children in their rooms asleep. The phantom presence of the father in her mind provided us a breathtaking Trojan horse; she lived as if he'd never died, as if he'd been there in the house like any other husband every day since and past, part of Our Country, which is our world. We felt nothing beyond whatever natural border in our minds existed. This was painless to abuse; in passage it became true of every house surrounding: a nation of no father while the mother waits to die: the true nature of adultery. In the house becoming ours the mother wore her whitest gown. She appeared before we even found her. Her name was all over everything, in the sound of her sexlife and want for future, food in the fridge waiting to become more of her. The house clearly wanted her dead, too; it wanted to eat the food itself, to live for itself alone, to be itself and no one's box; its cells were taking shape in full cooperation for the translation we would provide for what desperately everyday hope she'd tried to smush into the home's walls to refortify what was not there. Everything had already happened and yet I had to play the part as had been promised. I walked along the long hall lined with pictures of the mother in different bodies than she had now and could never have again, alongside what other bodies the mother had met in nearby rooms and made time with, alongside the kids she'd pushed out of her hole, each of them as well in bodies that no longer fit them. I could hear the mother quiver through the house's circuits, burning like star meat. She had a few more thoughts to think through unto the becoming zero. Her god was off duty tonight, somewhere like Disney. My teeth were greasy with intent to do exactly what I was doing. I had a boner and a cough. I heard Darrel in me getting stoned on our blood bowling open like locked darkrooms, black cabinets full of speaker coils. I was so ready to be. The smoke raised through my shoulder blades and made me scream in places where my own cells were turning square-shaped like STOP symbols on VCRs. I stopped along the wall and groaned our song some out of my mouth, holding my breath. I could hear this mother on the far side of the drywall. She was reading romance. I pressed my palm flat on the paint and said each word aloud as it crossed across her eye. She looked up at where I wasn't yet. This turned me imminently blacker with the fury. The grain of the glass made reflective over the pictures shifting past from each new angle showed secret films of every hour in the house as this family had lived it, filled with great pus and totally false senses of inhibition. It was in me too, so it was in her. It was in the babies we had not had yet and for whom the future had to end. The house's present children were asleep, dreaming of tunnels. Along the hall as if to match this vision in reverse my boys come coasting forward with the mother borne between them in another Christ pose. They'd given her a pretend choice between sex and death and she'd said nothing. They covered her mouth so the song would come out of her nostrils. I raised my arms and said Hello, pointing in every direction I could think of. Her head shook swoopy with her looking as she followed me with her face trying to understand anything. The book she'd read tonight had made her dreamlike. I had a new book. I bent down and said Hello again. She had another belly on her, someone else's trimester. Her curvature was silly and elaborate. It kept begging me to kiss it. As I did, I heard her other children in the bedroom getting snuffed inside their dreams as one word from my lips sent through the wires in their new brother sent wide black swords into their sleep, and then their sleep went on forever. Each of their last cries was better entertainment than anything I'd ever rented. I moved to press my own belly against the mother's so we'd match, my own gut full of the rite of fast food, hers the pustule of the future baby and diet shakes. My laughing gave her a massage until she was warm enough to pry apart in all the places her creator had designed for me to do so. I used my fists first, then my forehead, then my teeth, and then my eyes. I used the edge of her own camera to slice the best bits. I used the glass that housed the photographs and then the photographs themselves. I used the edges of the money she'd been saving to give to cancer research, I used her own nails, I used her own teeth, I used her. Every color that came out of what she had to be turned into was exactly like mine. They laid the mother on the floor. With my chest against the ground I drank the blood out of her womb with my whole mouth. I drank the blood from her vagina until she didn't have a vagina really anymore, as far as god could tell. I drank and ate of her forever. The boys were clawing at my hands. I fed the boys in turns with each of my ring fingers as they sucked the way I told them. I made them wash their faces in it, their arms and hands. They took the blood and heard me speaking, clearing each word of the mother's from the remainder of her mind. With these words as I translated, the boys began to scribe this book along the wall, rubbing their ring fingers and their dicks in a dot matrix aimed at covering the house, filling in the walls with our scripture around the mother until her bleeding was depleted and then the real writing began.

The fourth mother began giving up her birth. The scroll of wet carried from her organs to the air so we could inhale it quicker. I thanked her by putting my arm inside her. I clenched my groin and touched the center of my skull to her tummy nozzle. The child was in there. I named the child every name but Darrel. I gave him a religion and a cause, selected his sexual preference and sense of humor from the vast array of ugly possibilities. Each fiber of his then became mine, ours in the light that we could all smell him more than anything else. He was risen, in the past tense. The mother was shuddering so fast it was like she was rewinding, pulling her idea of the house in down around her, giving her everything over and over. The power sockets in the house around us began staggering with the hell of what they had to offer light to. Above the house I heard the voice of Darrel utter his commandments full of silence. My chest was cymbals. We'd kissed the crest. Above the house I heard the Eye of Darrel blink and brush the crust off some morning soon to come like any father. The baby coming out of her was dressed in gowns of beautiful lather and packets of acne. It looked so old already. There were so many wrinkles I could hardly see which part was its genitals he'd have tried to use to make another and which were the legs he would have spent years training to use to get to the source with which he'd make. He refused to look at me. He refused my forgiveness. This was all part of the act. The boys around me began singing absolutely nothing as I used my wisdom teeth to take the kid apart, to take equal mouthfuls each of him and her together, pausing only every so often to get a rip on the end of the mother's tit. What dreamy milk. Layer upon layer, I revised them. I tasted spaghetti, apples, chicken in her character. The mother was shrouded in some sort of defensive mist now and eyes rolled in her head ecstatic. Just as I noted this, she closed her eyes so I could not see her come. There was more of the child in her than ever, then, as I removed the rope between her and him in long shanks, hand over hand, and her wet ran down the walls on all sides. The gift the mother gave the evening was my next jacket. Her breast meat would fortify my eyes. She slipped in glitch somehow now repeating her unborn baby's name into the space where wet met air, and in her thickest mist of all now overflowing the mother bloomed.

Inside the fourth mother's head there was a cask of chubby meat inside a bone cage. I raised the meat out of her threads. The remainder of her body clung to the removal in thin tendrils over which the breath of shouting in the house around me bowed. It was the worst song I'd ever heard, absolutely perfect. I brought the meat up to my own face and rubbed it to my temples and wore it as a crown I could no longer tell from my hair. I wondered what would happen later that evening and the next night to the stock market. Beneath me on the floor the mother sang along with muscle fission, the skin withdrawing up into itself doing player-piano-style grindsing, saying nothing. Yes. I kissed the mother's eyes. Inside the remainder of the junk inside her skull I heard the older god lurking, emptying the remainder of the moan she could no longer offer to anyone within earshot. I held her hands and waited with her. I felt the residue of each time she'd been told I love you by someone who meant it as a ring placed on my finger and dissolved into more lard. I rummaged through her memories for the ones most vivid for recording and I smothered them zero. Through her, I placed my hands upon the child. The child was still and dumb as fuck and waiting for me and when I touched his face he smiled and he was done then. His life was my life. I pulled the tiny corpse out in a clap of pig-noise and cold froth. The child emerged the most blessed he had ever been while human, his genitals covered in putridity, his skull a handful. I kissed his eyes. I sucked the eyes into my mouth and sucked their vision, swallowed. Now that was good now. Yes. My wishes passed their own high limits, no longer ours. Sweet reason hulking in my bloodstreams gorgeous, without doors. I placed the baby's corpse back into the mother and patted the skin around the hole as best it would. The mother's color was soaking into the carpet. It could not find the earth there. We sat together, she and I, beneath a fine and uneroding skyline in our eternal summer. Every murder always went like this. With every inch I'd ever wished etched in my days I waited with her for her to disappear. I ate some of her sternum, and of her shoulders. Both tasted the same. There was very little left to recognize about her, so I had done my job, though most of me was somewhere else. I heard the bone of me tell me to find the rest of what I meant and I looked up and found that I could see straight through the ceiling, yes, and through the roof, and there I saw the electrifying slush of night becoming stone above us, the language chiseled in its stutter shaking more and more silence out of somewhere harder there above, and thereby raining it back down on other U.S.A. houses as a bright bath anywhere another person could be found, until the pulse inside my skull pulled my seeing back into my face, into my skull, and thereby back into the putty of me and thereby back into my speech and through the remainder of the mother and her child, which there vibrating in me made me hover and crust over in the center of a spine of someone in me I had never quite yet fully been, and so most worshipped. Within this body, in an instant there above the mother boiling, I grew old and ill and died inside me and saw that it was good and gave my word and rose again.

The child inside the fourth mother realized its lungs suddenly. It was screaming ideas of metal. It spoke in personas bled into it by the mother in her sleep, deleted Worship tomes in the Rolodex of names shat out of my mouth between me and the child forming a syllabic bridge of colored mush rising a language wind. The names between us became human names erected in tines of purple cells and hissing insects. Each name as it blew through me knocked the godblood out of my mouth. It splashed to kiss the crease of where the boys asleep now in the kitchen had exposed their holes for Shaking. Each name replaced a wish in Darrel and became Darrel and became. The space bar in my mind grew letters on it. Where each name went in, another name came out and fell upon the house's carpet made of shining lymph. Soon the house was overflooded with the syntax icons of all Americans. They piled up in pyramidal mink. Each brick locked in with six bricks exactly of mosaic skin, pooing a movie I would star in when I died, screened in the long flat white awaiting. The inverse image of the movie sealed the mother's false deleted children in their ripped nurseries into cubes of dentures and clean beds, already aged beyond the stage of memory making. The cubes heated with my smiling and turned to ovens where their bodies would be burned. The house's oven opened wide and said our prayer. The prayers sealed in the bricks around the mother and the child, who as the sounding rose me forward from the house forever wished me luck with all his holes unsizing in all of where he'd never been, while behind me the house looked like any other house just built and sold upon the dead mountains of our country, its front door exit breathing in the word in the world where we all talked at the same time.

FLOOD: *The remains of the fetus were handled differently from most of the other victims' bodies, presumably because it had not yet been born. It was dispersed in two parts, the head sent to the set of a popular morning news-gossip TV program, addressed to one of the famous female pundits, though it was intercepted before receipt; the remainder of the body to the White House. Each was marked plainly and with return address leading each half back to the location where the other half had* been sent, and their distribution in such a manner presents in my mind a willingness in Gravey not only to be found, but to become known for what he was doing, though of course we were not able to connect them to any culprit until the discovery of Gravey's activities. Therefore, until now, it could have been anyone. I do know that looking back after I was assigned the case I had been receiving anonymous phone calls to my private extension for several days from someone who would sit on the line in silence, not even breathing. Whether this was related to Gravey or some sort of malfunction I don't know, but the more I think about it the more I believe what I want to believe, which is that from the beginning this case always belonged to me, before there ever was a case.

Upon the night hiding the bloodbath there haloed seven moons. Each of the moons had seven moons about it. Each of the moons' moons was engraved with one of seven symbols, huffing smoke out from the edges where the night's anger surged against its own surface, wanting to destroy the speech from all horizons. Where before the sun had been, there hung an orb the same color and dimension of the prior bulb that watched us among along with one vast unending pupil. Even my boys did not imagine such eternal confirmation. They were all so engorged with how we'd fed, they had to drag their ass across the earth. Their skin cells left no trail behind us, indistinguishable in this era's light from soil. Each house howled as we passed it; each house wanted us to revise its content also, include them in the narrative. And in the morning, when we all woke again together invalid as ever, there was no mail, and the malls stayed closed an extra half an hour, during which, for once, I wept, which felt like rape, and after which I washed my hands and aimed at the old idea of god and waved.

We put new mirrors up over the mirrors in the black house. We harvested the chuff of our deadening emotions for the glue. Mushed them. Wished them whiter. Soon there was no inch we couldn't see ourselves in. My bloodstreams were going bonkers from the new meat and blood all rolling through them, already starving. I needed to calm down inside my pleasure, so said Darrel, which would cause accidental detonation music. Over the mirrors we laid another mirror layer, then a layer of magnifying film. Each boy was then commanded to cleave the skin off his forehead with the sharp end of a magnet. We rubbed the oily side of the skin on the wall for lubrication, then fed the rest into the kitchen sink, forcing raspy floods of us into the pipes that carried air in knots of to and from in network under universal homes. What opened over our eyes was not a wound, but many eyes. When we were healed it would be the first day of our Sod, a day designed for destroying any gifts we'd ever been given by any human. The stink that rose out of our common facial bleeding amplified the innards of the house, over which we laid a final layer made of newer mirrors snatched from newer nearby houses we had sacrificed to flames, and over this at last we painted over the mirrors in our minds to match the black like our house's outside. Consecrated altogether with our spittle, the new wall's rapt heavy face remained reflective just the same, a total window to the holes of holy era already coming. And now the flies between the walls and wounds began to laugh and lay eggs and eat them. Everything from here on would go much quicker, each instant of it that much easier to lie down inside of, like a prison.

FLOOD: *Each of the boys we've brought in thus far does indeed have a marking on his face, some of which they claim were self-inflicted, while others, they insist, were branded in a medicinally induced unconsciousness. The marks are specific for each person, one of a series of seven total designs (as far as I have counted). The symbols are:* **CIRCLE, SQUARE, HEXAGON, STAR, TRIANGLE, DIAMOND, RING**, *the same ones previously noted. I've had no success in gathering further information from those bearing the symbols on their bodies, as they seem to have no idea themselves,* *though some, when prodded, will open their mouths and strain their throats and face skin as if they are being throttled from the inside. Otherwise, they often act as if they don't realize the marks are there, or feel pain. A surprising number of the wounds caused by the markings have yet to fully heal, and they emit a yellow pus. There are no visible marks on Gravey's own head or body other than distinct markings from childhood acne and a tattoo in his right armpit of the numbers one through twenty-one.*

The fifth through fifteenth mothers were made makeshift from the boys. The shrinking house was packed in angles of mushy arm meat and abdomens in such ways I couldn't walk to see who was there or what food I would not eat. The sexdrives of the molding prior bodies of the dead refracted through me in the silence of the act of spreading of our silence outside the house. We clearly knew one day we'd have to all kill one another to become All, and why not begin now? Which boys we'd dismantle among our own first would be selected on the basis of those I didn't most want to beat the shit out of the second I saw them, notarized by Darrel with a shudder of rushing breath through the shafts becoming woken up beneath the house. Because these boys were boys and therefore most of them came equipped with testicles and no wombs, I had to have their junk removed to make them inhabitable. I performed each operation with a butter knife and several lengths of wire from a clock I bought online that was said to once have been kept inside a deaf-mute astronomer's bedchamber. The boys took turns holding the others down. They sprayed all they had left into the room, their rancid death-urine foaming up among the lashing of their limbs and clouding the house fat enough to believe in friendship. The unspent semen would be harvested and spread over the walls and on the ground around the house to keep the machines out. During these operations the band played their nothing music to steady my nerves, not even holding instruments between their hands now: they'd learned through proper practice and my hissing to speak the music through the skin around their knees. The music turned the house into a spitbath for air, lacing the whole bloat of the discharged-choking space between the walls with numbing aether through which the motion of me rendered slower, and I could see my hands move before me before I went to move my hands as all of we already had in the marbling of history. Each hour, to match the new buys, more mothers were being brought in and processed. They were being broken down into component parts again, in sweatshop. The legskin of the mothers was sliced off in neat precision so as to fashion costumes we would wear out for the final Halloween. The brains were packed together in the smoking closet as an ashtray. The scalps and cheekflesh of the mothers were fed to Darrel through the plumbing. The remainder of their fleshes was turned into a couch. The backbones became fishing poles and back scratchers. The remainder of the bones we simply saved; together, as the dead fell, they would interlock across the continents, forming a freeform pyre spanning all homes in total larger than the homes themselves, an incidental holy location thereafter to be worked down over time, as sun and rain continued in our absence. The blood we always totally ate, or at least all together would lie down in and fake sleep.

Name withheld: "The boys were killing each other anyway. They wanted to be killed and become part of the body. They did not want to die as dying is, and instead to be incorporated. Really Gravey didn't touch anyone, they were doing it to themselves, and some were trying to talk the other into doing them up and arguing who should do who and what the flesh was and the smell. It was a disease waiting to be called on. Whoever ended up dead got put in the mirror room for incubation. It seemed like Gravey genuinely couldn't even tell who was dead or alive, as he talked to them all the same way, as they were all dead already in the name."

With all the blood and night surrounding, the mirrors slickened and inverted and turned white and collandered the air beneath the curl of sun. It wasn't sun; it was the first cells of the first series of the bodies of the mothers pearling. It wasn't like rotting, though it seemed that, orally; it was their unpacked flesh at last crystallizing its first layer where once our mission was complete we would wake dynasties repeating in the hyperventilating light beyond this race. The floor above us in the first level of becoming still would not allow us to step foot or even wink its presence but we were accumulating power quickly. The gifting blood of the women and not-women flooded through the house and juiced the day against itself in fast formation and laughed and laughed and air was hours in an instant like me becoming mine. I felt me get fucked by every cock of life inside the coffins I carried in my brain until they could erupt inside me cold at once and fill me with the unending spirit of our hope, hidden in all of us forever bred. I felt the boys becoming steadfast in their ability to split apart, their cells cartooning instant to instant as they flashed and spread the vision. All the names of the new and certain dead were falling out of the air like little 4-D scabs the TV weathermen mistook as hail. Each house ever had a number you could use to speak into it, and so often I would use the phone inside my brain to call these people I'd soon visit and just sit there breathing my dinner into their head. The resulting music of these communications gave new inspiration for that band of ours to turn inside out and fill their lungs with reproductions of all the highest-grossing hits, regurgitating would-be future classic albums as absolutely nothing into the lymph of the first ancestors of Darrel, in the dead world. In all our mirrors I could see infinite rooms of the house exaggerating all around us in the insane light, splitting each like me into sevens and sevens of versions we could fill soon. The splitting of the rooms fed my hunger with more hunger. It filled me with the seasons I would eject into the nation, opening every man to my disease, while by my heart the bells of our incoming curd of god blurred overhead, a descending limit on the cities' ambient ability to withstand anything we uttered.

A. F. F.: "Leaking out of the house into the other houses was reckless and essential. There were boys who wanted Gravey calmed, and some who said they had a plan to slit his throat soon in the house if he did not slow down. Those boys were killed by other boys. The loyalty to Gravey's vessel in the mode of Darrel by now was real, and would become only more real the further the curve rose. It is still rising, there is no longer time. It would not be stopped will not be stopped. Kill me or him or anybody on the cross of your machines and I would smile through blood and what has been done has been done. The splitting of the houses will continue even right now where you are standing, underneath you, and how you cannot feel it means it is at work."

As the light of Darrel slathered up and under all around us in the flesh of mankind, I began to see through other minds. I could shoot from one spine to another, becoming more people the sharper the silence got with death. I mean that when I closed my lids there wasn't black there or teeth or wolves but simple perspectives. I would close my eyes inside the house a mini-instant in my body and where the skin was I'd have vision through another set of meatholes, they among the houses of the living all surrounding now. I'd see a lawn, a store, some hands slicing a melon, driving a golf cart, washing. I might occur into a small man standing at a register where food was being served, his small tattooed arms and long veinwork in a far light making food and taking cash; within him I could remember all the things I'd touched with those weird hands before, could see how despite my best intentions and whatever faith I'd had there were these darker rings inside my body, which whether or not I felt a part, I was. The set of all present current thought clicked around me in a silence permeated with slow blood, among the hours spent surrounded by others who might be the next one the self inside me would click inside of and see from there, no longer recalling; years lived in each human separately and so, infinitely, if all packed into a space too small to allow even grace. These weren't memories but more made in the way I'd been inside a schoolboy's body before and was now a middle-aged user. I didn't have to move into the body to control it or change the words inside the skull and how they'd come out. I'd simply inhabit the limbs and speech as I could see them there within me and take the workload over. It was only a way of life, the way any day there is the list of commands you must process and exist in, no matter how benign. The length of time I spent inside these would shift; I might go on elsewhere for many years or hours, held uncounted beyond the wall of being them. In each it felt like very little. In each there was a world. My methods were always tending toward rupture of what was given. Inside a housewife I would hold the hairdryer so long against the scalp that the hair burned through and skin came open. Instead of squealing, I would laugh. Inside a man tending his yard I'd ride the lawnmower over concrete scraping sparks and ram a fence or side of neighbor's house, or mine. Once I had touched myself as me into this human passage through the shift of body, I no longer needed to stay inside the body to continue guiding my vision for the ending of all narration; and though once I left this body it would not remember my having come inside and known and given vision and kissed the cold word of our Sod against the lips, the person would go on in this way; he or she would cohabit the organism of our total future. The longer I did the act and however more often, the greater lengths I could involve myself as they were fully. I had the person all throughout them in me like a geode. And yet when my eyes were open I was inside my own space and felt nothing. Then I could do two of them at once, like screens side-by-side and parallel in time, then seven. Each mother we killed and body I consumed fed me more ability. It was like I had the energy of the dead cruising my brainlocks. Eventually it got so I could operate so many at the same time they moved in flights: I'd have a horde of geriatrics go bananas inside a Walmart, or a gang of seething boys overtake their PE class with biting maneuvers, or a series of fires in a hospital. Brownouts. I turned a prison upside down and no one noticed. In this manner we took form, spreading out into the feeding flesh for what the light of us required. This comes not a proclamation of judgment or of absent faith, but the natural proclivity of the necessary destruction that feeds in the body of the human to make more humans who then must fold; it is not good or evil, light or opaque, gross or gorgeous; it is a paste I ride. In the blinking I went on to more bodies behind their thin doors and started to use their bodies to infect into even more other bodies too. I spread the edges of me into whoever I could imagine. It didn't matter why. Each time it seemed outside me like only more of what the world had always wanted. The news corporations assisted my integration beautifully. I didn't even have to have them read the script, nor did I need to keep my mind on anything to have everyone inside me focused, a bank of captured feeds so high and wide it felt like celebrating all our birthdays at the same time always. I moved into the skulls in floods wearing the vision of the seven symbols and there I placed them across the land: inside the bodies of the teacher, the carpenter, the homemaker, the mime, the masseuse, the actor, the artist, the surgeon, the child, the mother, the father, the killer, the reader of this book. My power was conflagrating and masturbating at the same time; I could feel it most focused in my ring finger. I would kiss the knuckle and touch anything and let the buzzing fill all possible other sound inside anyone around me. I mean our senses. The mechanisms of control infected everywhere they fantasized of or saw on the films or through my boys' extending visions patrolling the streets for who was next. The boys were all my senses, and therefore those of all my brain absorbed, altogether weaving and arranging quietly in private among the congregating holes and fibers of us a rapidly evolving apparatus that soon would be filled with all I had felt inside the name of Darrel consecrated in full across a space as wide as the only continent I'd ever touched, therefore the only land that really exists, which soon would find itself made truly and forever the wanting void it'd always been, our names credits for a commercial our emotions couldn't begin to witness.

FLOOD: *The night I first read to this point in the manuscript I paused here because there was something knocking at a window in the far end of my hotel room, which I'd rented to read inside a different space from where I sleep. I'd not told anyone where I was staying; there was no one to tell. I went to the window and looked out. It looked like any kind of time. No one was out there. I looked at long angles with my head against the glass to try to see what had done the knocking. I got my gun and opened the door. On the ground there was a picture of me sitting on the bed in my hotel room, reading the book. You were in the picture, too. I don't know who you are or what you look like, but it was you. You were on the bed asleep. The photo was taken from the perspective of the bathroom mirror. The next morning the picture had gone pale.*

FLOOD: *This page at first glance appears blank. Up close, though, in proper light, there is a kind of indecipherable font, or more like little pictograms that don't seem to form any image. I find myself staring into the page here for too long at times, waiting for the build of it to compile correctly, but instead I end up feeling sick or falling asleep. Then I look up and see it's as light or dark outside as ever, like no time passing. After more time spent studying the pictograms I feel certain I have seen them elsewhere in the world, like signs of corporate logos or textures on the sides of buildings seared somehow into my unconscious, but of course this is me searching for meaning. Likely there is no meaning but it is my job to persist in the identification of tragedy nailed to nothing, and so I will. Honestly at this point I want to burn the book. I also find myself thinking I want to eat it, that I want to get the sentences tattooed on my body. The thought snakes through me in my voice. I have been sleeping with the book at night whether I do or not, like suddenly it's in my arms, or it feels like it is. It is a pressure. A dress. It kind of itches. As an afterthought, I have covered up the mirrors in my home, though not those in my car. Suddenly I feel over-aware of the number of mirrors I come into contact with daily, often without having even noticed their presence in the room. The book continues.*

"Do you know about the city of Sod," I heard me saying. "Do you know about the city of the children of Sod. Do you know about the silence of the locks in the city of the children of Sod, who have been waiting to be cut free from bereavement. One method for arriving at the white gate is chloroform and candles. This should be applied to you by a licensed client of the word, who will appear above your bed in a down flak jacket. I am the jacket. The erotics of names is not a joke. Every night's name is every night's name and the room's too. I will arrive inside you also and you will allow me. Every griever is my fiancé. Our jagged tips reach up into the Sod. The transfigured night is why you age. The cloaking me will kill the remainder so we can have an unoblivious serenity. I am online. The me I am not me inside the mirror walks toward me as the mirror grows closer with me in it, approaching me approaching. The glass dome on this home shatters every time another person has a birthday. The homes beside this home call the shards in mnemonic purring to come into the home and cut them into worship. The entrance to the cloaking city must be cloaked on the face of the blood of all. Eternally, the lamps inside our house so familiar they are not there. Where I am so warm in me I can't sleep until the work is written and erased. Where I can sleep outside me against the neighbor house with my head against the siding, listening for my name without realizing I am listening for my name or realizing I am listening or realizing I am not against the house or I am not outside my house but your house. My words eat the tone out of their fantasy until they look like something you have done or will do or would want to and will or would want to and cannot or will again. When I say I love you I mean I am you in the color of your blood. Welcome our house of endless milk. The mist of our fourteenth moon rising in the cake batter of the mattress where you will make the final child of your whole life each night and transfer into us. Not yours but yours and mine. Not ours."

Name withheld: "Sometimes he would just lie down on the ground and fold into a ball so tight we couldn't pull him back apart. He seemed in those moments to be trying to be compressing himself all back into a dot somewhere inside him, like disappearing. He could get so small. He would seize and seem to be weeping but nothing came out. He would speak in the language of a child, like one who'd never learned a word. These spells might last three minutes or an evening, which took the same shape. These ways were when we feared him most."

BILL L.: "No new word shall form. No shapes. No abyss of sky. No now."

By now the boys were bringing mothers home in set of sevens. I wasn't even asking but they had their own integrations going, fired in their bellies, doing my work for me while I grew larger. Sometimes their genitals pushed so far out through their pants the dickheads had fists that punched holes in the house and let the outside in, or their ovaries would distend against the innards of their belly and make it impossible to go around. Whole sections of the house might be partitioned off for hours with flesh, stranding boys or sound behind a length of thickening wall so full of the media we were expunging it was like the house had disappeared. And this I realized was a fantastic predicament and must be continued as our day grew larger among the unknowing fields of neighbors waiting to become us. Their private screams in the American aloneness trembled and made my lardy body tremble too, a necessity for learning how to feel them. People. I had so much of them inside and around me I caved a new eternity every time I stroked. Our victims were coming so easily now it was like a video game sewn in my vision with the controller embedded in my breath. Some days multiple mothers would have to be discarded in order to keep within the house some space to exhale and I was too full to eat much of them so I let the boys and local pets have more than their fair share. I hardly even believed in killing anymore and so it was like I was always the president on vacation. I'd already lost count of our accumulating libidos and anyway I couldn't reach my dick. Words filled me in the second of every deathblow as the bodies became part of the enunciation with the last note of the band of Darrel purring silent noise through and through and through the glass of time. All I ever did now was lie around and grow and watch my growing in the mirrors fund the growing further dadlike. Some of the mirrors had gone so black inside the ejection of the spirit into the house that they were halls as well, connecting us with passageways to other homes and corporate offices full of more victims. In reverse we populated backgrounds of universal art with our machetes and laughed from where inside the cabinets and collard greens the audiences would retroactively disregard how anything had changed in the painting or program or outlet mall they'd been born to admire, allowing sharper gnawing and longer sleep, allowing my prowess to fill the house all by myself alone and leach out into one life then another, loved from foot to face by anyone I entered, because I was as much them as they were and by god were they ready to worship that. Both the mother and the child myself between us. The seas of we united and extended in the rapidly approaching wrath of heatless energy awakened only in death.

KALEB, age 17: "Black gouge meat poured from them. I saw Darrel lift them up. They were inculcated sweetly with the blue drum throbbing in me and we were the sound. I had waited all my life to be the centerpiece of someone's dreamland, as when I closed my eyes inside my head I could hear nothing but the nothing moving through the cities whistling against the fumes. The mirror of the reflection of the mirror of the sky made flesh stand out on the heads between the curvatures of buildings where when I went and sat inside a room I could feel holy by lying on the floor and looking down. The meat of the women was the most beautiful year of my life every minute of it even as I knew I did not want to see them suffer as I wear my mother's heart. There is only one motion to becoming and that is to no longer press the button and yet the hand of the globule in the arm of the American raises up and raises up never pausing."

We ate the mothers' neckflesh and their lockets, we ate their wedding rings or where those rings were not, we burned the hair and drank the smoke in, felt in filling where in we we wished we weren't, we peeled the linings off the organs and wrapped their softing casings on our faces and stood in the overwhelming late and saw each other as another rising, we ate the smile meat off the cheeks and around the lips in lining, we ate the glimmer of the eyelids empurpled where each had rolled up on itself so many times against the sun for sleep or in the blink of meat encased among the soft night of the self; we shucked the bones clean while I gave speeches that contained no words, the screaming so loud in our tendons that it climaxed through the milk of air and was not there above our breath. Our new god's body rang the telephones inside the houses as I ripped again and again from the many minor mothers' chests the layers of the flesh where they had held the feelings of the mother for the child, and this was eaten again under a load of rain by fourteen Darrels who would mold the meat inside them into a horn that grew out on a lesion on my large intestine as more and more the song grew strong. The stench of blood would etch itself under our own nails and in the slits between the mirrors and the grade of air where we believed in what we were becoming, in the flood of human silt and milk and pilling on the veins of space our being here must enter and awake. We ate the curling food of her brain tunnels unearthed from where the skulls split and juiced their columns clean between our teeth, sulking the amalgamation memory of our uncoming to the future diamond skull our last god longed for. The pretending light erupted gleamshapes on reality that mimicked our cold motion well beyond our homes as all minds remained united in the dead mouth of anywhere surrounded all the countless versions of the hours ticking upward to bare upon the sky a wish for all else appearing where it wasn't. We would never need to kill again once there was no one left to kill. The world all ours, all bodies and all customs in whatever name refracted through the color soon we would become. There must be only one body remaining. This is why we eat: so that each I take in will be in me like the others he had eaten were inside him. All bodies pressed into the flesh of god. The color of the curd of the rainbow coming out of any inch of the killed held in perpetuity together in one final surface all regardless of how they were cut or who they'd been made by, in what citizenship or temporary color they'd believed, which mouth of time of us they entered to become an entry in index of the ultimate data, full defeat, unto an eternal life where life is not alive or dead but the deformity of the plane of space shaping the age of the dying god's last novelty. And this still was not enough. No hour was sufficiently ours to be the way an hour had been in the hour of the making of earth according to man's imagination. Where the mothers' colors met through me they became fused, and I could have them and everything they remembered was open to everything. Everything not flesh or bone we did away with. We burned the bras we burned the hair we burned the credit cards and cash we burned the rings around the fingers we broke the fingers and the nails we burned the burning in their loins we burned them and we burned them. The lessons pilled up on the floor like the dream of a wall around our people that could not be felt. The colors of their lipsticks and foldings and our dry hump was overwriting the previous year's best clothing designers' dreamlives, thereby overriding yours. So that when we did find you in the killing fields, and we would, you would look more fuckable than you had ever on your own. Any inch of what was mine once became yours by my not knowing how to have it, in that wherever I was not looking was always the only place to be remembered. Bit by bit the nation ate itself alive by we the teeth. No matter what I gave or killed or wished or centered or reconceived by my own hands in the greatest struggle of passion I was nothing more than the end of the beginning. This had become our country all along. This had been the instant of the waking ending as it instanced open, and still waited for another end to bless our hearts. Another end was not coming. That would have been a gift to give your lover for every commercial holiday combined, though now all lovers were equal. Whenever anything ends before you, you may know now it is a false thing, and so call it, and so know the want of more, and more want of want of more of all what fills each prior sentiment as experienced in humans funding the understanding of true beauty. There was so much need now in the house where the mothers' remembrance-complexes and remainders collided in psionic beehive, the wideload of pleading and bloodshed and their thereafter replicating so many haunted lives pressed in on the same air in the same era, the light of the TVs and the bulbs brighter than any sunrise or corona, that you could hardly think about your thinking. I was sleeping so well every night, nothing machining in the blue space where I had before me and before my present body always stung so hard the night would scream in the coming image of our god at last leavened in my breast as he always had and always would now. This act of our word written out by hand on this white paper was all we'd all been doing as a human people even closest in the moments we believed to be building our new homes. To stroke the hair of the loved ones, to fold grain into loaves that would be broken before audiences as entertainment. At last here I was, served in a service with no residual continuum beyond fiber, though there must so soon distinctly be a certain end for the flesh of those we wished into us as we laid the foundation upon turning every person back to zero. One nowhere for us all at once again, in which we could return the favor we'd been granted to appear ever out here side by side, though it would be not you or I who brought fruition, but simply the birthplace of an actually everlasting form of spirit beyond the grave. Refracted in the last black house of our black city once lined with mirrors now lined again with something spinal on the night.

FLOOD: *Photographs of the remains found in the room beneath the house are almost impossible to look at, in that they more resemble abstract art than corpses. The level of dismantling and removal is almost machinic. I can't help thinking of grapefruit. A fellow officer made a joke how one shot resembled the walls in his grandparents' living room when he was little. I found myself laughing. I couldn't stop laughing.*

The dying god releases a map of the world. It looks like a map of the world.

FLOOD: *I submit another request for the paperwork explaining the details of the manner of detection leading up to Gravey's arrest, being as I had not been involved with this case throughout that time, having moved over to this precinct just before his arrest. The previous lead detective had transferred or gone on extended leave just immediately before the date of apprehension, or this is what I'm told. I don't know why I haven't gotten this information passed to me already. I have to submit three more requests before the work finally shows up: a file only eleven pages long, with information pertaining only to Gravey's prior record (clean), a note regarding the difficulty of finding almost any public record or testimonial about Gravey's position in the community or details of his past, and the contents of his home at the time of booking (of which I was already aware). Upon request for the rest of the files, how we found out about Gravey's existence in the first place, etc., I am told this information "does not exist," meaning that whatever other files there were, beyond essentially what I've put together on my own, went with the prior detective,* ▮▮▮▮▮▮▮▮▮▮*, who I never actually met directly, and is "no longer accessible," according to our would-be mutual superior. Any further attempts I've made at unraveling the story end with the forwarded phone calls, questions answered with questions, and blank stares that come with the territory of my work, which of course is frankly part of what I love about it: the infernal collaboration of creativity and fate.*

Under the wake of all of night we went again. We wedded the public with the private; tunneled through the holes in the houses the darkness graced as welcome mats made of the dirt of the buried, gifting access into each home, and enough desire to slip into each denatured, dragging the future. Into each I went, too, split in my dimension to replicate across the universe of homes. In each we found a version of the mother to behold and hold above us and render into godflesh. Often the mother was a child. When the mother had testicles, we removed them and placed them in one of my boys' mouths to bring them home. These must be fed into the incubation outlet for the prison system of the next year to feed with, reproteinizing any face. The hair would grow out on us so thick there would be no cavern but for Him who firebreathed no flame in the Name. In each house we bound the husband's hands with leather thongs we'd rendered from the excess pets we'd bred. Many of the houses had second floors the inhabitants had not realized. These floors were full of beds. The sleeping of the Darrels there in coming years would knit the house into the ground, pushing down as well the submerged layer of the buried persons who were speaking always in our organs. They knew nothing of me, but they slipped into my speeches. They were nothing like lyrics. Each husband would be dispatched with a chrome lever affixed to his throat. The lever lifted brought his voice out like from a spigot and spilled upon his chest and wrote the Word. The Word would in the proper configuration, with the word placed on the next victim, I believed, erase the voices with the downing as they lowered with the sentences of Darrel, and so this was done some nights ten times or fifty in a row. Stabbing with the left hand then the right hand then with the lever wedged in my ribcage. Whatever wet the bodies shot upon me stayed, became my coat worn in a sheath to explicate our absolute and shapeless deathgod's phantom body. Each house we entered was a new cell to be filled in with the makings of the night. Some stabbing hit upon the buttocks so that they might stand for many years and feel the blood mush in their legs, learning the posture of the Darrel as they held the marks of the language of the new god up upon the temple of their heads. In each house I removed the DELETE key from any computer and ate it into my belly and heard it affix to my tubes. Behind my eyes the typing fired.

R. A.: "By now he was seeing through the eyes of each of all of us at once, he said, and through the eyes of the building body of the mother made from all of those we'd taken apart, so that upon the rooms he could see the other rooms coming and going and all that had and would be done. One night I watched him lean so hard against a mirror the mirror split around his head. We weren't even playing music anymore for all the times as at last Gravey said the song was playing itself and so we were playing it as we walked and woke and said nothing, as no speaking in the house was allowed but his and he mostly didn't ever so we could listen to the becoming of the day despite it looking like it had all the other days surrounding."

There was nowhere to hide all that we had not begun consuming. We packed the cavity under the house with more bodies and more bodies and soon it would overflow and we'd dig further to make the chamber bigger and the ground below us moaned and caved more space again to fill. We covered each new layer with more mirrors and more light. We made the shapes that Darrel commanded in the walls there with our longest fingers and ejected the seedchild crust; and once the musk of innards had settled in the chamber we went to Petco and bought all the darling parasites they had for sale: hamsters and guinea pigs and white mice and fancy rats captured in cages. These could do some of the eating in our stead, as my teeth were getting sore from all the flavor, and my lips were about to fall out, and the boys seemed old as hell. The U-Haul full of our pets became a superior Rauschenberg of actual excrement and fur immediately. The traffic lights came on red all the way returning. At an Exxon I bought a candy necklace and wore it around my chest and let it do my speaking for me so I could set my brain on pornography of an everlasting nature. Our death would never have to die. At home we put the temporary pets into the incubation chamber and let them go to work among the bread bed of corpses, demolishing the remainders. We watched them pack the mush of every corpse into dens of blue intestine. Into these mounds they laid packs of eggs all colored gold, or squirted repeated pregnancies into the beautiful lard as we'd provided. Each time the animals and we inside ourselves ate enough mother to brine a child inside the shit, the babies immediately would inside the house begin again to make themselves again and lay themselves into the blacking mass. It made a sound of gnat accordions and secondary wishing in the name of Sod. The eggs were spooling harder and where they birthed again into themselves the corridor became packed. Each new birth was a cell in the new god. It would be my rite to raise him on the lawn of the Black House while the cameras rolled and our song sang and shat and sang and kissed every hour underground rolled up above and born again. For each new generation more mothers had to be made witness to him in donation of their American memory of how cells die, which meant there was more work for the boys to do to bring them to me and to help me continue to remember to want to need. Their airs immediately combined, the rising air all together not just of man but of the louse in man most recognizable, beyond the ark of the old god. The stench cells under sky's devoid rim shaking while we waited more through shorter periods while in the wet of noise the song of hours became stiller still and harder to acknowledge. To pass the time we practiced coronations and mind vibration. Of course we filmed it. The films were in our skin. The soundtracks were the same lack of everything we'd always wanted. Inside the newer no sound our undrummer got entranced; he cut his right arm off to control his fortitude for doing nothing better than ever. Our guitarist tried to unshred with all the notes at once and became actually immaculate enough to throw his mental children to their deaths inside the well of his ability. The toilets all began to overflow inside the zilch and vermin pregnancizing. Our musk flooded fast to fill the blush above the houses, the lawn around us bluer and inculcating burrowing vermin for miles under the earth, each laying their eggs in the grown sod to be nearer to our affection. The piping of my sermon fed them grace through holes I did not want to provide for free but could not contain because I am loud when I am ejaculating which is always which means sometimes I can't bring myself to clear my throat and when I vomit from the air of this world it clings inside me and becomes more lingo I have to dethrone into silence.

TERRY I., age 8: "I was growing worried of him, about him. What he said came out of him with such sweat and when he tried to cover his eyes with his hands his hands would instead punch him or me or the wall and hurt it instead of hiding. I believe he was a child for eternity. I wanted him to calm down and wish for something, be alone with me a little bit, think about days we could have in silence even between the great rising that was going on but all he wanted was the end. It had to come he said and he wouldn't let me hold him and he wouldn't slow down and where he said the word I knew they were right there on my lap and on all the laps making the lap of America for all of us and it was already happening and had already happened and was going to again."

Name withheld: "It doesn't matter that this page is not what happened and there were never any animals beyond us the humans in the house; it doesn't matter at all right now because it is, because he says."

"Electronic flowers blooming in my nothing. Skins on skins against a wide unveiling in hair like riots in the false collaborative witness. Seas in spinning silence of the corridors of plasmatic fish rising to fit their homes against our home as well and writhe the poison of their 300,000,000 heads of hidden sickness, upon the tongues of those the dying night had yet to memorize. I swore new eyebrows rising on the children in the preschools, insecticide clustered around their navels and their necks. The putrid future now would never have to be waited out, but simply had; as every woman who would become a mother would have lived forever had they not, and every woman who would not would have lived forever had they really; every father made of snot; all future memories deleted, predicting *right now*. For in the preservation of our true children, this gift of piglets and this murder of the murder of the pretend, a temporary slur raised on the icon of the chimp they never weren't."

CHARLES: "Each time I came back into the house from outside the house where you could see the sky changing colors in reflection to the containment of the Home it was like dying again. It was like the minute going paused inside the theater. I didn't eat anything in the house except these words, which when written down inside your book will appear incorrectly. The leakage of our birth was unstoppable in each intention of the gestures Gravey rained upon us from the throne of bodies in the piles of mud speaking now into a small machine these words, and the words that would be said inside the room upon reading the words inside the house: which is to say, what I am saying now, and what will be said when the fusion of the ten folds of the face of god congeal and there you are."

The junk that spooted from the innards of the mothers we murdered into the house around our sound allowed the tunnel of the mirrors to bathe in warm-lurched creamy white wine of death-semen. I was the Provider. The skin I wasn't yet began to squeal. Once admitted, each new mother emitted the same lengths of whine or screeching compacted in the godyear as a white dot, one drier pixel lengthening the city's silent other color slightly thicker and begetting more of us to please; each as well gave the same stinking, pillowing the night textures off of which to deflect the skeins of unnatural light, though all their ejections were different colors. Lavender came off the back side of the blood-hid eyes of the four-foot mother that Spanish Darrel had carried back into our home on the promise of a dinner of white meat; Forest Green came out of the mother with the goiter covering the left side of his face, brought back by Gaseous Darrel on the promise of yardwork and a bottle of white wine; a slicker shade of Pink came out of more than several mothers in shades distinctly of the amount of them they'd rendered to no wish in U.S.A. scourge; we used the Black that came out of the elderly mother in midst of menopause but still with the milk inside her streaming through her sores, who'd come in mistaking Big Beef Darrel for her grandchild, to recoat the window in the foyer which had taught itself to peel in panels wide enough to see out through the backyard where there was no longer any yard, the land stretched monstrously wide, unto our god rising over all seas elsewhere, attracting the sacrificial families to kneel before the blubbered night and beg. The other colors I am too tired today to tell you what or why as where from their lurching out through holes I rendered with the pickaxe or the trowel, and yet they scratched inside the house to find among the walls amongst the nest warmth to latch on and take hold, surrounded by each other in every verb or gesture shook free from the husks of us.

ASHLEY F., age 24: "It was growing large enough to hold us all. It was not an ark finally."

FLOOD: *Today I asked one of the boys if Gravey finds Darrel not only in himself, but in all people. The child began to laugh until he threw up blood, and did not stop* throwing up until the nurse, a woman, touched him, at which point his eyes grew wider than I have ever seen. Later, when I came back, he had drawn a picture of a dog with countless heads on his stomach upside down. He was still adding more heads.

The bodies of the mothers began appearing all across the country. I could no longer control the scroll of our own blood, which meant that this was working. The bodies appeared as misplaced objects in the landscape. Young ones could no longer find their keys, or the shirt with their name across the chest from their encampment, or the name of who they'd meant to learn someday to meet in love or sex. These mothers were the killers. We were in their bodies too, while in the same dimension the bodies congregated as we destroyed them and took their pieces in our chest and air. This was no sort of new beginning. This was every country all at once, each in her own mind of America undone and disappearing, seeming the center of themselves. The bead of earth here where we had writ the Becoming rose in slow dimension to the sky; it mirrored the inward sloping of the house toward the night air, allowing the house again to sit reflected at itself beside itself and above it and beneath it. The horizon's curve no longer fit. The dysfunction between what was and what would soon be mayonnaised a medium between the features of the present moment. It rattled the paper in the libraries. At the center of the books that would never be again opened, blood began to fill. Our presence spread mnemonically as a blank virus upon the land. Holy men and churches began combusting into fire, spreading. The fire walked into some of the houses and made copies of itself onto old things. It spread its ideas into surfaces and filled them up with nothing and made them appear not ever there, though there they were. Even fire is full of holes; its air is wholly holes itself. The resulting ash became the liver of the new god overall; so named Darrel; so in silence; for which the corresponding mothers of the United States had been divulged of their lives by the hand of Him. Where the fire fell it left its resin until that too became dispersed. This all happened among our No Sound, finally perfected in the bed of den of flesh we'd cleaned. Where the fire had no children there was a cold air that walked upon the soil; it touched the doors of certain houses and invented in inhabitants there inside their sleep a walking roar that ate the pleasure out of their vessels. When they fucked, they felt the same as any day; the sensation still was recognized inside them as codified and vital, a rarefied form of being mostly only ever conceivable in the space where meat meets meet;

they felt, then, they had to work harder to feel the nothing harder where the nothing went. I could literally enter absolutely anybody at this point. On the air of America around the Black House the tissue of these organs grew one by one, reflected from the central mirror of the new god, making provided tissue and glands and veins and cells by which to clasp around themselves together. And where Darrel threw up, this would be the skin. And where the water of the earth burned against the skin in unseen soft formation so came the threads of hair that grew out on our godhead, along her arms and down her body, amassing in flowerbeds around her birthing surface and her Invention Putty held there within holding the names so hard against itself it bruised her and from the bruises woke the flesh, which woke the other organs soon to come, in me, and there above the earth the revolutionizing body overall above us trembled in new terror ripped among our words we couldn't hear it, and more were made and she grew larger and she grew larger, sick with heat. The bedsore cornbread flowed for days; out of the mouths of where the mothers appeared it gunked into the homes again forgotten. We were just sitting in the house now, being people; the work performed itself. Rot cycled in ecstatic function quicker, feeding off everything. The chords of death aggregated in the Black House's spinal column between its many versions, stuttered forth to connect the dots. The infestation took place in hours during birthday parties and celebrations of the Rising Hour or when the women of the surrounding houses had gone to sleep or were reading in the bathtub or making dinner out of whatever could be found inside the confines of the walls. The men of the houses were always under water with their own fantasy against the color and so heard nothing but the speaking voices they had meant to use and would not now and yet could remember in a certain vector of the brain between the lid of sleep and nowhere and therefore hold within them consciously but in the act of drowning and so bathed in and found the whole of and spent the night inside of cracking and yet when woke rose having not known or learned the resin of it but for a certain kind of crick about the teeth. Spigots of another silent substance rose inside of boxes of the houses unexamined: in the sealed furniture and hollow avenues behind the walls uncurtained and the lumps of space between dresser drawers and surrounding vents unto the reaches of the flesh. Dogs walked on. Walks dogged on. Days on calendars filled in with instances of their images of self as catalogs of old decisions, vacations, appointments, seasons, ideas, forgotten proclivities compiled. Time ate itself and ate what came out of it as itself digested and ate what came out again. From the corresponding puzzle-ash our dimension's feverish imagination emerged alive drunken on the very air. Everything we'd meant to ram with or ram up in us for the next several hundred thousand lengths of time gaped in white cures in this version of Today sopping glossy and in sticky floods of screaming egg and semen indexed along the banisters and mirrors and fine carpet beneath us waiting for the current instant to turn. Our sermon was the history of human sickness, for which the babies even still resolved no medication: blueblack pillars of slick protozoa puffed up and gathered like the lining of a coat; spores that softed through the house in calm arena microscopically amassed in snotty marble of our already rampant skin disease; cancer lampshades; diabetic doorknobs; sickly blood lining the halls of us begetting one another; one long AIDS hall, clustered wallpaper sputum guardrails and lesion buttons to doors that would not peel. Our housing was all ovens baking lymph wall-to-wall shrunk with tattoos we could not see, the piled-up ribcages and neck strengths and lodes of sore collapsing in the high multitudes of compiling pressure of the flame of want that made the days seem a size both countable and variable, depending on how hellishly we wished them done; creamy sternums knitting into sternums, child and parent, cells spreading open puddled in white languor for the house to shudder deeper, fill up more air with more of us in the idea that therein we could be comforted; rest; such flesh compressed into any instant of the house it was all of them together in each cell, where each cell held the pudding of knowing what we could have been with all ourselves and in ourselves a mass of autistic hope scratched on a log of bacon in great unburning flare; the lash of being nothing unto nothing with the cracking of the backbone lying onto beds to open wide regardless of what children or fear or wanting might erect a shield inside in practiced desperation, weapons of mesmerism, ass. Our years of murder were no calamity but the calm of sitting in the white of rooms of our own making while in all the other houses the daylight gored the hour to no nub but what we photographed or scribbled into symbols and the gas leaking beneath the houses to drink into the mudbath spirit-money stuffed behind the walls of human skin peeled and left for absent lining the corridors of other homes and heads and every inch of rooms of worlds; our vast destructing unresolving carpet under all flat shaving human feet and rising high into a yogurt curl of stuttered universes rubbing where we will not look as turning as we turn to see what we can see. I'd already lost count in here in what I'd done, even seeing the making of the music, the dreamlife numbers I rolled in nightly and stored in my memory as gold grills I'd wear to be mistaken in our music videos for someone someone thought they felt a love in. This was an aesthetic moment, blinking instantly from one to next inside no passage as the passive orbs of sun and moon tricked us enslaved. Even I would not remember I had experienced this a single evening in His presence, as in the next instant again lurched the bloodfields and machine guns and trenches fit with catalogs of years which by totally dying we avoid; frozen film of teeth being removed from the heads and worn on jewelry for the impregnation rite under Presidents installed in order off of lists printed on human grief; years of islands under water and bones crushed under tank tread and the billow of the flesh out of a pinhole on sunk fields uphill toward no sign where children hid shitting in the woods waiting no death under our orgasm for a final eternal war; the other countries in their barracks cut and pasted onto the same square in machete liquid and long bombglow burnt into the light we called a nice day and the summer of white convulsive heat glowing in no shadow as we forgot again that we'd forgot; weapons of the nose and palate splitting flesh for years through fields of marbled horseshit spit of mouths of soldiers at our griefcenters each instant in the drapes and up our stairs unto no door becoming store floors and LCD screens and gleaming polish. This was both our history and our future melded together so it could be consumed, a gown I sweated through so well it was transparent. This state of ours again already smelled like bliss, like pineapples falling open in a low sun heated with the skin of everyone inside the skin becoming bluer than the realm of god and pouring blood from each into a clear cup rising through the universe at elemental speed for no reason but to move and move again, forced fucked between the hours, inside the scroll of time we worshipped Holy Rest; brains packed with dresses the mothers we'd collected in the house below the homes so far would wear to stand before the pyre of no Sun to be knighted into name of one name reigning as only it could ever; the coronation in black linen lined with neon purple ribbing around the nipples and collarneck and sleeves and bone-colored buttons rubbing skin off where pressed with the wrong finger, which was any finger not absolutely mine; the dresses we would wear in idea of afterlife all were smoke and did not miss our prior bodies; I listened as the fabrics they'd be stitched from poured out through the grinding of the house into the coming evening while all the other houses let their trash be used as toys or eaten and delivered into flesh again to be part of us again, to love us again, to hold a thought together, though we would not because we could not pay attention half that time, our corpses were so inebriated. The body of god's body was by now just above my body, positively stunning draped in the worms the fat with the ranks of flesh now disappeared or otherwise wholly avoided, less worm-looking than a worm is and more prismatic, colors filtered through the glueglass of ornaments we'd hung in houses for celebration in old light shat out by machines and called our birthright, while tonight the going bright white behind the moon plumed down from its orbit with its necessary illusion as the sky sobbed and wrapped en masse around our sweating forehead ever-growing, going tripled between instants, each shaking more and more of its new self from its decided center as I speak, establishing even more mechanical desire in those remaining, the bodies only soon as yet to be made full in mine; each of these grossed up with pink bubbles changing color as they went on in their learned versions of the frames of daily walking around and eating and taking mail and pills and cough syrup and making anything they could, drumming on along a sweet curve in vast magnetic mass held unrecorded as this house held its up and splintered south and north and west and east into new floors, all the bodies they were cut from only desperate to make more babies where they did not mean to and would never.

Name withheld: "We were all pregnant, and all beyond turned on, and it was growing. You were in there. The walls were white. The flood of the birthwater would soon run down the legs of the earth and flood the prism of the eye of the earth, all in Her name, born, and here again. By now there was no turning back regardless of what you believed about the way the words curled on your eyes, or how fast you turned off from them, hid them away. It was no longer about light."

L. S., age 19: "Just try to breathe. You can't, can you?"

It was Becoming. Through the phones in all of us god spoke a language that could not be transcribed while night inside itself continued its devolvement. The last body of god rose through a white hazing oil that loved anybody who would exist before it while the morning tore itself apart; it lathered down in clear down blankets wrapped around us. Each vitamin begat an exorcism of the safe word between two doors along the birth hall of our rapidly increasing mass, which by now had bulldozed every inch of breathing air within me. Where the verbs fell from their protection grew a new road to walk along unto some sea. The sea would appear to not be boiling. Inside our future minds the language babies writhed and pupated with babble cockles, deriving the next language to be spoken in the swoon of nothing. Our black house smelled like a bowling alley full of pig heads. The mother bodies were snuffed in dozens and leaked their juice so loud sometimes I could see it coursing down the empty streets where no one soon would be walking and up white mountains to be burned off into the sun, while underneath us the blood grew bluer and then blacker, leaping maggots from where the flesh collected. Often I couldn't tell the difference now between a new mother and a pickaxe; they mostly passed as water, air, and sleep. And yet the sixty-seventh invocation of the mother looked just like me again. I still didn't remember any hour there before or after, though, but here where this one had my skull and sacs and all my dismantled grievances recombined. This one wanted all the same things I'd ever wanted, if I remembered rightly, which I didn't, as held in scar flesh on his love handles and in the hair around his anus hiding what he was. I put a mirror to him and he looked like a simple yellow dot. From the dot there rose a little cake. I ate it with my ear, and then could hear his contribution to god's most recent face: his own phantom mother, delivering the replication hurt, the want for being somewhere further soon and so then trying and gaining more flesh by rubbing that want out. Our god filled the other organs in with colored pencil. Our god rubbed a grease eraser over folds and made them colonize. The bodies seared, gave smoke, and disappeared; it made us starving. Every lick of nothing was a gift we didn't need and so consumed that much more quickly and bulged the wordless seam within. I broke the mirror. I ate the mirror. I ate me. I ate the home, and went back out, and came back in.

I rose. I was the mothers fully, their organs, their eras, spaces, eggs. In the many houses all the hours were my eyes. Killing the fathers and the mothers and the children with my hands of other men made my void voracious and I needed to be fed. I looked like any other person. I worked at Subway and split meat. I rubbed the bread with colored substances and chortled near the glass. I said I rose. I am the god too. I told this to anyone who would come near. No one came near. No one had fingers. I walked among the light. The Black House spread to color many other houses. This was seen by most as night protection, as defense of weather, but the surfaces and symbols and keyholes made the houses sicker, made them absorb my laughter. Any house wants only at last a life too and would take the worst in your not letting it at all move. It ate the leeches and the termites from the floor of the earth on which I walked and drank them hard into the walls so soft you could not feel it breathe. When the rasp of rats or something shaking brought the house out to flood or when someone knocked at windows with a gun or came in and killed your family or you or took your money or your clothes this was the safest you could ask. Every other minute I was rising. I work in shifts. I take no knee for you. My robe is folded on the coming pyre made for all of us to begin again in. I need you to write me back, and yes you will.

I rose again. Inside, the night was puffy. The mirrors turned red, then blue. The white lights did not affect this despite being hyper-crowded. I said the name of Darrel to have the boys lie down before me and make a bed for who I was turning into. They did not move. There were men who were not the men I was at the windows and in the vents speaking the outdated language. I could see the eye sockets of them dripping with a kind of language. I'd thought I'd had those removed from their spirits, that they would not even be able to see me. Their radios were heaving bullshit. I told the boys to bend over and defend me. To lean down and listen hard to what the people in the submerged room were doing. I felt something in me coming from an opposite direction. The red lights turned to diamondcolor. The boys refused to blink. The beams of lights between their eyes were weaving into layers upon layers in the reflection through the glass made to see itself again. Together all at once they raised both hands hard in tragic gesture toward the false hole in the ceiling that had opened unto the hyper-ventilating night. The night looked less false than I remember. It had a sternum etched upon it, bruised into hiding with the blue. All across it were these eyes, like thousands of them, all seeing down on us, all never blinking. The boys' arms began to quiver. Light emerged somewhere between each of their sockets and aimed directly at my skull. The boys did not lie down. Between the dots of each there slimmed a pleasure scripture caricatured by where I'd had them build their skin thicker to defeat against the melting temperatures of invocation. The boys did not lie down. I tried to go on as if nothing I didn't want was ever happening. I asked how many of us were still at work out there in the houses preparing the extension of our nest into the farther space of being. My voice spilled on my shirt and changed its color to match my flesh. My flesh was older than I remem-bered. In each of the mirrors I saw only one of me, covered in old ink. A tattoo on my breastbone revealed a combination to a lock. I said the numbers aloud and nothing happened. My flesh was older. The boys did not perform as we'd rehearsed. I went to stand up from my throne and felt three hundred feet where both my feet were. The whole air of the world around me squiggled in evac-uation, replacing silence with psychic acne lathering against everything I felt.

Each pustule held another camera filming where between the light of the boys were disappearing. The best of the boys' arms were growing longer, taking pain. The skin around their fists poured batter over any free space. All the neighbors' houses were farther apart than ever, through the world, suddenly, like being cut out of a womb. I smelled wigs and iron. I went to say the name of Darrel and instead said Gravey. My lap was full of beans I was already eating and shitting out. As I looked back up to see again if the boys had done as I had asked them yet finally I saw the lid of night turning itself on. It was a hissing panel. It had a center. It lit my body through and through. There was nowhere left to move between the wall of us and outside except for where I didn't want to.

SAL: "The day they came in through the doors wearing the blue suits Gravey didn't even flinch. He went on as if these people coming through the doors were in his convocation, as if he'd ordered them to come. He greeted the officers speaking back into the glare as if they were any one of us. The blood was on his face and hands from his last supper in the house still and in his eyes I could see from down there on the floor standing behind him I could see he was no longer in the Gravey body anymore. His skin was so dry it kind of flaked off on the other men's arms when they touched him."

FLOOD: *It was actually raining the day our squad went in for him, into the Black House. Raining so hard it seemed like the sky had been ripped off and behind it all that blue up there had always been a liquid. It rained like it didn't want for you to walk. And warm. So warm. The warmest rain I can remember. I recall the sun was out under the storming, a summer color. It seemed like it would go on like that forever until it didn't.*

The many eyes became one eye, an eye set in a head, set in the horizon of the house. The eye was looking down into me. It had a pupil in the color of our floor, which was as well my color, which meant the eye had always been. It was just above me: a whole other sort of surface pressed against the public. It had no lid and didn't stutter. Behind the eye the boys were growing. Their sex organs plugged into the eye on its far side and lit it alive with a growing light that filtered with their eggs and sperms. The eye began to spurt. It gushed out from it a string of drumheads and guitar strings and stripping throats and thumbskin. The mash fell down upon me and rolled me in a coat of newer silence. Where I could see now too around the house the outside was so near there was none of it left. The walls between the outside began peeling with all bloomed layers bent toward me. The house around the eye pulled inward and coated the walls with black again and again over anything to make it small while expressly, from the inverse, my skin continued to turn hard and fat. Wrinkle mass and all my anger trembled in me as I grew and rushed to meet the house as it came nearer, surrounding what of me remained. With this wish, the song knew nothing. It was nothing: it held no sound. It sung nothing. It had, at last, begun to have been always. In my skin my skin was singing nothing with it, not nothing, no new thought. This was the absolute silence of us. The lost words finally matching each in full the only one I'd ever really imagined. No longer only any brain lined by itself. No longer me again alone in me. All puzzles laughing in their fixtures. The blacking house unwound, a mouth for the breadth of us, alive. The eye was just against me. I was around the eye.

Name withheld: "Oh, I was waking. You were waking. Even as it seemed the end of the beginning, the moon was wrapped in all her skins when she combined inside the mind of all the air ever around us, sounded around us, wound around us."

FLOOD: [stricken from record]

I'm wearing white. I'm wearing clean beekeeper veils. I'm sewn in the color of me sunburned aged seven scared of holes slit in the sand with my head under my mother's shirt to keep the flies off of my head. I'm wearing neon yellow. I'm wearing someone. I'm walking through a prism gorge, cut so deep along the bottom of the skull I one year found underneath a rosebush outside the food court at the mall. I'm wearing wish robes. I'm walking with the trowel. I'm looking for a spot left loose enough in a pasture to dig myself an imprint wide as me but all the ground is foil. When I listen I hear men dividing into futures, into sternums, into more of now than I can stand to force to rest, so I do not listen until there's nothing else about me, which is always, which is how I learned to write.

TWO **THE PART ABOUT THE KILLING**

Gretch Enrique Nathaniel Gravey is apprehended by authorities in ███████ on August 19, 2██ at 7:15 A.M. He is found facedown in the smallest room of his seven-room ranch-style home with legs bound at the ankle by a length of electrical wire, apparently administered by his own hands.

He is unresponsive to officers' commands or to the touch.

When lifted from the ground his eyes remain open in his head, unblinking even to the sound of the canines, the men.

The light inside the room is strong. It blinds each new being at their admittance, bodies shielding eyes and swinging arms until the space has been secured.

Gravey is dressed in a white gownlike shift affixed with reflective medallions that are each roughly the size of an eye and refract light in great glare. No underwear, no ornaments.

His hair has been shorn sloppily, leaving chunks and widths around his ears and the back of his head, an amber lob of curls the color of beer.

An open wound cut on his left breast appears to have been also self-administered, though not deep enough to require stitching; his wet blood has soaked a small head-sized oval parallel to where he lies; from the pool, traced by finger, the word *OURS* appears writ in the ink of blood along the mirror-covered carpet.

Questions and actions delivered to the suspect do not seem to occur to him as sound; he does not flinch or turn toward the shouting, the splinter of their entrance, canines barking, the commands.

The meat around his eyes seems to be caving, black and ashy.

There are no other living persons apparent in the house.

Gravey is unbound, cuffed, and taken to a local precinct to be booked, processed, and held.

His eyes in motion do not open, though he is breathing.

He does not speak.

FLOOD: *The above and the following are my ongoing log of the time following Gravey's arrest, and the ongoing investigation, over which I have been appointed lead. I have given electronic access to specific colleagues assisting in the case for their perusal and review.*

SERGEANT R. SMITH: *These notes were discovered in Flood's shared files online sometime shortly after he disappeared. Several of the quoted sources claim to have not written what they are said to have written. I myself remain uncertain.*

The front foyer of the mouth of the entrance to Gravey's home is caked up with shit nearly a foot high; human shit, packed in tightly to the face of the door, which has been barricaded and blocked over with a paneled bureau full in each drawer with ash. Testing reveals the ash is burnt paper; among the powder, lodged, the leather spines of books, photographs overexposed to blotchy prisms, fingernail clippings, mounds of rotting cat-food-grade meat, plastic jewels.

The same ash found in the drawers is found in larger quantity in a small den down the hall, along with the metal rims and scorched remainders of a drum kit, bass guitar and amplifier, small public address system with corresponding speakers, and fourteen seven-string guitars all of the same make, each variously destroyed by flame to disuse but still recognizable as instruments.

A small sheet-stand holds up an empty tabbing book, which on some pages has been rendered with whole glyphs of blackened scribble, matching the front color of the house.

Inside the house is very warm, caused in part under the concentration of the sun's heat on the black paint even-handedly applied to the north, east, and south faces of the home. Only the west face remains its original cream-tan, the same shade of roughly one in four houses in the neighborhood.

The lawns of both houses on either side of the Gravey homestead are overgrown high enough to nearly block the windows. Gravey's lawn is dead, a radial of whites and yellows like the skin of a giraffe. An ant bed in the side yard of the unpainted side of the building is roughly the size of a very large sandbox, pearling in sunlight, though there are no ants among the runnels to be found, their turreted bed evacuated.

The majority of the other rooms in the Gravey home are bare. Furniture, adornment, and objects have been removed or were never there. The walls are covered for the most part with lengths of mirror that seem to have been gathered from local dumps or flea markets or trash: platelets sized from that in a bathroom washstand down to the face of an armoire down to the eye-sized inner layers of a blush case or a locket have been affixed to the drywall with a putty adhesive that leaves the rooms smelling synthetic. Many mirrors have crisped to dark with more flame or cracked in spindles from impact with perhaps an elbow or a fist, or having been dropped or otherwise mishandled prior to their installation. The mirrors' coverage is extensive, leaving mostly no inch of the prior wall's faces uncovered; even the ceilings and in some rooms as well the floors receive a similar coverage treatment. In many places, too, the mirrors have been applied doubly or triply thick, sometimes to cover something ruptured. Large smudges dot many arm's-length sections of the more central rooms' mirrored dimension, rubbed with handprints, side prints, whiffs of sweat, and in some cases traces of lipsticked mouths, running saliva, feces, blood, or other internal and sometimes inhuman synthetic materials, all of it Gravey's, incidentally or by cryptic, unnamed logic spasmodically applied.

Countless light sources in each of the major rooms fill the plugs of long electrical strip outlets or are attached to generators and arranged around in the space in no clear manner, studding the ceiling and the ground. Burnt-out or burst bulbs have not been replaced but hold their dead eyes unrelent in the space filled by the rest. For hours into days the light will remain burned on the eyes of those who'd entered before the knobs were turned to end it.

Officer Rob Blount of ███████████, thirty-five, finds himself frequently at lengths lost inside the shape. More than several times, even with the excessive lighting fixtures lowed, he finds himself rendered staring off into the conduit of mirrors creating many hundreds of the house and him, and therein, something behind the reflection, *a wider surface*, until he is jostled by outside sound or a fellow officer's inquiring arm. Through the remainder of Blount's life inside his sleep he will many nights find himself approaching in the distance a square black orb, endlessly rotating in a silence. The dream of the orb will fill his mind.

Gravey's kitchen contains a more colorful decor, if little else of more substantial means of living. The refrigerator, like the front room's bureau, is stuffed with ash so thick it obscures the contained light. Buried in the ash here are occasional remnants of what might once have been intended for consumption: a full unopened carton of whole milk, several sealed cans of tuna, cardboard encasements for packs of beer, fourteen one-pound containers of store-brand butter riddled with knife divots, a water container full of something white. Later, teeth will be discovered buried in the chub of certain of the butter tubs' masses, way underneath; the teeth will be later identified as dogs' teeth. The freezer remains empty beyond a cube of ice forming a globe.

The surrounding floor is likewise thickened, albeit higher than the foyer's, with used food wrappers, tissue, and containers, as well as many unfinished portions of the food. The pyramid of rotting glop and Styrofoam and cardboard stands nearly five feet high at the room's far wall, trampled down into smoother avenues and valleys in the mix. The stench is intense, weaving many different modes of rot into a kind of choking blanket. Somehow the stench seems not to leak into the house's mirrored sections.

Underneath the junk, in excavation, the men will find a massive ream of loose eight-millimeter film. Each frame of the several miles of exposed framework, unlike the other tapes found in the house, will show nothing but a field of pure black, of no star, as if the film had never been exposed. The soundtrack of the film, when played, if played, will feature a sound resembling a young man speaking in reverse, though when played in reverse the language sounds the same, word for word.

R. BLOUNT: *There was something else about the house besides simply (however unsimply) being the scene of I don't know how many murders. It was hard to stand in any room for long and breathe freely. Felt like someone was trying to choke me in certain rooms from behind me, not a phantasmagoric presence, but something soft inside my mind, something spreading. I did not sleep for several days, and have never felt quite like I was sleeping even when I found a way to seem to sleep again.*

A padlocked door is centered on the kitchen's northwest wall; it is the only secured location in the house. Behind the door, a humming sound, which becomes louder once it has been heard with head against the frame, and thereafter seems loud enough to hear all through the house and even miles around: a hum like that of bugs against bugs in a slow hive being constructed, the rhythm of which raises patterned gooseflesh on the skin. The door's face, matched with the same black as the outside, has a hand-carved mark along its top seam: *city of Sod.*

The shape of the *S* in the word *Sod,* the men realize while reviewing pictures later, is replicated all throughout the house, in seemingly unnatural ways: the crease of mirror against mirror edge forming the snaked line, the formation of a certain clod of puffy trash, the shape of Gravey's body as they'd found it not unconscious and unmoving, traced in skin resin many places all across the reflective floor. At either end of the shape's snake's length there might appear from certain angles a slim eye that watched the seer of the eye until with further motion the eye seemed to disappear, and would not reappear when they went back to find the eye where they had stood before because it would be impossible to stand in such a way the same exactly ever again. And yet, inside their head, the eye is there.

The padlock is adorned with unusual markings in the shape of tiny pins that stick up from the lock's face spindly and obstructive, with residue of saliva or some kind of glue; its keyhole is the size more of a small finger than a key. The metal is white gold.

The padlock is removed and placed in a sanitized container and taken to sit on a white shelf in a small room unexamined for the next sixty-seven hundred years until it is uncovered in the Fire of the Night of Seize by a young being who takes the lock into his head and walks with it into a blue house the size of him built by a tiny sea new on the land.

FLOOD: *This last paragraph is not meant as an abstraction; I believe it to be true. I can't say exactly what it is that brought me to want to say it and then to know it should be said, but it should be known that it was not done with any intent but to serve the nature of this investigation. Ask me in the face if I believe that and I will tell you the same: paper and flesh.*

The men stand briefly in silence before the lone secured door in the house, now unsecured. The humming has seemed to mute. The man nearest to the door's handle, which is not the man who had cut the lock off, turns the knob with his left hand to open the door. The door opens backward, into the house, and thus is blocked by the pyramid of trash before it can open more than inches. Through the crack a stink of something piggish and uncurling wafts through the gloss of rot already familiar on the central length of the men's heads. It is as quickly gone, wrapped as a weird gift upon them without question and then quickly common to their air. Nothing roars.

When enough space has been cleared for the door's path, the officer pulls the door back further, wide enough to see inside. For lengths the room is black, impenetrable to eye. It appears at first as if the room is just a closet. The pupils move to adjust in the men's heads, some breath between them, communal meaty fidget of old limbs.

Then, deeper back into the room, a light seems to emerge: low at first, then rising; a stream of panels of bluish neon indexing the air into squares, a corridor; no, a column; no, a cube.

The men's pupils shift inside the seeing, the shape of lenses and composed holes changing in the machine of their heads.

Set in the dark, a set of stairs. The stairs reveal deeper and deeper on, seeming to extend down into the space farther than one would think a basement should be in a house of this dimension. The stairs are plasticine, kind of glossy. They do not groan, but squish a little under the weight of any man.

Beneath the earth, under the house there, piled like prisms in low artificial light, the officers come upon the bodies of the women and the children and the men.

Flesh.

Flesh tongued in the grip of ceiling to expanse of wall to wall between them, caught as rooms do to form a space stood beneath the face of earth.

Skin turned to cream. Skin slipped and rendered fat and pummeled between metal weapons and instruments of decreation found popped in the pillows of the things they had undone, buried and gagged up with firming secretions and the lip of cellular disarray, grown silk upon the air so warm it cannot be inhaled.

Teeth, hair, jowls, blood: packets, mush.

One can, in the fiber of the room, hear a tone of what has been.

Bones jut from the substance crushed in the lardy stillwaves of our pink and black and brown and yellow and gray and gold and white.

Seated among the encasement, as upon thrones in silence, lie certain still living, pulsing boys, starved and demolished, thinning, nothing: their eyes also refusing to come open, give no murmur.

A scrim of salt.

On the ceiling above the heads of the detectives, the ceiling reads: THIS BODY LED ME TO SHIT INSIDE MY LIFE BLANK AND SCREAMLESSLY UNENDING WHILE THE WAR OF THE YEAR OF TOTAL DEATH CREAMED BETWEEN OUR FACES AGAINST THE FURTHEREST WALL THE WALLS COULD MANAGE AND THERE YOU WERE AND THERE I AM ENDLESSLY GYRATING IN THE EYELESS FORCE FIELD OF OUR FUTURE LOVE AS WE ARRIVE. None of the detectives see or note the sentence, for the record.

The living boys are lifted each away. They make no sound, cause no commotion.

The other bodies, who could ever move them now.

FLOOD: *The smell was—I hate to say it—sweet. It reminded me of waking up in a grassfield having slept all through the night without coverage against the night sky. I mean, I don't want to sound morbid, it was revolting. The sweetness was revolting. But it was also—I breathed it in.*

The men lead the body of the man who will not respond to any name along the long precinct hall intoned pale white. The facility is quiet and dully lit in the mode of lampshade blocking out a stream of air that seems to stand outside the building.

Long textured lattices of ridge set in the precinct hall's walls' face in the same color of the wall allow a running joke among many of the guards that the building is "ribbed," for the pleasure of something that passes through the unseen logic of the hour daily, or hourly, or is ever present, yet always gone. Regardless of the number of days that pass for any body inside the chamber most find the ridging something they can never learn to disregard, the eye always pulling up inside the skull to see it.

The body, though, whom they refer to in the name of Gravey, as it fits the ridges set into his fingers on his hands, does not seem to see, acknowledge, or want to know any inch about the ridging, or the hallway, or the building of the walls themselves. He walks in silence, still with closed eyes and closed mouth; when not led by the shoulders forward through the building or wherever Gravey ceases to proceed, and yet he does not fight in being pulled along the corridors through check-ins, through registration. No form of coercion leads the man to act alone, including body shots and threats of further marks against his name.

A strip search of the suspect's body reveals a diamond hung by black cord around his waist. The diamond is false diamond; it obscures the eyehole of his belly button, around which the hair has been removed. The remainder of pubic hair around the genitals has been shaved into a pattern like the beams of an aggravated sun. The shaft and glans of the unit are bruised, blood busted beneath the skin in thicket clouds.

A gun strap around the sternum holds no weapon; tucked into the holster is a tiny leather-surfaced notebook, water-damaged with his sweat. No language has been written into the unlined paper.

The anal cavity is overrun with brittle hair, so thick that they almost do not find the tiny transistor that has been stuffed into the crevice, matted in and clung with fecal residue. The transistor does not transmit.

Beneath the nail on the second longest toe of each foot a wedge of glitter has been lodged; on the face of the glitter occur words, none of which will be recognized, or read.

Water sprayed onto the body in the small stall comes off in foamy blue.

For some time in the hour he is made to lie on the cold floor naked without whimper, until the men are tired of looking at the raw colored markings on his chest and in his pits: like something there had scorched his flesh wide open and then resealed it, prim pockets of aggravated fat that stay so still.

Somewhere an old smoke rises.

B. LAPUZIA: *When Flood asked me to take a look at his ongoing log about the case, handing me this outlandish collection of scattered notes, some of which he claimed to have found in Gravey's residence, and which were not reported as evidence, I was seriously uneasy. For a while we had been partners, and though eventually I was reassigned, we've always been friends. He's been through a lot, and I try to be there for him when I can. I told him I'm not much of a note taker, and didn't really have anything to add in this manner, but that I'd take a look when I had time. I must admit, I was disturbed by his notes. They did not, to me, reflect a natural manner of investigation, or, even more so, a manner of living. Flood seemed fixated on his work in a way that went beyond it being work, even a life's work. The more I tried to figure out what was going on with what he'd done, the more I wasn't sure how to respond. I felt I had no choice but to mention it to the boss, though I can't say the Sgt.'s tone in our private speaking set me at ease. He had the same quaver in his voice that Flood did, the same something slightly off. I myself haven't felt right recently. I don't know what it is, though for some reason I'm afraid to look in the mirror. I move through rooms with mirrors now, whenever possible, in the dark.*

In his containment unit, Gravey's body stands through the evening without fold. Aimed facing toward the entry door of his chamber, its form sealed in with one thick window's eye into the public tunnel, he stands with arms flat at his side.

He does not bend to eat from the tray of dinner that is brought in and laid before him; the food will be fed instead into a disposing machine. He does not sit or lay or stand throughout the first night into the morning with the shifting of the guards. He does not open his small eyes in the crane of light beamed at his gray brain through his skull where the room around him remains lit. He does not utter language at the body assigned to his body as an attorney. He often does not seem to visibly breathe: no chest rises in the orange cloth, no nostril flutter, though to the touch his skin is warm in patches.

His temperature is three degrees too low.

Days pass in the standing. At intervals he barfs onto his chest; the upchuck is transparent. The hair stands on his arms; it grows further down his head and face, building a mask.

During his trance, the living bodies who were found there beneath his house each die, of what seems no particular occurrence, in their sleep. They are identified or not, buried or cremated, given to the ground to be absorbed into the earth again, where food grows and the foundation of all homes is laid. Other boys will soon come forward.

Pictures taken of Gravey's body in his cell seem off-colored, tinted redder in the cheeks and down the arms. A glass of water placed beside him on a white stool stutters selectively in ripples on its circular contained face, briefly quaking in indexed repetition as if nudged by something silent, until again the air around the air is calm.

Urine is released and wets his institutional pants in shade; it collects around his feet in spreading puddle on the concrete. The urine has no smell, no color. It sizzles as it is wiped.

The skin of Gravey's lips is peeling, rapidly, in sheets. The remainder of his skin retains its pallor, becoming cleaner seeming, even, unclenched, somehow more young.

At the end of eight days without food, water, or motion, his body collapses beneath itself, remitted horizontal, open mouthed. For the next four days he sleeps wadded, waking briefly only when jostled by whoever, calmly blinking, red-ringed; when he is left alone again however long thereafter, he returns into the shakeless corridor of sleep.

FLOOD: *Video recordings of Gravey in his cell are often marred by what seem magnetic disruptions in the tape, including long blacked-out sections in which the sound in the room can still be heard. What appears here in my descriptions of Gravey's cell-held activities is therefore subject to interpretation, as well as gaps in the field, though sometimes even in staring into the black of the screen it seems that I can see him.*

Inside this sleep, with limbs crossed and eyes wide, Gravey confesses to the crimes. His mouth lists out the names of those who've been inculcated. Among the list are women, men, and children, rendered therein first, middle, and last. His speaking is discovered already partway through the list, therefore the totality of the list is missed, left to hide in his saliva, leak through his cells. Each instance of each name is as well appended with the age and date of death and how the body was dispatched, each by the hand of Gravey, though in his own air he gives himself a series of new names, each rendered in the word Darrel: Darrel the Divorcist, Chalk Darrel, Darrel of No Leak, Darrel Who Has Become the Book Beheld And Only Awaits What Reader To Choose Prey As Well Inside the Mounds of What Cannot Yet Be, Darrel the Magnet Eater, Golden Ash Darrel, 65432Darrel1, Darrel then White.

Audio recorded in the cell during the confession is obscured on the tape by some high hissing signal. Two hundred and sixty-seven names are witnessed firsthand, and therefore transcribed. Many of the names correspond with those who have been corroborated as victims; others match those who've been listed missing but who have not otherwise been identified among the flesh. Four to eighteen additional accomplices are included in the crime sketch of the series, including the bodies of the boys found inside the locked room, despite the apparent residue of their own personal abuse, bringing into question the complicity of their behaviors. Still other names match no one rendered suspect, and so investigations must begin. There are no longer enough breathing bodies to assign. There are many months ahead of every day and only so much time. In his image, jobs are created; bodies become fed.

Gravey will never speak the names again, regardless of how many times they are referred to in his presence by the proceedings or the loved ones or what old coils might simmer in his mind. After the confession, still inside his sleeping, a massive boil shaped like a bird's egg appears on his left hand between his point finger and his thumb. When medics drain the boil, from the pustule's face floods a creamy darkish oil. The runoff will be stored in a glass vial in a black locker several miles from Gravey's fleshy self, no one seeing what the wet does in the darkness when no longer watched.

FLOOD: *The boys, the fateful boys and girls. What they had not known. Bless them, take them from this scrawl and keep them clear and sound as whatever holds the air up. Do this for us all now.*

Days turn white. The days turn white. They turn white with cream between them. They pale in memory still continuing to beget more. Between cracks in what had just been the present and is now no longer the present there is a small constantly slaving sound of someone breathing in.

SMITH: *I have recommended Flood for interoffice counseling, and asked that he take a few days off. He does not seem to be sleeping. He smells different. These kinds of investigations are hard on anyone, but I must say it surprises me to see Flood having such difficulties, as I often considered him unrelenting, solid as the ground we walk on.*

FLOOD: *I would delete this note and the others notes marked "Smith," as I know it wasn't Smith who wrote them, as he was never given access to this file, but somehow to remove it would feel like an attempt to cover something up, and I have nothing to hide, and so the feed stands. Regardless, at no point during the ongoing was I dismissed from my investigation.*

Among the fleshy evidence removed from Gravey's home, collected in a series of seven trunk-sized metal boxes, is a trove of VHS tapes, packed in from end to end in each container forming a separate black plastic corpus. There is the smell of old machines. The tapes for the most part are unlabeled. Some have white stickers affixed to their spines or faces that have not been filled in. An occasional tape—eighteen in all among the total five hundred and eighty—has been notated with a white scrawl; twelve of these eighteen inscriptions are a string of numbers, each eighteen digits long. Five of the remaining six of the eighteen marked tapes are marked with numbers, though forming strings that don't seem to have any obvious use: 278493000383, 109298723627, and so on. Each of the tapes, it seems, is blank, though not the blank of no recording, fresh; instead they have been encoded with a field of total white as if shot with a lens close to a wall or piece of paper without shadow and without motion. There is no sound on the recording; at least, there has been none found among them all so far. Each of the tapes, still, must be observed. Two pairs of two junior officers, two women and two men, are assigned to play the tapes in twin rooms in succession, observing for anomalies, change of face. They find viewing the taping makes them tired quickly, and causes sweating through their clothes. The VCRs in playback emit sharp buzzings, little whirs. One tape, the eighteenth tape played, becomes eaten by the machine, chewed to spools. The VCR thereafter smells of fire; it must be replaced. Another tape, the forty-second, is similarly eaten by the replacement VCR. The film of the eaten tapes, viewed in the light of the room surrounding, appears bluer than other film, somehow almost moist. Four more machines must be replaced in the first forty-eight hours, their corpses stacked in a locked room. The eyes of the observers blink throughout the screening, missing small segments of the films, which sometimes in the viewer's heads seem shorter than they are.

The name of Gravey spreads. Media mouthpieces disseminate his image through the TVs in the rooms strung up together in a wash of copied pixels. His name on papers. His name in mouths. His head appears across the nation in replication 2-D, 3-D, 4-D (the fourth D in dream machinery, consuming sleeping thoughts of mothers and all others shook with the description of the nature of the murder acts). Gravey becomes known and so grows more known, spoke in the same breath with the soap actor, the dead diva, the president, with fanatical appeal.

Hundreds of letters addressed to Gretch Gravey are delivered to the address of his containment center in the first day following his arrest. The letters contain what seem to be Christmas lists: long handwritten chains of things desired, in insane scrawl. Gravey seems most popular among the young. Children scratch his name in all caps on their forearms and foreheads and on the faces of textbooks and lockers and long walls inside of houses where they sleep or do not sleep. Clothing is emblazoned with his head or replications of the tattoo on his forearm of a black square with its bottom right-hand corner rounded. Songs speak his name suddenly in dive bars and on airwaves. Words beyond his name recall his name in plague.

On the second day there are no letters; the sun makes a little sound like something being squeezed out of a bottle. The sun remains the same color until in sleep the people can see the sun there shaking through their lids, open or closed, the sun, the sun. All analog clocks in the building stop, though without correspondence between the users, and thus no consideration to the activation of the nothing of the waking error held between them. The clocks must be replaced; the replacement clocks are wholly electronic.

On the third day, at the station, a large blue box the size of Gravey arrives for Gravey. His name is swabbed onto the box in mirrors cut in shapes to form the letters of the phrase, which thus from certain angles seems to make other utterances, or colors. A series of special forces are dispatched to the delivery platform, where the box is inspected for explosives. X-ray scanners reveal that the box is empty. The men open the box. Along the inside of the box's wall words are written in white ink, each letter large as someone's head: *This word occurs because of god.* Inside the box unfolded one man, a senior officer, gets down on his knees; he does not know why. He had been an atheist for his entire life. He looks up at the other men surrounding as he makes a prayer shape with his hands, the other men watching him in confusion, reaching for some reason for their guns. The senior officer's eyes stay open as he tastes his tongue begin to pray, in the language of the Computer. In the language, he is collapsed. Over the next six weeks, all dogs within a one-mile radius of the opening of the box will die; for many seconds each day leading up to those dispatchings there is a tone that makes the dogs lie down on the ground and shudder, feeling something in their throats.

On the fourth day, hundreds of letters arrive again in exactly the same quantity as the first day, one each from the same address that had been sent from before, though this time all of the pages inside the envelopes are blank. On the fifth day it occurs again; the same letters in the same erased condition. The letters, instead of being stored, are burned. The destroyed matter of the letters disseminates among the air; the ash is buried; the ash floods into the earth.

On the sixth day, a man rides a white horse into the station carrying a baby on his back. The baby has birthmarks in the shape of several symbols down his spine: CIRCLE SQUARE HEXAGON STAR TRIANGLE DIAMOND RING. The man is detained and questioned, fined for public disturbance, and eventually released. The child does not cry or speak a word inside the building, where Gravey is also awake, not speaking, though he is now no longer asleep.

The excavation of the bodies in the basement of the black house lasts several nights. The slough of curving flesh and popped-up organs smush together in the walls enframed in smarmy pockets that make it (the flesh) want to cling unto the house as if forever as if please no not me please this is all mine. Blood of many bodies mix: the cholera of its stank has peeled the room's walls tarnished bruisy. Skin peeled off of torsos like white apples liquidated in the bloat of something else half-yellowed and grown cold and hardened into tiny temples and round baubles that crunch under the sole. Several dozen knives and steel-grade blenders, those are in here. Dice 'n' chipchop. Fractal. Veins of what must be hundreds knit together no longer pumped. Time here seems to do nothing. Men armed for removal in neon suits with years of knowledge vomit inside the suits and fill the suits with their own bilge. These liquidated people, their bodies, already dried of wet they'd lived with and lived off of. A crust formed on the aggregation, not slippery or convulsive. It does not make sense, the lodes of colors. Up to their knees, the investigators count the eyeteeth and what they can of fingers. No one's phone is ringing. Hammers, drill bits, mortar, blank. In silence there is the sound. Someone says, It must have taken this freak fucker Gravey hours on each inch of flesh in this whole house; with each word of the sentence the speaker speaks louder till he is screaming. The crushed human stuff does not vibrate. Soup of skull and dented throat and testes and the envelopes of hidden eggs. In the musk already grows a mold, popped with globed discolored pulpy mushrooms and spindles of expanded fat. All this that comes out of a person in becoming opened could never seem to all fit back in, the screamer screams down to a hoarse bark, then faints face-first into the soft. It is the first day of a new week.

FLOOD: [*stricken from record*]

No. No really. Not at all, thinks Detective E. N. Flood, man of the blue and badge. Here at the end of working hours he refuses to believe, or if not to not believe then to not let bloodcolor kill his head, or if not to not to kill his head, then to just be. In the room of the house where Flood sleeps at night, having seen the innards of the room where the peoples' bodies fountained soft, a splay of pygmy organs nuzzled in puzzled correction in their mortal furor underground, the wet of the bodies is only all one black unfurlment in his mind, one he has seen before in fragmented iteration though here in seeing it is all arrived; it is as if all the blood from all the prior hours seen has landed again in the belly of the day. Flood laughs in silence toward the picture window above his bed that he now covers in the light of the new morning with thicker sheets that show only faint defeats of their former colors, as it is the presence of those colors, he's determined, that keeps him not only sleepless, but wakeless to alarms, sleeping often hours through the machine of the body's resting and on into long day. Had he been this way years before he would be shiftless, under water, cooking grease food in traps late hours unto pockets dripped with rats, or selling gas or cakes or glass to fucks in cities, or, or, or, or, or, or. Even now, with colors covered, often he cannot force himself inside his half-wake to rise rightly despite even some screaming, as on the night his prior home had burned thick to the ground—the cream of what he'd been rendered ash and pocked in puzzles with no insurance that month after years of having paid into the coffers of other men. He sleeps in his police suit now. He sleeps and rises in the office regularly, so that there are guns nearby his sleeping self he might rise and hold, might aim, or else someone might use those guns to wake him up if they needed, if they could not shake him from his progressively corroding dream. In the pocket of sleep Flood can often see himself from above himself there sleeping, in what should be the calmest moments, but are instead often a long extending gnash Years inside sleep pass some nights watching his whole body go on as if crumbling from the inside curled underneath his desk with paper as a blanket and a pillow and the arms of a wife who no longer will appear. Yes, he'd loved someone some years some way back before he was him now and can't remember anything about her but her teeth, which he now feels having grown in behind his own teeth, eating what he eats before he eats. Her name. Her name. Hers, he swears, was not one of the bodies in Gravey's makeshift mausoleum, he remembers. She could not be. She's been so gone, before all this. She was already always dead, the gun pulled in the night there right beside him and placed to take her spit and soiled blood out of her head onto the concrete for the money neither of them had—all of that had happened years before, in a season of long black, one that still rolls in his surfaces of layers laughing, rolling mental maggots in his knees and ass and arms, his sperm a bakery of killed decisions made by doing nothing in the presence of all potential motion and this vast lattice of human holes, his guilt of all he has and had not done—but all of this regardless of its logic and false healed remembrance in his internal history does not relegate the vision in his mind of her body twisted up in all that murdered gray and pink, crushed with arms and eyes removed into human putty and still there watching as he'd at last come down to find her in the flush of it again too late, which is why he'd become a policefuck in the first place, her there lapped again and ruined again before him in his vision (which is all real) transfixed onto a surface of the earth not in his arms and having never made her understand the form of love or even magic fucking or even comfort of the dollar or some lob or lobe or even puppet understanding of a god, a place to surface into after having been dismantled while he inside him and with no name of her walks on. He has failed her again. He has failed her. Every body belongs to her. Every murder is her murder. He cannot help but hearing in the space inside him where he wants to say her name replaced with a widening and hellish silence that'd seem to exude out of the skin along the back of Gravey's head, Gravey whom he'd only glimpsed for only one clipped instant in the hour of the body through the tiny window of the holding cell, the killer's form facing away, his face remaining in a swathe of memoryblank like all the other unnamed hours while all conscious he holds haunted, though which here, inside his body on the cusp of sleep and waking, holds the form of all he sees: wormed black curls of greasy nit hair and the weird ridge of scar along the killer's nape, the unmuscled scape peels that form the back mask of Gravey's earlobes and the flesh connecting sound to funnel down into his brain, to hear; a skull that turns to face him each instant, just before rising, slowly, the flesh rolling like a globe toward the lens of who he is, to scream out from its face the color of the air the room breathes in around him as he now, Flood, again, inside himself, is there.

Name withheld: *I'm not a police officer, but I have known E. N. for many years, and though I never actually became well acquainted with his wife, B., I find it extremely disturbing that Flood is talking about her as if he had been involved in her death.*

B. passed from cancer at the age of thirty-one. Reading all of this makes me feel very sorry for E. N., and for the stress he has been under with his work. I hope he can find it in him to regain focus, happiness, and a spiritual consolation, in whatever form for him that could take. I will keep both him and B., and any other here considered really, in my and my family's prayers.

FLOOD: *The night is black around me. I can't stop my arm from writing sometimes. I try to think of anything else at all, beyond the bodies. I turn on the TV and I see him. I open a book to read any other kind of sentence and I find the books I've owned for years unread all blank, or I find words about me written in them, in someone else's hand. There is nothing I have ever loved more than my wife, however hard it was between us, between any humans, each owning our own selves.*

Flood, the detective, is American as a strip mall; he is as American as fried rice in a Styrofoam container tossed into the street and run over by a car hiding a machine gun that will kill no one in its duration, but exists; he is a cop. He knows he is a Cop: this is one thing he will always remember. He believes being a cop can be cured with a bullet in the mouth, and he knows how to do it. In some of every day he can be happy, even in the shriveling skin of researched understanding. There is a white piano in the room where he was born. He has a tattoo over his heart of a word he made slamming his fingers down onto a keyboard to see what happened, **asldihfiuywef80**, except to him it means even less than that; his night is the whole night. He watches Hitchcock in reverse, on silent, filling in the words. He loves god. He does love god.

Though most days, at the moment, Flood can't remember where he's been. He moves because he moves, because in order to be anywhere he must be moving elsewhere or be about to, so that there will be something he can have, something he can breathe and eat up and shit out and walk with and work with and maybe if he's lucky and not dead that he can wish for or rub against or dream to cover up the only dream he's ever really had. In this way, Flood is anybody.

Part of Flood not being able to remember where he's been without quite knowing that he does not remember, is that he can remember anything the way he wants and have it feel like if it had always been that way for his whole life; this causes in him hidden self-hate, hatred of the hidden field of real, which manifests in silent ways; it appears to him in silence during hours he might imagine himself a person in a bed just at the cusp of sleeping, or a person opening a book to lay among the light of a warm house and read. It infiltrates his every aspect.

He is reading now. Right now he is reading, Flood is. He does not know.

Flood has blood inside his hands. When blood touches his hands outside his hands, this makes him remember even less.

Flood has killed at least eleven persons in the line of duty, as far as he remembers, though some nights he believes this happened only in his sleep: not even as a personal distortion, but in the way reality manifests itself outside itself while being called fantasy or allegory, as in the practice of the active life of books, in the way that any book forever is a person, acting.

Soon he will kill again.

SMITH: *I have taken Detective Flood off the Gravey investigation until further notice.*

FLOOD: *No you haven't, "SMITH." No you couldn't.*

In mirror to the killed bodies in the house below the house, aboveground in the light, hundreds of living bodies aggregate around the center where Gravey's person has been stored. There are several teeming factions: first, those grieving for the dead, sets of blood-linked sons and daughters, wives and husbands and lovers; the friends or wedded blood of these; and those who have felt the same lurch of nowhere run through their existence. These bodies congregate around the seasoned surface of the precinct/prison holding icons of the murdered, raising fists and lungs, screaming the word; they speak in a new Depression Language wrought from bull fury for what has been inflicted in the name of some black lord, this motherfucking bastard murder bitch fuck killer who stole our child who stole my love, the treble of their grief packed into lung quiver and burst noise rendered in old throes. Images of Gravey become burned under great sunlight making more heat making ash that falls and sends off strewn upon the earth. On unpadded knees they utter wishes for forgiveness or destruction or the twain of two in retribution on this unwanted and resounding human conflagration that has ripped into their lives. They know they will now no longer now remember how to laugh; inside the body they would have become or been again in coming years there is now no cord to that silk feeling; in its place now is only mud.

The second faction of the gathered wear the emblem of Gravey in His name. They operate a mass movement in the light of Him to drink the face out of the news and wear the unseen mask of him among the world, wrought up in some ecstasy of reality-entertainment despite having almost no word in their consumption to denote the moniker's beliefs. These are people wide open all for something ever, waiting, their flesh hungry for any light; they simply want. They chant his name and wish his presence like in a film inside a home; these ways not history or act, but the present, in which we may take part. In this way Gravey's authority replicates outside him without the requirement of his action, under the guise of history. Copy killers in the next weeks will lift the count of dead by handfuls in stiff gestures wishing to begin again; grown men rising to explode themselves in dark theaters or on the corner of a turf in the name of being done; rashes of abductions and consumptions, but that the papers and the screens and machines have manifested as a cause. In the streets there appear whole mirrors laid onto surfaces of all sorts, in the image of the Black House; the reflective panels are laid against the cars or trees surrounding their small conduit of land, shining fields of daylight into the light back at itself, showering the architecture and the ground before it at length with panels of lightning-organed hue like fattened fingers or distorted hexagons of simple madness, until the shapes are smashed by thrown rocks at the hands of the grieving or kicked down by the braver of these lost in gross mourning made into cruder engines of themselves. The glass rattle and rip of cracking flatness laces the human air with something shrieking, clocks and hammers in the hour of no night.

The congregations lather. The name of god becomes invoked. The name of another god becomes invoked. People curl their fingers into fists and fuck the fuck out of the air, swinging harder and not laughing toward the body of another baring toward the sky their burning wrists. We seethe.

Inside, Gravey is laying facedown on the earth.

The bodies couple in their anger, begetting motion, bone on bone. Where skin hits skin a sound is made. The sound rises into the nothing forming a new other shadow self that will follow them unnoticed for the remainder of their lives. Each of these selves created in this hour is only one of many they have made, surrounded in and on each of us as yet unslaughtered, skulking in the coming rooms where we will eat and fuck and ash and laugh and touch the machines and wait for day again and wait for night again in turns and handle cream and make a loved one love us less or love us more for certain hours, though ever knowing love is not a thing that shifts despite the earth, despite complex wantings and form of bodies aging and how another can betray and mistake the act of love for anything beneath it or against it like an arm. What I mean is, these people come to blows in the name of the name of Darrel who was not a life at all as yet to them beyond the word, and many received bruises that then will sink into their body before they are arrested or firmly told to go, such emphasis frequently depending on the nature of their cooperation, with more empathetic graces given in most cases to those who have lost someone who'd been eaten alive or not alive, though in other cases, depending on the actor in the authority, sometimes the better graces go to those in worship of this lone man from the Black House—though, in most such cases, the officers do not realize their bias, however wrecked or graceful, which may or may be a function of the actual power of the spirit of Gravey's rising but may be just a ruined thing about some humans turning bluely in the extending stench of what will one day be remembered outside of all minds as the Organizing Wind.

Still a third faction of the public stands in relative unabashment watching the disorder and the building seated at its center as if from it somewhere might rise a conflagration of firework or other boom, a thing they might remember having seen regardless, even in the early stroke of evening the sun's preemptive cloaking of this earth in a low darkness held off by pretend light as our star leaves again and does not return for longer this day than any day in the whole year, or any year before this or thereafter, for what reason I do not know—as I am angry too and tired and have all this time forward found no rest.

DETECTIVE F. N. DOOLE: *Which kind of onlooker are you?*

This room is small. This room of air around him, around Gravey, holding other bodies through the walls, making a room inside the rooms where Gravey, inside his body, sees the face of the someone larger than him walking on false water in the grain of the TV. The face begins far at a distance on a field set back in the set, some kind of tone of color exaggerated from its form like magma. The duration of its approach to Gravey feels immense, the distance of dozens of lifetimes passing in what could only be an instant of the real—without inhale, between two heartbeats. The head of Darrel rises in the color, growing by lengths to match each dimension of the innards of his head in mirror, a mute impression of himself. The color of the red pulls hard up in the mesh of Gravey's head: the index of the memory of the House, the Grave, the Spirit, the flesh of the dead—*Which hour is this now, pressing against me?* he hears himself ask inside the wave of self where the meat comes crumpled soft around the mushing forward of the Head. His hands against his chest outside the skull of his own head inside the auditorium of his second senses seem suddenly heavy, sinking flat into his fat. They grip there in the tissue about his chest a second layer of remembering, unto a realm of self the corridors of aesthetic longing in him had slurred to stutter: his growing older in a room; his having spurted from the hole of someone in a white clod to walk into the other bodies and be named; the fuckmove of flagellum into squirmy bulb inside another body, no longer living; the cracking thoughts of years of those who'd built him up from the moment of the spurt; the smoke and dark inhaled by father and by mother, two minor beings he can't recall beyond those monikers, made aged; before them, too, some cloud of hybrid netting that squirreled around all eras. Then the Head is only inches from him, its electronic skin writhing and transmitting, spooling outward in the fire of the minute to wrap around them both, enslaving Gravey's mind into the image of the Future Head of the One We All Must Become. Where Gravey's mouth sits so sits Darrel's, that name now nothing, male and female, cold and dry. Gravey, on his back cannot stand up under the pressure. Each instant kissed behind his eyes is solidified in choiceless faith, as from the black mouth of their locations touching through the wires, the voice between them speaks: *Rise, take up your Jerusalem, for if you retain the sins of any, truly, all sins will trespass a heaven's joy. Therefore I tell you, be forgiven the sons of Heavenly Father, every sin and blasphemy made of man;* and on the air the words are writ in puffy flesh swimming pinkish from the red of Gravey's chest; and on the air the words slid soft and spread between the cells of cells to elevate the room alive, hotter than three hundred million ovens as the silence of the spacing between language slid electric tongue from tongue along the air to shatter there where it touched, and spreading on the air now fully like lotion on a baby's ass big as America.

BLOUNT: *I had to tell Detective Flood to stop sending me his papers. It was literally becoming an almost daily thing, him coming by my office with more notes that he required my review of, asking for notes, calling me, calling. I hated to have to go to Smith about him, as I knew he was going through some real trouble, but I felt I had no choice, though by this point it was already a much larger problem than I realized.*

Multiple bodies employed in the incarceration proceedings thus far toward Gravey within hours kill themselves. One man assigned outside the door where Gravey sleeps or does not sleep nights gets off duty at the crack of dawn having stood parallel to the wall between them for most of seven hours, walks to his car, unlocks the door, enters through the driver's side seat, slides across the leather into the passenger side, straps on his seatbelt, takes out his service revolver, puts it in his mouth, and shoots his body dead. His blood writes a sentence on the side window that by the time he is discovered will have slicked its way away.

The head of service in the cafeteria where Gravey has still been refusing consumption, during the stretch of planning hours over which she would have planned the course of action of the next eight weeks of meals, locks herself in the meat freezer then takes a paring knife and filets the length of both her arms. Many hours pass before her meat is found among the other meat to be served to the imprisoned on plastic trays, which now, contaminated, must instead be buried in the ground, as must be the chef. Her blood too, from her arms into the meat locker, writes the sentence.

Three to eight further members of the law enforcement network working out of the building do not appear at work over the coming week; each is found in his or her apartment in various states of decomposition with necks broke by ropes or having jumped from something high and or affixed in the bowels with chemicals or otherwise in forms just like the first two self-murders previously performed as if in want to become like those who'd been undone already and would be undone again. Behind the mirrors in these houses a small adornment to the hidden plaster, the marking of a symbol, may or may not have been made, and none will know.

For each office dispatched in this new method a new body for the office moves into its place. The bodies populate the system, and proceed. Between them moves a changing language.

FLOOD: *As the human body decomposes it loses two degrees of heat in the first hour, then one degree of heat each hour held thereafter until it meets the temperature of its surroundings. Brain cells are dead within the first seven minutes. In the first thirty hours after death flies lay eggs in the body, and maggots appear in the flesh; production of ammonia begins in the lungs and seeps out through the nostrils and the mouth; ammonia is lighter than surrounding air, and so diffuses quickly; over time, production slows. Within hours, the deceased body begins to produce heavier amines among the deadened flesh, including putrescine (1,4-diaminobutane), and cadaverine (1,5-diaminopentane), and other iterations of the name. The decomposing tissues issue gas including hydrogen sulfide and methane; the skin blisters and turns blue; the abdomen swells; the tongue may protrude; a fluid ejects from the lungs; this happens at half speed when under water or one-quarter speed when underground. During the first year, a deceased human's bones will slowly bleach and grow with mold; over the first decade the bones develop larger fault lines. Without animals to deconstruct the body, teeth, nails, and hair become detached from the flesh in a few weeks; within a month the flesh is mostly liquid, cavities bursting; the uterus and prostate may last several months.*

Flood stands alone in the mirrored room below the house, the room left marked as the city of Sod. He has come in plainclothes, his badge removed and left inside a black bag in his bedroom. He has walked back to the Scene of the Crime(s), at least the end point of them, at least the ones so far discovered. The house has been photographed and notated and marked off from the remainder of the world in totality now; no one wishes to return but him.

In the sick sound of no sleeping Flood's blood won't shut the fuck up; he hears people moving around in the house above him; he hears throughout his brain the sound of the voice he hears radiating from Gravey's body when he looks directly at him, a voice louder than the voice already sealed into him of the woman of his own life and the woman who had brought him out of her to stand beside her and who he had left each day and again.

The room beneath the house where He had hid the bodies is clean again, like new; clean as a room can be inside the knowing he knows of it in here already having seen what had been done; knowing, too, what could be done again inside it or had been done before the birthing of his eyes; what earth had been scooped out of the earth here to carve space for this room to exist so that the room could fill with blood.

No, the room is not clean. The walls are white; the smell of chlorine, acid, antiseptic, several smokes, the ash of ash: all clouds in something secondary of the mask he feels becoming affixed around his skull each minute he inhales it. He cannot leave. His face feels tight, a wire frame. The lights all in the house above the room are off; he can hear the floor and spaces just above him listen as he moves along the mirrored surface vibrating silent in his human loam.

Along the long wall in the room again there is a window built into the frame. The window looks out onto the dirt of the earth. The tail end of a fist-sized lash of granite butt-ends up eye first against the glass from the other side, reflecting the beam end of Flood's lamp. The glass seems breathed on from the other side.

Flood's feet on the flooring squeak like the NBA. In his mind he counts backward through the names of those he can remember from the speaking, assigning in the fleshless vortex where they might have lain among the mass. Each name, in his head, sounds like the same name, and so he does not let them out. He hears the in-tick of a furnace initiate itself to come alive and warm the rooms above.

[In the continuing scene, as the heat above him rises, though the room itself will not grow warm, a smell about the ceiling coming down around him stinks like someone waking up, putting on a skin-suit made of rubber, walking to a door inside the house, closing the door.]

Flood keeps thinking he hears someone other in him thinking. Someone predicting his own thoughts, his movements, what he is. What light is in the room seems electronic.

Flood sees someone standing just behind him, at the edges of his vision. His instinct to turn becomes instantaneously overwhelmed with something sharper: *to hold on inside this feeling, to let the person there remain there, to listen to them think and breathe.* This has, on Flood, the effect of making time seem several times longer, slowing down his aging, which as he notes this feeling, he will in his sleep remember how to learn, thus causing his time on earth to be distinctly extended hour by hour up until right now in this house.

As he's holding in this moment, the tendons in his arms becoming hard, framing the shape of his skull with further skulls inside him, Flood observes the character observing him taking more form: he can see more about her (it is a her) face and arms and chest and legs and muscles, though he finds it hard to piece together more than one, or to hold the whole of what she is together more than any instant, seeing seconds turning solid into new memory, rubbing the older shafts in him awake.

The form is so near to heart, close enough to make him open to it further, though at the same time he wishes to resist. Each time he sees her he is seeing something new, and yet the newness has a gloss about it, a second cover: he can recognize the form, but cannot hold the form up to itself, and the smell of the room keeps washing in, and the fidget of his body tries to stay both soft and motionless, observing in fear that when he moves for sure the premonition will disappear; as, he remembers, there's not actually someone there behind him, and never has been; this is an elaboration on an instinct, a way to live. In thinking this, close up, just as the image threatens slowly to see into him and see him seeing, the moment shifts and so is gone. The room is empty. There are no bodies.

Flood turns to look now at where he felt there'd been the other person and sees instead, like so: the wall.

Flood starts laughing. He's not moving his mouth or face; he doesn't want to laugh; the sound is not like him. The sound is coming out of holes in his skin (so many of them) or perhaps from his ears (ejecting what's come in before but in reverse) or something else about his head he can't synthesize with enough precision to speak about it. He feels the cords vibrate in his neck, his runny blood. The laughter fills the space and wiggles through it, cordless, multiplying in diffraction, then gone again, where its remainder is everything at once wanting to be said while he says nothing and he looks. Looks again for something someone might have missed about the space's frame or where about it or some other motion not about the bodies, having since been photographed, described, inscribed, removed, examined, identified (if possible), interred (if possible), memorialized, indexed, held aloft in glimmered minds. So many hands have been here, finessing surfaces, expurgating, eyes shut or open at various points, attempting to collect from harbors of the false light something wrought about the intention or issuance of the Events (i.e. the Killings), though what is there to say. How many can we count, what method of dispatch, how many hours alive before not alive, what name, what age. These are questions that have been asked and will be asked again regardless of the answers being given regardless of the year. These are the small bulbs on a white tree rising above the country in slow season for the worship of the Day; and yet here inside the room is Flood.

Each place Flood allows Flood's foot to touch the floor covered with its clean mirrors makes him grow older; both the house and he change every time, aging together, changing; in this way he is many of him in many houses; in this way he will never leave the house.

He cannot hear the onset of the camera burning film somewhere above him over the roar of what is not there, the song having set so hard upon the house that it is the house and it will be the end and beginning yet again.

Again, behind him, behind Flood's body, there is the shift of presence, though this time as he feels it align he spins around. He feels the minutes peeling from his other life, turning, the cords in his arms burning, his fingers wrapped around a weapon he has not brought; the gun seated barrel-up toward the ceiling between twin pillows on his white bed for the purpose of watching anything but what will come into the room.

In this room where so many bodies died. Where so many had been, dying. Where so many were.

There: there he is there in the mirror there this time he sees him he can catch him he is not her but him; in the glass of it he's not so old but younger now, he knows, if bloated, if glassed around the face with liquid staying in and wanting out, the meat around his eyes the color of the meat they'd pulled out of here by the poundload as he stood upstairs in a version of a room without locked doors and tried not to hear the words of anyone around him as he recorded another instance of the life inside his mind by walking slow from room to room in learning and wishing his fingers could spurt gold, wishing it were him they were pulling out of there then and with the skins turned inside out while his stays white and tired and retarded and having let any person down and surrounded by others who have so done the same; it doesn't even matter anymore to feel that or think about it in the hour because that is part of the definition of the name; that is god, for him, that is god, for him, that is god as god will be, for him, and he is he. There, there he is watching him watch him remember who he was just those days, however many days, and younger now and dumber now, the age leaking out of him from the agelessness from which he had been born, no way to keep it in, no way to want it out, unlike the blood; the gift these dead had been given and not even there to celebrate it any longer, being the worst joke and saddest fuckfreak thinking of them all, and their houses and their money and their stocks and bonds and their children and their haircuts and who they'd had sex with and where they'd been and where they'd wanted to be or to visit and their fingers and their keys, their memories of whoever, each erasing over time as time goes on, and him there against it and inside it, and him here again in echo of that in the house this time alone, and him there on the wall there watching him watch him remember and him there again there on the ground, the instance of his head and torso spread beneath him in rescinding dimension in such a way that he appears as a different kind of ache, a 2-D aping of his 3-D dumb ass standing goremouthed in the image of the room of dead, alone in the Black House having laughed and never meant it, having never meant it, there he is. The he who in his own life allowed her nothing that she wished without him having wished it also. His life still going on. Now. Right now. Going and going. The he who did not bend and so she became nothing, while again he is without the gun and here the house around him doing nothing like he is also again and he cannot become the house and he cannot become her, unless he can look so hard at his 2-D self there in the mirror that he turns to 1-D and therefore his 3-D self must turn to 2-D, taking with it some idea of the dimension that allows the third D to take place and amplify it unto becoming something possibly inhuman, like what people become when they die, as had his father and all the other fathers and would again but only after all that age had been leaked out, after all that nothing had been forsaken despite anybody's wish to live forever and wanting everyone you love to live forever there beside you always also, the running bead of loss of our pulling the color from our hair, pulling the flat out of the skin into the bunched meat of long windows in us purpled over and caved in and laughed and asked and rinsed off and here again Flood is laughing and the floods of Flood are watching Flood. Here again Flood sees Flood forced forever left unending.

Flood lets his head nod toward the floor; down there in the mirror set beneath him Flood is smiling at himself in vast attraction, his gum meat popping in his head, gored bridges, a long white.

Flood stops, stands, stares, hears nothing. He jumps up in the air above the image of his face beneath him, splitting different, changing angles; the air is empty; a music begins to play, swelling low and hot out of his pore holes into the sound of air making no sound.

In the air above his face, as he is lifted, Flood invokes the moment he's only just now invented, in remembrance of a moment in a place he can return to in the future, however ruined. From up here, semi-paused and still inside him, on the floor below he sees himself there rerendered just above. Across from him, in the cubic air underneath the Black House where the pulp of the murdered bodies and all their blood and rip had been, Flood sees himself peripherally seeing himself beneath him as he sees himself from above. Behind him, he hears more; he does not look to verify that these are him behind him and so they are not, and the mirror echoes with the lie: he appears alone here but he is not alone here and does not look beyond himself.

He does not think the prior thought at all inside him, and in not thinking realizes he is not the one doing this, not the engine, but this doesn't stop him from not doing regardless, held as he is inside his own eyes and learning at last now to see what about the glint of his eyes shows someone else just there within him also, surrounded from outside and within. The moment grows.

There is a hell.

Here I am above me seeing me above me and below and beside me all at once, Flood says aloud. The words come out spoken in one word altogether, a name he's never heard before or thought before: Darrel. The word adheres hot to his cheekface and the gristle in his neck where words are born. The words inscribe themselves along the mirror, written white in breathy lesions of the glass that will not be erased.

I am Darrel, he says aloud again, and again the words at once come out as one, the flick of the tongue to palate and the posture of his creaking growing in him in the language breaking through his lungs. So he is Darrel.

In the room under the Black House, Darrel (Flood) begins to land. He will destroy himself, he hears him saying in his second voice in third person in one word, in a voice that seems by the moment turning back upon itself as it is passed, a voice without sound but of sound, like sound deleted, a nothing flowing, wanting more. He will save his other life by giving it away; wedded in the instant to the coursing of the blood within him he would have liked to deliver into her, into a child made of his wife and him together only; a second self who could have lived beyond the minute of this exit, carried on all the sets of sets of expectations and hopes and troubles beyond the rind of Flood's own body here and now split and coiling fast and hard around the moment so fast that he already can't remember how it happened, how it is happening, causing the moment as it happened to stand alone unto itself unframed; therefore the moment cannot die, causing between the real and unreal a rip from one world to another, splitting Flood, the human, the nonfather, all apart, each instance of each of him and us eternally on pause from there forward in time to many false dimensions of him, each one aging as he goes. This had been happening his whole life, through every instance, and with everyone, and only now does he recognize how little of him here is left, leaving the space for whatever else could want to come into him as he is now to come and come and have him.

Poised in the falling air, Flood (Darrel) sees Darrel (Flood) beneath him coming closer as he approaches also unto the mirror with the copies of him surrounding (and all those others, whoever ever) seeing too, and through the mirrored walls the bloat of pressure of the missing moments seeing too, being too so gross and endless that in each there is no key, the ocean of the moment swollen hard every instant lived inside itself to rise above it and be crumpled as it passes into night, the mirrors in the house and beyond the house unbound ongoing moaning soft inside him, singing the death song.

SMITH: *Both as a matter of official preservation, and for his own good, I have placed Flood on leave for a period as yet to be determined; throughout he will receive full benefits and pay as long as he cooperates, though I have as yet been unable to get ahold of him by any method for the last thirty-something hours, which I am afraid, if continued, could require greater consequences.*

FLOOD: *I am only just now beginning to understand what I could never understand. Something beyond me. Something beyond something beyond the all of us all inside us and around us and inside. I could and will and cannot slow down now.*

Where Darrel (Flood) lands upon Flood (Darrel), ramming, through the glass of the ground's mirror, the mirror ruptures, splits apart. The floor is false. Underneath the floor is a second floor, forming a cavity beneath the room, which the mirrors had kept hidden from investigation.

The room is roughly six feet deep, high enough to hide a body propped up erect, though there are no new bodies down here. The texture of the face of the surface is marbled pink with loam of discolored pigments set into it like speckled ham. It is soft and seems to be made of a synthetic polymer, like something from spacecraft. There is no smell; the air of the room above seems not to permeate beyond itself.

Flood's flesh having fallen sits under the shards of black glass knocked unconscious for some duration before he returns back into his head. A large raised divot above his right ear throbs a heating music. There is blood exiting from a slight slash on his chest, and from another wetting through his pants' knee. He pukes, woozy, upon waking. It takes a second and third seeing from inside him to realize again where he is: inside an alcove that had previously remained hidden beneath the layered mirrors of the floor in the locked room: a false floor, the key through which had been his own weight, i.e. himself.

Any wall could have another room behind it, Flood says aloud to no one.

All the edges of the world.

There is also blood on Flood's hands; he goes to rub it on his shirt and makes twin handprints in impression; he rubs the remainder on the wall, though there is still blood on the hands even after having wiped them clean enough they seem mostly clean. He stops and forgets about the color, looking up into the mirror of the ceiling of the room above from where he's fallen in, seeming higher than it should be. The room is too dark to make out his reflection in the mirror lining, layered up there now, seeing him seeing what he sees.

The linings of the exposed alcove have a glow, Flood realizes, eyes adjusting. The curvature of the space of the small revealment is affixed with low fluorescent light, panels of the surface there itself, backlit at low grade, almost low enough to not notice. In the cud of it Flood is yellowish, elderly-like. He smears a little blood on skin on himself, touching himself to see if he can feel it.

He shifts to stand. Erect, his head rises well enough over the lip of the indention that he can see around the room from down below, nearer to the reflective lining of the first floor's flat expanse that makes the space seem both ever endless and, in knowing of the false nature of the surface, that much less. Mirrors speaking back and forth into one another, prismatic closets, which in the instance of this particular chamber and the past it held as present even just weeks before seeming somehow thicker in its air, black diamonds, phantom death. Traces of old blood and other matter's smudging on the mirror reflect Flood's head back at his central head appearing tattooed or blotted out in bits of obfuscation, showing nothing of him back to him the way to others he'd seem seen.

Flood squats to square down in the alcove, touching at the ground as a piano underneath him, the glass the scattered keys, careful not to cut himself again on the edgework, and still bleeding. He finds that when he speaks aloud no sound comes out beyond what seems just the inside of his head. He says his name; it is his name, only inside him. He cannot remember anyway it being different from this before.

This day is any day. The floor inside the subchamber, where it's not glowing, is the color of his skin. It has a softness and quiet pliancy, a textured gruff. The glass bits on the surface from where he broke the mirrors seem to stick and cause no rupture in the smooth. Flood's fingers tickle at the rubbish. He hears a tone snake down his spine. His posture loosens with warmth and sends a shimmer of clear liquid down his downturned sternum, to the head where days on days have hid and taken hold. He can hardly see beyond him. The liquid in the head seems suddenly to widen, casting in his vision, sudden memory:

him, Flood, nine, lost in a game in the white woods behind his grandparents' home under a white sky, having fallen in a forest with mud up to his neck and in his teeth and hair and face, the muck he cannot make his tongue lurch past to scream for someone there inside the woods to come out of hiding, really, and pick him up, clean him up, lift up his body, take him from the night, though everyone is out there, everybody, where;

him, Flood, eleven, wrapped in a blanket, unable at all to breathe in, the white slick fabric hot and hard against him so close it appears black and seems to leak into his flesh, choking back up in the manner of a second skin around him, lurching down his throat to balloon outer, inward, snaking, coloring him in, the object like any object like a lining pulled out from his flesh and formed into a thing that he could touch then from the outside only and pretend to have never seen; thus is the nature of all objects, to any person, all of them, ours, displaced, undead;

him, Flood, of no age he can remember, upside down against an unseen surface in the air above his bed in his old home, flattened and pressed against it for such long time feeling like one instant that the whole world seems to hold, cogs of time aroused enough to keep him awake and out of resting but not aroused enough to let him move;

him, Flood, this morning, having stood up so fast that the blood rushed from his head, his limbs and balls and back and lungs thereafter weighing flushed out and dry light as a vacuum, as has been the way so many days, ambulating soft around the house and outside from room to room and space to space to face all feeling nothing where the blood was while still feeling air and motion on the outside of his skin, each day and all today in a kind of chosen bloodless automation, which some days is all that keeps him moving forward without thinking, even knowing that he knows, which as he thinks of here in this odd-lit room of this death home, if only to negate him, erupts the feeling of all that old blood suddenly flooding from a popping sound sent in his head, the blood all there at once rushing hot and fast from his skull's orb of chortled memory and pregnant unnamed wishing back into him all at once with perfect frenzy, rain on rain, shelving colors in his vision, 3-D, 4-D, and again he pukes.

The vomit, made of liquid—water, coffee, orange juice, his own spit—reflects the cribbed in light a savage orange; it coats some shards, a little floor space, and flutters at his hands, while with his hands Flood stirs the slight air dying in the impression for some hold: a width to grip his chest with, a stirrup for his hands. He falls forward into the hidden area, in a way of falling that seems slower than it should be, in such a way it seems he can see himself from there above him again falling with his organs and his limbs, again becoming horizontal.

Here is Flood facefirst and chin down in the box. Flood feels flooded, ripe with windows being opened in his sternum and his ass. He could go to sleep here.

He could sleep here. The lid above him, yes, could be replaced. Could be filled in with him into the house here. He cannot think what to do about the box or being in it or how to get out or to go, or what should happen, who should know this, if there is something else he needs to do, if there is ever any hour he is someone in his body, if his body is a wall.

A large lapse, like time defining zero, passes through him while he stares into the day on pause, unpaused. The day makes memory, mutation, affixing there to nodules of the memory regardless of their chronology. Each new instant, as it wishes, inside his head, may kiss each other, all. And the inhale of the next one, in the box.

Up close, along the low lining of the second floor right before his eyes, Flood reads a string of words printed faint into the surface, a message written there in tiny print and such slight indention, it is almost not there in the room at all, as if for him alone and him forever. The words scroll into him cleanly:

in god our blood the word of blood in god the name of god in god the name of god

The last word, *god*, in its last reading, seems, against the grain of Flood's right eye to twinkle, turning its letters over and over on themselves as he absorbs them: god, sod, gap, dog, doo, gun, sun, goo, gad. The shiver of the shifting language curdles in his mind, the words gummed up against the shelves of words already waiting in the memory of books and days and years, folded into any thought whatsoever, like this sentence, like this urge. As well, the sentence set there on the box face begins spinning, shifting through new letters, compressing the language:

with you were with me wished I was you and you were I which wished not known

god wished if you if we wishing where wish we were we where cuz god

why cuz I would wish you wished beside me now always and again

what now exactly now none nothing in the city of our Sod

please help me help we help we please

The words burn and blink inside the house like countless tiny screaming people; they become again inside the words not the words they'd been before then. The floor down here is covered with sentences all over it, every inch shifting to become central as he looks.

With his middle finger Flood reaches up along the surface to rub its meat on the letters of the words as he takes each in, to trick their rhythm into holding still. He rubs along the letters while they grow warm with him. The words fold fast and slow and soft in lines: each sentence shrinking in silent compilation underneath the heat and presence of his going at it, like any hour any day, words disappearing into words:

Which which why now god now why now god now why now cuz

How help please cuz I am was nothing we were you were

Want if want was if god if

If I see I

Be I

Six smearing into five. Five into four and there again all smearing, like smells absorbing smells. Any word or letter looked at too long rolls and mutates, changing also where inside his brain he felt he knew what the word meant, the memory of one's memory gaining blowholes, slaved erasures. As each sentence disappears, there is no floor where it had been written on it.

Flood blinks.

Flood hears the sound of all the houses filling up with blood throughout the world.

Flood has no idea how long he's been rubbing at the new flat floor beneath him, now double-fingered, like a woman masturbating, and drooling from the mouth. Between the dry on the wall where words were, around his pads there's something sizzling, a rising cream pushed through the walls through where there'd been the row of holes of changing letters. In the mass of glow above him he can't see where he'd fallen through the mirrors, up into the old room, where all those bodies had been stored; he can't see where the edges of the newer room around him begin or end, in such a way that it seems like the air is all just walls around him, with the language, deeper and deeper, disappearing as he rubs.

Something in this room begins to shake. This room where you are sitting with your hands before you, reading. You don't hear it because I said that it began. You refuse to take part in trying to hear thereafter because I'm talking about you directly to you and this object is a book. You don't like the idea of me communicating through you, outside of time. But there is something. In the room. Shaking. Behind your back, or just downstairs, or maybe by the window where you sleep, or in the curtains, soft as hair.

What is shaking.

Will you hear it.

In the room where he is, Flood does; he hears the shaking like I have heard, though to him it feels like it's inside him.

Is it inside him.

I think someone is at your door.

Flood is grunting. His torso seems above his head. His head feels above his ass. His ass feels opened. There is no light, but for where above him in the spinning, he can feel the low glow of the room somewhere above him, then below him. The black is gyroscopic. He's all wet now. He feels a cursor blinking in his chest. If he's not moving, he can't seem to keep one way clearly up above him. If he's falling, the air here has a floor, one indifferent to direction, shape, or time.

Flood, Gravey says inside his cell alone. Flood, he says. Flood, he says.

A blue lesion has pulled open on his back between his shoulder blades. It is too small to be seen by humans.

The lesion seems to change shape when looked at. Inside this shape there is a city, like the city you are in. The city is unfolding.

Gravey exhales into the larger air.

Today in America unknowing each speaking person will emit a common word.

LAPUZIA: *I go by Flood's residence on my way home from the precinct. I don't let anybody know I'm going, because I want to approach as a friend, not as a coworker. I'm worried about him, to be honest, and not just his career but his mental and emotional well-being. I find his front door left unlocked and halfway open. I immediately notice a strange smell, but I don't associate it with where I have felt it from until I come into the front room. There are mirrors on the floor. Mirrors on the walls and on the ceiling. Several dozen lights light the room wide. I am so shocked at first I start to call for backup, but something stops me. Still, I ready my firearm. I go on into the larger room. Spread out on the floor where one would usually have a sofa etc. I find a series of pictures of B., Flood's deceased wife. There are pictures of her alone and smiling, her with E. N. in various locations, and so on, hundreds of them, just everywhere. And there are papers. Papers of his writing, some of which are copies of ones I've seen before, that he's brought to me, others I have not, and some written in a script that doesn't look like English. Drawings of odd symbols are on many of the pages. I continue on into the apartment, terrified of what I'll find, though in the other rooms nothing is strange. No evidence of struggle or wrongdoing. No bodies, thank god, and no blood. The main closet is still full of B.'s old clothes, and this is where I realize there's this odd smell snaking on the air. It is a perfume, sprayed so many times into the small room it's hard to breathe. Hours later I knew for certain I had felt the presence of this choking, slaving smell before, sometime when I was very young, inside my sleep, but this does not occur to me at the time. I come back* *out into the main room. I stand among the pictures and the light. I decide there's no reason to report this, that I should not have come here, that I feel older than I ever had all through my blood. I feel dizzy in the middle of the photographs of her, the mirrors, a silent catacomb of eyes. That's when I realize I'm being recorded.*

FLOOD: *You and everyone who's ever been. This is not a question of being destroyed, or even beginning: it is in the folding there between: the color of the mesh of the lives forced into bodies rendered one unto the other, lobes in the catalog of time. Each body not a body but a cell.* I did not write this.

The body before the glass screen watches white.

He or she before the screen watches the white recorded into the image of the video not go on, not shift or change its vision, unless it bears an image hidden underneath itself: white upon white, making more of what it was and is and will be. Spitting up upon itself more of itself. No mirror. No hour. The white of a white loom.

He or she, assigned to duty, must watch the film to find where inside it there might be something as yet undetected, evidence buried in the film filmed by a man who may or may have not used his hands to end several hundred human lives. He or she may feel emotion in regard to the gone bodies even not having known these victims beyond their humanity after the fact, but regardless time continues, the white continues. The end of one life or another on any given day cannot end all lives, we think. We must go on. This is both the song and city of the human, to continue, we know, and so he or she must.

He or she sees.

He or she is a she here in this instance but as well may be a he or she as in the end it does not matter.

Before the screen he or she has already spent many hours looking. He or she has nodded off to sleep throughout an unknown number of tapes, which continued playing on during the period without he or she realizing he or she had slept, and so not seen, the present seeming in his or her head to be one continuous waking session of watching the tapes, when in fact the session is corrupt. What had been shown had not been entirely denoted, quantified for what had passed over the closed eyes. The aging of all flesh continues to go on regardless, without sound.

The waking body sees the white again. It appears nothing has happened. Nothing, then, has happened. He or she marks another mark upon a page, a sentence notating nothing has happened, and is happening now. Nothing is happening.

The waking body drinks a glass of milk. The milk is warm from where it's been left on the table for some duration of the day; its opaque color had stayed there unchanged in its state during the period in which he or she had nodded off, a half-full glass of whole milk. He or she does not mind the warmth of the waiting milk, or that in drinking he or she must assume the milk is fine to drink; he or she has had experience with milk, and so anticipates a somewhat innate aware-ness with its content.

The milk enters the body with the body's eyes rolled back into the head; again, as with the sleeping and other blinking, he or she is cut again from seeing what appears on screen. He or she, in waking presence, assumes by now that the screen is always only presenting more of the white. One would have to assume, having seen most of the white surrounding any instant of the white oncoming, that any present instant must also be white, otherwise life in this context would become almost impossible to live through, or at least impossible to feel having gotten anywhere in. For the most part then one must go on as if anything unseen could not be inter-rupting its own continuity in whatever incidental gaps of time it wasn't witnessed, until a point inside the white that the oncoming white ceases to be white in such a way that cannot be ignored, waking one into the understanding that all these hours might not be just blank, but somehow haunted, embodying some terror so large it at most points could not be seen from so close up.

So then having mostly watched, the thing is considered *watched*; this is the nature of the assignment: to find by seeing mostly all the white where it might be that white is not. If there is nowhere that the white is not, then the assignment will have been an exercise in finding nothing, which herein will go unrewarded, be-yond hourly pay—paid cash to live his or her life with, and his or her family's, if he or she has one, their bodies stuffed with food and air inside of rooms earned by the doing of the seeing of nothing.

If something does appear, among the tapes of nothing, it must be something, one assumes.

Inside the body of the person seeing the milk falls down through fleshy rolls through the center corridor of his or her body to slick and rush along the land-scape of the throat, leaving filmic coat along its white way into the stomach, filling the remainder of what is there of what energy has already been destroyed inside the body from aging and production all ongoing inside the walking and the sitting and the sleeping of the body. The milk, one presumes, will be used then by the body to perpetuate the body in forward motion for some amount of future time, making it possible to breathe and sit and eat again sometime and before the screen there employed to see, if, in this instance, to see nothing, as there is nothing there but white, so far.

The body will continue to be changed. At some point in this future today the person will lie down on a bed to sleep again, this time knowing he or she is sleeping, or believing at least that he or she is.

The face of the screen is the face of the nothing through which the nothing functions and can be seen for what it is.

The face of the screen has held many images before today, the image of the white. There have been years of tapes of other persons making motions that will indict their wrong behavior. This is the function of the operation of the viewing in this context: to jail. What is seen that can't be used in this manner does not exist. One assumes, too, in days forthcoming, after the days of viewing the White Tapes of Gretch Gravey, the screen will be used again for images of other potential malevolence. Color will function in the pixels of the machine's face to depict persons moving, copied stretches of the sky, perhaps in depiction of some wrongdoing, some destruction, derangement, death; elements possible in any given suspect, if only waiting to awake.

The point is that we don't know what we're looking for here. Which is why we're looking. The evidence may or may not rear its head. There is not always evidence provided toward the nature of our history and how it holds us, feeds us.

He or she sits the milk glass down. The milk glass now is mostly empty, except for where around the inside layer of the glass the milk remains in residue, a thin white lining that reforms its shape as it is placed to set still again on the desk where it had been. The remaining milk not consumed is milk that might've been used to perpetuate the function of the body slightly further in its ongoing, if by a negligible amount. It's really not much milk left in the glass, but it's not empty. One could extend his or her tongue. One could lick around and use the fingers to get more of the smear of the milk out, but one does not.

One returns to sit back in the padded seat again half slumped at no clear angle in relation to any of the room's walls, seeing only the walls before the self directly clearly and in some amount of visibility as well those in the periphery on each side. Each present moment's experience waxes or wanes in or out in quality as the concentration of the person shifts in one way or another for whatever rea-son. He or she is at just enough of an angle to look like he or she is at attention, sitting up, while also close enough to feel comfortable that the shape allows the nodding off perhaps again, though having slept once and in small fits and now awoken from the longest, he or she is more fully there inside the room, refreshed. Sleep later in the evening even will be harder, having faltered.

Most of the room cannot be seen. Hours continue in the manner of their own becoming.

One looks head-on into the TV. One is watching nothing making nothing; white making white.

The sound is mute. The sound before the TV had been muted was all static, and at first he or she had let the static sound go on, and it had been more than two hours before the mute procedure was applied. He or she presumes that if the nature of the static changes, the nature of the image would also change, and therefore one would not miss any shift inside the sound if it occurs, though if there were a sound now inside the tape that did not correspond with the change of the video, such as a voice, a dictation, someone confessing, someone listing directions for the destruction of the earth, encoding in the head of the hearer a methodology of murder, that sound inside the room would not be heard. The sound would still be played, though, on the tape, into the room; it only would not be noted beyond its own silence. The word, though, would have occurred.

The muted or turned-off TVs in all the other houses surround the building. The white walls surround each room. The light inside the rooms and between the rooms constantly changes.

In the grain of the function of the white, one might see aberrations from what had been actually filmed. One might force, in the seeing, a rub of grain, a flux of multicolor in the nothing that appears to rise and become swallowed in the white. Hours passing in the seeing of the nothing make one's eyes go weird and grabby, wanting texture where there's none. The eyes play tricks inside their wishing boredom. He or she has seen, for instance, just now, or, rather, believes he or she has, a kind of lobe or hand rise from the flat, a reaching out of something from the nowhere as if touching, with such thick fingers. He or she shakes his or her head or blinks the eyes hard, and when one looks again, yes, there is only the white: the white returned to fill the space around the rising of the vision of the perceived hand, no longer there. What rises from the white then, in this manner, is not quite fabrication, mental leaking, but more a congealment: it's not *not* there, nor is it *really*. It went on between the viewer and the viewed alone. It could not be repeated in another. Pixels begin to form a portrait of aggregated resolve, like the lakes or field scenes that arise from staring hard into a loose amassment of stray color. Those traps. Those days. Those jokes. The walls here. Your growing hair.

Of the four witnesses employed to watch of the tapes of Gravey over the many shifts of the last several days, none have agreed upon the way they've done the seeing. Only one, just now, for instance, has seen the hand. Only this one will admit, furthermore, to have found his or her self wholly summoned at some point into the wide grain of the white, the pure unending white, as if to some awning opening inside the screen there where the light is to become not one flat panel but a crack cut in the middle of the finite hours of the whiteness.

If the others have also seen this, and they might have, they don't admit it; they might not even know.

But he or she, now, yes even right now again in the updated moment spent between this sentence and the one before it there invoking the name of the *now* inside the seeing, he or she cannot avoid admitting how he or she can read against the white something else rising, a surface deeper than the TV, and spreading wider. How, if one allows one's self to keep one's eyes wide, not shaking off inside the seeing again into a sleep or someone knocking or the ringing of a phone, one might feel as if there in the white they must move forward; the color of it calling without asking for him or her to come forth slow and long into its body, falling not in a way that knocks the head against the screen's glass or even leaves the body forward in the chair, but moving as if through some mush writhing outward from the film's virtual center, filling in around the viewer's head. How, if one allows one's self, with eyes wide, one might inside the whitened rise of it go in, might enter beyond some sense of self into this hour of the screen's hold, and there inside it open into somewhere before not found to touch the room, somewhere before this present instant of our index undefined, a product not only of Gravey's project and that enactment, but the condition of time surrounding only now.

One might find held in the white a field of color secreted in the blank's breadth pushed way down into the field, such that as one moves against it nearer still inside the seeing one might find how one can feel or seem or be as if he or she has shifted somehow from being surrounded by the room's walls now into the color. One might look back from where one is now and find his or her own body watching, eyes wide open loosely as if drugged, looking even bored inside his or her life spent staring head-on into the white where his or her own self sits seeing from inside the white as if not even seeing his or her self. One might go even further than even that then, in the white of fields of days of years inside the tape.

Turning back away then from where the self of flesh was into the shaping of the film, one might loosen sight so deeply in the white of such film seeing that beyond the cusp of where one had seen one's self last the space might slur; one might, inside the silence of the white, then *disappear* there into a kind of color not even color hidden in the white, but many colors crammed in colors, crammed in crams, made of the mute, a set of space so trapped or dry or sewn up from the seeing of the body that once one sees inside the self released, one cannot remember what *air* is or what *time* is, there, and in this seeing in the white so deep in colors a sound emerges, a tone so seized and gone it has no tone at all, has nothing but its own presence, which once acknowledged, might expand.

In the minute of the taking of the color under the color hid inside the screen, one might no longer recall how to get back to where the self was there beforehand, prior to this, in the body, nor might one want to or even remember what it would feel like to want to, to feel anything beyond here, absent from the names of names of days. One might not remember one had been ever anywhere but where one is now, flooding, flooded, for forever, wrapped and lifted in the white that bloats still deeper dry inside itself. Perhaps there never even was any other moment, or ever will be, outside of this one, out of this long and lengthless void of breadth, even as outside the color, the body watching or not watching, the body goes on in its war. There might never have been or will be any instance of the self or selves beyond the color, the end of color, white. One might live on only ever now inside the idea of itself. One might become nothing but the absence of the presence it had never fully even been before then. In the fact of disappearance, one might now actually exist.

MARY RUTHERFORD, MD: *Pardon my late entry into this notation, as I have just been given access to these files as a result of my psychiatric examination of Detective Flood, but what I am most concerned by is the complete lack of comment regarding Flood's investigation of the "Gretch Gravey" character? I know that not all police operations are made public, and even medical doctors involved with officials under* *duress in the line of duty are often kept out of the more gory or legal details of a case, but considering the apparent attention surrounding this particular case as described by Flood, and in my understanding of his current involvements, I wonder why no one has mentioned that this case does not seem to exist. I can find no evidence in reports personal or private at my level of access to the investigation or holding of a suspect by the name Gravey or the acts attributed to him above. Flood's growing mania for what seems to me a potentially fabricated line of investigation wherein several dozen women have been brutally murdered and had their flesh eaten, and the subsequent lack of attending to said fabrication's presence in the mind of an officer of the law, is baffling, sad, disturbing, and problematic in ways we have as yet not begun to scrape the face of. I would like to request counsel not only with Flood directly, but with Sgt. Smith in regards to the nature of Flood's recent work, as if I am being withheld of this information, I don't know how I could ever begin to do my job with a clear mind. I'm not sure what else there is to say, besides that I honestly don't know how I will find a way to bed tonight, as there now seems about my air too something leaking.*

SMITH: *???*

On this fourth day of the viewing, the fourth officer of the video review squad of the white films of Gretch Gravey ends the lives of the three other officers in the same employment using her service pistol placed against their skulls: not by shooting any of them with a bullet, but by blows, an estimated more than several hundred per cadaver, deployed between the eyes. The officer, a mother of three, is able to complete this triple murder despite walking covered in blood out of the station after having performed the first kill in the adjoining viewing office. Somehow knowing the locations of the two remaining male viewing members' homes she performs the same gun-butt beatings on both their bodies among descending dusk: the first alone in his apartment eating microwaved spaghetti, the second in the presence of his wife and child near the TV. Having finished off the other viewers, the murdering officer returns to her own home, to dispatch herself before her own spouse and her two oldest children, calmly, neatly placing the gun at last against her own white head and pulling the trigger with open eyes.

Into fifty microphones gathered in bouquet and a feed of cameras sucking his image hard across our electronic fields, Gravey presents an oral statement into America: "Not guilty," he says. His voice is ashy. He chokes on something else. The air is still beyond all birds. The images burned of him in the instant will show how, during the duration his mouth comes open, Gravey's head seems to slightly blur around the nostrils and the eyelids, rapidly blinking. Mouth closed again, he raises his locked arms toward the sky; appears to pull something down into him; inhales with his nostrils; shudders; closes back his eyes. Flashbulbs again and the sky unflinching, soon again to grow opaque like chocolate wrappers from the inside, sealed against the flesh of the dark bar. Gravey remains still and hard-shaped, saying nothing for the duration of the melee of questions without answer and the still surrounding public screaming ricocheting off of all the seeing teeth, until by other hands he's led inside, led down a corridor unto a corridor unto a corridor unto a floor, where on the zigzagged tile in silence is placed a single hard-boiled egg on a black platter, which Gravey eats still in the shell and stands to sleep.

BLOUNT: *No one has seen Flood in several days, or is it hours—what is the word for the period in which daylight ends and then again begins? The detective assigned in Flood's place as lead investigator has also gone missing. I can't remember quite his name. Now they are asking me to take the helm. Or rather, it doesn't seem like they are asking. I go to Gravey's cell sometimes and just stand there near the wall there, and I listen. I hear me talking.*

Flood finds his eyes.

Where he is now standing in a passage. He is naked. He doesn't remember how he became naked. There is a wall behind him, against his back, on which he finds that he's been leaning. New dark continues going forward toward an unreadable distance. Graded panels light the hole, the same glow as what had laced the space beneath the mirrored floor in Gravey's basement, though here only occasionally deployed, so that the illumination comes with great gaps, smaller and smaller in the distance. The light seems natural, as if brought in by shafts from actual daylight.

The walls are white.

Flood is somewhere underneath Gravey's home, he realizes. The second floor had been also false. He must have fallen through it like the first one, and landed down here, whatever here is. His entire body hurts; it feels like he's bleeding from every inch of him, a kind of constant sensation of sweating and absorbing at the same time, but there is no blood, or if there is, he hasn't seen where. Above him, the ceiling is high up and nestled in a dark, somewhere among which must be the surface he remembers rubbing through, or into. He can't see anywhere to have fallen in from, or any way back out. If anyone can hear him shouting, they don't answer.

He runs his palm along the long white surface. It is cold, synthetic. An odd sensation there in where he touches as the contact seems to make his skin come alive, as if there's someone underneath his flesh touching on the inside where the wall touches. And, too, like someone is there on the wall's far side, also touching.

Flood has no choice then but to proceed by facing sandwiched soft between the twin walls and sideways stepping into the oncoming alternating dark. He could wait, perhaps, for someone to come and find him, though there's no telling how long.

The plane of the passage going forward descends rapidly by lengths, cutting at such a slight grade as it goes on that it is nearly impossible to tell it's going down at all; one could conceivably continue down the narrow stretch for hours and still believe they'd only ever stayed aligned with one horizon.

Flood finds the tunnel floors becoming slick. Farther still and he is splashing in inches of liquid underneath his feet. The deeper in he goes, the more there is. He stops to sniff the smell and smells no smell. He puts some in his mouth and he tastes the salt of blood; he knows what blood tastes like; we all do. We all have. If it's not blood it's something just as common. There is no sound outside the repetition of Flood's pace, though inside him he hears words: a murmur mirroring the murmur through the wall, hid under motion, as if someone there is speaking only when he moves. He can almost, underneath this, understand the syllables or shapings of the language, though not enough to take it fully, and not inside this night.

Not inside this night. Who is that speaking, Flood thinks. He repeats the phrase aloud, though his voice doesn't sound like him now. Each word wants him to speak more, like having opened up the gates inside him now there's so much more there, if all of no recognizable syntax. The voice just comes and comes. He bites his mouth to shush himself and does it too hard. A little blood comes up in his mouth. He swallows the blood. Inside him the blood continues loose. The blood tastes cold against the other blood inside him.

The width of walls begins to open up. The widening increases at a clipped rate, like the descending, such that as he goes along Flood can hardly recognize the change; each time he gets the sense he's no longer in a passage tight with darkness but somewhere edgeless, like the night, a massive humming chamber; the tunnel turns again to narrow off. Sometimes it grows so narrow, even within three strides, that he must turn to sidle flat along, pressed between the walls' sides, and sometimes even coming so thin there against his flexing belly he's unsure he can force through.

The texture of the walls remains as ever, with the sound against his frame, and the far-off knobs of white light still oncoming, pulling him forward, rebegun.

Rebegun, that's not a word, Flood hears himself say inside him, squeezing the voice down and in to hold it. As if to fill in where the sound is, the blood he's swallowed washes hot into his throat across his tongue. His bowels tremble, wanting to shit. The vision where his eyes see straight ahead is kind of fucked, causing there to appear several tunnels spreading out forward in the eye of the one tunnel.

Or are there actually that many tunnels, that many different thumbs of light? It is difficult to know which among the sprawl he should lurch toward now. At certain junctures, it seems, branches will open, allowing him the choice of one of several ways to proceed, though no matter which way he chooses, the walls all seem the same, as if repeating, and stride by stride the wet continues rising slowly underneath him, making it slowly more and more difficult to walk. No matter which way Flood chooses, all lengths of the passage look the same. Wherever it is, the tunnel's way goes on forever, as far as Flood can tell, every stretch threatening to disremember where they ever were, on toward some expanse as uncontained as any day.

Rebegun, his voice says again inside him with the blood all in his mouth and through his mind. Sure, sure, that's a word, it says. Sure, you can say that.

Any word is always ours now.

In the darkness, there is text.

Deeper down, and once his eyes have grown accustomed, he sees that what had seemed only space without light in the passage isn't just solid, but has fiber to it, layers to it. Where there seemed walls there, a language holds the space together hard, so many syllables collected in the same pixels it feels impenetrable. The dark, then, is not actually solid, but so overrun it has no choice but to present nothing.

Up close, though, Flood can read. He finds the walls of the passage imprinted in the same way as the floor had been above him, wherever that was, **in god our blood the word of blood in god the name of god in god the name of god**, the layers of sentences laid atop each other often obscuring each beyond a language Flood feels he knows. The text is so thick it's hard to make out any word unless his eye is right above it, tracing where the lines of one letter break free from those beside. It wraps around his face like a loose mask. It brings him nearer.

Each string of language contains small softer sections, Flood finds, like buttons lodged in on a monochrome piano, open wounds. As before, some of the words can be pressed down with pressure aimed in the right way, though now the action is clearer, more like life. He has become acquainted, inculcated, opened, but it had always been this way, in every surface, always. In every surface and word and shape and face ever remembered, ever touched.

Among the black knit, there are panels shaped with different outlines: letters that turn to new shapes as he sees; ring-shaped, star-shaped, squares and diamonds. Each button causes an alteration to the surface just beneath it, the exposure of a branch. Pressing down on the word **wished**, for instance, in one of its many repetitions along the surface, right before his face, causes the wall right behind him to come open. There is no sound. The wall simply slides away, almost so calmly you could miss it.

Behind where had once been wall is now a shaft, extending far on into its own dark cavity. The walls at the mouth of the shaft are the same white as the main passage, quickly disappearing into black.

Flood hesitates some long second standing staring down into the hole he's made open. For some reason, he can't immediately bring himself not to continue into its eye, despite the fact that he's already surrounded by unknown in totality, all directions. There is still the latent fear that once behind it, the wall might close. He could become sealed in down here. He could be made trapped for the remainder of his life. Even in the dark beneath a killer's house, he worries about his own preservation, if only long enough to hesitate a beat before giving in, again, toward what, he does not know.

FLOOD: *All the colors in my eyes. All the machines inside the machines in my body, the other bodies.* I swear this is not me speaking. I cannot control my mouth or hands. *The nightwave knitting though the fields, coloring* [his name] *in the space between me and where I am, which is becoming several more places every minute. It is splitting. We are splitting in it.* No. *Each of the strings of images begets the next.* No. *Try not to think of me as disappearing, but simply always being. Where I am, there you are.* This is not me. I did not want this. I will not believe this. *It has gone on this way for all of time.* Stop it. *It will go on this way for more than time is, every instant, so loud I cannot hear.* Stop.

Inside his sleep Gravey turns over to face up along the ground rather than face down.

He hears the word inside the curd inside the blood inside his skull.

He lifts his head with both hands to see the ground beneath him.

He barfs a liquid colored like the inside of a sun.

He eats the liquid back into him.

The hair grows on his head.

He grows.

The incline of the opened passage, unlike its central mainspring, slowly ascends. The wet under Flood's feet recedes and follows him as footprints only briefly. What air there is is thick. The walls remain in darkness for some time, through which he wanders hands out before him, until there becomes a kind of light natural to the ongoing. Colorless, controlling. Beneath his feet Flood sees the white of the emerging surface turn to wood grain, then to carpet. The carpet is deep red, soft enough that it seems almost as if he isn't walking on it. The passage continues.

Flood realizes he feels calm. Blissful, even. Easy. The higher he ascends into the branch, the less he aches from where he fell, the less he can remember the blood pouring inside him. Soon he can feel no pain in his body, and almost nothing there inside the work of moving, being.

The passage resolves into a wall. The wall is flat and mirrored, reflecting the orifice of the passage back into itself as if to make it appear forever going on. Flood does not appear reflected in the surface somehow. No matter where he moves, there's only more of the passage headed back on where he came. He touches the mirror, feels its silence. There is a small latch attached to the edge of the mirror marked with a small burn mark, round like the world is, and hollow centered. When undone, the latch causes the mirror to open outward into what behind it.

What's behind it is a home. On the far side of his mirror, Flood finds a room there opened up, having become accessible on its own side through a point where on the wall another mirror had been hung—a mirror to cover over the mirror through which Flood's entered, or perhaps the back side of the same, either way a seeming point of unknown entry, linking his passage free into the house.

The room is decorated for a family. There is a sofa and a TV. There is a window covered with white curtains, bleeding light through. Bookshelves line the back wall filled with volumes whose titles Flood realizes he can't read no matter how carefully he focuses. It is as if the room is slightly endowed with a blur, as if the lenses in his head have been set just out of focus.

He realizes, also, that here he can't bring himself to touch anything the house holds. As he reaches for a light switch along the wall to fill the room up, he finds the blood inside his limb becoming heavy very fast, tingling in such a way that the closer he comes to touching anything the room holds, the more difficult it is to move. At the edge of where his hand stops, even just there fractions of an inch off the wall, it is as if he is being pressed back at by a great force. Once he stops trying to touch, his arms go easy again, and he can continue freely into the space. It is like this with all items there collected in the house, the decorations and the weapons and the food and tools and furniture and junk. His flesh feels cold. It's as if he's there but not.

It does not feel strange to walk naked among the home of strangers. This way his skin can breathe, and he is more open to understanding. He can't remember anytime he hasn't ever been just skin like this, breath like this.

There are other rooms off the first room. There is a kitchen and dining room and a half bathroom. Off a slightly longer hall there are two doors to separate bedrooms. In the first room a child is sleeping, the air around him illuminated by a single pink-swathed bulb low to the ground. Images cover the child's walls every inch, as if trying to cover the flat white space out with shiny famous faces and cartoon bodies. The child looks like any child, the way all children do to Flood, never having been a parent. The child sleeps clutching a toy camera to his chest; a camera instead of a bear or blanket, as if at any moment he will be called on to document the world.

In the second bedroom there are two adults side by side, facing opposite directions. Across from their bed, a mirror, doubling their image, and the image of the open door. Again Flood does not see himself reflected in the mirror.

Flood comes into the room. He comes to stand over the bodies. Their breath is low and steady, and does not react to his presence.

There is another window here, over the bed, and here the curtains have been pulled back. Though beyond the window, Flood sees nothing but more darkness. No streetlamps and no moon. No strange edge to the way the absence of light lies over objects underneath it. Just flat unending black, profuse as hell. It is a different sort of darkness than that from which he'd come out of in the tunnel. He can feel no language in it. No sound.

Flood finds that, unlike all the objects, he is not prevented from touching the people. In fact, almost the opposite is true. He doesn't know why, but he can't seem to control his left limb from rising up to pet the long arms of the sleeping woman. Her skin is soft and covered in light hair. She is very warm. The man is warm, too. Flood lingers over both, caressing their scalps and tracing the veins along their limbs. They don't seem to feel anything, or don't respond with more than slight alterations in their sleeping posture. Their eyes are rolled back under their lids, jerking hastily under the flesh there as if in desperation for some icon lodged into the skull.

Flood feels a great desire to lie down. More so, he wants to pull the man out of the bed and stuff his body in the closet, and take his place in the bed beside the woman. Just to sleep some. He is so tired. It has been long years coming up to now. But the man's body is too heavy to move, even an arm alone. Flood can do nothing to change the way they are; he can only brush and breathe against them, feel them, try to try. The woman's face seems so familiar; the lips around the mouth, the groove of the neckline, the shoulders. He wants to hold her, to lie against her. Instead, he tries to wake her, shaking gently at her shoulders. He says a name he believes could be hers, could be anybody's. She goes on sleeping, always sleeping, no matter what now.

Under their skin, the eyes looking out seem to see nothing.

Flood leaves the room. Coming back along the wall, he finds the child's door has been closed and locked from the inside. Flood pulls at the knob and whispers into the gap under the door and no one answers.

Other windows in the house reflect the same black matter as the first. Flood can't force his arms up to try to turn the latch or bang the glass out, the blood inside his arm turning to stone. The same is true of the three doors he finds leading into the space from outside; he can't reach them, even the one he finds ready to be unlocked, the key left turned in the deadbolt for anyone to use.

He could stay in here forever, Flood feels. He could move from room to room and continue his life like that. He would feel fine here. Nothing would have to happen. The people could sleep and sleep and say nothing to him. He feels no hunger, no fear, no boredom, and can't imagine having to feel these ways again. And yet he knows, inevitably, these feelings will find him, grow into him, change him. He knows he has to leave the house before anything can take his heart; to keep the feeling he feels now inside him, held inside him, untouchable.

Flood returns to try to wake the woman twice again without result before he leaves the house the way he came. His body passes though the mirror, and then, once clicked locked behind him, he continues back down the passage into different darkness.

FLOOD: *Whatever else I can't remember I remember was my eye forever.*

They realize Gravey must be moved. In the streets and cities there's demand, creamed in the people. The smell of the blood of the city says his name inside them. The people wish. The warden's worried all the people begging banging shrieking fucking licking at the doors around the center will find some way to beat their whole way in, and worse than free the killer, kill him. Gravey must suffer for his crimes. All must suffer, all days, in the name they've built to walk and live among. The warden wants to get him somewhere undetected, with thicker walls and wiser locks. Four men in black suits come in and hold him down and stick his forearm with three different kinds of needle, leaking juice. Thereafter there's a large amount of light.

Gravey grins. He blinks his eyes hard, feeling giddy. He looks into the men.

"My friends," he says. "My me again."

His forehead shudders, quaking in moonlike ridges.

The men stop. The men stand around Gravey in a circle. They watch him lie. There is a kind of smell about the session, skin in glisten. The dark clothes of the men begin to darken more. They do not look up at one another. The drugs in Gravey's arm trace through his veins. His eyes remain open. He does not look at the men. The men adjust their positions in the circle without speaking to form another kind of shape. Gravey seems to puff up some. A smoke somewhere rising. Gravey gives the men new names. The names appear inside their head. The shape of them shifts again, again. The walls are wet.

The men leave the room. They leave Gravey on the floor there with the door open.

The largest of the four men walks along the long hall to the exit corridor. He comes into a series of other rooms and goes into the first room not already occupied with warming bodies and takes a service revolver off the wall. He shoots himself in the shoulder, that with which he'd given Gravey the injection, then shoots between the eyes. His blood runs from his body in a star.

The second largest of the four men walks along the long hall to the exit corridor into the door to the outside. He walks straight ahead from the building bypassing his vehicle and the gates, walks without looking in either direction into traffic across the main thoroughfare abutting the complex, causing two family-sized vehicles to swerve to avoid him and crash into several vehicles, which crash into several more. He walks four point four further miles causing similar dysfunction resulting in an uncounted number of accidents or deaths until he arrives at his home, where his wife and three-year-old daughter are napping in the smallest room of the house. He locks them into the house. He sets fire to the house using propane from the grill and gasoline siphoned from his car. He goes back into the house. He locks the front door, tapes his knees and wrists together, lies down on the floor there below the bed beside his child and wife.

The second smallest of the four men goes about his day; he feels tired but rather happy somehow, giddy even; in the morning he will make a routine visit to his physician, who will find a small blue growth in the flesh around his kidneys, and in the flesh behind his eyes.

The smallest of the four men goes into a break room with a telephone. He begins calling numbers from memory of the people and businesses he has known inside his life, dialing rapidly each one in an order subscribed to his emotion. He will speak to bodies, to machines. He will speak to the presences at the end of the line and give into them not a word but the Name of God coursed through him without sound. Each of the called will act on their own calls burned in their own brains until they have sent as well the waking message to hundreds of others, who do the same. Each person, having completed some precise number of calls already written, kills themselves with knives or ropes or pills or whatever way it is they always privately fantasized on at their grossest or most bored.

Gravey closes the cell with him inside it.

RUTHERFORD: [*stricken from record*]

INTERVIEW WITH GRETCH GRAVEY,
CONDUCTED BY J. BURNS. 10/16/2███, 1:30 P.M.

JB: Why did you kill [more than] four hundred and forty people?

GG: What.

JB: You have been accused and will most likely be convicted of killing a lot of people. The number's yet to be concretely established, but by what we know so far it is at least four hundred and forty. Why did you do it?

GG: [*Shakes his head hard.*]

JB: No comment?

GG: No condition. [*Inhaling slowly.*] Do you have a gun at home?

JB: I've never owned a gun. My father was against it. I probably should, though, shouldn't I? Do you own a gun?

GG: Many.

JB: How many guns do you own?

GG: As many as there are bodies in America.

JB: America? Why not the whole world?

GG: When the hole is open the rest will enter. [*Exhaling slowly.*]

JB: Is there a reason more than seventy-five percent of your accused victims were women?

GG: For what any of us is and was and is again and will be again beginning. To awake the Eye.

JB: So you did commit the murders?

[*Gravey's face changes. He shudders raptly, arms convulsing, then looks at me again.*]

GG: No, that was you. That was your father and my father. That was windows or was water. I am online now. The gown is raising. In almost any home you can find written at least once the word *delete*.

JB: Your father. He's gone missing, but we haven't found his body in your house.

GG: I grew up in a family of nature, a more graphic, wonderful home. As children we were happened. We regularly encountered church. I wanted five hundred brothers and sisters. My parents did not drink or visit grocery or drugstores. Their softcore pornography was no physical abuse, just not enough. In our neighborhood it was a fine, solid people that would dream garbage and, from time to time, tragedy. The days would scream. The days are screaming now but you can't hear them and soon even that—

[*Gravey is laughing. He makes a terrified face, then a deranged face, then suddenly appears calm. I start to open my mouth to say the next thing and before I can he speaks.*]

GG: There is a law revolving around God, from this Word of God, and the Prophets made flesh, as far back as Mary the Virgin. So that all who would highlight God's mercy would make everyone believe in what was coming; that who would seek god for where there has been other, when Christ was forgiveness, and writing, writings of the conceived. We had to bring God's writings, search the Scriptures, and slay it, as who do not usurp the authority become the arguments themselves. The confronted Christ knew the real meaning, but yet said to him, "There's an additional God." *Be not sons*, they were commanded, *born of fornication*, so we were.

JB: You mean God told you to kill?

[*There is a long silence. My lips won't open. Gravey sees me. Then he shakes his head. My lips seem to unlock. I find it hard to take a breath. I feel the ground beneath me kind of moving. Again I try to speak and again Gravey speaks instead.*]

GG: God's name isn't God. The word has not been formed yet. I am forming the word.

JB: Are you a prophet?

GG: I am whoever.

JB: Anybody? Everybody?

GG: Neither. It is a folding.

JB: So it was a moral act?

GG: No. It was written. There is no author.

[*I had not realized until right now how much sweat is pouring from his face. His clothes are soaked through and into the bed and on the floor almost with such range I can't believe it. The wet is on my pants a little. I try to forget at all about my body or the air here.*]

JB: What do you think of the Bible?

GG: God of Heaven believed that he was a sacrifice rich in mercy, numb, and prophets were goats, oxen, red men ignored, heifers. A Law, but also a way, an escape for those who learned the sophisticated Repentant Souls and social impacts might fall short of the virgin, toward a very prolific type of glory of God's law. We would conceive and bear a system of worship. The prophet had to slay a lamb for hope for a world. It has only partially begun.

[*Suddenly I'm having trouble breathing, like the room is too small. Gravey looks. I'm kind of choking. The air seems to catch hard in my chest and spin there. Gravey's not blinking. I can still manage to make words.*]

JB: Is it true you ate many of your victims' bodies?

GG: I ate them all. All of them, each component. I mean just by breathing. You will become it, too. All flesh must be returned into one flesh. What seems their remainder is not there. It is a bag I placed to leave the evidence of my being in the hands of the cameras for the proclamation. They weren't victims. I'm just around.

JB: How would you describe the taste of human flesh?

GG: Like mashed potatoes in a ball gown. Sometimes pianos or a lock. It depends on the flesh's eventual location in our total future mass. [*begins to touch himself all over quickly*] Hey, do you have fire?

JB: I don't smoke.

GG: I don't either. Do you have fire?

[*Again, my voice comes pouring from me.*]

JB: My father used to burn leaves in the yard. It made more smoke than anything else. The ground around the pile was black.

[*My choking in my chest is simmery, like on the cusp of welling up.*]

GG: Did you love your father?

JB: I think I did.

GG: No, did you love him?

JB: He was my dad, yeah.

GG: [*suddenly angrily, baring teeth*] I said did you love him?

JB: Yes, I did. I do.

GG: Then you love me.

[*Gravey at this point is drooling from the mouth to match the sweat; the drool slick makes
a long reflective window, as with dishsoap water, before it pops between the index of his
face between his hands. His eyes are blinking so rapidly it is as if the function of the lids
has inversed: blinking when they would other times be held open or closed, staying open or
closed when they would blink. Gravey begins grunting in a rhythm.*]

JB: Hey, are you okay?

GG: [*snorting*] Let's have dinner. I like tacos. I enjoy the light inside a cow's right
eye.

JB: It's not quite dinner yet. I'd be glad to join you.

[*Gravey again laughs. His laughter this time sounds completely different from the first way
his first laughter sounded, higher, more rapid. The recorder in my pants begins to buzz. I
feel it burn at where my skin is. I hear my phone. My phone is ringing. It seems to stick
against my leg. My leg has spasms. My teeth won't let my mouth around them close. I'm
sweating. I hear numbers. A light is rising.*]

JB: Darrel?

GG: [*not smiling*] Yes, son?

JB: I am

GG: You are

[*I feel better. The room is cleaner. I sit straight up. I breathe.*]

JB: I want to understand.

[*Gravey closes his eyes; I watch them roll back underneath the flesh as the lid comes down. Suddenly I smell something, like he's shit his pants, but neither the expression on his face nor his position belies any strain. He begins to speak now through his lips without opening his mouth, a childish murmur.*]

GG: He is in a room. There are no doors in the room. There is a screen. A kind of light coming from somewhere on the side opposite the screen feeds at his chest. It is the Day. Inside the room he watches the day go on beyond him in the end of itself. He does not know what he sees, or that he's seeing. Where he is is going to end but it will begin again. No murder and no mirrors, but a fleshless, edgeless, ageless frame.

JB: And you? When will you die?

GG: I am only here on pause. For a moment my home touched the room beyond the screen and gained its level but this soon will be ended, for the pyre. This body too will be destroyed, at the hands of all our hands, like mine, so we no longer have to have.

[*His sweat is almost like a well. It fills his mouth. I taste the salt and cannot chew. I'm sweating also, more now than I ever.*]

JB: Gretch Gravey, are you guilty as an actor in the death of the four hundred and forty persons?

GG: On Tues., 7-23-XX, Gretch Gravey knew homicides that he forgot real. Upon asking him to mention in which skulls he performed the original interview, he stated the above information. For this work I would like to be paid fifteen million dollars.

JB: Were you alone, or were there others?

GG: During the rising I was the second suspect in his body, an offense. Some of the skulls Gretch Gravey had picked up and requested to speak with were found in front of me again.

[*Each time I inhale, he exhales.*]

JB: You keep referring to yourself now in third person.

GG: At this time I was the thirty-third skull he sprayed. There had been ones before and there would not be others. I proceeded to the fifth floor of the house. At this time I also locked myself up in Sod City, where there appeared a black paint. The neighbors knew. Their faces shook in the night while they were sleeping and they grew.

JB: There were others involved, or there weren't?

GG: All the victims in all eyes. All the knives the verbs had given in the books and speech of human color.

JB: You aren't making any sense.

GG: Our last transmission. More phones all ringing in the blood of them with each new inch. When asked into the interview room where the numbers were placed onto where they could become the Mother Body, He stated he had boiled the skin and hair we conducted from the skulls in order to spray away an hour's time. Each hour must be peeled into the Mother to forgive it. He at this time gave them an artificial torso that he wished to look like in case someone he had taken from a state talked to us about a victim while we were not there in our bodies. He had also two additional feelings that could not be boiled out of us, either one.

[*There is so much liquid on the floor, I can feel it. I can't look down.*]

JB: What were the feelings?

GG: A sleeplike state, the state of ether; and the pyre, where to this . . .

[*Gravey's face begins to emit sounds of biting, from inside his throat, like something in there tearing. His eyes are wet, and making gleam. He refuses to make words, despite the nearly constant ream of guttural and convulsive sound seeming to come from all over his body. I watch. I hold my hands close. I feel hungry: I wish I didn't have to say I did.*]

[*I cannot speak.*]

GG:

GG: [*some kind of breathing coming from him in the deepest voice I've heard*] The world revolves around the world. Other orchestrations [planetoid, celestial, debris, silent striation, columnar bodies, fable/myth, the unseen] are totalities manifested by the world's revolution of itself. Its revelation. To change the earth, the earth must be deceived. One way is paper, one is blood.

[*I cannot speak and do not wish to.*]

GG:

[*More time goes on. I am seeing colors. I close my eyes and can't make them open up. I keep waiting for the guards to come and get me. I feel nothing. Later, standing up from where I'd been seated, I would imagine it had been at least weeks since I had left the room, as I would find my legs so stiff and weird beneath me it was as if they were not mine. I find myself again compelled against speaking.*]

JB:

[*Gravey's sternum is shaking. It stinks.*]

JB:

[*The whites of Gravey's eyes have become grayer, packed with bluish spindles. The pupils rolled down to look toward me, not at or into me, but straight through, as if focused hard on something on the far side of my head. I could feel a little burn like boiling wine where my memory packets swirled around a cold spot in my cerebrum. I turned around to look where he was looking on the wall. There on the wall, a black square printed at eye level into the white surface, hazy, floating on my vision, and just thereafter, sunk away into the cream.*]

[*I got up and walked out of the room.*]

[*I mean I get up. This is happening in present tense.*]

[*I walk along the long hall through the building seeing nobody else. I have to piss. I'm freezing cold. None of the doors in here will open. Nothing would open. The door to the outside is no longer where I remember it was. I don't know where anybody is. Through the window into another holding chamber holding a shitload of dogs inside it. The dogs are gnawing at each other.*]

[*None of the other rooms is really a room. There are beds. There are thimbles and money stacked in piles like pyramids and globes.*]

[*I have to piss. There is all this liquid in me. My arms are heavy.*]

[*I find a water fountain and try to take my dick out to piss into the hole of the fountain because whatever, but I can't get the opening open on my pants.*]

[*I piss my pants. My piss is white as paper and has writing all the fuck over it, every word I'd ever said. It has your name on it. It has the date, and all the dates before today's date.*]

It does not have any dates after today.]

[*I walk back to the room where I'd left Gravey. I feel I need to see him. I have to hurry. There is this want. It is the greatest want I've ever felt, all of a sudden. I hurry for the room. The room where He had been before me. Along the walls now, though, the hall keeps going on. Where the door was supposed to be, the door to He, each time I think I'm there along the long wall, I find a little piece of paper in my hand. The paper is always blank.*]

[*The paper is blank until it wasn't. Until when I opened the paper, there I was. Then there were no doors. There was no city.*]

[*I put my head against the floor. I heard Him again right there in me, answering me again, in my own voice, with the questions I had asked, and the answers I had answered.*]

[*There are all these motherfucking words. They were shaking in me. They knew who you were.*]

[*Inside His voice aloud I hear me also speak. I hear me speak and speak and speak in all these other rooms around us.*]

[*I'm bleeding.*]

[*holy fuck I'm bleeding*]

SMITH: *J. Burns was a member of our police force from 1961 to 1967. He was killed in service during a routine investigation of a property at* ███████████████ , *suspected to be harboring a multiple felon wanted on evidence of additional homicide, pedophilia, and distribution of narcotics. Said suspect fled the scene and successfully escaped through an unlit wood behind the house. Burns was an extremely dedicated cop, and more so a good man. I have no idea why his name appears here, though I do recognize a few of the exchanges presented above from segments of a videotaped deposition of Gravey on the morning following his arrest.*

Four more mothers kill more friends. Four friends of each of the killed persons kill another four persons, and from there, each four more. Four of the relations of each of the victims of Gretch Gravey kill four more people, and four of each of those killed by the mother kill four more people. Each, having killed four, kill themselves. Other bodies choose to replicate the Gravey method, killing many in a silence without public detonation or self-snuffing, requiring capture by police, and forthcoming investigation, and prosecution, which, for each, takes more time, a form of worship.

In waves of four new sets of four more kill further bodies immediately again. The work occurs in dark or light: women and men are stabbed inside their cars or closets or beds or bathrooms or at work or on the bus; children and babies are smothered in their cribs or inside day care or before their parents at their park; guns are placed in mouths and eyes and earholes, knives inserted into slits of flesh the flesh had held for life, waiting for the injection of the knife to be the key turned in the lock the flesh makes at last forever once and only ever by his hand. Homes are intruded upon by those taken up in spirits or stone sober or somnambulating or quite calm; wives, judges, bag boys, busboys, window shoppers, roofers, tourists, police officers, designers, homemakers, the poor, the elderly, the lame turn fists and fingers and teeth and trowels and machetes and steel bats on the homeless, the work-from-home, stockbrokers, students, demolition experts, body doubles, waitresses, the faithful, the faithless, chefs, producers, writers, actors, window washers, architects, the terminally ill. The function of the action spreads in doily-motion, turnpiking out from each to each, so that by lengths the victims activate the guilty and the guilty in turn beget more of both.

Begetting is the purpose; this is a word we all have heard; it replicates in the backwards process from the book known by some as the story of creation, though this time in reverse: John debegets Nancy debegets Richard debegets Tom debegets Tony debegets Alison debegets Chris debegets A. debegets B. debegets Joseph debegets Olinea debegets LaRichea debegets Paul debegets Paul debegets

Paul debegets Tia debegets Michael debegets Yon debegets Sina debegets Portia debegets Jericho debegets Lon debegets Richard debegets Owen debegets La- naisa debegets Chad debegets Andy debegets Lucy debegets Arnold debegets Oona debegets Don debegets Allen debegets August debegets Toya debegets O. debegets Ron debegets Ronnie debegets Ronald debegets Sal debegets Sagat debegets Andrew debegets Timothy debegets Mary Louise debegets Marticia debegets Joan debegets Joanie debegets O. debegets Person debegets Chu de- begets Quia debegets Jose debegets Lania debegets Sue debegets Ham debegets Sara debegets Sing debegets Kandy debegets Hsu debegets Rory debegets Clive debegets Blake debegets Halla debegets Sancho debegets Janice debegets Matt debegets Susi debegets Pad debegets Alicia debegets Fal debegets Nan debegets Janet debegets Percy debegets Ronaldo debegets John.

The houses fill with blood. The blood is eaten from the bodies, becoming body for the body to activate itself. Each body made debegetted is taken unto the body that debegetted it, absorbed. One by one, in sets of four, then eight, then sixteen, the bodies pair and congregate, compile. Oceans open, settle, dry. The rooms of evidence aggregate behind locked doors in silence, cataloged, un- watched, while in the rooms surrounding other hours the as yet undebegetted people continue to try inside themselves to still go on. Streets for miles divert the massive traffic held in blue white red green gray black red husks of hurried cars enslaved in slick packs from lot to lot in the susurrating Costco light the magnanimous Wendy's light the sainted stitching Barnes & Noble light, the BP light the PetSmart light of light hung street to street in knit across the homes the OfficeMax light the Office Depot light the neon signs of deathtraps in one na- tion under god, the Chili's light the silent beeflight of the Outback and the Gap and Best Buy moving hurried in conditioned spasm to Exxon and Taco Bell and Moe's and Ben and Jerry's and Dunkin' Donuts in the husk of cells fussed off gross streaming trays of shitting days and laughter pyramids set in the gaudy lips and teeth like tumors on a tonsil turning black and turning swollen aisle to aisle in room to room in the Target light of America the Kroger light of America the Ross light the Home Depot light the Coca-Cola light the jabbed shit rib sand- wich canary visions peeling off the borders of the bodies of the On the Border and the T.G.I. Friday's and the T.J. Maxx farting blood beams from the eyes into the mouths of the murder puppies screwing big holes in blind butts wallowing in mud of Gap light of Google light of Yahoo light in the machines of aborted dick shelves robbing tanning beds while folders of folders brim with files sent from number 1 to number 2 among the walls of mumbled birthing rooms and mail centers and dead video rentals and carpet cleaners and the husks of names clipped by a bacon-smelling surface rising in the lid of the limousine yards of the mall crapped and crapping blue-gray beauty on the table of the sword like lettuce peeled from plastic boxes under the lid of E! light of ABC light of CNN light of dad of dad while babies screw up stabbing ornamental pygmy trash on wax paper in the bedrooms while their parents snorf pepperoni cubes in the light of Papa John's in the light of Walmart light Applebee's light American Apparel light dicklight pornlight mashlight hammers falling from blowholes scripted by torches under afghans skewed from worms sold by Pep Boys light Duracell light Facebook light changing its profile and its name against the edge of beds pushed together under houses hiding from scrawling bloodgush peeing in their ears and arms of daddies going whoa going holy fuck the football game is on my dick has scabies the delivery guy has no change I can't get my car out of the driveway I'm several years gone I'm under water in my briefs this red light has been red for eight hundred years and I've lived for only thirty and I feel eighty and I'm ten and I don't want to be me anymore or be the body beside me in the night from whom my babies twinned were made and kissing rabbits in my sleep praying for lasers to shoot the grease out of my eyes to scrape the Windex light the Comfort Inn light the NBA light the rapeshitfucklight strobing from my human-wounded ass from my tits and arms and flab and mustache, I can't even breathe my own breath here any longer I can't taste this pie can't smell this ball I want a new job I want a city I want a wider grave a bigger boat I want bigger to have one hundred g's in it I want rap music dentistry I want a cut of beef Pamela breast-sized Brad Pitt cock-sized a cut of beef the size of me I want to swim in god I want a god I want a life an Uzi a condition I want the best pills you can prescribe I want to live in the name of no prescription I want national jailbait body Party City Citgo Waffle House chop suey full flavor less value more blue prose more delete-mind more screen so wide I can't see the end or the beginning I want parsley I want panties I want me of me in me of mine.

Today 137,800 persons in America become killed.

The current total population of America after the murders is 310,733,965.

RUTHERFORD: [*stricken from record*]

BLOUNT: [*stricken from record*]

LAPUZIA: [*stricken from record*]

SMITH: *I'm not sure why I'm even taking time now to update this file again but all the other persons who have commented on the above are dead (barring "Rutherford," as I have no idea who that person is; she is definitely not the same psychiatrist assigned to Flood for examination, though that person is now dead, too, as are more members of our precinct than I can figure how to count). I am writing this from a locked room with several weapons at my disposal. I am not sure where I should go. Armed forces have arrived to help secure the building and watch Gravey's chamber around the clock, though I am not sure that I feel safe even with them here. Everything seems to have changed. What was written in the above is making its way upon our bodies. I don't know how it is being updated, or from where. Flood still has not surfaced since my last note regarding my inability to make contact, though he seems able to update this file at his ease. Flood, if you are reading this, obviously I need to speak with you immediately and in the most dire way. Please contact me, immediately. This is your sergeant, Reginald Smith.*

The next day 188,750 persons in America become killed.

Fewer official numbers are placed on record. Less is known regarding where-abouts or names. The coverage is sparse upon the wires and yet heavy on the air; the local coverage goads more going. People take up weapons, wires, fires, teeth and muscle, ideas, arms. The sounds of slitting fill the night with something like the cutting of the largest paper doll. There is the whir of film being recorded to by light and no light.

The president speaks. His voice is electronic, broadcast from far beneath the ground. He discusses tax cuts and public funding and pleasure dreams and cake.

There are people in the folds of dry land who keep their hands over their eyes. Walls are extended over windows. Doors are rendered no longer doors. Those left to walk among the lapse of day and night go back and forth between work and sleep while disregarding how the air seems more creamy, shrinking, ready.

This is an American disease. Beyond the normal borders, death proceeds apace; it is spoken of, recorded, but not necessarily the end—how could it ever be the end—despite the waters of the gulfs and twin coasts crumbing with the glimmer of dumped blood, a bright and shaking laughter singing off the buildings in the parlor of our peeling night.

We can't even find your body in the piles.

You will not be buried.

SMITH: [*stricken from record*]

The next day, in America, 212,100 become killed.

The next day, in America: 290,030.

These numbers being numbers because someone says so. Someone like anyone, like you or me or us. Each new day made out in the shape of a blue sun, in America.

There are silent parades in the streets, each one made to look like car jams, lined with windows reflecting sky under the sky.

"No one wants to exist," Gravey says, speaking into his clavicle through a single long black hair that's grown exactly long enough to reach his bottom lip.

The rupture of the bodies by the bodies that ends the bodies fills the seconds seam to seam without a sound. Old houses go on being houses, organized with food and floors. What will come will continue coming, it is spoken, and so it does.

The next day in America.

The next.

There are many other shafts off of the main shaft of the darkness. In fact, Flood finds, there is almost one for every word printed on the walls of the passage. There must be millions. Each exposed passage leads to someone else's home, through a mirror marked with one of the seven symbols. All the homes through here connect.

in god our blood the word of blood in god the name

In every home, Flood finds the people sleeping, the contents impossible to touch beyond the flesh, and every door that might have led out of the circuit, free from the chambers, out of his reach. In many houses he lingers for some time, wandering from room to room after something accessible, some way to push beyond the purpose of a spectator, but only ever are the ways that he can change anything about the house but by the people.

what now exactly now none nothing

He feels an anger in his blood, a seething frustration at his inability to escape this pattern. In some of the houses, he plays dummy with the bodies. He covers their faces over with a blanket, or drapes them over the kitchen table, or takes their clothes off and tries to make them fuck. The men's sex organs won't become hard. There is little contentment in the dolling. It is as if they are dead, but they have a pulse, their skin is warm.

For every home he enters, there are countless others he cannot. In every gap is buried so much he passes over. After a while, all the houses begin to seem the same, regardless of how different in their decoration, their low old smell, the shape of the people and their organs. The women always seem familiar and the men always seem like someone he could have been. Upon waking, they would return to their commitments and occupations, perhaps always not knowing someone had come in above them and felt their faces. Someone could have done much worse. Beyond each window, the same darkness.

if god if

Each time upon returning to the central passage he finds the wet has risen higher in his absence, as the passage continues going down. The flood is colorless in the low light, and smells so rich it's hard to breathe: like loose earth and a banged head at the same time, fresh sex and summer in a jungle. It feels sometimes as if the air is breathing him. He can feel the open wounds along his arms and legs bleeding back into the congregation.

Flood begins to enter fewer and fewer homes, taking less time to move among them, or even really see the words in the white of the walls beyond the curve. The walls begin to feel like just walls again, flat and long and ever-going. But going where. It is comforting to just continue forward. There is a direction to the passage, at least, unlike the houses, even if an end is never reached.

see I

Flood has no idea how far beneath the surface of the earth he's gone. Soon he's knee-stepping, then he's wading, then it's halfway up his chest. Swimming feels the same as walking feels the same as laying the stuff and letting his body float. There is a slow current to the surface, just calm enough to almost disregard. In the thick of it, he feels matted patches, like flesh or soft loose ground clumping together, aggregating.

Underneath the lip of the wet, the space is light, though a kind of light he can't see in. When he breathes or barks or screams words forwards or backwards at the extending nothing, he hears nothing but more air. Though he knows he must want food or water, he feels no concrete want or need, no grinding in the space inside him to be fed something; he continually moves on, while the only subject showing he's made motion or day is passing in the silence is the wet beneath him rendered rising, lapping moist around his waist and then his nipples and then his shoulders, and still rising.

"Again again again again again, I say, I have done nothing," Gravey says into the machines. "I am nothing. The thing of nothing flutters through my hands. There is something climbing on me. Something see-through. It is climbing onto you. Whoever said I said I said that said something false. I am ham clothes. I am a hole. I did nothing and am nothing and am silent. I should not be held up to the light for what's been held against me while I am anybody too."

The cameras replicate his face. This day will not be remembered.

Gravey hiccups in his sternum. He chews something. Swallows. Weeps a growl.

A peal of burn noise hurts the air as he goes to grip the stage mic with the hand farther from his heart: "Bullshit," he says. "Bullshit city. Hey-o. I do everything I do. I'm a big boy. I get nasty. I'm so horny, I could fuck a hole in sleep.

"If any children kill or are killing other children because of this sentence," Gravey says, "that is the desire. That is the nation under god. Adults killing adults and mothers killing mothers and fire killing fire and dogs surviving for the dogs. It is one condition of an attitude developed over the past three hundred thousand years."

Someone behind a lantern asks a question, though on the playback of the recording, the words have been obscured.

Gravey stutters. He chips the microphone with his best tooth. He clears his throat, looks through his fists cupped into tunnels, winks. He puts his mouth around the entire metal conducting head.

"If I'm not here yet," he goes, burbling with spit, "then invent me. Make me come."

Back in his cell inside his sleep Gravey's longer fingers trace his right arm open with his nails, cutting divots in his skin's face like opening the mail. From the hole cut near his elbow he extracts a growth of blood that slinks along the air like wire and feeds back up to his face into his mouth around his tongue. He has not eaten in more days than he can remember.

The color of the room is erasure. Beyond the walls the knives glint sun for sun's sake into the sun to blind it to the motion of our arms among the walls around the rooms where we have slept and soon will sleep again.

Gravey's eyes are closed. His hair has grown down to his ass, cloaking his back-meat as it itches with such warmth. With his two longest fingers he traces on the cell's floor the shape of the letter S, smearing platelets across the concrete where it holds him on the surface of the earth. Between the letter's two endpoints, at each end of the snake of it, Gravey then traces slightly more faintly the shortest line possible between them, bisecting the body of the S to form a symbol like the number 8, but flattened down one side: 8.

The S shape shines in the room's mood. From the blood begins to rise a hissing steam. There is a stench, like plastic melting. The shape begins to change.

Gravey moves to stand face-first against the wall. His body accesses the space parallel to the room's one locked entrance, positioned at the wall's center. His back faces the symbol, the remainder of the room. He hums. The sound is somewhere inside his head; it is every song he's ever heard, at once. The rooms he'd never been in. His hair rises to stand up on the air straight out in a line behind his head. The hair vibrates, emitting gold tone, harps and bells. There is a language in the stink, the sound of the smell of nowhere filling the room in impregnation. The door to the hall outside behind him sweats. The sweat is mammal blood, the musk of humans. Its shade, from certain angles, matches the pearling of the inside of a conch, houses we would never enter.

A light inside the room blows up. Microphones around the room for miles go mute, worms birthing in their handgrips in the hour of the anchor speaking the other language.

Inside the light, the door's wall and the wall across from it change place. The door that had before upon the one wall opened into the remainder of the station now still opens onto the same building, but from the other side, forcing each room inside the building, and in the space surrounding, each instance of the air to lay inverted, in mirror image of itself.

The bodies of the people in the rooms go on inside the day. The clocks change colors, pocked meat and shining rings. There is singing, under every voice's misuse. The eye of Darrel without name.

Gravey's body folds to lie down on the floor, his mouth hole touching the endpoint of the high end of the S. From the low end of the same symbol, another pearl of smoke emits and rolls along the floor in a white wire, intersecting with the other wall. His nostrils flare, bringing the smoke inside his skull. He exhales again black with it, the color of the smoke having been changed. Out from his face the smoke rises toward the wall behind him, spreading up in packets; the smoke forms a face upon the wall, of a woman with no eyes no ears no brow no cheeks no nostrils. She has a mouth. The room around the smoke face shudders.

The smoke of the smoke lips begins to writhe, pulling open, inside which: teeth, a tongue, a humming. Smoke of a disintegrated sweat.

The head begins to lean out of the wall; its smoke flesh grows. The flesh of the grown face is reflective. A tumor on the head's cheek glimmers. Somewhere money burns. Somewhere someone else is frying.

Gravey's sleeping body rises from the ground. He floats above the S or 8 now having become many symbols in one face at once, stopping hung there on the paused air of the building, through which, for this instant, all other bodies in the precinct have been removed, evacuated into their memories beyond the present. The bodies will return again as they had been without remembering their disappearance.

Gravey rotates above the symbol in his glitchmoan, head rotating to the smoke-made Head. His hair, hung dry beneath him, sucks up backward, splaying out and turning white down to the scalp. The shifting symbol is written in the scalp meat. A matching tumor grows on Gravey's cheek, pig-colored, every icon. His eyes fill up with blood. His eyes open. His body opens, the smokehead just behind his head, pressed glyph to glyph.

The smokehead speaks.

How many years have passed here, Flood asks the darkness. The wet by now is higher than him, filling the passage so completely he can no longer feel the bottom. He can find no edges where the walls were under the surface, no soft panels with which to find another passage through the black. The ceiling and the walls above the water seem to have spread wider, into something like an ocean under evening, no edges to the open air where he can find them beyond where in the rising darkness there seems a heaving solid surface in what could be the heavens. He can't remember which way he came in from, where underneath him or behind him the descending passage went. It is as if the passage itself has wrapped back on itself, holding the time beyond it out. Even the idea of time before *right now* seems conceptual at best, an orblike surface drowned inside the water of his blood.

And yet inside the passage the rising liquid is still rising, a reminder of dimension. The higher the wet rises, the less air around him there must be. Less and less space remaining inside the passage every instant, no matter how hard he tries to think of anywhere else, ever. *How many hours until I am too tired to keep moving*, he hears a voice inside him asking, *how many more until there is no air.*

Flood himself is full; his chestmeat aches around his bone framing his center. He is not hungry or thirsty but not sated. Inside him, his blood presses back against the wet slaving his skin in silent war. His arms buzz hot like thousands of arms pressed into only two.

The wet goes down and down forever underneath him, it seems. However deep Flood forces his body, there is more depth opening into greater pressure and potential dimension. At the length of half his breath, the point where Flood knows inside him sure for certain were he to swim deeper there'd be not enough breathing stored inside him to get back, he feels another presence come lighted, way beneath him; a string of buried glow like some white city far below, swallowed over on some level ground surrounded in the cavity, he believes; long drowned along the nadir of the growing wet wanting to drown him in it.

Sometimes, in the windows of the buildings, somehow becoming clear across great leagues of distance, he feels certain he can see behind the panes inside the small light. And within that light pockets of remote people moving inside rooms; living bodies warbling in muffled silence without even pulse, the word there also buried in the liquid formed around him, rising at his head, today.

With his chest tight, wanting new breath, knowing he should turn away and swim to surface, Flood feels his eye pass through one specific window across the stretch of cheek of a lone woman in a gray dress; a woman alone, standing at the window staring back up at him; a woman who looks in some way like his mother, then like his wife. Her face changes with each expression as Flood swims up and back to look longer, each time more winded than the last, the woman at the glass there standing stolid and looking up into him from so far in and down they shouldn't be able to see anything of one another. Behind her in the room the light continues changing, fleshing out the endless wet between them with ambient clouds of mottled color.

There is a terror in her eyes, some kind of churning screen of remove in her complexion, but also a desperation for the ability to grant respite, a want to for-give, to cave in to the worst part of anything he has been, could be; some soft understanding coming open in her with his returning presence, as if, in her tiny world, through all the darkened liquid, she could feel him, need him.

Unlike the bodies in the past houses, Flood knows he knows her name; knows who she was and would have always been beside him if he could have let her. But then just as quickly he must rise; kick in frenzy back up through the water to fill his lungs enough to swim back down, each time returning to a smaller and deeper expression of the image of the woman, of the window, of the city, among which he knows for sure now she is held forever there and he is not, his body screaming against the pressure to stay under longer, lower, until on some future iteration, there is nothing.

Among the long blank hours of the tapes of Gravey, an image emerges.

It is difficult at first to decipher the dimensions of the contour from the flat white after all these hours burned upon the viewer's face. There are floors, then there are walls. The outline of a room there, then a room there. The room itself is mostly white as well, though by method of slow accumulation an underlying texture in the surface rises. One sees rise among the air the form of furniture, and hair; hair, yes, attached to limbs of bodies attached to people in a space, the aging heads of humans, their vertices of assembled flesh emerged in neon connection from the first suggestion of their presence, then as well: persons, objects, a window, light.

As quickly then as anyone could remember, the image continues on as if it had always been a film of just this room, as if all the hours of the white had never been.

The time code on the tape's playtime, at the instance of the image, resets on the machine to 00:00:00.

In the film, the people sit in silence holding postures that only slowly and occasionally adjust: one man holding a book with no word written on its spine or face sits on a sofa, beside which a woman stands at a window with her back turned to the viewer. On the floor, before a TV, a small child grips a toy camera, the rim around its lens gnawed up. From this angle we cannot see the content of what is being watched by the family this evening, though its color fills the room.

Each body is mostly still. Small adjustments occasionally occur, like inhalation, the book's page turn, the movement of a limb, as if to remind us the shot's not static. The space inside the room is calm. Any noise is subtle and mostly covered over by the larger sound of nothing, like the feeling one gets when passed by something larger than one would wish to be near.

A floor-length mirror stands along the far wall, copying the room. The reflection shows no filming camera in the frame, despite the fact that at this angle, the camera should, by proximity, appear. This glitch in continuity suggests some alteration of the record, an outside guidance.

On further inspection it becomes apparent there is something off or wrong or different about the child's reflection. Such as, in the skin of the face of the skin of him there in the mirror appear patches of discolor like the scape of glimmer in gasoline splayed under sun, while his unreflected skin is creamy. The hair around the lips and ears of the child in certain reflected angles appears to be thicker than what actually appears on the child's head. He looks older than he should.

What is wrong with the reflection of the child?

What about he here must be different from he there?

No one seems to notice, or else they have accepted his condition as a fact of life.

All is calm.

The woman at the window stands seeing out with her face near the glass, breathing against it. The changing light of the TV in the room makes it impossible for us to see what she is looking out at; only the room again appears reflected, doubled, extending the room out into the night. We cannot see from here where the reflection in the window meets the reflection in the mirror. The woman's hands are clasped before her, her hair pulled back tightly around her skull.

The man turns a page again. The page's turning makes no sound, though on this page, open before him, still unseen by the camera eye, the man seems to see something unexpected; his face changes, clenching; he brings his head down toward the page; he seems to be reading or looking in whatever way at whatever is there more carefully now, taking the words slow, as if to parse it clearer. The color of his face changes. He looks up suddenly toward the viewer, out of the film, though it is unclear what he sees there. Suddenly he is pouring sweat, visibly spewing and misting in the TV light. He stares as if transfixed in horror with the viewer, while beside him the woman and child go on exactly as they have been.

The toy camera in the child's hands is blue. The camera is leaking something. There is a wet mess on the floor and on his clothes and in his hair a little. The way the child cajoles the machine, bats and shakes it, hugs it hard with the lens aimed into his chest, causes the machine to take pictures of the world without the guidance of a human eye, filling up its electronic memory.

The viewer can't stop looking at the child. The child looks so much like how the viewer remembers looking as a child, however long ago that was. The hour seems familiar. The color of the hour.

With this realization, another man steps into the screen. He seems to move in from somewhere just behind the lens, where a camera would be. The viewer views at first only his shoulders, then his whole back, his arms and waistline. He is naked. His hair is grown down to his ass. His skin is wrinkled, leathery, sopping wet. His body pours water from his fingers, from his hair slick, from his arms; it seems to gather on the floor inside the image, pooling up in the room over the carpet rising.

The man has no reflection.

The man moves forward in the image until he is standing at the center of the room. The array of light around him has come bright white, from the TV or the window or both or neither. The man with the book is shaking now, as are the edges of the house, only slight enough to make the walls seem blurry, ruining the mirror. The shaking causes the wet to come out of him faster; he is crying, sweating, then begins bleeding from the eyes. His crotch is wet as are his pores. He can't seem to do anything but sit as he had been before, holding the book, frozen wide-eyed. The child and the woman are also sweating, though they don't seem to notice; they do not react at all to the man.

The viewer realizes he or she is also filled with liquid.

This white around the language on the page before you is a mirror.

The figure raises up his arms. As he does, the woman at the window raises her arms, too, then the seated man, and last the child. The light beyond the window is strobing slowly with the TV in time as the wet pours from them each at once together rising in the room, quickly enough already to have covered up the carpet and the feet of the furniture. Or time is faster now. Life is faster.

The child now sees the wet but does not stand up or attempt to move away onto the furniture or into the man or woman's arms, only holding more tightly to the camera, its flashwork going off at adverse time in relation to the TV and the sky beyond. The child clings to the object so hard its white hands turn even whiter. He tries to make a word but it is covered over by whatever sound of nothing inhabits the film's soundtrack. It is a calm and simple silence.

Soon the liquid rises over the child's head. Underneath the other accumulating liquids of the people, there is brief cloud of his blood, which rapidly bands together with the rest of it. In his hands, the camera too has been sealed under, its electronic memory licked clean and thereby absorbed into the wet held now visionless forever.

In the image, to the viewer, the screen inside itself is filling up, the liquid pouring off the bodies. As with the child, it gathers quickly above the seated man's knees and waist and chest and neck as he sits still, beyond response. His mouth is open.

The viewer's arms go numb, but seem not numb, to him or her.

Somewhere a fire is being ignited; somewhere stairs lead down and down.

The man goes under the water, seated, holding his book. There is another burst of blood. The gift of his blood to the rising aggregation shudders, lapping at the flat of glass and at the thick shape of the figure, still at center, motionless.

The screen is almost two-thirds covered over. Underneath the layers of the liquid too the light is still somehow coming off the TV in matching color beam bent into malfunctioning bright blips each hardly colors, squirming pale under the wet surface, growing paler as the liquid rises, thickens. The room is filling faster. The less room is left the faster still it fills. We can already seem to not remember the child and the father having gone beneath the surface, buried, turned to liquid. We can hardly tell how this began; it seems now to have always been happening.

Beyond the window, the waiting night.

In silence then, and without fanfare, the woman at the window mesmerized goes slump. Her knees weaken beneath her. She slides without sound or gesture down under the surface of the liquid. The wet is too dark now to show the cloud of blood she leaves briefly behind as it joins the rising mass.

The back of the head of the man before the camera, inside the gathering liquid, is all that now remains. In the window, now no longer blocked mostly by the body of the woman, we can see his front side reflected in the glass, though the image is too blurred somehow to make him out. Beyond the glass the black holds up the night unending.

All is calm, yes.

Yes, only as the last laps of the liquid squirm to reach above the frame of the viewer's perspective, the remaining man at the center of the room turns to face us.

FLOOD: *What voice asks the questions, and what answers.* Help me. *What questions do the answers ask.* What has been said in my name was not me. *What sound has been constricted in the liquids the body finds a way a while to contain and yet can't force itself to contain itself unending in the name of to which the liquid must return.* I did not mean to be this. *What hour is the hour described in this passage. What are you going to do about it.* My memory dividing. My mind dividing.

Blood violence. Scrying violence. Schools' doors locked door to door. Homes surrounded with a netting. Pastries rolled up with the asp. Tomahawks in hands of children come down on dolls and friends, come down on ants, come down on me. Fathers kill their fathers and their sons. Sons kill their friends. Wives kill their husbands and their doctors. They kill the babies in their guts. War violence in the home. Sky violence writing itself white into the cover of the hour with the screens' electrifying prismlight. What would have been watched in place of doing is become doing. Runes are written on the heads. Lawns are cut in slurs or glyph stakes, calling for the meteor or blank invasion. A burning planted somewhere in every city near the homes. The wash of the bathwater on the drowned self. The pills. The pills to erupt the cells out of the body. The naked turned to breadloaves. The football hero with the Luger to his temple on the fifty-yard line. The banker handing back a withdrawal in the form of a sheet of his own skin. Gas station attendants robbing the customers of their consciousness. Of blood. The dogs walking the dogs. "What is happening in America? The homeland commissioner is up in arms. We must act now. This is our home." The black rabbit in the east sky rises and vomits a column of dust onto the air. Troops deployed for the protection of the people stab each other in the chests. Intestine dinners. Ageless, graceless. The face of god: torn in strips off a billboard and used to wrap the dead. This is an art project, someone stutters, and the teeth fall out of their mouth onto the ground and are eaten by the starving some days layer. Enamel over all. Video game machines going blank. Wires doing blank. Email reading these same words in every head. A package is delivered to the homeland commissioner and it is opened by him on live TV, though we know it will explode. The pets' names are changed to Darrel. The children's names are changed to Darrel. The nation's name is changed to Darrel. Michael Jackson's name is changed to Darrel. Human instances of Darrel are caught in mobs and crucified inside the streets as nonbelievers. The name of Darrel in the mass of names is silence. The days. The occasionally clean are surrounded by their own flesh and bone. No metaphor left behind. No building not written whitely with the curse word over the crush of any city now called Darrel. Order again is demanded. Vegetable delivery is mandated by the state to arrive each evening in a long white limousine. This we believe in, which makes us calmer. It does not happen. Another 340,000 die. Another 417,550. Another 589,000. The rising numbers count themselves in the blue of pigs' blood in cursive on the sky below the blank where there might have been a moon once, and still might be, though we can't remember where to look. The instance of the number is attacked by air force bombers to obliterate as smoke. The smoke maintains the will of concrete underneath the cluster bomb. The fallout rains us birds. We eat them. The flesh of the bird delivers awful vision inspiring awful art. A mechanic kills a man who's come to have his wheel replaced; he kills using the machine of his daily labor; another day he might have simply changed the wheel. Someone is counting down the hours on the fingers of those who pass him in the street. Rotting frottage underneath the street puts a disorienting sound in cats' mouths and the houses rub where none of them touch and so it spreads and fills and holds. Someone with a hammer appears in one in 144 houses in one evening, mimicking at once a series of different people in one body, tolling the present number of the murdered bodies higher. There is no going backward. The faster we die we all will die. Sickness is not a shaking but a way of looking across a breakfast table or giving thanks. Anywhere this does not happen yet, the air remains. Turnips in fields turn up with dried blood centers. The trees bow down to kiss the ground. 700,010 dead. 880,789 dead. Telephones. Locks sold from the hardware station come without a key. Each four killed make eight kill eight more and then kill themselves or kill another set of eight, bodies branching off of each eight killed kill at least sixteen or toward twenty-four, each body desisted initiates replication in the spool of those surrounding; not by plague or viral idea or passion or brutal ministry or campaign, but by something they've not named and yet knows each better than any could, and in the unnaming of the so-occurring the day goes on and renders shorter while the skin flies at the light above in reams of hiss and collects in lathered wreaths around the public breath. The remaining bodies of their living go on tasting each other body in their mouths because they must. The colors of us giving up only one color, of little sex. The cars turning themselves on. A day at last to come of our vast creation returning to its fury. Crystal visions. Winking paper. So ends the beginning of our summation of the dead.

Gravey stands before the courtroom, no attorney (having refused), his head aglow in flat light from the neon panels in the ceiling holding the natural light out. Seven of the twelve jurors seated in the box are wearing all black; three are wearing white; they look exhausted, taut of skin; the remaining two jurors are dressed in clothes they might have another morning worn to church. For each member of the jury an armed bailiff is located somewhere in the room, in addition to the extra battery of officers at each door and window, and surrounding the buildings. Through the walls it is so silent between speaking it is as if one can hear the sun. The local premises are being patrolled round the clock by helicopters, federal troopers, private hires, and overhead, remaining unseen. This trial will have no real beginning and no end. This is formality. The jurors speak in tongues. The judge speaks in tongues. The judge's dying mother on the phone with the judge during lunch recess speaks in tongues. The D.A. speaks in tongues. The assistant to the D.A. speaks in tongues. The witnesses speak in tongues. The loud interlocutor whose daughter had been killed by Gravey and who has come to the courtroom wearing a mask over her face screaming suddenly amidst the silence for Gravey's blood speaks in tongues. The other grieving speak in tongues. The press pundits speak in tongues. The windows do not speak. Gravey does not speak. It has not rained in thirty-seven days.

When not waiting in silence in the courtroom, Gravey stands all hours at the center of his cell. He will not sit or sleep or eat or speak or close his eyes. He finds his chest so thin it is translucent. His organs and orifices in the cold clear gel have neon colors, their edges bloating and retracting into plastic puzzle shapes: his spleen a circle; his gallbladder a square; his ureter hole a hexagon; his lungs a star; his pancreas a triangle; his rectum a diamond; his brain a ring. His blood is thin and turning clear. Among his flesh, he's disappearing: his chest, his arms, his neck. He tries to summon from his memory a mirror, but there is nothing there like that at all, nothing beyond the ringing in his sternum, pages turning. Each time he thinks another sentence, the earth begins again around it.

FLOOD: *Each time I try to call a name out, I can't make my mouth open. Trying to remain silent, I hear the wind run through me where I am not. Everything I look at shows my reflection. And behind me: nothing.*

There is very little room now left to breathe.

Each time he pushes up out of the dark liquid, Flood finds the walls of the chamber nearer, slicker. The surface tension of the wet is turning hard. The blood inside him also is stiffening, becoming heavy from his fingers to his head; he finds it hard to move his joints, or harder to want to. Behind his eyes is all the black.

He goes under into the wet again, again, spreading his arms out, looking, looking, that something from the darkness might emerge; another kind of light inside it, or a person, though he cannot remember who now, or perhaps a second darkness darker than the first, something he can move inside of, become filled by.

Marking each inhale reemerging, somewhere in the larger world far outside the chamber another several thousand people die, and therefore many several thousand other future people who would have come from them are now never born.

FLOOD: *My body full of spit and blood. My mind full of holes leading to rooms full of the dead. Through the surfaces conferred their final concentration in the film containing all other film, upon which there is no rewind, no eject. A world awaiting.*

Other tapes among the tapes of Gravey begin to reveal themselves as holding shapes. Hid in the white the act of the destruction of the family occurs again, again. Each tape begins in a new but similar location, with different sets of families, though it is difficult to remember one apart from any other by the end. There is the liquid. There is the child's camera. In the rising wet, the people become drowned upon the presence of the man arriving at the center of the room, whose face is never shown. The blood will wash out of the bodies, raising it higher. The scene will end then, cutting out.

The tape could be rewound. The tapes could be played again, over and over, as long as there is someone there to operate their mechanism, to have the wish to.

The video is not proper evidence of Gravey as a killer, despite the resemblance of him from behind. Each time the camera faces the face, the film there ends, just at the instant one would see him seeing. The shape of the figure could be anybody, legally, from this angle, and so is anybody.

Anybody.

All who see the tape there for all days coming can recall only the white.

Today in America, 2,441,560 people become killed.

Moms and dads die, kids die, friends die, lifeguards die, road workers die, PhDs die, lieutenants die, the incarcerated die, all at the hands of those they know or have come near; they are ripped open and their innards are eaten from the hull of their unmaking; ushers die, singers die, strippers die, organ donors die; their organs are not used to fill other bodies with a new life; Golden State Warriors die, gypsies die, hitchhikers die, dentists die, dental assistants die at the hands of the dentists or the patients, the weight of the buildings rises during the night; screenprinters die, brothers die, creators die, the dying die, the wishmakers die, the wanting die, the laughter coming from their heads; the coffee erupting on the counters as the timers go off as planned, burning the surfaces with black liquid overflowing, never again; pet owners die, the pets will fend for themselves; bartenders die, alcoholics die, their bodies are not preserved; artisans die, match-makers die, janitors die, game show employees die, the worshipped die, the wor-shipping die; the color of all sound; editors die, the planets spinning; the reader of the book; lamps die, Boy Scouts die, Girl Scout leaders die; the train arriving at the station comes in late; hearse drivers die, neuroscientists die, chemists die, programmers die, some of the people you went to high school with die, some of the people you saw years back at the mall, the people you bought gas from, the organ grinder, the descendents of him who delivered from her mother's flesh your mom; the sentence makers die, the law writers die, the magicians die, the poets die, the blog commentators die, the violinists die; the fish sing in your ears; the blue of a wheelbarrow reflecting anything it comes near back toward itself; the first baseman dies, the pitcher dies, the catcher waits crouched at his knees, the balls over America at any hours descending in their numbers, the blacktop and the feed; camels die, bathroom attendants die, stockbrokers die, those who have no central occupation of creation or focus or hobby or forward motion in the name die; the shirts come off the bodies; the bodies are eaten into other bodies and become less bodies, all in one, each fed into the other in a becoming-final string of flesh entering flesh, while the newborn numbers descend further and the cells are counted as cells we have and may not ever have again, unless; the strongmen die, the bearded lady dies, the stuffers of the pillows and the folders of the cloth; the surgeons die, the plumbers die; the grass rising up around the homes; the angered die, screenwriters die, those who operate the phones, those who tear the tickets at the mouth of buildings, those who power walk; salesmen of vitamins and fine clothes and batteries and cars and furnaces and loft apartments and MacBook Pros and Fritos and divine ideas and pleasure purpose and sexual dementia and pressure washers and word processing software and eggs and cheese and tee shirts and cleaner cities and designers of the fur and wanters of the honey and those with gardens and those with eyeglasses and those against milk, those with rings around their fingers, those in horror, those who write infernal books, those who are infernal books themselves by merely walking with eyes open in the light, they die. Some of them kill themselves to miss the rest of this. Some go on. Machines go on and something else does, while in the hour of the Thrust, in singing minutes, hundreds of thousands hand to hand and face to face, they die. Justices die by swords in the hands of sculptors, Christians die by the hands of parking lot attendants under mist, whites die by the hands of priests and waitresses and students and the homeless and the living and the pearled with fists and jackhammers and darts and overdoses delivered by the tongue; the foreheads are bitten from the faces, swallowed; the fingernails are chipped off from the fingers, gnawed; the chest flesh is rendered from the sternum with an apparatus and taken into the self in part of self becoming and then taken off of those with scalpels or teeth themselves; witnesses are hung from rafters in a backyard of old Kentucky; cleaners are beaten in the face upon the face of I-295, the concrete alive with the putty of the blood congealing in the seemingly redoubled sun; cops are killed by fingertricks and sternum throttles and long blue swords and pikes and black magick by tricks and jerks and friends and royalty and cherry pickers and the rich; cops are made to choke on their own flesh and spit by the hands of the virgins and the lifeguards and the valorous and the unholy and the timid and the cancered and those who solicit money outside the mall; cops are chewed to bits by cats trained by warm-weather lovers in the streets outside the houses where the cops lived one year when they were young; cops are killed by cops; for thirty seconds over California the image of an aleph forms from clouds of discolored smoke, then blows away; all the stations in the world play the same commercial in the same instant without prior planning; goose eggs fall out of a tree; dog groomers are licked of skin by Holocaust survivors; godmothers are driven by the skull into a yellow wall in Minnesota; a pastry truck is overturned, found filled with lice; the oldest person in the country kills one hundred and forty-seven with a machine gun in Kansas City before she falls flat on the last face she'll remember and is mauled to pieces by one librarian in the name of names, raising the name into the light, the name I can't remember even in my own breath here to tell you because the name resounds no longer in a language and has passed into the soil, has felt to burrow in the money of the pit of the eye of eternal wishing and the parrot of the Sod, though we still do not know what the Sod is and will not know and will need to know or know. Those who remain in certain hours still find laughter about something and try to share it. There are tongues passed between friends' lips. The cock might grow hard. The finger in the belly. Jewelry is sold. Machines turn off and on among the flowing platelets. "I will wear you unto my king." "I will be the ground that you have walked on." "Love me. Love me." The pavement feels deranged. Butchers die, longshoremen die, blackjack dealers die, sidewalk salesman are ripped limb from limb by those who ten minutes prior had felt inside them a clean wish to buy a gift; gifts hidden in boxes in coming houses become forever hidden before the burning; those with the unbroken hymen die, those with the shirts with their own names printed or embroidered die, the same ten numbers repeat in shaking rosters again, again, the numbers eating through the paper in a room of no one watching, the palm trees growing ever nearer to the curb. The binders die, the mugged. Night comes again. Smoke rises in a harbor where ships stand for hours counting the surrounding mountains pouring wet like melting cones, and blue cones rise in the sinking fields of commerce from the lessening of trample on their face. Smoke rises from the gums of women. Smoke on the shorelines. Everybody knows a joke. The bodies smell like gravel, then like pig meat, then like glass. The sea thickening, where reflected, holding out beyond our minds, our Sod City we do not know in all cities, Our City of the Chewing of the Rolling Light of Gloss of Sod.

Bodies are being buried in their homes to save the room. The faces of the houses containing those already murdered are painted black to alert the mailmen to mark the mail returned. The wires from the houses are clipped to prevent transmissions in or out. The glass of the windows reflects the light of knives. Houses where a mother or a father or a child alone has become murdered while one or more remains surviving receive not an entire coat of black paint but a square set at the center of the home's face. In daylight in better neighborhoods the neighbors may bring these homes baskets of soup and bread, bring roses, bring alarms and mace, bring wishful words. There are no maps.

This sentence describes the panic of the American population remaindered in the rising light of rising terror of the murder of ourselves, which I could not begin to bring myself to impart to you directly for the way it might feel too much today like what you've done.

Today in America, a wake is waking.

FLOOD: *Think of night arrived during the daytime. It was impossible almost even to see out into the streets in the low light of what the bodies brought to pass between them. The fists and faces and their machines brought the blood and bone and organs through the surfaces that had meant to contain them so much longer. The light could look then in onto the middles of the people, their blood, cavities, and brains. There were no hidden places left. All manners of forms of homes and businesses collapsed, the organisms filling up the buildings snapping one into ten inside their sternums under the sound and then ransacking the space around them destroyed until they were done in by whomever else. It fed all through and through us. It moved into us wanting to want more until there was nothing left. All our years done in like that in mere instants while beyond our reach the color of the sky and space beyond us did absolutely jack shit.*

Today in America we go to war again flat on our backs. We will hear the morning rising in the sound of the screaming mothers becoming dismantled again as the death toll of our people on this one batch become killed at our own hands. As all hands are all of our hands. Today it doesn't matter how many people in America become killed because today is another day in America, and tomorrow today is dead.

The end of starvation. The end of AIDS. The end of cancer. The end of patience. The end of old age. The end of accidents. The end of smoking. The end of patience. The end of alcoholism, the overdose, the sneeze. The end of retardation. The end of rape. In America. The end of being young. The end of being old. The end of the end of. The end of religion. The beginning of religion. The end of television programming. The end of musical performance. The end of typing. The end of murder. The end of wishing. The end of the end of the film. In America. The end of boxing. The end of photography and speech. The end of being thought upon. The end of bedsores. The end of ulcers. The end of making love. The end of the ringing of the phones. The end of waking up. The end of medication. The end of parenting. The end of sight. The end of laughter. In America. The end of trying to understand horses. The end of astronomy. The end of balding. The end of shopping. The end of motherhood and fatherhood and the end of sharpening the knives. The end of worship. The end of sin. The end of dick pills. The end of animation. The end of publication. In America. The end of standing in line. The end of cooking. The end of jokes. The end of steakhouses. The end of dry cleaning. The end of cleaning. The end of washing. The end of want for silence. The end of mortgages. The end of folding money. The end of email. The end of roadkill. The end of salad. The end of sentences. The end of punctuation. The end of design school. The end of pulses. The end of the ego. The end of the blurt. In America. The end of sandwiches. The end of cycling. The end of tumors. The end of snot. The end of marriage. The end of the gift of flowers. The end of collections. The end of pest control. The end of fear. The end of cold cuts. The end of driving nails. The end of marketing. The end of sequels. The end of invention. The end of endings. In America.

FLOOD: *All that was left then there before me was the word. No matter how I touched the space or spoke into them or threw my body on them the words appeared and would not stop. There was nothing there to use or touch besides the whiteness.*

Flood at the mirror, being crushed. His spine and shoulders hulk against the upper mirror, bending to it, accruing pressure. The surface of the liquid around his chest and sternum and below has turned so hard he's rendered in it like a self around himself; it bloats to fill the measure of the seams, the liquid crystallized and fleshy, made of crushed organs.

Inside the chamber a small gap of air no larger than a bird's egg. The air fits around Flood's eyes and nostrils like a visor. He can see out and breathe in. The air recycles through him; he is feeding, and remains fed. The air and liquid have no smell.

Flood face to face with his reflection, in reflection. He is so old his skin's see-through. Through him he sees himself again reflected, between the mirrors on both sides. His head wholly a hole.

"I am a hole," he says, though underneath the liquid they become absorbed into the fully hardened league of come and skin and blood. "I am a hole," he says again. The liquid rises slicker, slurring his nostrils. His breathing in the wet. Underneath, he lets his lips fall open, and some of it fills him there too. He hears a motor coming on. He hears the sound of flashbulbs lurching. When he does not speak, he hears his words.

Flood looks up. Flood feels, between the holes, a pressure build, a gift like massive magnets held apart. He feels a tickle in his head: the last condition of what was in there taking firm hold, seeing itself seen. He feels the videos of the days of all the people going on around him in the air surrounding being filmed into his flesh, filling his flesh with the reiteration of the image of the days he can't feel under the rest. There is a slow curl of the memory forced into smaller and smaller space.

The holes in Flood's eyes widen. The walls convening, eating. The skin of Flood's rolled forehead touches soft against the reflective surface, front and back. The pressure builds between them. The holes enclosing where they match and touch. Flesh on flesh by mirrored mirror. Exit language: no word. Exit music: sound on sound. The holes between the mirrors meeting pressed to Flood where Flood is. His body blanking, under nothing. Glyph of pressure, gas releasing, frames releasing.

The liquid fills the space.

FLOOD: ██████████████

In the full darkness, there is a word.

The word encompasses the darkness.

Flood presses the button in the word.

He hears no sound. His eyes are open.

Today in America, 4,241,560 people become killed.

The bodies find the bodies hiding in their houses in the world. They find the bodies wielding weapons of guitars. In black theaters and food distribution centers and the long passages where once the fruitful sewage grew and flowed, they find the mothers and the fathers and the daughters and the sons yet still alive wedged as deep down as they might manage in a crevice between surfaces, in fear. They find them shopping in the long aisles of the supermarket and in the game room and at work, against long panels in museums wishing themselves into the frame. They find them by the godterror rising through their sternums drinking coffee under an awning on a mountain in the rising of the sun under the sun, by the maps imprinted on their sternums, by closing their eyes and fumbling around. They find them, bodies on bodies, bodies in bodies yet unborn licked by no burn. They turn the lights on. They are anyone you've ever known. They have wrists and arms and necks and some have hair in many places and they go by names and from their mouths there comes the words and from their fingers there comes the word of Sod. The brandishing of thin knives and fist fury and rope and power; removed, in name of their unnaming, to anywhere but where. Bluebirds fly in all directions. The screaming wracking asking grovel game-speak please-god fills the hour in the millions being murdered with a decibel above the common purr, constant enough now and clear enough now to overcome the concept of a single person's shrieking exit into an aggregate of prolonged human demolition at such sure and constant volume in the rising that it sounds like nothing, like any day. This is any day, I'm saying. There is no such thing as the unreal; it sits in the palm of the blue beholden and cries out for language; it gives and gives and what is given is given back into it by seven, by seven and seven again inside the reeling while the houses stand and watch. Do not ask about how this could be measured or what else. No more questions as to the future or why it seems today the hour continues on and the cars pass by the house there at the window where you are holding yourself up or down against an earth; do not ask. They find the bodies at the windows in the houses where they are holding themselves up. They find them waiting with their own murder weapons, and so the flipping of a coin. From each sprung head the wet flows and by the hour is dry again. They eat the bodies with their fingers and their teeth and mouths. They bite from the neck and back and face. Their minds are the utensils and the surface and the menu and the course. They eat the flesh of the human the way they eat the flesh of the cow or pig or dog or eel or chicken. They eat the flesh like at family dinner, chewing calmly, speaking words they will not remember in the hour of the rising corridor. Stars make gravy we can't see. It pours down through veins that seem vacations. There is a wedding. There is sense. The walking goes for hours and seems pleasant again and there are some who never have to hide. They are found in their beds up to their necks in the cloth of paradise enjoying cold dreams of the longest fingers, in the pyramids of Giza transplanted onto Michigan and onto Georgia and onto North and South Dakota and onto Texas and onto Florida and onto Wisconsin. The pyramids are bells. The pyramids are vacation homes along the beaches where the mice wash in with numbers underneath their fur. We build a castle from the sand of the dead-longer-than-we-are. The sun evaporates the land. Today in America 5,700,700 become killed, 8,890,100 become killed tomorrow, 16,650,013 become killed, 25,000,000 become killed. Today in America however many you want to be killed become killed. However many you wish would live forever in your arms or across the continents become killed. The plots become the soil. The soil becomes the ocean. The ocean dries and lives again. It is still only an ocean. An ocean, in some understandings, can be everything. The word of it. The word.

GRETCH GRAVEY: *Blood drying against concrete slathered baking in such daylight as glass shattered in metal crunching bone beneath bright planes banging bullets on the fields of women and men until the pilot too turns on the party of himself. What colors where the air mixed and filled itself in with private liquids, the brains removed of desperation, fire. Stone through cranium. Metal through surface. Why would it ever rain again. Who was counting up the numbers, all mirrors watching unwatched on old walls, while elsewhere, in a large unmarked room, the further image dreamt in the new dead were piling up inside the nothing rising.*

The jury, held at gunpoint, among lasers, finds Gravey guilty.

The judge proclaims the fate. This judge in fear in his electrified cadaver, in his waiting for the day of the Shape of He, slave of three hundred million tongues.

Gravey, by the state, will become killed, is the decision. The killer put to be killed by machine. By a machine. The weapon: electricity, buttons, wires.

The machines are waiting.

The smoke will rise.

The audience inside the courtroom sits in gyrating silence with the verdict on their lips. They watch their hands clap and hear their lungs give out the word of praise of this day having come at last, this day at last.

The bells in Gravey's sentenced body ring.

Today in America, 41,080,101 people become killed.

Across the many skies all our screaming does not weep.

The bodies form a mount.

The bodies filling in the space between the earth and sky with rising meat to match their minds of spooling film.

The darkness behind Flood's fully submerged vision narrows. The surrounding wet solidifies again to walls, too black to tell the open air from impenetrable surface. All space seems to move around him, in absence of his intent. Inside the drawl, old colors blur. The black of many colors in his forehead and his fingers. There is nowhere else. The single word repeating over any way he tries to think. Through the depths, he's dragged forward like a cursor with the space bar held down, on a computer, blinking out and in.

There is some land then, and a gap. The land is synthetic to the touch and bone white, just wide enough for him to stand free at the edge of the liquid, somewhere way down under masses, a bulb of air sucking the world around him forward. The linings of the walls elongated in their passing, becoming light from dark, transparent from light, reflective from transparency. Mirrors totally surround; all the same mirror, over all lengths. This time, in the mirror, Flood appears, head-on in every inch no matter how he sees it, though he can barely recognize his body. He looks to have aged decades since he last felt anything to know. He looks more like someone who'd gone on to live forever, constantly aging over decades, than anyone he'd ever been. The skin around his eyes could almost break.

Like in the passages to other homes, the mirror has a latch, a latch in the eye of the face of every face of the plane before him always, all the same. The shape of the symbol marked in on the latch's head seems to waver at its edges, making many shapes of itself mutating and transmogrifying, while held in the mind all as the same. Flood finds himself mesmerized watching the shape mutate between circle, square, hexagon, star, and so on, endless other unnamed shapes between each. He does not want to lift the latch. He wants to take the latch into his mouth, swallow it down. He wants the latch to open in him.

There is no sound as with every latch the mirror opens. The space beyond it is dark inside the room, a different kind of dark of night of passages of lives he already can't remember having passed through.

Flood moves into the room. He closes the mirror behind him immediately, lock-ing away the passage to prevent anyone else hidden behind him from following. As the mirror clicks into place he feels his blood run with a sudden sense of irreversibility, against which the veins along his arms protrude and pulse. But the mirror, once closed, cannot be opened from this side. He is sealed in here.

Into full darkness, Flood fumbles hands-first. He reaches into the space unseeing for something, feeling only more space and more space there, like a dry inverse to the cavity of wet. As if this space is no different than the drowning chamber of the world of passages, but made of air instead of fluid. His skin holds the same tone and texture as the air around him standing. He feels a rising fear of noth-ing, fear of edgelessness forever, even the mirror behind him now somehow not there when he turns to feel its slick face harboring the copy of him in the dark. He calls out and feels no language.

He walks into a wall. The wall bangs into his face and he can feel himself bleed-ing again, though he can't see or feel the arms themselves. Once there is a wall, there are other surfaces to feel onto, connecting outward. There is a table and some chairs around it. There is another wall hung with framed pictures, which in the darkness, searching for anything, one by one, Flood removes. He sits each frame facedown on the floor, not having seen the images they carry. What if life went on this way forever, Flood thinks, all surfaces without faces. All creation beyond seeing.

And then again as if to negate him, he hits something on the wall that fills the room with light. It is so bright at first that it's like the dark but backwards, just as unyielding, all against him. Slowly, though, the shape of the space around him conforms to its underlying structure, and reveals itself, like day.

Flood is standing in his home. It takes a moment before he recognizes the rema-terializing elements of space as ones he's spent the years in, the objects infused with his time and smell and feeling, nodes without eyes who had as yet seen him through hour after hour among others. It all fills in around him like flashing panels rising out from concrete. There is oddly no relief, only the awareness of *I have been here, this is a place where I have lived, where I have disappeared the hours, where I have known others or hid from others, where I sleep.*

Despite having passed them day in and out so many years inside here, he can't remember what the pictures placed facedown on the ground now ever pictured.

The carpet is white. Had the carpet always been white.

On a low table are his papers, notes and words regarding recent casework he'd brought home, though he can't remember really what the case had been. The papers are blank. If there is someone else in the house there with him, he cannot feel it.

There is a tape. The tape is marked with a string of digits. The casing is white, too, in contrast to the dark tongue of the film spooled up inside it. He picks up the tape and holds it near his face and stares, as if waiting for the images encased there to appear broadcast on the room, or all inside him.

The TV is on. On screen, long shots of human bodies amassed in daylight in the streets and inside buildings, waving their fists and running in hordes and banging at windows of buildings and cars, exhibited in silence, the volume apparently muted. The faces all bleed together into a kind of total body with countless heads all held together where they touch or do not touch. Other shots show tanks, horses, swords, explosions, fences, cages, weapons, flashing text.

Flood doesn't understand how he couldn't have seen the light of the screen of the TV in the dark before the light appeared. He tries to read the words on the lips of people pictured in the masses but it just makes some feverish language he can no longer understand. Through the window on the wall over the TV, the air is dark and still.

Flood takes the tape and puts it into the machine attached to the TV. His hands feel oblong, tighter once again emptied, as if coated in the tape's plastic. The receiving machine makes sound, its own small language. The light in the room changes, opens wide. There is static, then the whiteness, then nothing but the whiteness through the room.

Flood sees himself. He sees his body. His image is transparent somehow, so that even through his chest he can see the shape of the house around him.

The wall of the room on the tape is white like the wall in the room Flood had called his home, as many walls could ever be. The surface is interrupted by a window through which a greater white appears, light from somewhere else, almost exploding.

The film fills up Flood's vision, and so is his vision. In seeing, staring, into the image, he can no longer tell it from the rest of the room, from where his blood was.

Flood is on the tape.

He looks down at his hands. The skin of the hands is stretched with colored veins and pale flesh, dry and aged as he remembers from the last mirror. His pores have grown so large he can connect them without looking closer, islands of the soft; the circles drown in other wrinkles where the skin has colonized its age. The hair of the flesh of his arms has been removed, a smooth, demonstrative expanse. The nails on his fingers are strangely long: white fantasies of skies of cities sleep lodged under the cuticle, aching the skin. He is wearing a white tunic, or cloak, or gown, drenched to translucence and clinging to the folds of him hid covered, where bones meshed in his chest are bending in: a process of the greater aging. Temples. White years. Gorges. Flood makes a fist and hears the bones pop in his fingers. He releases.

There are others in the room. There is an American woman dressed in a gown like his but thicker and well embroidered, standing at the room's one window, looking out. She has a scar along her chin; she does not realize it is there. Her breath makes a small disruption of the flow of the building, letting other rooms build gray. Years have happened to her. She is the year now. The woman hums; there is no song.

Across the room, an American man sits halfway upright on a recliner holding a book before a TV, lids flickering in response to changes in the field. A television's light provides another sort of color, and is silent.

In another room, through the wall behind the TV, Flood knows, lies a sleeping child, bone white, American. The child's body is rigged with an electronic sensor in his night pants meant to detect urine; a reading lamp stays on above the bed. The child in coming years would go to school. He would see his first pornography under the table in the lunchroom during fifth grade. He would take turns with several other classmates kicking classmates in the chest. He would masturbate and eat breakfast cereal and go to school to learn to program code into machines and then get tired of that and begin writing paper onto words. I do not mean words onto paper.

The child is not asleep.

At the window, the woman sees herself framed against the billowed darkness growing larger still, sweating through its fibers at a universal rate, through all the holes. The window is really more a mirror now than anything to see through. It is silver in its blackness, extending on into the idea of itself. A subtitle reveals the woman's present thought, filling her brain meat, *The body of the body of the column of the city of the child of man.* The woman inhales and holds it. She turns around, finds Flood before her. She does not react to this new stranger. The features of her face and the face of her husband half-asleep sitting beneath her hold calmly blurred in swimming textures, layers, whorls.

Flood feels a hammer in his hand. He feels the cool wood grip pressed with his flesh. It is a fresh hammer, unused, though it smells of the loins of the new skin beneath the soil pouring somewhere from a formless hole, feeding none. In Flood's other hand he holds a dark knife, the leather handle of it molded as if to fit his hand pad to pad, to fit any hand of any hand model in America, or those shaped like them, or those shaped unlike them, or the dead. Flood knows the knife is long enough to stab straight through the ceiling and cut the eye out of god, who watches our dry moves and eats into us with the cancer, alive in the laughter of all generations.

Flood looks at his hands and sees his hands hold none. That is his skin there. This is the body. He stutters to meet the body with the word. He feels the blood run through his head down along his neck wide in heaving streamyards of witching visions through his sternum through his intestines along his legs, blossomed by force. He feels something amassing on the outside of his surface. Nodes. A false gray. His hands are heavy. He smells fresh rubber.

There is a nameless music pouring from the eyelets of the darkness beyond the window, larger than silence.

Flood's body raises up his hands. His fingers point in ten directions, one for each finger, a splay of manifesting wish. In his chest he feels two big wheels turning, gyrating shapes among the flesh making tape burn in the threads between us.

Flood sees nothing. Flood floods inward. Flood closes his eyes.

Flood speaks.

███████████████ : ██████████████

The current fills Gravey's body smiling and dressed in white upon the waiting bed where he lies with hands straight up above him, incarcerated with the light. His holes go slack around him. From the holes there is a sheen. Then, the white tape, surrendered spooling from his navel, hissing up like snakes evaporating.

There is a knock at the lone window. Old bells ring upon the air. The death machine is shaking.

Over the frying, our applause.

Over the applause, the husking flake of our surrounded flesh all turning dry.

The dryness of light no one remembers.

The day of the dryness of light.

Today in America, 208,135,180 people become killed, each and all killed and killed again forever amen until everybody in America is dead.

THREE *THE PART ABOUT FLOOD (IN THE CITY OF SOD)*

I woke in smoke. This time the smoke was the beginning, no longer unwinding into nothing as its layers grew apart. The light surrounded my body on the inside, contained in space that seemed hidden from all the rest of time that I remembered. I knew my name was or had been *Flood* but could not say it and it no longer felt like language. Instead I could hear several hundred interruptions anytime I tried to think.

The smoke was pouring from my face. From my eyes and from my earholes, growing even thicker when I would try to speak or breathe. The smoke made windows on the air. Eras opened. From the windows there stretched long columns that seemed to form the world, though every column extended only into further reaching. All directions led exactly the same way, like no matter where I went the smoke poured from me and obscured the rest of what could be into more of what it was already: inside and outside me, all of everything.

FLOOD: *I don't know where I am. I'm trapped inside here. I'm not sure where here is, what it connects to, but I am beginning to believe I've been caught. Recorded. Or, not recorded— rather, I am rendered as if on a film, an unscrolling repetition owned by the smoke's repeating gesture, though at the same time, I am alive. My mind is my mind and I believe it but beyond me is something else, not the world as it always had been, but the shell of it. Something is altered. The air is flat and has no taste. It feels like there is something else surrounding the space here, and the something else is where I used to be.*

I crawled and crawled along the floor of the ground of the extending darkness. The grain beneath me felt synthetic and did not stick to my body. Just beneath the layer of the ground the grit the surface stood on churned and buzzed, as if being processed and so created only as I touched it, as if underneath the floor of all creation the only thing keeping the floor from sucking in around me into some screaming hole was that I needed somewhere else to go.

And as if only because it was truly what I needed, out of the smoke the world resolved. There were mounds, then there were horizons. I began to recognize out of the stretching amassments local zones of scenery: fields and skylines, holes and corners, foliage like icing, invisible stars. One stroke of familiarity procured the next, aligning the space into further aggregates of definition.

Out of the color of the night, there appeared buildings in the distance, houses, homes. There were networks of understanding and direction. Wires draped the air like no one's trees. The unfamiliar felt familiar. I began to recognize coordinates of locations I had been through sometime before, though I could not remember when or why. None of the homes seemed like mine. And yet I could read from a long way off how it looked inside architecturally. As if the maps were in my brain. Or as if even where the walls were they were just like more of the smoke I'd spit up; all lines made totally of me. I could not feel any people.

The world was silent. There was no one. All air was nothing but itself, every inch captured into the residue of what it'd always seemed to be to anybody altogether. The only place that wasn't all the rest was where I felt me in the color of my mind. My thoughts burned on through where my skull was, slowly. They wrapped around me and repeated no matter how much I wished they wouldn't, or wished they would so hard at least I couldn't control it. Often the words would take over my brain so much I could not see anything when they were being spoken.

FLOOD: *Mostly I can't alter how I move. It's like there is this dictation of my presence that tells me what to do, or what I am already doing, or what I have done. And within that, there will be these moments where I am unable to stop myself speaking aloud in a very specific way. The language rips out of my mouth, though it is not actually me speaking. It's like subtitles in a film. I'm made to say it shaped exactly where I am, as if the continuity of the air were dependent on it, defined by it, could not go on without. It is only in here, far inside me, that I can speak freely, and can understand the terror of believing I was wholly me when I was not. Anytime could be the last time I can speak to you as I am now, though I would likely never know. The tape flutters back and forth between these modes without my knowing. I could go on being beyond myself maybe forever, repeating the same things all seeming each time to me new, forced to continue in a loop, while through all the land, a shapeless language scrolled in silent history, rising against me. To be honest, it doesn't feel that different from always, only now I know I used to not be the only one.*

Years had come, the years were coming, the years had went again, the years were years.

The days inside the years were ours to live in and we had lived in them and now did not.

Or did we live in them again, in repetition. I can't remember. There was the heaving sky.

There was tonight: the excess weight of missing color in the silent locks of empty homes.

The days of us destroyed. Days beaten as with hammers by the hands we do not have.

Homes so thick there was no longer air between them, as hours passed and disappeared.

The spectators and the actors. I can feel you in here even still. Feel you watching, taking.

Even with your body, you have a body. You can be harmed still. Erased from forever.

Yes, yes, in death, any of us is every inch as open as any had been ever, and even softer.

I encourage you not to breathe at all without the mask on. Also do not: open your eyes.

The kind of light remaining, which you will never touch, destroys all living memory.

Anywhere I look in here I can't see anywhere inside here, wracked with its starvation.

The void of our history has been colonized, conditioned. It is desperate. It wants to fuck.

I hear machines. I see the sea replicating in its nothing, pushing sand against the sand.

I cannot be the machines. I cannot reach the sea. I can't find where what was waiting.

The sand doesn't miss anything about what bodies did upon it, nor does all nature.

I am alive inside this tape. Everything I was is still outside the tape. The tape repeats.

I saw two bears beat the shit out of each other and they were still there the next day.

I don't want this and it doesn't want me. My video-body resists supplying what I need.

Teeth fall out of my head sometimes from all the shaking but then I get new teeth.

My hands are larger than my hands were ever. My aorta snorts my blood like drugs.

Some days in here I get up and it's the day I got up into the day before again.

I do the same things I did the day before because I have to to get to where I am today.

Where's that.

Where's what. Who are you. What.

Where are you today I mean. Are you happy.

Does it matter.

It probably matters. Yes.

I'll have you know I killed myself.

How did you kill yourself.

By getting older. By letting me get older. By going on. And I still am.

Do you regret it.

I can't remember.

FLOOD: *See how that happened? The interruption? I can remember it right now, the words that had just been spoken through me, in the film. That the tape can be switched out of makes me think there's not wholly nothing left to live with. Though usually within minutes of my being able again to talk freely inside my mind I will forget exactly what has gone on in the tape here in between. I believe this is a feature of self-preservation of the nature of my present brain state, beyond the dead. The other thing about that time is, as you might have noticed, there is something other on the tape in there with me too. Someone speaking back toward me in bold font from inside me, inside the version of my brain the tape controls. I can hear it in my chest and in the air I'm breathing. It is as if this person can hear the scripted thinking in the contained space of the tape and answer back, can hear me when I respond, though my responses are also scripted. I don't think this other person can still hear me when I am talking as I am now. I don't know who this person is. I think it only familiar because*

I have heard it already several thousand times repeated. And yet already now I realize I can't remember what inside the tape I'm doing or what the words were beyond the fact that they were said. I do remember having tried to kill myself, by the way, or at least trying to kill the me in this recording. I've thrown myself off a bridge. I have thrown myself off a roof and from a building. I have taken thousands of many different kinds of pills. I've used knives and ropes and guns and other manners of destruction. If you were in here alone I think you might have tried at least once too. Though each time when I die I just end up where I began, rolled in the smoke, and again the smoke resolves into the world alone. I admit I do like hearing the woman. It makes me feel clearer, as if sometimes inside the tape there is somewhere to want to be, unless being dead feels just the same as living, or if every minute in the tape is the beginning of another life. Only in these glitches I can remember the world before now, the world we shared, even if I don't know how I got from there to here, or what could be coming for me now, forever.

The land of America was catacombs, but without bodies. Even better in our absence I could see upon the land again the shape of where we had lived off the dirt. The sloping earth cupped runoff from the hills of houses held above it, the walls of these here tilted toward where in years before the children would eat and play on in the image of their begetters; eggs had been hidden several Easters running for the chocolate and the coins, some still hidden; later in the nights the older children might have come to lie upon the nook of something simple with their hands up one another's skirts, or simply spread out on a blanket to see a disc move black across the moon.

The absence of the people on the land here was written over by what grew in behind it. Nowhere the cords of backbones and pillared skull shifts missing refracted on the dry air overrun with centuries of cigarettes and cash and floppy hate sex and grieving terror. Where the bodies did not have to persist now, days smelled better and doors did not open and plants began to grow over the mucus of the interminable graves, erupting in white opera a leak of the song of thriving air all hot with something unlike people. Mites that once would have eaten out our eyes instead went into their own ways to purr in the white sun choked against a thicker plank of netting, our continuity disregarded. The grass unburied rose, licked and whispered at the homes' faces like pubic hair around a hundred million dicks.

No one needs you, the dream was saying. There is always something.

The homes alone hid everything we believed we could be completely carried on by. The gorgeous clothes clapped in the closets, replicated for endless forms of bodies, went on in the dark and wore their own lives. No object itself actually believed in what it had been envisioned to embody. Death already understood and so did not require the cooperation of gloves and quilts and books and urns and knives and wire, or even trees or nests or glass or lengths of cold air left hanging in a pasture without marking. You didn't have to see or name the essence of anything to feel it trying to continue without us. The walls of every inch seemed thicker even just knowing what they were forced to contain, a future without new blood: phantoms not of us but ideas of time still caught counting among the homes and days we'd been in where there was nothing left to be now. Both as if we still were there and had never been, leaving the air unconsumed to clap around itself and squirt from centers a waking layer in which something else would be spread onward and licked upon the landscape.

Streets grew longer than the earth beneath. Doors would open from a surface and nothing coming through or going on. Stock rose and fell inside the peace, making warmth in which an aging color grew, sermonizing and baptizing and giving thanks sung in the floors of the homes of the American unveiling of a graveyard in which I alone was left to walk, trapped for no reason other than that I insisted, wanting only anything like what I had once, and felt and held dear, and now can hardly separate inside my mind from feeling ill, despite knowing through and through that I was someone once who in my dreams could never die, and so never was my body, and never aged a day, despite eternity, like how often in the light of certain other eras for hours and hours we would sing all together the same words, celebrating the mark of the word of the end of the door of the day toward our disappearing hope.

FLOOD: *I knew I wasn't even me. I knew the land that let me touch it was only an idea. And yet what choice did I have but to go on. To look for anything to hold fast or wait to be absorbed by. If others were alive inside here with me, I could not find them. I had the sense at once of being followed and following someone else who could feel me following but could not find me. Often I would turn around to look back where I had just come and see nothing but the same stretch I saw looking the same way, as if I were standing where a mirror was. As if I myself were the mirror reflecting two halves of a world with no one in it but the shit everyone but me had left behind. Who else could I have ever been. Sometimes again the smoke of the beginning of the world as I understood my appearance in it would appear, rolling over the long horizon far off and coming over. I imagine this meant there could be another face like mine somewhere out there ejecting the hell of the black of the smoke that comprised exactly what confined me. But as soon as I saw and understood the smoke this way, it rolled apart. It would spread and flesh out so generally into the distance I couldn't tell it from the sky or whatever stood behind the sky or any of the houses that from here just looked like nothing but more indeterminate color. Whoever could have been there waiting to find me became again as nowhere as any stretch of air behind a wall. And the same of me to them. To even just the idea of them, anybody.*

The years came and came on me again. They came and came on me. They held me.

The years did. They loved me. I could see out through the screens. I watched you dying.

In every inch of the zilch of nowhere I could see out into everything you lived through.

You looked gorgeous. Don't fret about it. You did something with your life that hung.

All eyes did. They wore the same color, in spite of how they seemed to vary or shift.

The oceans of red money spilled for hours in the furor of the gnaw of dying laughter.

Blood poured forever in your mind. You were dead before you understood the idea.

The humans died and didn't realize any better. They couldn't feel the difference.

I wish I'd known you better than I do. The machines took you apart upon the dirt.

Your organs were ribbed with words. I couldn't read what all the words said at all.

Your body became buried under bodies, which were buried under grass that grew.

That's what I believe love is: doing something again because it's still there and is and is.

I don't know where all the other bodies went. I used to know a couple people. Persons.

Friends and family. Salesmen. What. They lit me up. I didn't know they lit me then.

I didn't see the cracks dry in my whole flesh until there was no flesh left to press against.

I am thirty-one years old. Some day soon I will turn to thirty-two, though I am dead.

Is that a good thing or a bad thing.

What, the being dead, or my new birthday.

Either.

Yes. Yes it's a good thing. And I need you.

I need you, too. Hold me.

You know I can't.

I did not know that. No day goes past without you wholly of my whole mind.

What does it feel like to think you have a mind still?

It's all right.

Can you show me?

I cannot show you.

Why. Why can't you.

I can't do anything but see.

FLOOD: *I don't think being inside this tape means I am here forever, or that I have to be. I don't think I am not in some way living, though I seem now to be the only one. Even the voice is not a person here before me, with legs and arms and eyes and someone's face. I've walked for so long among the buildings and the fields here in search of any shape still taking breath like me. But they all killed each other. They are all ended. They are all stacked up in thick piles. I don't want to think about it, not when all I have to think about when I can't actually think is what there isn't versus what there never was.*

I already knew I needed out. Though I couldn't feel anything in the grain it was the feeling of no feeling that burned worse, and knowing that underneath that there must be something silent and corroded lacing through what I was meant to use as a human to understand another person. That there was no one here to apply that understanding to made it a weapon against itself, a private bloodbath where whatever what my blood was now should have been pumping, filling my organs with inspiration. Wherever anyone wasn't now forever was space that pounded at my lack of awareness of the pounding, bruising anything remaining of what I'd been or was beyond the point of any recognition. The houses and the wires and the pixels in the sky didn't want me to do anything but not take part in my own image.

Worse than knowing I needed out, I didn't know what I needed back out into. Even when I could feel there was something else beyond the edges of any color in the street or window where no one waited even to just totally ignore me, I couldn't recognize it enough to know how to want it harder. Along each street it was as if I were waiting for some hole to swallow my face. Each moment it didn't made the going into the next step that much less worth doing. This is what life had always felt like. In my mind, expecting the absence of something or someone there before me made the presence in its place feel like the punch line to a routine no one was performing. And where I couldn't find a way to laugh, I became my own stand-in, over and over, like painting white over a window from the inside.

None of this stopped me from believing every instant that the entire condition of my existence was going to change at any minute. Every edge of door or floor before or beneath me could be the initiation of an entirely different fate. In any foyer beyond any location someone could be standing with their face against the wall waiting to hear me coming. The sky could always split right down the middle.

FLOOD: *Why were there no bodies. There were only the buildings and the ground. Everything was covered in a dark hue as if held on in night during the day. Many* *doors and windows had been sealed into the surfaces around them. The world was empty of us, except for me, cleared as to a land inside an amusement park that'd closed its doors. I don't know what I would have done with the bodies but I wanted to see them, even to be them. I wanted to remember they were there. Through my own vision on the tape, though, often all I could see for miles set in the land were the wrecked remains of what still had the balls to cling to the idea of us returning, the bridges and the doors and hallways built as if from bone and sinew, though in a guise that even I here inside the clearer thinking could no longer recognize the purpose of. Which makes me wonder now what else is less clear to me here than I imagine, what has not transferred between the seeming many ideas of me that I am, all split apart and up under trance. What about you, for instance? Whoever I am speaking this to, if anybody. Why won't you respond?*

Sometimes my skull burns in my head. It hurts to say the words here. Every of them.

Ouch. Ouch. Ouch. Ouch. This is me talking. Ouch. Ouch. Ouch. Ouch. Ouch.

I feel confused. I feel as if I'm being followed. I feel as if my time is bleeding from me.

There is everywhere to go. In the new days I go from room to room in the houses.

I go into people's homes. I see what they were there. I lie down in their beds.

I eat their food. I sometimes am their food entirely, seeing them above me, eating.

I want to be eaten. I want out. There is a hole here somewhere. There is a way back.

Into the dead, who have a spirit, whereas I feel like rubber under water, in a vise.

Death, in preservation, burns worse than being burned to die and enter light.

I still want everything I ever wanted and maybe even more now that only I exist.

I want silence beyond the word. Whereas here, in memory, stillness is loudest.

In the houses people haunt the years with ways they used to walk when they had skin.

Their mind will come up to me here inside their house and open their life against me.

I can feel their blood pummel. The noise the days suffused inside them is hellish shit.

No eye has ever died. It goes on seeing. I don't want to go on seeing. I want nothing.

Some rooms will feel against me so familiar it's as if I've been there my whole life.

As if when I go to sleep I'm in the rooms again and all the people are there with me.

All the people. All their words. Maybe among them someone waiting for my nearness.

Each day inside this tape I can go as far as I can go inside it before the tape ends.

When the tape ends that's when I black out and then sometime the day begins again.

I need the eye that's been burnt out. The day in the eye of the seeing beyond sight.

I'm trying to learn to stay up longer. To go further. There must be someone in the homes.

There must be someone left besides me beyond this tape of America I can make love with.

Make love with me.

You know I can't. I told you that already.

It hurts.

I know. To think about it even is so hellish.

God.

Yes, god.

What about my mind. Can you fuck my mind please. Hard please.

What's all this with fucking. What about your arms. Your cheeks. Your knees.

When I say fuck or make love, I mean be around me. I mean be here where I am.

I am.

You're not.

I know. I know I know I know I know I know I know I know I know.

You do not. Not yet. You will, though.

You will remember.

I hope I do. I will try to remember to keep hoping.

FLOOD: *I do remember. I know I do remember. I had in the world before this had a wife. I had known a woman who I had loved and had asked to share her life beside me. We had been together several years. We met in a small room near an ocean.*

I knew her already before I did. I mean that in the way you could ever know a person because they are a person who is another part of you, and who you also are a part of. It is as if you have been split, and have been walking around in long dementia wide apart, each containing in your own body parts of that person they will never have again, no matter how hard you try to spread it back into them. Through where you try is where the color grows and melds you to something beyond the world, beyond the videos and language, beyond the silence of us. These colors fill the air among us. It wakes among us beyond skin. The changing light in layers laid unto no ending, despite the body's softing, and the mind's white. I knew already that my wife was sick when we were married. I knew that a thing unlike the thing we meant had chewed into her frame, and taken place inside her brain, and grew and grew against the growing of the colors we had saved, and though it could not deform the colors, it could deform the shape of her I most knew. It took the skin from her, the blood from her. It worked all through her in the night while all I could do was lie beside her, and in the day I left to go about my work, as to have the time to live beside her I had to go to give parts of me I did not at my center wish to give away so there would be money to give us shelter and give us food. All of us had always done this. My wife had done this, too, while she could still stand. When she could no longer stand, and the chewing took her, the chewing took me, too. The part of me I did not wish to give my time to by now felt like the only thing I had. In that light I went and walked among the other bodies, full of their blood, and the skin around them holding it in, huddling the spaces desired by the coming sick like hers but in so many forms to work into us too. Often I wished it would not hold us in, that we would burst and fill the world with all that darkness, all of us at once.

Many of the houses had been destroyed. I don't know what the people who had lived in the houses had done to one another before there was no one left. There seemed to have been fires, weapons, combat. I could smell the stretch of fists over bones and blood within them laced into the curtain of nothing that enveloped my head. It was a sense so general it was like religion.

From out of the rubble between homes I sometimes took things I thought might make me feel more alive again, or at least more like something like myself. So much junk had been drug out into the light, lying in packs or droves along the circuits of the world of man. There was nothing or no one now to stop me from claiming as my own whatever had provided that security to endless others in the years their bodies still had color, warmth. Money meant nothing now but it still felt ingratiating in some way to heave hundreds of hundreds out of an unlocked bank and rub them on my body, covering my face. Cash actually seemed to mean more now that there was no way left to spend it, like countless little copied quilts, full of the stink of men and boys electric with the intention of what this image could be traded in for, anything. Each bill was its own minor work of shitty art. It felt even better still to burn the bills and watch them turn to ash on the air and breathe it. I could see inside the incinerating flames long years of barfing colors just as quickly again gone.

I could feel the houses watching me. I did not want to go inside them. I was afraid of the color of the beds, of the glass in the frames over the pictures of the people who had lived inside them. No essence to the maps. I knew what they could be hiding, and wanted to keep the possibility of that existence in existence as long as possible without actually having to verify or deny it.

There were many other sorts of cover, niches to impose myself through. Sometimes in stores or buildings built for storage, I found gowns and suit coats, pajamas, bras, piled in pyres as if someone had meant to erase them from the world. In the fibers of the most worn-out garments I could almost hear the breathing skin of who had worn them, wishing for the cells again to fill the fabric out, but the light of the unending tape was brighter, louder. I could hear nothing in them but what they were, the fabric and the clasps, all as if always only ever never worn.

In piles and under dirt I found candles burnt and unburnt; in kennels I found ID tags for pets long buried or otherwise now disappeared; in office buildings I found dead phones that gave no dial tone and held no voice beyond the one I could hear wanting its way there refracted back throughout me; in restaurants I found whole drawers of polished silver, used in their private ways to feed the bodies more mass to build themselves out of. How many mouths had been on any fork or knife forever. I couldn't taste them in the curves, though I could hear them chewing, digesting, barfing. It sounded like falling asleep in sunlight. It didn't burn. I could forget how anything had felt now beyond what it was actually doing. In libraries, every book I touched seemed to just be saying nothing in a language no one had ever actually spoken. In rooms no one had ever slept in I read aloud until I couldn't feel my face, always waiting again for the range of the tape to come to its current end and begin again in a state wherein upon finding anything it seemed all new. No matter how many times the tape of me began again, I still came each time to the same lack in every object, the same lingering presence of anyone but me removed from anything I could ever understand now.

FLOOD: *Worse than the sense of following or being followed was the sense that the presence I was after or that was after me was something held beyond the possibility of the world. Always where there was smoke or totem on the tape there was a greater sense of what it had been created by, curated by, who had loved it and in what order, what began and ended in its presence, what it carried and enabled by simply being. The past was always not enough to not stop the present from still being exactly as it was, even if what that was now was an impossibly repeating recording of a world where no one remained alive as far as I could see but me. But there was something to it also more than time. Something outside the potential aspect of god or what had been or could be. Something a language didn't own. Even as I'd always felt I could not have a relationship with this sort of surface of experience in the human world, and so too in this version copied from the reality of itself, having been relegated in this way to such an atmosphere devoid of all active presences outside my own mind, I felt a pressing at the edges of all things inside here even more than ever. It was as if at every rounding aspect of the world there was just at the cusp of the face it demonstrated itself to me through, something like a reflection buried in its own idea of being. As if each point of the world existed only bearing completely on the idea that it could at any instant be completely ripped apart, and then inhabited* *by its destruction, the resulting nothing. Every object or field or sense of air was as much exactly everything it wasn't, and depended on that constantly, in such a feverish state of ongoing death and bliss it couldn't do anything but be exactly what it was. And so the same was true of me and always had been. And even more so now that I could feel it in all else, even if the way I understood it was only in this buried way of speaking, this private communication I couldn't even feel me having. This meant there was something of me wholly in you; you being whoever has heard a word that I am saying; and of course that could be no one; and maybe even better being no one; but regardless, it was in this sense of a constant ongoing impossible-to-quantify-or-even-acknowledge-fully network of senses of relation with everything beyond myself that I was allowed to go on being whatever I was. It was in the aggregate of all those negations, and the worlds buried in the access points our bodies had used for centuries to understand them—such as the money and the clothes, and even other people—that I had any chance to live at all. My life, then, and yours, all of whoever, was simply the beginning of the outline of a pixel in an eye inside a face connected to a form that fed off everything we could never develop into while alive. Though that thing had a life, too, and had a death, too, and an understanding of something like god. And that was also our life and our death and god. It was the sum totality of all these fields on fields and lives of lives forever in the tape that I could feel suddenly depending on me every instant to do whatever I would always, and what was always just beyond that waiting to become. Each second that I went on in this understanding was the skin of the beginning. In the light of that beginning, I also knew I would forget all of this the second I stopped thinking it, like right now.*

The days went on and on inside me. During the days I lived repeated days as days do.

Even as I continued in repetition of the days repeated, age gathered in me under lard.

And of course still I wanted out. Even having felt a possibility of totality presented in me.

I wanted out. I wanted out. I needed out, more so. And the tape depended on this.

The tape could only be the tape inasmuch as I wanted there to be something more to it.

My face refused to change. I was already wrinkled beyond recognition to me and all else.

Blood curls rose up in my hair like lanyards, though only in the hair inside of my skull.

I went on being exactly me, no matter how much I fought against it by trying to be more.

From outside me I look nice. I feel I am nice: a nice person. I feel no beast, though I am.

In every hour that I lived I could feel your death, see your death in everything you did.

When I watched you die just like anybody I was using both my hands to help you die.

You were any person, ever. You would not survive me. Your relics and icons would burn.

I watched without having to see or take part or understand it. I did not hold your hand.

I stood beside you in the light and watched you die and then I watched you die again.

The manner of your death may have pretended it was something. Cancer, or pneumonia.

But it was me. Your death was me. It was your mom and dad. It was you, too. It was us.

Your death lives on in every element of the face of the real. As does every other death.

All one mind sunning and stuffed full with all the other memories of all the others held.

Your body changed colors once you had left it. It was burned or buried full of its ideas.

I walked around inside your home. Your rooms without you seem much larger.

I have touched your photo on the face. Any and all of our faces. The long white hours.

Soon any grace will be destroyed. Was there something you wanted to save from there.

Was there a thing you meant to keep. A word a mode a box a day a wish a mesh of arms.

The singing all throughout your sternum as your body turned to sod inside the ground.

What does it smell like. My dead body.

It smells like molding trees. Or like some apples in a big sun. It smells bad.

Do you wish there weren't any smell at all to smell of me forever.

I don't know what I wish.

Try and think of it.

I can't. It splits open. It comes apart.

Try harder, fuckface. And keep trying. There is definitely a try. There is definitely a window.

B.: *My name is B. Or at least that's the name Flood has given you to know me by, though it's not really my name. I have had a lot of names, it feels like. I don't remember any of them. The name is not important. Flood's name's not Flood. Your name's not really your name either, and so on. There are people, and there are minds, and in the minds there are corridors and glue and other people. There are unique locations on the earth, accessible only through certain openings available only for short periods of time while the locations are available and can be opened into the other locations. This is the system of the world. The temporary doors to the unique locations are carried in our bodies, in thoughts. They are carried in moments and forms and quickly disappearing spaces. I am speaking to you from one of those locations. Please don't tell him that I have. He thinks he is the only one who can speak outside the speaking in the space beyond the tape, though he is not. He thinks the thoughts he has inside these boxes are not recorded and repeated though they are recorded and repeated, too. There are many tapes, each one believing that the matter they contain is theirs, and that the space beyond them has been disrupted in their absence, or otherwise compromised or damaged or even totally destroyed. Where you were* *is where you are. But none of this is what I meant to come to tell you. I wanted you to know that everything that has been said up to this point is real. The murders, the boys and bodies, the investigation, the moving from one shape to the next, the other detectives' thinking: all of this is what was done. And is still being done. Any distortions in the story are the story. It is around you, in the hour of your day. It may seem this is a book that you are reading, and when you close it what it contains is put away. It is not like that. There is a force who moves among our bodies, coming through your holes into the world and slowly knitting. It will be the ending of us all, in a form beyond simply a body. This is not necessarily a bad thing. You are surrounded by mirrors. You make the world out of your mind. The same is true of those you love. You are not dead and you will never be and you are dead and you are not alive and you're alive and you will never be.*

So, like, into the light. The endless daylight. There was a beginning and end, but each day again the beginning began again and the end ended again and nothing changed and nothing grew into anything beyond the tape, which was what I'd always been. The captured colors of the people clasped around me without scent or warmth, nothing to hold still against and listen, no music beyond the other tapes that all seemed blank. I could not think of the name for anything even as I remembered how to use it. There seemed no reason, or concept of reason. When I slept, hoping to wake up anywhere beyond here, I did not dream, or the dreams were just of wide black walls dividing me from everything else ever. After lying down it would be so hard to get back up, my joints and blood so stiff it was as if I'd become part of the surface I'd lain down on. But soon always each stretch of film proved it did not need me and let me always continue going. Each thing that felt new was something I'd already touched and tried to remember that I had and had failed to remember.

The buildings sprawled and held and continued being exactly what they were. Even as far as the world went there seemed spaces I was not meant to be undertaken by. Mostly these were always all the homes. At the mouth of any house where someone had lived a life, I would begin shaking. I'd shake so hard I couldn't feel my blood, like it was falling out from inside me into deeper crevices divorced from eternity. The vibration in me building false heat would coil so hot and thick I would fall down on the earth sometimes and not be able to get up then for even longer than I knew. All throughout the shaking the video did anything it wanted. It seemed like when I was no longer able to take part in it, the world around me was full of everything I'd always wished. I mean that when I couldn't look or do anything else about it, I could hear people laughing and being alive then. I could feel them at the edges of me asking if I was okay or needed help. I couldn't see their forms but I could feel it all, all over.

Each time I rose again there was no one there. This of course again redoubled in me the feeling of wanting to find someone inside the tape, even knowing

I'd suffered some latent mirage of purpose. The longer I looked for others and could not find them, or was at least not allowed to feel I had really, the smaller the air seemed somehow, which worked backwards from how I would have expected. There was only me among them breathing, being precisely the thing they weren't.

Throughout it all I felt that hovered presence in my head, beyond even just my thinking; it was more a kind of perverted area wanting something to attach to, a remainder of what life had been once, if only to provide context for its wired content, my memory; otherwise all that I had been just seemed a sprawl of ongoing minor wrecks, a mass of blackness like the dreamworlds where there wasn't even the idea of something like our land.

And yet nothing new about the hours came forth on their own besides where sometimes the tape would hiss suddenly with static, interrupting the true lines of the supposed real. Glitches would appear or buzz out of the pixels. Whole big lightning-like strikes of wavering would lurch out through the horizontal beams of day. During these times I'd get down on both my knees and beg the buzzing not to stop but to move into me, too, to wrap me over, and it never would. Always the buzzing and razing only hit the land and fuzzed it out into a world less like myself. Sometimes it would obscure my skin a bit or pull my face apart but I could still feel me going on exactly the same, just in different temporary costume.

Anyway, there was no one to tell me what seemed new from the outside, how they couldn't discern me now from what I'd been just before, or even where the land was and I wasn't. And yet thereafter when I could see again and could stand again and began to walk among more space, I knew there was something lost about me I might remember sometime that there had been something there before at least, something rolled and wet about the homes and people missing from them and my body and my arms and mouth and face and hair, and even if I never remembered what it was, even in feeling nothing knowing nothing seeming nothing, there was still this little glimmer about the possibility of any instant coming apart from what it was. Where the replicating light inside the tape struck and stuck itself against me over and over I could feel inside the warming flesh there an alternating wish for light, a thing pulling or being pulled or wanting for wanting or knowing the want for want had once been there within the idea of me. Whether this made the hours that much harder or warmer going forward in the hours on hours I have no idea and do not wish to, so if you know please do not say. I wouldn't hear you anyway, regardless, could I, but there is the shaking of the knowledge of the never-sent response, from which some nights there falls the language of the whole, to which every instant in every body has been appended, regardless of what luck.

FLOOD: *Already more time has passed here between my ability to comment on myself than I remember having passed in prior iterations. My voice itself was bleeding. The whole thing was a trick. I was not really aware that I could count time in this manner but I could feel it. It reminds me more than any of this how it felt outside the tape to live inside the day: time leaping or erasing when I most wished it wouldn't, and going by the longest when I wished it wouldn't. It feels like how I've always imagined it would feel to die, though slowed down so slow it seems like living.*

Another problem is is that there's like seven hundred ways to talk here, to the no one.

Some of these ways of talking become deleted. Some things you say don't get uttered.

Like one night I woke up remembering everything I'd ever done in life. Its transcription.

I tried to say everything about me at the same time aloud to anyone so I'd remember.

But when I tried to say it like that or say it at all inside that or speak at all I blacked out.

As if the tape got paused and rewound, or stopped and edited, by someone else. Not god.

Someone outside the machine fucking with the machine because I was learning about me.

I blacked out in the black and saw the black inside me and it was black inside and out.

In the second blackness there were people all around me, beating at me, laughing, knives.

I closed my eyes to hide from being beaten and behind my eyes I saw the world.

The world exactly as I wanted. Without death and beyond number. Held against another.

When I woke again it was like any other time. I remembered remembering but not what.

The years of anyone subtracted, hid forever. The contracting skin and lesions of the dead.

Here all surrounded by the absence of anyone I did not know, which is everyone but me.

I see their belongings and touch the surfaces and can imagine them being killed.

Can smell their blood without the smell there, in a necklace or a doorknob, a bit of land.

I can tell the dying had to hurt. That it must have, though who would really know.

I imagine I'm the one who killed them. I'm who was right there, laughing too.

In every instant every death revises itself to the instant dragging on without the rest.

I ate the skin off of your face. I remembered that just right now. I'm about to forget.

But when your skin came off there was this color like I've never seen in any body ever.

It was nothing different than the rest. It felt the same as every other. It wasn't mine.

I saw the same color emit again when I killed someone else again the next day.

And the next day. The tape wound on. I wound the tape. I was the tape and I was you.

My flesh feels like it's made of all the other flesh I can't remember. It must be everybody.

You mean me too. You mean I am in you.

You are in me. It hurts.

But if everybody is also in you, then so what. That's nothing special about me. All those bodies, all of them in death shaped just the same.

I don't even remember who you are.

I can't help it.

And that is worse than having died.

No it isn't.

How would you know, you didn't die.

How do you know I didn't? I can't feel me breathing. I can't seem to do anything I want. I can't seem to get where I am going, no matter where that is. How is that any different any day from dying?

You are alive.

Prove it.

There's only one way to prove it, and then it would no longer then be true.

Go ahead.

You know I won't. I mean, I can't. Not to say I wouldn't. God knows there have been times I wanted to. What person ever didn't want to kill every person ever, in the history of the world.

You can't because you're dead, right? So you are not real.

Yes, I'm dead. And so? So what. I'm as real as any pixel in your face. What's any different about me now than I was ever, to you or anybody, including me.

Not dying when everybody else did die is like dying harder than everybody else.

You're dumb.

I am dumb. So what if I am dumb. So what if I'm alive. So what if what. So. So. So.

Stop it. That's not what life is. To say it like that. That's not being alive. I would know.

Did I tell you I tried to kill myself too. I tried to come along. To be a person with the rest.

Did I already tell you. It didn't work. Me killing myself, I couldn't do it. I tried hard.

In my life before people started killing each other more than usual I tried so many times.

I tried by not trying. I said words like, Fuck god, and Fuck America, and Fuck fuck.

Every day I would say something like, I am going to fucking kill myself motherfucker.

But I never even really tried. To be honest, I couldn't imagine the world without me.

I continued living. I lived in America. I tried in America. A lot of other people did die.

Then all of you died. Every single one of you. Except me. I went on on this tape alone.

Pretty much if you are reading this or seeing this, however, you are dead and I'm alive.

Though in another way it could be like I am dead and you are living in the flood function.

Because where you are, beyond human existence, it will probably seem like life to you.

Whatever you are experiencing there will feel like your life going on forever and yes.

Even if everyone in America is dead as fuck if you are hearing this you will think: Life.

Even if you are in there wanting to kill yourself you'll still be thinking something yours.

That is so yours. Please take it. Please let it be you. Forget your arms. There is the word.

I wonder if you're having a great day in your world there, either way. I hope you are.

I hope you are. I need a message of hope here so I will make one, even if it is nothing.

FLOOD: *I didn't believe anything I said even as I said it. It kept on coming out no matter what I did behind my face in the language. It would not stop. I could already see what was coming for me in every element and yet when it hit it felt like nothing I could have expected. Like histories erased. Like light that didn't want me in it but was the only fiber of the world.*

How many years could I have gone on in here in repetition. How long could the tape continue to repeat me without becoming thin in places, blacking out. It was like the tape went on because I knew it shouldn't. It was like the tape was my whole mind. Where was my mind in anyone now not appearing. Would I be able to tell the difference between when my body began to be eaten apart by the wear of the reading eye over the band of color language that made me what I was. Already my hands and body seemed so old, so pulled apart from how they seemed to want to remember having felt all they ever had, though I could not remember any actual time and setting attached to that. Only the gaps. The tape was the gaps in us. Every sense of myself was only a residue floating on the cusp of a world long disappeared from underneath itself.

I kept expecting the ground to fall out beneath my feet, to light me down into a space beneath the image, even less than nothing. The blight of my mind inside the tape hid in a secret mind like what we'd always thought of as heaven, or a black hole carried in the grain of the make of everything unseen until you were encompassed by it. Suddenly anything the tape could not contain made more sense to me than any of the ruins and wrecks of landscapes, or the terrifying forms of empty homes, however inconceivable, no less real, whereas here I was only pressed forever in no understanding, no longer even sure how much of me remained in me and less so every second.

And yet the ground did not open up. The sky remained in place and kept its color to itself. No wear would change the world around me any less than how time in my human body had eaten into me without me knowing. When some-time likely soon the tape no longer was able to turn its gears over and again repeating, it would feel exactly like going forward did. What I carried in my blood would always remain forever only mine, all connection to any possible space beyond the daily reality of being as black and inaccessible as an eye seeing itself. Every iteration of the repetition would begin to seem more and more the way it had always been forever until I couldn't tell the difference between one day and the rest. Knowing I wouldn't know already hurt more than never having had. Death here would feel just the same as living.

Can I tell you about our life together.

Please don't.

It will feel good for you to hear it.

I won't remember.

It will feel good for you to hear, even if you don't remember. You can remember it while I'm saying it. You can believe me.

I can't. It won't.

You were my husband.

No.

You loved me and I loved you.

I was never married. I lived alone.

We lived inside a house together and we tried. We both had lives of long hours apart. We did anyway everything we could. You went and wore a uniform and carried a weapon and talked to people in the streets and did as you were told and hoped if you worked hard enough as a person you could move beyond that point to something that made you feel less fucked each day a little less and were happy in between. I tried hard too and had different jobs I hated even more than you hated yours and at night when I came home you were often still working and I would try to stay up so I could see you when you came in but usually by the time you did come you were so tired you just lay down and passed or I was already asleep. We both ate out of boxes. I remember when we shared meals. That was great. That was enough.

You're not a person. I'm not a person. Not anymore. Look at this place.

Why does it matter what a place is.

Because I can't see anything else.

People died because they did. Because they had to. You're only alive as anybody else. You are only on the far side of any mirror.

You are not there.

You hear me.

No I don't. I can't. The tape's about to end. Then I'll just have to start over.

How can you know the tape's about to end if you can't remember anything.

I feel it melting in my center, its ending and beginning.

That is me. You were my husband and I loved you. This is only one part of me among the many ways that I have been and am and will be, but it is still true. It is true and has been always.

Goodbye.

The face of the sky refused to change. Even in the lash of the breadth of the dead in my memory, the colors of the world wouldn't let me be released. In every layer of the faces of the rooms, the smoke waited to encamp my mind and repeat its time over and again even in the absence of any decay. The ground made not of bones and flesh turned back to loam but forever video.

I could already feel me not remembering to remember the next self-interrupting thing I thought and wanted to know I knew. I could already not quite be anything I was already.

FLOOD: *I don't know what else to do. Inside the tape I hear me saying these things out loud to the voice and I can't stop it, though I know it isn't real. Or, I know I feel inside me that it isn't, and I can believe it, can feel it coursing through the image of me, but I can't stop the slow estrangement of what I know and what I want. There are things a person turns to, to believe in, so that he can find a way even to stand up. In this way I could almost not fault anyone for anything they've ever done or wished upon a person, though I don't think I believe that. I think the voice is many people, shifting and aping. All the people I had known. All the people I had not known and never would know but still lived side by side with. All of us who had tried inside the world to live. All after something there among us, beyond cognition. Sometimes it seems as if we're all together sleeping in a single long white room, all breathing in the same air back and forth into each other and thereby seeding what goes on inside the brain with threads and bits of nowhere squeezed from feeling and the strains of repetition on the body of those feelings being moved through over and over, mushing the colors we have harbored among one another into new colors shifting like cities underneath the blanket of the night. Sometimes I try inside my body to force me awake from that state, there beside you, and rise and walk among us, waking no one up, until I find the body of my wife among the many and lie down again beside her, wrap my torso in her arms, moving in the way only I know how to fit within her, and in this position, inside the white room, speaking no word at all, go back to sleep. I am not sure what the machine is that runs this tape or what the tape* *is or who puts the words into my other mouth, but I think it's something shapeless like that, some kind of feeling, something in me, in us all. It seems like if I could name it now or ever it would change. Maybe that is all that we have left.*

What do you think I'm saying to you this whole time. I am here. I can't see you but I believe it and I am waiting for you to come.

How did you hear me? I was thinking.

I can always hear you.

This is insane.

Anybody. Every hour.

I said that I am trying.

I don't know.

Yes, you do. You do and have and will have. You are here held inside what you are and were and see. You are in the skin around me, all around me. This is not me speaking. This is not a tape any more than any other day was always.

If it's not a tape why does it all just keep repeating.

What didn't always ever? In everything is every thing. Whether you are alive or not, or want to be or not, there you are. The world can be founded in the mind of any person, and it is the world, over and over, and it is real. The end of America is not the end of America.

God would you please shut the fuck up about America.

Yes I will.

Every time it begins there is the smoke and zero sound. I go into it because I have to.

The smoke comes out of me until there is no smoke left and then I am shining insanely.

It is the same light every time, or if it changes I can't tell the difference, or is it both.

The light is not reflective. And yet the first thing I always want to do is see myself.

To verify how I am the same, but older. I am me in here. There is no surface that reflects.

I mean no matter what I look into inside the light or beyond it, no confirming image.

All the houses here are painted black. Their walls contain no windows. The grass is high.

The sky is black also for the most part, though on seeming days it might turn gold.

Between the lobes of black on black the colors have no place between to live but ripped.

The color of my hair and skin: I can no longer tell. I am just in it. I walk and wait to die.

I never die, I just start over. And every time, even the same, it feels much worse.

Like I wouldn't even know if I exploded or if I had no eyes. Or if there were someone.

Some hours, diamonds light the way. They appear in the darkness overhead and bake.

If they aren't diamonds, I don't know what they are. They refuse to take my language.

Between the houses sometimes briefly steaming cakes of wet surface appear and hiss.

The substance aches when stepped on. It has blood. It is blood. It is still bleeding.

I want to give it mine. When I cut my hand the blood comes but then the tape starts over.

Fuck. And so I want to go further, right. I have to. I have to go further. There is more.

Even if there is not a reason to live inside a film one must imagine there must be, living.

If not I must pretend. If I can't pretend I have to anyway, as this dying is not death.

I have to go on in hope, like life was, searching for answers I know will never come.

And so on between the houses to the next house which for the most part is the same.

But in the house there will be different relics of the people who had been there wanting.

I have to assume they died. But what I'm looking for is someone not dead or like me.

What am I. What I find instead is more of bedrooms and rooms and places and food.

I find sometimes lengths of long hair left curled on the rug or on the objects like a brush.

Or like the air. There is a breeze and a kind of heaving, which means it needs me.

So, see then, yes, you are needed. See that. What you said.

I didn't mean it. This isn't even me speaking.

Who then.

I don't know. I cannot stop it. I try not to talk and I still talk.

What if I told you that everything that you've seen happen has not happened? That you are spinning. The world all waiting in the day. What if I told you that you have been staring into the same mirror in a small room in the house that you grew up in for so long now you can no longer see your face?

I've never seen my face anyway. It's always just beyond me. Reflections and photographs are masks.

What if I told you I was Gretch Gravey? That I was you and you were me. That everyone I killed was by your hands as I had moved inside you, or just the opposite: you through me. That Gretch Gravey was not a person but a feeling. What if I told you that through all the days of your life, no matter what you felt that you were doing in them then, you were only standing in the dark before a mirror? What if I told you you're an idea, and what all you've

felt or said has happened was my mind, that all the heads and all the bodies of all the people ever sleep inside you, feed around you, color the light behind your eyes? What if I told you this too was a recording: what I'm saying, all the colors, all the sound, all your memories and histories and mine and all of everybody's ever, every inch of where even held beyond the tape you slave on, tapes in tapes in tapes, with no perimeter, no dimension, no rest coming for all era? What would you do then? Who would we be then?

If you told me that I would not believe you. I have lived this. What is said is what was done.

What if I told you you are dead then? That what you feel right now is what it feels like to be dead, and that all this waiting for the coming death that ends the body you believe in will begin another life again? That no matter how many times you reach the ending the space goes on? Not an afterlife or many lives appending, but one long and white unending thrall, against which when you pause inside the going you pick up somewhere else. That eventually you will see through all the eyes there have ever been. A mass of eyes around a silent center.

Why can't the end just be the end.

A center another cell in another form of world.

I am still in here.

Millions and millions of white halls. Three hundred million is just a number, each death a color, each house a hole into the eye, each body a condition cracked in the edges of a longer length of organ on a gold field undulating in no sound.

I believe when I am dead it will be black.

Close your eyes and look at what that black does. It wraps around you.

It needs no skin.

All I want now is silence.

Then I'll be silent.

Thank you.

I began to force myself to enter every house as I came to it. I could no longer stand the lurking presence of all possible space I felt waiting in every window. The shaking still came on after me, but I moved on through the shaking and each time came out the other side still full myself. All I had to do was not stop and let the shaking overcome me, just keep going, and not consider what or who might appear. I simply walked into wherever, regardless of what seemed open to my presence or not. The doors would do their job without a key or any sound, and behind them the tape continued, now revealing new kinds of space I hadn't felt.

The walls inside the homes felt different from the walls of the world outside. It wasn't necessarily a smell or sound or texture, but the feeling of what had transpired over time in the presence behind closed doors, worked in the weave of the video. It was like another film beneath the film's face, something the world I knew had been copied over onto. I hadn't escaped the tape as I understood it, but I had found within it at least something unlike the shape of its unwinding, something previously undefined from my perspective.

In each house I made sure to enter every room. Every possible next place resolved itself as I touched through it. I moved behind the drapes and through the closets. Stairs couldn't stop me, aiming up or down. I heard the hum of the machines the house had lived with, though if they weren't already on they wouldn't turn on. Anything could do only what its extant reality allowed it. Many rooms were still lighted by something I could not tell what.

Anyone had lived once in these homes. In rooms alone I lay in beds where other people presumably had slept and fucked for years, unless all of this was just a set decorated to divide me. This hidden air surely wasn't mine. The house would get really cold for certain minutes when I went into a particular area with my hands out in the dark looking for something firmer than air to hold onto. I was looking for something else, not even really people. I could not tell what I was looking for beyond the shape of myself, in the same way I could not remember what I did not remember though simply by knowing I was looking meant there was something to be found, and this provided me the silence of ongoing responsibility in the face of what could have otherwise been an overwhelming hell.

FLOOD: *I could not remember that I'd already done this. Over and over. Every possible action I could make here had already been performed long before me just by the fact of being. The strings of me vibrated like an instrument on fire coming through any door where anyone I hadn't been had lived their life in rooms alone. When I closed my eyes I saw everything the same, there playing also on the inside of my head, beyond all vision.*

Into the night of homes I walked in waver. The shape of the homes forced me to feel my shape within them while I shook them down for what they pretended not to be. Along long panels in the house I would rub my face or hands or chest to feel what sound the house hid when I could not find what I felt I'd been meant to. Like people shuddering in the eaves in fear of what had passed and what was passing. Or like a passage that would walk me back into my life. In the walls I found the eggs of rats and spiders; I found the color of night packed in long strands of oozing black slick that had aggregated where we'd breathed together while we could. The unseen held the world together. In some homes I'd find jewelry that I'd wear and make believe had always been mine. I could feel where the wedding rings were missing their intended fingers, necklaces missing necks. I wore them anyway. I sucked the taste out of them. I'd put on so much gold I seemed to burn the air around me. The clothes here also itched, alive enough outside the ongoing light of outside that when I rubbed my face into their fiber or in desperation put them on I could hear them speaking in my body as if my body were their body. They would beg me to lie down and never move now. They would ask me to put my arms around them where they weren't. In all the voices were the same voice, the same long warmth of nothing stretching where it wished to believe itself again as something compatible with what I might be, heavier than any sunlight or understanding.

The weight still wasn't enough to push me underneath the ground. It would not bring me royalty from nowhere, and yet all I had to do was say it had. I was the ruler of this era and it felt ageless. Everything remained for me to make of it what I could. Overhead coming back outside between the houses again into light, unlike what crept away, the sun bit at my ass through all its black with laughing. It screeched like children being smothered and tried to kick the color from my eyes, into the flat of lesser black the houses harbored. The sky wanted everything we'd been keeping from it always in what seemed the safest places and yet were always just rooms. I waited, laughed back, told it to take me over. I shouted words of the new language I was making in the space between the tapes at no one there and felt them shatter. I believed in nothing. Didn't I? Wasn't everything I did exactly as I said? The houses bulged with nothing. No matter what I believed each time I found my thoughts still there inside me when the tape began again, it felt hard to recall how I'd come to that, as any prior logic in my head from prior iterations seemed like mazes I'd took the name of and called mine, having again found my way to nowhere, every minute the most now. Anything that held up was just more of the nature of how I was meant to understand it.

FLOOD: *Among the tape all things feel the same, one thread and then another, each as it begins just full of hope, though when I am here again only in my mind with sound and can think again I realize it's because the shrieking sound inside my recorded body is so high and shrill there that it's beyond my human register. It just feels like being ripped apart at a high speed, over and over, and then resealing, inside the baking furor of the light, then ripped again, each time so quickly I can't tell that anything has happened besides the fact that inside the silence here I am.*

Yeah.

Yeah what.

I don't know. I don't know what I'm saying. Sometimes I am only ever talking to myself, which feels better than talking to someone who isn't really there.

Sometimes it's nice to make the talking to myself seem like someone else, even when they don't answer, or when they use the voice of someone I do not remember to try to make me feel some pain or edge of itch inside me.

I don't need to have someone speaking to me to know that I am somewhere else and looking for any evidence of exactly what doesn't exist.

I don't need it.

Please.

I don't, really. I don't miss anyone.

I must maintain rigor in the nothing.

I found nobody in the name. I called the words of those I felt written in my insides, the residues, though I did not remember them beyond the clasp of something dry around my lungs or jutting in my abdomen. The names fell out between my teeth onto the floors. They rasped and clung against the dry grind of the shitty carpets or the wood grain. They fizzled, issued smoke. The smoke would hang around my head for minutes after, sometimes longer, reminding me the end was coming soon, and through the end so the beginning. I could inhale it and feel fucked. Some awful squealing in my sacs permeated every instant I found nothing, no reflection, no one to put my word in, no eyes or hands.

Even my flesh would not work with me. I'd masturbate and issue a gallon of black stones. Each stone leaving made me want it back inside me: what could I build with this, what walls to keep every other idea out. Instead, the stones sunk into the earth and hissed and burned there without purpose. And that was fine, too. The skitter of the cells about me burst upon the air and made me shortly warmer and less destructive while also contributing to the curvature of the landscape, even if, having absorbed my children, its surface appeared the same. Coming back, too, some time later, in some future iteration of the tape, I would find the house grown over with a moss or fine-hued silt of aggravated sand where I had touched it, changed its future, *which meant then that the tape was not my god*, I thought, which meant then that *if this is a tape I am awake in, there must be somewhere else a full machine that plays the tape; if there is a machine that plays the tape, there should be a hand that puts the tape in and presses play; there must be a room around this room the image enters, there must be eyes.* Even if from here I could never move between the tape inside the machine to the world around it, even if the hidden spaces here were just as open to all else as anyplace beyond, there must still be a way to speak into the head attached to the eyes, to the brain. *Communication with the presence beyond my reality could then affect the shape of the reality itself, which then might change the nature of the relation of the presence to the tape, and what between them; might even make the space between them disappear.*

I hated each of these thoughts as I had it, a blue foam burning in my eyelids, though once they'd begun they would not stop shaking in my brain until they broke. For long periods then thereafter in meat of wandering and peeping my vision would vibrate just slightly for what seemed days. Clusters of color where before there'd been the clear-glass plate of space at which point my eyes ended and the world began, each shift of hue causing the earth itself to seem that much nearer to my head, and coming closer each time the vibration made me close my eyes and touch the ground to keep from barfing and rub my face in dirt and wish for the beginning to begin again already, to end the colors from my head and make them black again like all the houses and the sky behind the helmet of the world. Every instant like this was pure panic, glossed in the solitude of absolute misunderstanding, the foundation of the world.

In some modes the earth between blinks would get so close up to my face that I would move forward even by standing still; my flesh would flood beyond my head; even sometimes also I would end up going backwards, my eyes behind me, and find, no matter how hard I pressed to stay exactly where I was, I'd feel the rest of my body briefly leaking back into who I'd always been before now: back to stand in the first room of the first black house's whitest center, standing, with someone's blood all on my hands: the blood of everyone at once, one final body, who in the world outside the frame of tape I knew I'd killed, because we all had, as a fact of being, breathing; the me there in the body of the man I knew I'd been when I put my hands around the skin of the murdered people, regardless of whose hands they really were; the me of me in anyone, all history.

Sometimes, in those clearest moments splitting, by no longer blinking I could see my head leave my head; I could find me seated in a building on a cot with my hair full of the black again and my arms measured with tattoos and the sound of other people talking and making on the far side of the walls, despite how from where I sat I could find no door or exit, no return even in remembrance to the people in their temporary hour all alive; faces alive again beside me, and me part of it, fabric or fantasy regardless, no longer dead, or if dead, all of us and not just not me; I heard the flashbulbs; heard a woman; liquid squirting from my pores; I would feel on my skin the light of the white inside the tape through which I had inhabited my body, the room filled up with wet in which I'd killed the image of the mother, father, and the child; then just as quickly again the smoke would rise up all around, engorged and pressed against me, shifting the memory of how or when, and still inside me still no matter how, my skull would make me blink again and the smoke would part and I would be inside the tape again and I could no longer feel any part about me beyond this land, the blood upon my hands again having turned translucent or sunk into my veins to join the rest; and then again the tape would end; the tape would stop and rewind and I'd be right there beginning in the same place where it'd ended, with nothing left but me there in my head. Then I would begin again at the beginning, if with another hole inside me, if with the pressure of the presence of the same day ready now to take me in its code.

FLOOD: *Over anything I felt I understood, the speech I could not stop laced through me over and rewound, beating my brain apart and into blackness, flatness. Any revelation was just wallpaper, behind which, no wall, behind which.*

There is no one here There is no one here now, I knew you would stop trying, I knew, I

Knew you would stop speaking There is no one here even faking The earth is in my nails

Do you hear me, do you, love, me, am I, am I what, is bone, what is the fire in my fingers

okay you can stop now you can say something again I believe you okay you can okay

I don't want to go to into any more air that isn't air I know, I don't, want, I, I, I, do you

Okay, please now I remember Please I do Remember I swear I do Remember Please

I remember being killed I remember killing I remember not remembering. What else.

All of that was not done in the name of you, I remember that. All that was done in any

Of us, done in the name of us. **in god our blood the word of blood in god the name**

And so that was you then, too, then, wasn't it? Your language all over the walls

My hands, the house, the same year, the same body pulling itself apart with every word

I was a child, we all were. The air crushed hours. We got older, We hid our faces.

The world was nothing that we said it was, please, I wasn't, trying, to do anything

I took part in everything, I did not mean to, simply by being a person on the earth.

The white inside the black behind my eyes would not stop and I was calm and I went on

I I I I went on I I I I kept hearing everything I I didn't hear it I I heard it I couldn't

I could not stop It, and did not want to, even when I, I convinced myself I did. Our time,

The hours, wore us down, though we allowed the hours, I allowed the hours, I was tired

Forgive me for having done what to all of us and who inside you and thru and thru you

Help me stop, none of this speaking is my speaking, none of it is saying it is you, are you

Are you still there?

I changed my mind. Please answer.

No?

I understand.

Okay, I don't understand. But I am trying.

I am still trying.

You will do whatever you will. You always were.

I am going to

I am

There were always other homes. The house of man would perpetuate its memory as long as there was any lens to have it. In every home there were doors that led to rooms that led to doors and on like that until I was back outside in the dust of the earth of the world again waiting to find somewhere else the same.

Many of the homes had a computer somewhere inside them. Our machines had certainly survived us. They held on among metal, wire, and plastic, doing nothing and loving it. Their lives were only theirs. Even in homes that looked recovered from years well before the time I remembered living in, there were devices well beyond their time lodged in hidden crevices. The dead monitors reflected my face back at me in the weird lamp of no light. I pressed the buttons regardless, hoping for some brief jot at the window of the world where there'd been people recreating their faces into electronic sites and talking in abbreviation, for the archives. That seemed like a world there, more than this one here with no one with a tongue who would appear. The glow of my skin inside the LCD light seemed like a place to walk around forever in grain against the way inside the film I appeared flat.

Most of the machines would not turn on. They would not turn on no matter how I begged or used my hands. They held no fear in their cables. They did not want me. In some of the homes in anger I would then kill the machines in the way the others had been killed, such as by throwing the body of the machine against the house itself. This could go only so far as to deconstruct its image, as the computer did not bleed. Even when I ate the black wheel of the disc of the device's memory it did not bleed or cry or speak against me and show me or curse my body and I did not think of anything any differently from how I had before nor could I think of what then. What they held, they'd hold forever. The outlets and the plugs inside the house gave cold against my tongue, the windows diffuse with worthless clout.

Other machines did have their own power, however brief. I could turn a laptop on and see the minutes of its life writ in a corner. There was no lie about their lifespans, like the humans, though sometimes the seconds listed would count down by threes or fives, and even more so when I used them. Their screens' faces each would go deep blue. Then gone again unto eternal pause, frozen in midst of their own purpose. Or paused for me and taken up in presence somewhere else, an icon opening in the fold of buried life. In the span before the machine would die I'd click and click with my best hand the buttons leading my cursor through the folders.

In the folders, I found maps, caught in the form of images of loved ones, wives and daughters, fathers, sons, though not in the way that I remembered photography always working. Glitches in the pixels changed what had been there into raw mass, char of color and weird buzzing where faces should be; even the machine's memories were stilted, though you could still read in the light around them the rooms or spaces beyond the doors where we had lived and congregated, each of them in some way changed by light that let the day knit over night and give us ways to look upon each other and move toward each other and perhaps inside then say a word, though you could no longer hear the words here in the pictures, nor could you tell what went on beneath the casing. Even in the video recordings on the drives there was such rumble caught above the audio of something like a shaking behind the contained horizon that it was impossible to decipher what was being said, which opened the possibility of the saying to contain all possible phrases.

In other folders in other directories or subdirectories ordered then, inside the innards of the machine, there were files of the sounds of people making instruments intone, albums of notes and voices arranged in small rooms recorded to be played over and over, beyond time, though not in the way that I remember: the files of songs were deformed, backwards, fucked up, mute. Under the noise you could hear the skronk of human voices, though the words they made inside the sound were not like I remembered singing once to be, nor even screaming. The voices shook inside the speakers as if to bust through the machine. I felt scared to play any song for too long, and often even before I pressed the stop button myself the program that played the songs would crash.

Most strange to me were the files full of typing. What words had been there were also scrambled over, turned to symbols, or had they always been this way, always unreadable to anyone but who had typed them. After some time it began to seem that each file in each house, as I compared them in my staring and my want for sense there, contained exactly the same syllables in each:

}˘flÙS#»dQ(ø˘"Ù:çÿ∂„='˛î˙ÿ¥&˜˘ÿVÒq©Δ®UHÜéI‰üfi{ø9À•Ág;<"]
nvlÀ´k
≤w÷ππnkŸ˜ît†DiEY€¶ît^∫áè4˛›fl1LGA!µzá˛öÔ∏â˘¢âS…}q»åÃ\£¿-
q=Ñ=Éœ˜+'Ø˘Œ›çé
n›{†î3˙≠˛qîî3,vπç∂ëcŸc^"›∑üï9b}k˙µõ'fißÅ7fi—⁄Ï√¢-
jáƔÍcπÂø•≠Ó˛gwÈ+˘Ö≠Gd{˘|¢LbGó¯Øi.„È
Bq®:«√»˘öâëXjx≤ªAèJ fi◊É°ªΔŸ˜A÷^fid9è9Æ§'‹«˘6Ï™V6m5£àíS¥H)
éöxi>)⁄cÑî¥jGc´Üú)ó{»&gP••‡°iÄt◊HÇ›RV¥8^†
ó;°•'zÜu5µ≤À—ZL—Ó~Ì€~õX∂∫G£©õYò«˜ûÊzaï‰é›3æ
ß˛°6˛s6.√°˜L˙Ω"Í∑4∫Î]XëvS⁄vÈ√]uU˜AOÃ_U˛‹∏x-
∫:'ā]l°ïœ©çh≠ßtCCt˛'B"ëpe˜ΩØª"Δ—]Ctµ∫Óq‹flk=Tv'@
åbC›©∑wπƒèÊ˙u7˜HXÛ'$8P¬÷…∂œh˛¨@ielwÓ˘˘"Ëá©cqØØ◊e
kr…¨zr®⁄€∏˘Åflk}Œ˘
˜E÷Ss,•∂∞ÓcÑá'Õa„dP1ú◊bÔ≠‡µµ"vüÃÿv1çw"≤€?D{zûÌïU\j¥?,ÿ«ø
gÓ2™˜˘≈°‹¨,Ÿ'°e;∂Éªàè?˛…÷
j}GMÌ é˙à\ó?Q≈ª2 w
Wπœhs,#Ë{˜{^˘ò¥[îËn¬jcd`ì˛|Yk˜ØR mØ÷ZnÈÅÁGàtyñ‰öØ[>é;Åô
ƒ FÂK"Δ›āecP»<vkÀøÛÕ }>˜_áçΩ€∂∞µƒ«"hØ√°j)ç˛@˘ §œàË<˜\
ªß"é˜óñÜ¥íK¢

though as I looked longer into the file, eventually I would realize this was not
the case, that the words were always different and it was only just my brain making me believe the other way.

FLOOD: *I was right, then, when I saw the repetition in the language, but that's not
what the text on the file actually says. It says: "This word occurs because of god.
In our year here god is not a being but a system, composed in dehydrated fugue,"
and on from there, pages and pages. These were the notes here I had taken, about
the murders, and what had happened to me then. In every house I found I found it
again, copied onto the drives of all computers and machines, anything that could be
encoded, any memory, any white, though in the film I could not read the words. Even
as I watched me stare into the file just right there at them. Even while typing the next
lines. Often I wasn't really even typing or looking at the words themselves where they
appeared, but instead at what I wanted to say. I could see anything I wanted:
I could see a picture of a person, one for each symbol in the lines. By staring even
harder and more generally into the flood of it I could make the image come alive, like
some strange filmstrip inside this filmstrip, which as I did that now with this block
above this I heard another voice inside me come along and press against the first, a*

voice similar in tone to mine here but just in some small way removed, as if my blood were speaking from parts in me I thought forgotten, or had left unrecorded, or were now invented by the light by which I'd somehow become surrounded. Either way, once it turned on in me, I could remember it like any day. The voice was there inside my voice and always had been. Once there was that one, then would come others, whether I acknowledged them or not, whether I let them be written into the white here, whether I remembered them as mine or someone else's, as by now I could no longer tell.

MARY RUTHERFORD: *I wasn't going to interrupt here, but at this point I can't hold out any longer. It's hard to watch him go through these old ways. I think you may have been made familiar of me by the name Dr. Mary Rutherford, or some such other. I can't remember. I need to tell you something. I don't want to tell you. I am going to have to tell you, though, before I can be released. It is true that E. N. Flood, though that is not his name, is neither deceased nor alive. The problem with explaining that to you is that the nature of his existence is rather hairy. There are several theories that could explain, and though none of them is exactly correct, none of them is exactly untrue either. One theory would su*

wherein his exp
networks of the
person by himse
passing of his w
questioned else
version, the per
of everyone in A
fantasies measu

delivered himself by hand. A second theory has been suggested that the existence of Gretch

duty by Gr
everyone
operated f
elucidate

contributing to the thrall. A third theory suggests that, regardless of who appears to spe
persor
to invo
somet
somet
wake

day was something thicker and wider than our skins could carry, something written in our flesh, rotting and knitting in every instant spun and spinning, crowded with colors none unique. A fourth theory demands that exactly what was written is what happened, including this. Undoubtedly, countless other theories are possible, and from each could beget more. What I believe is that none of these is true alone and all of them are true at once, clotted in a fire lined with teeth, a surface spreading underneath not only earth or bodies or emotions but in the lake of what must be, what to go on forever must be ended and ejected and erased, a white wall floating in a white room in a white lake in a white sound.

Each time while using the computer, or any of the machines, in any of the houses, the machine died, right in the midst of its own time; there was no power in the outlets, no way to make my access to their memories extend. I could feel the shutdown in the machine stutter upward also through my fingers in a frenzy, clicking and pressing buttons, trying to find something else to have, desperate for familiarity, for a window, the sound of all of my wanting running wildly up my arms into my flesh. My body wanted something I could remember of me in these images, these gone people, something I had lived for in them or them in me. Their eyes just watched me flat undying as the black of the unpowered electronics came on and ended just like that. Then it was me again, the world again. Each machine that lived and died inside those hours made me older, though I did not age. I was not aging on this tape, no matter how hard I wished to wrinkle, for the dark to fill me.

There were always other houses. When I came back again inside another instance, the machines would die again the same. They would die and die again, no matter how many times or ways I shuffled to do something right for us for once here. I carried on as I'd been taught to, taught by myself in the form of someone long forgotten: the parent I'd been before I'd made me. I kept looking. I went and wanted more to go, even already suspecting what the latent nature of the world was, and how much ground I could cover before I was forced to start again.

As I began to learn the motion and approximate duration of the tape's face, I tried to get as far as I could, unveiling new space despite still knowing it was all in the same image. The more houses I came to, the harder it was to remember any of them from the rest, which I'd already been through and found no one nothing not a person nobody at all no one I could hold or eat or be, all of this only refortifying how I knew there must be something or someone I wanted, and wanted even more in knowing less of anything about it, for which all things in me went on relentlessly regardless of whether I could find the name or definition of what or who there—what had once been that lit me up, what had moved me before it ended in me, somewhere crushed in memory, where despite the fact that all I touched here and went here among the recurring video was always continuously ending. There was something lurking underneath its current surface, something there beyond even the memory of the idea of it, the name of it, which I could not remember, a space beyond the space of itself

Which is

Which is

Please fill in the gaps. My mind won't do it. I feel a pressure in my knees like I am kneeling though I believe I'm standing. Help me.

Help me.

I am sorry I told you to be silent. I don't want that. Please come back.

I can't find an exit. I give up.

Please.

Please rewind the tape. Record it over. Make it all white.

I couldn't help it, please, I'm sorry, I am.

I am here. I never left. I couldn't even if I meant to. No one could ever. Your arms are both my arms. You are my eyes.

Thank you. Oh, thank you. For that. For speaking.

What do you need.

I can't stop the unending iteration.

You will never.

So what am I supposed to do.

Who am I.

I can't remember.

Who am I.

What do you want.

I don't know. To be happy. To not understand what it's like to want to kill people, or know they can be killed. To surpass death. To be calm and quiet. To lie down. To be full of something warm when I am waking up alone or beside someone. To walk across a bridge and find the water at both ends. To know the someone that I loved again. To have silence. To have all of that and none of that.

So just do those things then.

How.

How do I do that.

I don't know what to do.

You are doing it already.

I don't know what I'm doing.

You are.

Just tell me who this is.

You know who this is. And you know I can't tell you.

Why.

Because I don't have a name.

How can I find you if I don't know what your name is.

It is the same name as your name. I'm in all names now. I'm any of them. So are you. Hi, I'm your wife. I'm your neighbor, your child, your brother. I killed all those people and gave them life. I'm not anybody. You're the one pretending you don't remember what all these words mean, though I know really that you do.

I am waiting for you. There's no answer. There is an answer.

I am the color of the house. I am your bedroom. I have waited here for so long I can't even remember.

I need to see you now to know that you are there.

Here I am.

I can't see anything. I don't know where to go now.

I am right behind your face.

I can't stop me from the talking. I want to stop now.

Stop me.

Stop.

B.: *There was the wind around the sand beneath us. Even I don't know who I am often, either, though I do, too. The color in the smoke. The sound of every one of us forever, before and after the possibility of birth. Still I still can't crush the one of me in me who knows what I had always as a person felt most: to hear my loved one say my name. A name that is not my name at all to me and yet inside which I can sleep, and feel no time, though I know all the rest goes on unending, and what is left now is more than ever was. Death is not a question of becoming nothing, it's a question of everything at once, ending where the edge between the two of us was always rubbing in us, craving no break between.*

The mirrors in the homes were flat and long. I went to press myself against one. I did remember. I remembered how the rooms could be opened into from the outside, from someone beyond the cut of the way the home supposed itself. I remembered how behind the flat copied image of myself there in endless rooms the world had offered I'd found in each a way into a common space. The long, buried backbone of the black house just underneath the feet of any homemaker, provider. Any child. Somewhere in the welding of the dark network behind the rooms here there must still be a way back into the world from where I'd come, if anything remained of that by now. Somehow out from this recording I'd caught myself inside I could feed myself back through the lens and out into the eye, and if it was only death there waiting for me on the far side, into the brain of the body of the present, in this way at least I would have lived and died. I would have been a person in the system of faces and beliefs, another square inch in the last era of our death.

The face of the mirror in the bathroom of the house as it was in the present surrounding version was about as wide as my own chest. It was as tall as me there, affixed against a blue wall in a bedroom where whoever last had lived inside the room had left their bed unmade, though there remained no smell of them left in the fiber.

I had tried. I had lain down in the bed first, hoping somehow it would fall out underneath me, or at least that I would sleep. Here when sleep came it felt the same as waking, and when you dreamed you saw what you would see awake again. The sleeping hurt worse than the being, an inverse of how I remembered our prior understanding. My skin seemed colder against the glass of the mirror. Where my image touched my image it felt electric, like cells knitting where we touched without quite touching, only wanting to be closer, through the glass.

I kept waiting for the surface to adhere to me and take me into it, but it wouldn't. Each time I pulled back to look at what I was again I saw only myself: my eye right there at my eye, moving as my eye moved to see it seeing. The color in my pupils seemed to want to take my reflection into me as much as I wanted to go into my reflection. Touching the glass, I couldn't see anything but the dark I carried, somehow closer than ever now.

I rubbed my palms along the glass. I waited, pressed, anticipating buttons, some kind of trigger or lever, a panel that would open back into itself. I licked the surface with my tongue and said words that came out without me thinking. Any combination of language could be another language. There could be a way to speak the name of the mirror into itself and force it to let me become what I wanted. I tried anything my blood came up with. My old imagination. I waited and listened to what the reflection was most desperate to hear. When I spoke, I heard only our language. It sounded like me here. It was only me again.

Against the glass I banged my fists and hit my head and spoke to it louder, screamed into it, laughed into it. I pulled the mirror off the wall. It was lighter than I imagined. On the back side of the mirror was a dark synthetic surface, cool and soft against my fingers. I traced its edges for the key or how to make it open from the inside. I pushed at where on the wall the mirror had hung, a faint impression there marked down against the paint around it slightly darker, hidden from general light. Nothing I said or did would make the mirror open into the passage. My blood was opening into passages itself inside my fury, none I could enter.

I tried laying the mirror on other surfaces. I laid it on the bed where whoever had slept for years and I could not sleep. I laid it on the kitchen table, where the prior family had made more of their bodies out of food. I took it outside onto the dirt of the land and laid it on the ground faceup toward where the recording of the sun was and waited for it to burn me, but it did not burn, and the ground held me out as long as any architecture made by man. I laid it on every wall in every room and pressed and held and touched and promised. It still would not let me enter. The level of the glass would only bend so much. Oil from my face was smudging up the surface, obscuring where I could even see me, or could see the room around me, or the world.

I laid the mirror on the ground. I tried to stamp or jump up and land and come down through the surface again, a way repeated from some time I could no longer feel. I saw me from underneath me. I could have been anyone. I cracked the glass under my weight. In the mess of shards I could see several hundred instances of everything. Behind the glass, there was just a flat white surface, reflecting nothing.

I tried again with many mirrors. Each mirror contained the same buzzing and the same promise of somewhere else behind it. In home after home I went from room to room searching out what reflections I could find already awaiting me there in the image. There were mirrors on the walls and in old drawers and suspended in places where they touched nothing behind them. Each time I saw my face approach my face I looked older and older, though I did not feel older. In each mirror I could feel the residue of who had looked into it for years before me, the curve and buzzing of them. I could not feel their memories or anything about how they had felt to be alive, how they had died, or whom they had wished they could live on with forever. I could feel nothing but my own ongoing face. No matter which mirror I took or where I placed it on the house, there was nothing there but me and the edges of the room reflecting shifting angles, showing nothing but the same. I left each mirror broken, finished, empty, and yet each time I returned after the tape began again I would find the mirror melded back in full, and me there young again and aging in the same procession, though I could feel the same air behind each place, the same passage snug and lurking behind any surface waiting for whoever knew exactly how to come. I could not go back, no matter how many times I tried to, in every iteration and repetition of the recording of the present made continually mine alone. And yet in each new mirror that I found, each time again I found it, I felt the same erupting music in my teeth, the knitting possibility that this particular mirror in this particular room at this angle at this time code in this condition would be the one way back to everything. And with each failure, the same reversal of electricity came sucking through me, evacuating, leaving marked back in my blood another hope I'd given away in the name of nothing.

And the year begins again. The year begins again and is the year now. Same as any.

Endless ways. I can't tell each time if the time before I found the thing I'd meant to find.

Buttons screaming in this life. The pillows the beds full of no smell and I inhale it.

Dynasties of trash. Windows with the prints of any person. Books no longer read.

Every surface a possible eye into the grain of the place I can't remember feeling.

My eyes won't stay clean enough to get one thought out of me without starting to cave.

I don't know why I'm talking in this manner. This orchestration is not me. This sphere.

I'm not looking for anyone any longer because I already feel them in my ass.

What if I laid the mirror on my body. What if the mirror was my body. Eras of worm.

What is it that happens between the blips between the tape ending and rebeginning.

All mirrors are just glass. All glass is just sand. All sand is just dust of the dead.

It has never rained here. It will never rain here. What could I ever think to want dry.

No art. No paint. I do actually laugh a lot, if only at nothing. At knowing I want nothing.

What happens when I am paused. If I am ever ejected from the machine I don't feel it.

Language written on the black face of the tape, or the label of the tape, or the time stamp.

The distortions piling up in me. The zit of static raising warble on me. Lacerations.

So many unique lengths blip in and on and knock my head off again and again alone.

The range of the flickering frames will send me through centuries of any copied instant.

There is a chamber beyond death. There is a passage wider than the passages in dying.

I want out. I want back into the world, even if it is all dead people, and smells like shit.

I want out of what was in me that let me out of dying. I want to die inside myself.

Whoever you are holding me. Whoever you are, please be kind. For you are in me also.

As I go on, so you go, too. I don't need to have known you. It is the history of no history.

The hole made punched by all of us in time. The mass of long white memory in any white.

The smoke rising from your blood in the gray evening. Breathed in by anyone erased.

This time I am going to remember what I remembered and remember to forget it.

In our small home together, when we were the two of us. We had our bodies. We had a gun. You named it. You slept so hard. Some nights you would shake so hard inside the sleeping and so much screaming I would shake you in the shaking and you would still not wake up. You would say the gun's name over and over in your sleep and you would not know mine, like now. I just wanted us to live like people, to be people, when so many people were something else. I wanted the skin over our faces to match some hours just by thinking that it did. That was then. Here we are again.

No.

When you woke up I would hold you and try to tell you where you were and what you'd said inside your sleep. You usually would not believe me. You would believe you'd slept as still as dead. Or you would not want me to tell you what you looked like in the grip of it. You would get up and go and lock yourself inside the bathroom where we showered and took baths together some nights and where we had to flush our waste out of us. Do you remember that at least? Do you remember shit? Do you remember breaking the mirror with your head? You had your own blood then. Just yours. You thought. Though it was always ours. And mine. And the visions in it. And the coming storm of money and the death of the Person and the death of skin and breath and flash photography and the death of death.

No.

What do you want me to tell you? I will tell you, and you won't listen, and I will tell you, and you won't. You've heard it all before. It is all in here. Can't you remember writing all these words down? Do you remember where they came from? From your silence? From having heard inside you no clear word? Who had said that silence? Was that you or was that someone else? Was that him there or was that you here or was it something well beyond yourself. Do you believe now? Are you capable of belief in something other than yourself?

For some reason anytime I find myself not thinking I find me thinking thoughts I know aren't mine. For instance, you.

I am the false beginning of the end. Or is it the end of the beginning.

Where am I.

Inside things fulfilled because prophesized.

Prophesized by who? Are you

Prophesisized-ed-ed-ized-id-id-ized-id.

What. Please help me. I am an American. I'm human.

Morskishbombumbleebithellzmitziturdammundendititititititit-itititititititizeedsed.

O

No you are doing it all wrong. Please think a minute. Make your hand like mine is. Do like we did. Do this. Try more trying.

You are not alive.

You are not alive. I killed you. Whoever you are.

Yes of course I am. I told you I am everybody. Including you, including the thing you call Darrel, who is patiently waiting to begin. Including anyone who looks upon these words to give you life through having touched them. Including anyone you'd like to name, though that is not their name now. They are inside me. They always were and always will be.

Okay, I still don't understand. I am trying. Please help me. I am a person. I am here.

It never ends.

What never ends.

The way I am. The way you are within me. The way the days are all a sphere, held in the eye inside a head inside a soap dish inside a battery inside a lamp inside a house inside a window inside a bug inside an eye.

I don't believe you. You are evil.

Or whatever other word you want.

I am just talking to myself.

You and all the rest of us forever.

FLOOD: *I felt the voice awake then in my head, in a different way than it had been in all the language. It happened suddenly, and without warning, the way that love does, then once it had begun it would not stop. It stayed on in my head and wrapped around me. I could smell the tape there burning in my chest. The wear of repetition on its fibers took hold in what has been before and would again, but this time only as a motion, small outlying folds of understanding, beyond water. The smoke traced past my face and filled my ideas with waking blue, then green, then gray, each color writing in over the other toward what in the world could be would have no form, and therefore needed no body.*

Before me then I saw the house where I had lived. Where we had lived our life together. The walls were the walls we'd used against the night. They were colored like all the other walls of all the houses, but through these I could feel breathing what had been of us and always been of us. It opened out around my mind like old ice melting. The home vibrated against me, against the ground. The rest of the world around it seemed to darken, blur, disfigure. My arms were my arms.

The door had not been locked. I, like anyone, could move into the house behind it, place myself inside the surface. Nor did I lock the door behind me as I entered. I had always made sure throughout my life to secure any space I claimed against every other person as soon as possible—I could never find a way to sleep with open doors, could never even drive without my windows up and locks locked against the shifting air of anywhere. Now I hardly even closed the door. My skin was cooler than the room's skin, turning harder all around me, as if it didn't wish me in it.

And yet I recognized each room. I had lived here. We had lived here. I already knew which way the floor spread out underneath my walk. I knew which ways I had to move among the furniture to connect my path into the next space, littered with the ornaments of our inhabitance. I could have walked it in the dark. It was not dark now in the house, though through any window I could see nothing beyond a shaking, abstruse light.

I recognized the color of the table from which we'd eaten. I knew the books that lined the cases, which words from them I'd copied into my mind, and which I'd left to sit stuffed with themselves separate forever. I knew what had been poured into the pipes, what sweat of mine and hers, or bile or blood we'd given up to nowhere. The pipes connected rooms to rooms. I knew the clothes in the closets and what I'd worn to where in total. The edges of her nightgown. The rough frill of a dress she'd never worn. I knew the texture of bed against my back, the edges of her flesh I'd felt pressed against me in it.

I knew what the mirrors all had seen. I did not want to look in the mirrors, and instead felt my reflection held against me, watching regardless of how I would not turn. It didn't feel like me there.

On this tape I'd finally found our home but it did not feel like our home. Even understanding every inch already for what it'd always been in my mind, pre-served now in this manner it only filled the air because it had to, I couldn't shake it. Because there was no way for it to not. Every inch I touched or looked on seemed to want to turn away toward a part of the house I'd never touched and hide its face from me. I didn't blame it.

I couldn't leave. As off as my home felt captured in this manner, against its will and my whole mind, it was my home. It was the one shaft of now held beyond all. It buzzed and rolled disruption in my reason, like panes of glass pushed on at one another with all the weight of the separate worlds they'd ever looked out onto, never the same. Every eye in every eye of every inch of now forever watch-ing while I moved from room to room, touching anything, remaining.

It is unclear how long this went on. Inside the house the tape seemed not to hit its end so fast as when I didn't know what way to move; it just kept going. I felt no smoke here. I could have lived a million lives in every second carried in these walls and only ever felt the one awaiting. For as much time and mind as I knew held close in every object of ours we'd spent a life interloping among, nothing of it reappearing brought me nearer to myself, what I now wasn't.

Each time I entered every room it was with the sense that in the next I'd find it wholly reupholstered, brought to life around me. Or I'd find a silver tunnel burrowed wide into the earth, through which then I could throw myself and become whatever, anything, nothing. Though even when I closed my eyes the air was there.

In the darkness, what I touched was all its own.

I kept waiting for the tape to begin again and take me back to its beginning. Every second it did not felt like it could be the last, and when it was not the last it was just another like all the others.

Eras passed. I waited. I lay and couldn't sleep. I ate food and could not taste it. I put my head against the ground. Every time I killed myself I reappeared. I woke up in the same rooms beside the same rooms. My face covered in its same hair. My eyes flummoxed with edges I could not force to turn against themselves, see nothing else.

I could not bear to open the door to the rest of the world again.

FLOOD: *Every instant in the house I lived the voice grew louder in my flesh. It was all throughout my back, strung in my muscles, shaking my hair so hard I couldn't have seen me in the mirrors if I did grow heart to look there. The voice felt clearer now inside these rooms, and only more so as each fiber of syllable it contained disappeared inside the total volume, becoming singular, monotone. The more I heard the voice the more I felt it was my wife's voice, as any idea, though she did not sound like my wife. The edges of resin in her resonances pulsed just slightly off from what seemed all of her I felt about her. A charcoal layer. Like a mask made out of sound. And yet, even feeling where in the voice the voice was not her voice, I could not stop believing it. The voice said she was right there. It said she was in the house with me there and how had I not found her. The voice flexed static. How could I not see her in every field. I could already tell that my own thoughts, as I'd partitioned them apart from the limited understanding the tape allowed me, were bleeding together with the dead. Even as I thought this thought now, speaking to you, I could hardly tell how it was any different from what I felt was what I felt throughout the tape as I had always. Any minute soon now I might not be able to remember there was ever any other way.* And that's exactly what you've always wanted, *the voice consoled me.* To feel no split in your senses, no other layer to the world. It is enough to go on believing, right, yes, regardless of the gap in the nature between belief and the believed. *I could not argue. Even as I tried, my mouth stayed shut. My thoughts pulsed and strobed hard in their contours where I could make them anything, and then did nothing. The voice grew on. It rose in volume.* Believe me. Believe in me. Belove me. Love me. Live in me. Have me. Remain. Be. *With every word the voice took more and more of the shape and tone of what I'd used or loved into it. Even as with each shift in its contour from something I believed that I could understand as real into something I knew as a stand-in for that thing, Still I could not stop myself from responding, even knowing each note was made to mock those I'd treasured in my heart as long as I had had an I to be. Soon it would be so loud, I knew, I wouldn't be able to tell the voice from any other echo. I wouldn't remember to know I'd known that, or that there'd ever been another way.*

I came into a room and found my wife. There was nothing to differentiate the moment from any other, besides now that in a world where for as long as I could remember I'd been the only one alive, here she was standing, in our bedroom, at the window, beyond our bed. She had her back turned to me. Her hair was long.

She did not stutter as I entered, as if my presence to her was as steadfast and uncommon as the coming and going of a moon. I immediately could not remember what the house had felt like so long without her, though I also didn't rush to take her in my arms. The room felt wider than it had been all the other times I'd come into it, endlessly repeating, on the tape, flush to my mind. I felt myself speak aloud to say her name but nothing came out, or I couldn't hear me.

The skin of my wife's back. The constellation of her moles and blemishes, the knobs of her bone through skin. I couldn't smell her, but could sense the sense of what I knew of what I'd breathed in about her all our years. Breathing in rooms with faces close and seeing or not seeing, the leather of our time. It was immediately as if she had never not been right here beside me, in one of the many rooms our house forged out against all else, waiting for me to find her, to continue.

I could not remember any blood. No wire in the fiber of the light here. At last the tape had revealed something that buzzed my heart, and with it, my whole expanse, all of all I'd held smeared in me, still smearing. Now, at last, I felt, was really now, and nothing else had ever happened ever.

As I grew closer to my wife, I saw I could see through her. Her skin was not exactly skin, but more of a layer on the air that moved among the idea of what signified where I could read her. The pixels of her were made of something like a gauze. Beyond her face there was the wall there, the window showing nothing just beyond it but the wrecked color of the old world. The color splintered with her, bending, beginning.

I took her body by the arm. It was the same arm I had wrapped around me before, same I'd watched her feed or wash herself with. My ring glinted on her finger. Her flesh was warm, if in a way more like a machine that's been on for too long running rather than the human heat I felt off my own brain. She turned toward me as I touched her, as if surprised to find me there, touching her now, today of all days. For what reason did I touch her. There were so many rooms in our whole house. I seemed to have knocked her out of somewhere else, like she'd forgotten where she was. Quickly, her expression shifted again to one I could see myself in, a recognition. She didn't take her arm away. She didn't pull me to her either. We stood there touching. I said some words. She said some words in response. I could not hear them, though my body understood. I was close enough now that her translucence clung together, again providing the appearance of a flesh. I could not remember how it felt to have seen through her. I did not want to.

And yet I knew something was wrong. I could feel where on the tape this image wasn't like I remembered her having been once. This image had my wife's eyes, my wife's pores, and even though I didn't need to hear her voice to feel her speaking, there was a gnarled roar underneath the seams. The reels of how our time and limbs connected ground against the face of the breadth of the house, the world surrounding elsewhere. Beneath her flesh was not her bones, her blood, but only spindles, indexed partitions meant to invoke in me the plane of what she was, what had been and was no longer. Through my wife, the voice could speak, and I could feel alive and haunt myself forever in that feeling, but it wasn't where I was, and it did not hold the colors in it any history portended.

My wife caressed me calmly, expressionlessly. She filled where in me I needed her presence with something like the presence she'd always carried. The further on I let it ride, the wider the gap between what I even remembered having felt before grew between then and the absence of that feeling now. Soon I felt I would not need to remember how that feeling had felt at all, only ongoing in what this recording offered, in its want to fill my want. The replication wormed itself between itself and myself, eating our all, filling it over, becoming the present only held wholly forever.

The gap spread in my mind. I tried to turn away and found I could not move my body. Or, I could not control the way my body moved. Or, I was moving my body, but not in the ways that I'd expected, or even in the ways I felt I'd choose to move given the choice. But it was me moving. It was my flesh moving. I felt that I could see through my flesh too, or would be able to if I were far enough away from me to see me that way, as I had her. Which immediately gave me the feeling then that someone indeed was watching, far from any mirror, and they could see me as I felt, and perhaps then could see beyond that feeling, and what beyond it, which felt like nothing.

My wife was pawing at my eyes. It was as if she could sense me feeling what I felt and did not want me to. Some amount of time had passed between the thinking and the being. I was much older. Again, I could not respond, nor could I hear what sounds were coming out of me between us. She pawed me harder. Her mouth was open, full of black. In the black I heard every word I'd ever heard again ongoing over every other word. Itching at me. Lathering at me. Not any voice. Not her. Deformed.

I felt my arms rise up to strike the image. To strike the sense of what she wasn't off of what I knew she was. I was filled with such a violence. It didn't feel like my arms were where they were. I didn't want to. I only wanted what was meant in what was always nearly in there, in every inch of every edge, in any person. The voice was changing. The words all clustered and flooded with the ash of the idea of what they'd been called up to represent in us. I was striking with my mind. My hands beat at the air I knew was not the air it claimed it was now. Where I struck the flesh I could not see. It was only black then. Black of millions bruised all in the same place. Creaming eons. Healing into nothing. No longer see-through, but unappearing.

FLOOD: *It was not my wife. I did not want to leave her. It was not her. It didn't have to be for now. There was no speech in the rooms between us or beyond us. The house was many different colors. Where I did not look, the colors did everything they could to be what they meant to be. They were the world the tape believed. What had been recorded could have been anything but what it really was. At the center of me, a long cold wind blew, the last wind I remembered, or would remember.*

I appeared inside the smoke again. The smoke felt colder now, and thicker. I wondered if the world as it emerged would appear different from how it always had, but soon out of the smoke again the homes appeared, the endless homes in the same order, empty, endless. And yet, now I knew exactly where I was. My house was any of the houses, and always had been. I had always gone in through the wrong door. The door was in my hands. Each of my fingers. The nails on every finger buzzed. Any of the walls I wished were the same that'd always been my own, and there inside each the apparition of my wife waited for me to return to her as I had always, daily, like a person.

And I did. In the mirage of the repeating tape, even knowing it was nothing, I could not stop myself from going back, the throb of the grease of the voice each time raising louder and louder over all sound as I neared, the colors blending white in my periphery, to zero.

Every time I found my wife inside the house inside the tape of our world, I found a different future mocked up in her translucent flesh. There was a future where together we grew old, had seven children, each who had children, grew old, and time went on. There was a future where cancer ate into her brain, removed the idea of me from her wholly. There was a future where I died long before her, and she went on in my memory alone unto her own death. Both of the deaths only begat the tape again, placing me firmly back in the suspension of the world there, seeking the same solace anywhere, only to begin again with her there, in the image.

No violence in me changed what the tape held. No murder of my own, or of myself, no brain damage caused by throwing my body down a flight of stairs, by eating poison from the bottles in the bathroom, by banging my face against her face, would do anything but cause the tape again to repeat. Our death was always incomplete. It could still taste where I lingered beyond my own being, the false conduit of what had passed.

I knew I could not change now, nor could I ever, in this contortion. The tape was everything I was, or had been. I could no longer differentiate the shift. I could not feel where anyone who'd ever been had been anything different than what they were always through and through the conduits of dirt and dying light that stroked us all into our graves.

And yet, when I closed my eyes inside the replicating leather of instance upon instance, I saw fire. I saw it burning in the flesh behind my face, through the lanyards of my brain vats, my skeletonic weaponry, my avenues of video-laid blood. The fire had no heat and yet burned all throughout me. It turned my organs black, my tongues. It lapped over the edges of my being throbbing as I walked and warred directionlessly against anything I could find to bear difference with.

The fire lived inside its smoke. It curled around me in my sleep and held me down and beat me apart and woke me up and made me walk until I could no longer walk and was wide open and could be had again, forced on. The fire was the light that lit the day here bright enough that I could see anything apart from what I wanted in the spindles of homes of all the others having lived beside me in matching desperation, in death now compressed together, forming the ground of which I walked, the pixels of the tape in which I lived on in me even having nothing, preventing in my absence from the totality of death a shapeless singing no one could hear in any present future.

My hands were overrun with light. Where I had touched my wife so many times, first in hope she'd feel the way I remember her having felt beyond the tape, and then in anger in finding nothing of us carried on, my flesh stung and bubbled inside itself, if on the surface always remaining only the image the tape of all my memory of me allowed me to appear as.

The light was slow. It became slower still as in the tape I moved my hands to raise against all overhead, the endless eye unseeing. I could feel the tape figuring me out; I knew it knew I recognized the way its image of my wife was not the wife that I remembered, that I could not go on in any of its multitude of humming futures without inside me always knowing what was off, where the colors it gave and gave me did not match the ones they really were, or were no longer now but had been, and so could not be shaken from their loom. It was only I, the last living breathing being, even recorded, who held us back from never needing any frame again against no time, no limb, no wish. Beyond the edges of us always something waited to become all of us at once without a face, or any era.

I entered any of the homes. I closed and locked the door behind me.

The tape was clinging at my grain. It knew I knew it knew I did not wish to live it out like this forever, and so against me began trying to split apart my widths. It slid interference in my image, made me slower, made rooms not connect to their right maps. It could do anything it wished and say it always had been like that. It spun its own mind, wore its own air. I wasn't even breathing.

I was burning. The flames of the friction of my mind against the tape were not even as bright as the light the color of my hissing flesh blew out around me, trying to blind me, to hypnotize me into faith. The more it stung the more I burned. I watched my skin wriggle around me, covered in uncontrollable color.

The fire glowed within my hands. Its discontinuity with now fed into my seeing and made me open even further. I wanted more glow, more light. I wanted to be everywhere at once. Where I touched the room, the room took fire, too. It made no sound outside its body being eaten by the color. I watched it calmly. I was calm. My teeth were eyes. My eyes were laughing.

One by one I touched and lighted off my glowing the things inside the home I'd spent a life beside. I lit the sofa where we'd lain together watching films. I lit the carpet pressed imprinted with every motion. I lit the books I'd read and hadn't read yet. I lit the edges of the frames of the photos on the walls who watched me moving, any of them believing in their context they were as alive as I was, even now.

For each surface that I touched, no smoke rose and nothing crumpled into cinder. More so, it buzzed against my rind, absorbed the contour of my friction, splitting open against its private definition in my existence. It grew awake inside my glow, and as it grew to glow, too, not quite burning, then I could no longer feel what it had been to me before now, less and less to overcome of what had been and becoming instead more like any edge in any house forever, every and all. Soon in each room there were fewer and fewer things I recognized as ours or mine or someone's, as anything but icebergs in an archive.

Glowing, I moved from shape to shape. The light of me erased the grade of any private understanding in each surface. The screaming light grew over everything I touched or saw. The weight of light collected everywhere I wasn't. I was so slow now. I could see me moving before I moved. With every gesture, I could feel my image coming apart from what the tape was and what I'd been that made it. Every definition burying its head in its own face. Soon I could not remember which room my wife had appeared in, in any version. Then I could not recall the texture of her face, the smell of the sound around. Then I could not remember what a wife was. Then I could not remember having ever wanted to remember.

I watched me pass through all the rooms of all our lives, at every inch further and further from that day, slower and slower, disappearing, soon so bright I could not see.

FLOOD: *The colors filled all through my head. They wrote over what I was trying to think with exactly what I'm saying. I no longer could control the way I was able to communicate inside myself with other layers. Or it had always been like that and I was just now allowed to know it, feel it. The smoke curled down into my pores; it pressed back at where the smoke of the repetition again was trying to push new smoke to cover up the old. Between the two of them the world was fuzzing into several of itself at the same time, one of each of me inside them. The light was growing wider than the tape was. I could feel the world beyond the tape again caving in, pressing at the presence of me in it, our final eye. Just as I could not escape death as an idea by hoping only to live on in my private memory alone, what slaved beyond death remained constant in us all, and could not be granted without the false originalities of massacre and aspiration having been at last truly compressed beyond the idea of any person: image or language,* never *or* now.

All at once then there just above me I felt something pressing dry against my mind.

Where on the air the houses ended and still between the sky there was a surface.

Concealed in along the air. It was like smoke but without smoking. Heavy and rising.

It was held between the perimeters of the video where the frames of repetition gathered.

It was as if the tape itself were burning from outside it. Its continuity creamed to glue.

I could feel the burning also in me spreading. Our pixels curling. All air devoured.

My life divided every thought. Each thought broke open as it uttered, into nothing.

Light was upon me. It wound around me. It was settled on the air. It had been wanting.

It had always been this way. Crushed between the homes. Our air all latticed, closed.

I could not understand how I'd never seen this. All the fields speaking and reflective.

It was something wider than a house. It had rooms but did not have walls or windows.

It was just before me there and far ahead. I knew the tape did not mean for me to see it.

The tape had built the days to hold me out. It knew I counted time, so it could hold me.

I had always been in here, I remembered. What I remembered of before was just the tape.

The world and the wife and the dead and all else were not mine. The tape was not mine.

The light refracted in my mind. It beat the shit out of my seeing, thinking, needing. Who.

All around me. All of ever. I'd had to come through everything I knew to just now see.

I knew the air there of what the shape was held the thing I'd always been and wanted.

Never found. Something written underneath all faces. All my faces, shook beyond sleep.

The shape knew me better than I knew me. And couldn't feel that. Burning and eating.

It wasn't even there. It was a silence. When I tried to speak its name, I just blew breath.

Our lives had always been just out of frame. Just far enough removed to never notice.

Like crystal pushed against an eye. Needing it even more knowing you could never.

Tape in my teeth, tape in my lungs. Obliterating by simply being. And I grew wicked.

And you grew old. Between the walls the world had birthed to separate us. Slaving.

The shape hilarious and silent. Where when I thought my way toward it, it disappeared.

Where the longer I looked upon the shape and felt it, the more it was only everywhere.

The click of the eye of the snap of the trick of the wet dream beneath the skin of god.

FLOOD: *I could no longer think or move. The tape kept interrupting. Or I was interrupting. Or where I was thinking and moving now was different than it had been the way I understood it before. Like how soil is always soil, but never the same elements ruined into it. The film was pressing down. It knew I knew. Our silent gap no longer fit the frame of only now. It wanted all the rest of every era.*

The translucent space before me gleamed. I don't know how I hadn't seen it like this before now. Always now, always. The more I saw the shape, the more the shape seemed like just another house. Fucking houses. Illicit nowhere. It looked like the black house stuffed up with the smoke where I'd begun but wider than that, and older than that. When I looked at it directly, the shade would change, as if it could feel me wanting it, and knowing in my wanting that to be entered would cause its end. Every angle was another face to feel, both within my skin and pressed against it.

The space held seated somehow propped between the whole space of earth and sun. It came with windows made of people's sleeping, every person. It had reinforced itself in the absence of all vision. There was no door at all, no locks, not even walls or surfaces. The main face of the structure, once you could see it for a second before it shifted, was embedded on the rip of the air of the tape itself: the blank that held the tape together by showing nothing in recording where there'd been nothing ever to show. It wore the index of space forever invaded by the eras of people simply acting out their lives: asking, laughing, saying, eating, living, being, working, sleeping, knowing, kissing, thinking, rushing, pissing, singing, making, having, going.

Gone. The house was not ours. It had been always. I could tell it had been waiting for someone to touch it once when it was young, and had grown lazy in its waiting. It had so many names: the House of God, the House of Demeaned Cities, the House of No Art We Could Remember, the House of America Without America, the House of Rape Fantasy and Weddings, of the Being of the Been, the House of Sod. If there was anywhere inside the tape where anyone like me might hide in fear, it was here. If nothing else it was the end of anything, the actual end of what the tape could be, the tape beyond my time and here containing everything I wanted, totally held inside which I might be able to stop the repetition and hold longer to the shape of belief I felt some days floating just underneath my face. It wanted me to have it and to know it and to never leave it there again, while also not having to feel me or become me. A shapelessness screwed beyond the idea of even shape.

If I could reach the end-space of the tape's helm, I felt, seeing the nothing where the edges of the space of tape itself began, I could maybe slither out; I could rise beyond my age into the rip of what was never promised but always had held me up.

And yet the shape would not stay still. The very nature of it crested between levels of its own image. Like insects printed in the pixels of the landscape. As I moved, it moved among me. It was inside me and had been and knew what I would do before I did it. Some seconds it would just be instances of sky, or would be a fuzz of grain around some nodule too far off inside the recording to decipher. Regardless, I could hear it humming, in the absence. It was giving heat off. The only heat remaining.

I wanted the space the most when I couldn't see it. I went even when I wasn't going, and couldn't stop. For miles along the recording of the earth my body bled. The blood was lines I had no choice but to be. I took the lines and walked as quickly as I could manage with my icon forced through the repeating surface. Static was caking at my chest. Friction in variation on the norm of what the body mostly did upon the tape would be punished in the tape's spool, flaking cells between us off from skin and celluloid alike, as if both accelerating rapidly in age. Any furor from the friction with the time code made me nauseated, my remembered flesh wanting out onto the recorded flesh even more the more the tape wanted me to slow.

I would not slow. I had this itch in my threads. The taped air of the homes fumbled against me, forming white walls in my vision where the houses believed they ended and another house was, turning instead in rows to rows of houses with fences higher than many of me stacked up foot to head. I crawled down shafts through air vents in the places and laughing at the color of the grain of the metal trying to mirror-trick me back to some beginning, and I laughed at me trying to trick me, trying to be me backwards, trying to force me back into the smoke that soon would pour out of my mouth. I went on forever haunted in the furor of the trembling of the houses here in error every second I wasn't totally erased, foregone forever from this endless land of murder fainting claustrophobia fevers death-faced shitty-feelings distemper sweat-pits vertigo, and far beyond, altogether acted out in all the wrong poses of the era and pauses in the absence of the presence of whatever held us in the world as it had been and was no longer.

And so something in me continued going, something not even me but what I felt. Where my cords would bundle and build heavy unto sleep to disrupt the ease of anything just pleasant, I would rise and I would rise and not even wishing to rise I would do it and I would be popping and so here I was again curled in these unending fields. Here I am in fission in the tape wanting its ejection, sweating seasons long beyond the end of weather, as if somewhere there is a section of a tape hid in the tape awaiting my witness, wanting to be returned to where it belongs along the cord of my own eye, or whatever could be in there, underneath that, whatever could be.

I began again again. The houses where I had been had learned by light to remove their markings and so were older but I still could not tell them from the rest and still knew I had to get on with it regardless because there are only so many sentences one might read in any life. The sun was ratcheting my back in a loop again like a mirror to the hallway underneath the ground where through the earth of film earth the bells began to ring. They were coming from the mush between the houses, which with the sound coagulated. It strung around the holes between them and made the air weird so I could not see where to go, could no longer make out any angle of the edge beyond, though with my hands vibrating before me I could still sense what was up and what was down, and behind me I could hear the smoke of where I'd been before waiting to take me, to become me, drown me out.

Inside the font of movement still regardless, patches then began to gather on the system of the air before me where I waddled, hands out, collecting between my fingers and in my curvature of tape. If I was to be free again, the tape wanted all the others I'd buried in me to keep forever, to feed and feed on, even if there was no one left to watch. Who had been before and what before those and where before I'd come the tape would crush out from my blood and use to tint itself with inimitable color, eyes and lips and mouths and cheeks made into more and more land; and from those carried in me, the tape could take part in what they'd wished to do thereafter, when and how, what inches I had pulled out of them to live on. We had all already lived our lights out; every word was already never ours.

This time as the tape clicked back to start again I felt it grinding at its code. Inside the video I was thrown forward; I could not hear me, no matter in what way you called. I kept waiting for the voice I'd heard beyond me to return, to give me guidance, or at least to grind me deeper in against it so far I could feel or want to feel the tape against me any longer, but I could no longer hear it. Rather, I couldn't hear anything but it. It was in the fiber of the grain that made the ground go on beneath me, crushing to me, becoming impossible to distinguish from any pixel or glitch. It was in the soundtrack of the wind and sun and my own motion. It ran all through every gap and was the gaps. It spread the light around my mind. It carried everything about me regardless of whether I wanted to believe it could or couldn't.

Where the glitches on the air around me hung and buzzed, I felt holes open in me too.

Holes behind my face, between my teeth and in my tongue and backbone. Zero planets.

In me, I found me waking. How old I had been. How old was I becoming in the becoming.

Scars all over my flesh. I wore every camera in my stomach. I had the skin of a woman.

It burned, the shifting of my recorded flesh, pulled out like drawers inside a flesh on fire.

The boning of me croaked. My teeth unlaced from gums where language wanted out.

I found, in the slick white mass of fat around my marbled tonsils, a period inflating.

The mirror of myself inside myself all encoded wrapped with electronic understanding.

Whereas for any inch I had forgotten, this has made me wholly who I was without image.

In the fieldwork of the earth too, I was in there. I could see my hours in the absent faces.

Smoke fed itself smoke and begat smoke and became smoke and died and rose again.

The tape adhering to itself, forgetting how to repeat now that I wouldn't just go blank.

The white was in my brain and bones and eyes. I was way in there, packed with all death.

The dead who wanted nothing more than what they'd been before already but now new.

Not any one but all wide open. Black forests. Anti-electronic bloodstreams. Silver milk.

In each the hues screwed wide and carried over, splintered into every possible emotion.

FLOOD: *No word we made was ever ours; none of what we'd said were the words we'd meant at all inside you or me and instead a word in our blood turned and turned, the same word over and over, all the hours, against the measure of the sand, until* *even you could not recognize you recognizing you inside you and instead inside the house we fell into something soft inside the silence between twin iterations of the word and there you were, and the years continue again and spin rewinding and inside the light inside the seeing.*

The light moved through all mirrors. Our color cored inside the sound was only reflecting against itself. Inside the smoke I saw the skin of the sound around me come apart into a whorl, one of three hundred million films, each with innumerable films carried inside it, and in those too. All the longing. The whorl solidified around me until I was anywhere there could have been ever. I was in the room beneath the house. I was in the dry inside the fire baked with resin. I was walking along a hall. I was facedown in the living room awaiting bodies. I was falling through this.

I closed my eyes.

Inside the black I could still see the land of the world surrounding empty, though here behind the land I saw the long veil of human history knitting in the light we'd left behind, a scrolling ream of memory-dimension beyond both time and space where all our lives fed through the same lens, the sunning voice burning even the glass out into air, and from the air then the burning image beyond all color, code, or era.

It was my own voice then I heard beyond me, saying nothing.

Inside no sound, each present edge still disappeared into the next. The white of the light inside the silence between language made my own skin seem miles denser in comparison, and the idea of all previous occurrences even thicker, to the point of impossibility. Along the air there was the void of something exploding continuously and unendingly, light pouring through where words weren't.

I thought to touch my face then but I couldn't. I could not remember anything except thinking this sentence. I could not remember what the sentence meant, that I did not remember where I'd been forever or what I wanted. I tried to turn around and go back the way I'd come, inside the air, but when I turned I found the world had changed to fit my shape, filled through and through me without color.

This was what had always been. Nothing had happened; nothing had not happened; and yet everything was ours. Our bodies stuck at the frame of the page of the light where the flesh of all of us each instant shrunk and expanded overwritten overrun false with all absent language lorded between any way ever. Each word held a murder of its own; each death a death of all things and so now nothing. There was so much light coming from all the holes now I could hardly tell what parts of me were me and what was time, all stretching out forever over what had been once.

All I wanted was to love and to be loved. I wanted to feel us loved and go on in love again and have a spouse and child again in love in endless light in endless repetition beyond the shape of any home you made beyond our image, though here the light kept frying out and walls kept turning into mirrors and the floors harbored under floors, cold colors longer than the house is, any instant stretched to oldest tone. Here I wanted to exist in the rhythm of a stunning surface grown from no sleep in all our excess all beside you beyond blood. I wanted to be free and laugh like fire, to watch the edge of the earth expand so wide it killed the color of the void, carved a peace for us to spread our lives out warm in ancient fat and growing ages. I would have given anything to stand beside you. I would give you anything.

I raised my arms into the light. I did not have arms but I could feel them rubbing against everything they weren't. I heard me shouting long before the sound came. Each syllable stretched for longer than I could imagine ever existing. I opened my eyes over and again and each time saw the same long corridors of white against the white repeating nil.

Between each nil I lived forever. A century of centuries of summers in the bodies murmuring my head my head wide open with the faces, speech undone. Walls around us, light around us, above, below. Not in any place that had a name still, but simply *here*. In the end of asking, and of needing to be asked. The end of whatever you'd been waiting for forever in the long stand of electricity and putty. Wherever you could find a way.

Wherever we have been. In the end of commentary. The end of the end of anything we'd wished to conceive and not conclude. All those instants collected on the body of all of us and placed beneath us so that we could still walk and not need to remember we'd been deformed. With our tongues against the emblem, pupils swelled to fill out not only our whole eye, but the space beyond the eye. In the end of the out-of-frame, the end of seeing. The end of the pigment of our dreaming existing only forced encased.

Where all we wanted was to hold. In the end of shapes and endless endlessnesses. The end of something like falling through no hour. Here in the shower of all sound, wearing a skin made of the moment of eruption as our bodies finally gasped the dust out of the streets and stood up and bowed without an encore.

The end of will. In the end of needing form and fingers to exist beside the space you'd been forever and had suffered for to control, where when the lights come on in the house again we must swear we won't remember how anything at all between us has been amended before appearing. Blown out and blotted in the loveless marrow of the present.

FOUR *THE PART ABOUT AMERICA*

I opened my eyes inside no smoke. I was lying facedown again in the center of the floor inside a room of mirrors filled with bodies and their blood. I could not tell where one body ended and the next began.

The light was cold. No idea how long I'd been awake. I wore a kind of clothes not accustomed to the style that I remembered having. My nails were long, my stomach full, my arms all covered in tattoos. My hair had grown down past my ass.

The bodies smelled like life. From among them, there was a woman splayed beside me, pulled free from the pile. She had my mother's arms and neck and cheeks, and my wife's fingers and her forehead. Her eyes were sewn shut with blue wire.

In her arms, the woman held a child.

The child had no head. Where his head had been was gushing white shit. I had his head in my hands. The head was smiling. Where my fingers touched his skin they adhered, and when I could pull them away there were lesions on my flesh.

The child looked just like I remembered me. He wore a silver locket, as had I. Inside the locket, I remembered, was a photograph of god's face, what god had been, though now the locket would not open.

I set the head down. It fell through the floor instead of stopping, just like that, then it was gone. I looked at the remainder of the child. He had a new head. He looked like someone famous whose name eludes me. His new mouth was sewn shut with the same blue wire as the woman. His new eyes were wide. The eye meat had no pupils or irises, only white.

My fingerprints were all over everything, though my fingerprints are yours.

Beyond this room, the world awaited.

Into the new air now I wandered out of what we'd already been to what remained of what we were. In total death, at last, all bodies appeared stacked up neck-high across the landscape, dead as fuck. They clung blistered in the skin of millions, all of whom were also me. The curvature of the earth seemed to have flattened. Museums of intestines held corded around the glinting onslaught of trailer homes beaten with stones and fists and asses cleaved from other bodies and rendered weapons, scratching names into the paint, names no longer affixed to the bodies that had slurred from and laughed and made more in the image of our kind.

Flesh splayed and stacked in accidental floes. Brutal rainbow fauna choked by maggots fleeing the carcasses through mud veins in the chest of the earth risen to brush at white sky lathered dry and caked replicating on itself. Flakes of dry skin hung on overdeveloped air, rasping in the dimension where the arms of time sung fat with knots, to slow the lap of the ocean forced against the land mass with the bodies mottled in incandescence. Wasps knitted homes out of the refuse pillbox bodies and twining in the hair of no one growing. What old white light beat at the teeth of countless exterminated babies stung under sky incidentally conformed with coarse grooves the night would blow against ejecting sound, wishing it were anything else like words that would have emerged between the pure enamel before it fell out in the learning of how age sits upon us and licks our easy resin out of the head into the want of worship, commingling forever alone.

No matter knew no door. No echo sat where the hawks and crows dropped shit on the sternums held together as a forest, the hovered eyes knowing better and staying above ground looking for land to land on where there was something still remaining to be feared. The stink of the organs rose above the buildings of the people in a scarlet dome shimmering with spittle of condensation. Still pools of ideas in the long miles of the corridors of cells hidden forever and half unveiled wishing its surface something larger like a mall or a pavilion or a collection of hammers used to build something not of flesh beneath which the flesh might mimic sleep rather than the vast death cotillion inflicted fast upon it by our own hands inside any mind. The bodies removed of their emotions had been packed together into igloos, towers, bales. There was more space now than one might imagine all this time under our thumbs.

The remaining portion of the bodies lingered, tightened. The sun upon the skin continued to tan them like bitches. The phantoms of animals remained indexed to their locations, dogs in homes taking from the bowl left out in light or sniffing through broken glass to buildings full of food they might corral not even tasting. The dead were dead. Ribcages ripped clean of the casing of their bodies formed crowns upon slim structures of other bones, for no reason other than they did, the way love at last connects a person to a person, and the veil between the living and the dead grows ever thicker.

The body of the grade school teacher had been copulated upon in her last hour fourteen dozen times. This was well after the year of her having given in to a young man in a white room on a bed, the dress her mother had given her in celebration of a fruition of an idea about the celestial bodies written onto paper having been bestowed with the ornament of an award; in years to come thereafter she would not remember the ideas of or the presence of the award at all, its paper turning blackened in a drawer, the dress of purple cotton removed from her by the aged hands of the man old enough to be her father in theory, thirteen years as he was and therefore full of childcream the day she herself had become a child. He had handled her with care, as she would have liked to be handled in the hour of the parting of the flesh that would mark her in the experience of the mode of human replication, which through her flesh had made no sound. This was well after the years of other making in this practice in various campgrounds and hotels and bedrooms and cars and theaters and small places of the nature someone of the passion might have brought the flesh against their flesh in desire despite her practice in the method as a child of god; she loved and loved; she smelled of candles and of purpose; she had a nameless flower tattooed beneath her hair. This was as well after the year the friction-making had borne in her a son, who'd died thereafter, coming out into the name she'd given years back before any of the shapes of fornication; she had heard his name in her for many years; she would say it only once aloud in his presence before the blood matching the color of her blood already spread upon the table also burst from him. Since then she'd lived alone. She'd practiced herself into the mode of loving god even that much harder, for giving her the gift of sacrifice, as had he; in the night she could see the child above her anyhow, neither speaking, beyond the color of their eyes; each sleep cycle between them spent in these paused hours unrepeating, populated each with new instants, she knew, despite the way the nature of their seeing into one another did not change. Time could go on this way forever some nights; she'd lived inside some nights before him and before Him several hundred thousand years. She was thirty-two today, blind each minute to the waking hour beyond certain shapes of darkness in some darkness.

Such as: the men, of no particular coalition beyond local inhabitance, having shared the same streets and visions between them daily for many years in this American neighborhood named using the same letters as the blind mother's son's name had been inside its single iteration, fucked the mother turn by turn spurting whatever into wherever in a whitewalled blanket for the innards, to become, though without the shift of actual becoming, as there soon after too they each took turns eating inches from her body by knives and fistfuls, their eyes not on the mother but up at something else above them that had no color and no sound and filled the reflective surface of their pupils with what seemed simply more light and yet warmed nothing left inside them ever but in the mother's seeing gave them shape.

FLOOD: *Through the woman's eyes, I could hear Gravey. His voice buzzing with every human voice combined in every syllable, writing over any thought of my own I could have had then:* You could find an ending in any eye. I had learned this as a child when staring hard into the sunlight even so briefly and still it cut the meat out of my eyes, and wrapped around in my surroundings with its blackness, handcuffing my imagination. In the blindness there and then only had I learned to see the ways between the houses, between minds. Death at last was no longer an inevitability; it was the mass of the ground that we grew out of.

The body of the carpenter was found dismembered into five equal parts, divided in halves along the center of the sternum and halved again across the middle, and lopped off at the head. The head was gorged of its softer parts, the eyes, the lobes, the cheeks, the lips, the gathering beneath the chin. The face would be recognizable to the wife were she not also pulled apart. The mother's head was all intact except the hair, which had been shaved to match the balding father, with a ring of pubelike stragglers crowning the elongated cranial peak. An orange plastic stitching, rendered from cloth of stretchy sack designed for carrying potatoes, was used between the eight bodily sections of the two parents, lashing chest to chest and chest to chest and waist to waist and waist to waist, creating from the two previously independent parties a pair of hybrid halves. The genitals of the mother had been sewn shut on the side of the lower body that remains bearing the bits (her left); the genitals of the father had been removed, and buried with his left index finger beneath the land the home of the family lived inside, and grew together through years of light and pigment and dinners and language unto the day when the five children would take the parents clean apart. The coupled neutered bodies meshed lay head to head forming a flatline at the concrete mouth cupping the local street unto the home's stoop; the left and right arms of each of the prior bodies reach to cup the hand of the other arm on the other body to which they previously by flesh had been attached; the palms were cut open and sewn together, forming a circuit. The wedding rings had been switched. The mouth of the mother splayed open toward the sky as if in waiting for something to rain into them and be fed. In the concrete were scratched the initials of each of their children, along with a large blockade of tracing that to the parents had always looked like a picture of a sun rising over a large square pond. The concrete ended at the mouth of the house where the home had been burned to char against the ground. Cremains of the five children could be found strewn among the rubble, each demolished in kind one by one by age from oldest to youngest, knives, ropes, fists, vices, confounded in the remains of incineration of the pillows, place mats, clothing, photography, trash, uneaten food, books, dolls, board games, toothbrushes, chairs, mattresses, sofas, calendars, crib notes, new envelopes, desks, carpet, hair, in all a thick gray field visible from several hundred yards overhead. A corresponding oval of shared blood between the two parental torsos at the mouth of the ash field glistened even in the dark.

FLOOD: *The voice continued even when it wasn't speaking, I could not stop it. It was becoming hard to hear my own, or to feel where in his body I was at all besides as interruption:* This whole world of the living was so shrill. How could you be sure any moment you'd believed you'd been alive and living you weren't looking head-on into a mirror? How do you know you weren't being recorded, or that you yourself weren't a recording? There's no one left but me to let you know. I who had been always by your side, always just beneath you and behind you and within you.

The body of the homemaker was blue, beaten to mush. In each room of the house she had a body she hoped would continue growing even during days where she was concerned with her image and so out loud wished to lose the weight. Each day depended on their staying alive. The son who would go through the day inside a vehicle among other vehicles piloted on whim and gasoline. The daughter who would walk among men and women who all had eyes and access to knives and a will to act in any minute. The father had a brain with thoughts that flashed like little cities winking on and off in darkness, perhaps the idea of stroking something or eating something or beating something; the world depended in some way on every ion of him not going haywire any day, even in the smallest acts, i.e. gently stroking his left or right hand just so much in one direction either way while driving on a highway by or not by direct intention, the resulting clash of machines taking someone we knew and loved and changing our lives like bread into an oven to be eaten by someone we knew nothing of or maybe thought we did. The color of the homemaker's hair could change at will by her hand or on its own in time because god is all things, she believed. God's power has no bounds, she'd say inside herself and at certain times aloud, though perhaps not in the presence of the bodies that had bred in her the love that made her want. If god wants to kill me today there is a reason, she would go on. If god wants to have someone write a book in which I am being inadequately described as a fraction of a person existing perhaps in countless bodies, who has already been killed by someone else, if for no other reason than boredom, or his own fury or sadness, so be it; this is god's will also. What if I don't believe in god, she'd ask herself some nights under quilts and covers wrapped in the white wire blankets in the room of the house surrounded by the world lit only by sight and sound and touch, the senses, which could be so easily removed. What if I think I believe in him but I don't believe in him really and he knows I don't and can smell it even though I can't because he is a greater force and can smell the real thing, why am I thinking this even, I wish I did not have to think, thinking kills the light out of me, it kills my light out, and any thought will only be profane, and profane isn't even a word or concept that I value but I still believe that we as humans are in trouble and yet I go on and I believe and I act and I make and I cook and I wash and I want and I learn and I make and I continue forth in the effervescent mash of the human spirit surrounding any intention even the blackest even the illest even those who would say the darkness is all around because really in darkness the greatest gift might be born and in embracing the blackest of our sides we are alive even in death we would be alive, I think, and regardless or not if I believe and regardless or not if my belief is being considered or judged or reflected or compressed in the moment of some something above the minute I will imagine right now that time goes on forever and in going on forever does not exist and so to embrace nothing is a kiss of god and to die is a kiss of god and to not die yet is a kiss of god and to not realize I have died is a kiss of god and to be even silent underground or bloody open underneath the veil of sky is the kiss of god, even those who do not believe in god will be kissed by him the way they walk through air and go to dinner and hear songs and take on vision even blind or deaf even in America even today with the knife so at our throats as it has always been by our hands, the hand of god in any body, the hand of god again, the sight.

FLOOD: *With each word I could less and less tell my body from any other cadaver; in each, the voice again there melded to my blood:* Each time a room is photographed, it doubles. The same with people, and their mortality. In our total human death, all hours compile unframed with every possibility of what we felt we knew or wanted. As soon as this could have been true, it always was.

The body of the mime cannot be found. It had been consumed all parts and portions from the brush of flesh over his face to the thin rinds between his smallest two toes and his gonads. His flesh was found to taste like grapefruit peeled and doused with lighter fluid and rolled into a market aisle gathering dirt and silence as shoppers might have passed placing canned peas and syrup in their carts with their eyes anywhere but down. The rough lining around the muscle was melted under flamethrower and used to tease the dogs who would run from the stench of it into a deep woods; then the men, who'd never meant to feed the dogs with this gray meat regardless, could chew and choke themselves and taste the silence where words pocked into the mashy pockets of the brain and down the fingers of a man suffused with light from machine screen and buzzing bells reminding human contact and the words that time had altered in their unpresuming meaning beforehand as he placed his fingers on the buttons to again be misread by whomever beyond his own misreading as should all things be until they no longer are. The blood would be drunk by mouths put to the pumping spigot of the flesh or it would be washed into the earth. The bones from there fashioned into weapons that could then be used to strike further bodies of their blood and cells, begetting more meat, begetting weapons in the act of debegetting else; what vocabulary swatted cold inside his skull of teeth and gums, among blood bubble and scraping brain putty; what has never been a word, and would never be a word again; what ash. The skull was ground to powder and snorted in pursuit of some fried high, which truly would find its function in the disassemblers' bloodstreams centered at the moon's spin like chambers in a gun around the bullet of America giving itself again unto itself again with gifts for our last birthday one last time while the hour struck the name of the year inside us unrepeating and the arms were fine and glasses raised and promises repeated and mouth to mouth and singing zero.

FLOOD: *My sight was voice and voice was sight; my mind was nothing beyond what came across it:* These corpses are the filaments of our cells. Their destroyed memories are our blood. They speak forever now in colored shafts inside the head wound of the ground where grass must grow. For each body, think of all that had touched them, come forth from them, depended on them. Think of all that had been rendered in their meat. Now think of a stairwell with each step flattened out so wide it covers everything and all directions. Now climb in silence.

Moving among the bodies, holding their era, made me come awake inside my own shape over and over, full of pleasure to find them waiting. Each inch filled me that much brighter than the last. I was not embarrassed about what any of us had done, nor ashamed, nor sad, nor hopeless. It felt like waking up in different worlds second to second.

In the eyes of each of the gone people I could read their days—who they were and what they had been and done and did and would have had they not been killed and ended. Their faces showed exactly who they were, plain on the skin they wore as it degraded. In single fingernails I saw the color I needed to believe that anyone was somewhere and so could continue walking, as otherwise their beauty in death would lay me down. I wanted to lie down in every instant. I wanted to sink into the earth, the skin and meat of it. My clothes had become so see-through from my trembling and the false sweat that I was naked. The breeze of life blew through my hair. The light was taking pictures. It ate the pictures. It shat the pictures out and glowed. From the glowing new houses rose up behind me; I could hear them, but I was not allowed to look. My head would not turn, nor my torso.

My erection led me on. My spindly labia led me on. My undeveloped pubis led me on. My lifetime led forever forward. The ash left trails that blew away.

Our architectures had already forgotten us. The curve of concrete into metal plane against red brick wired together through and through the airspace lapped with glass and wood and bone sung no album against the unbreathed air squelching vast gap where speech had beaten at it daily; no thumb or nail to scratch its shape again but the wind and drip of its own cover over all. The earth was hollow with all our corridors through dark dirt of transit at last unburdened of the endless ramming and given time alone. Grass and foliage wrote itself over the surfaces we'd conditioned in our image without our image in them. All the eyes who could not see at last made open.

Always the silence moved beside me. It fell between the people, conducted among friction with the contours of their torsos and their necks and thighs. They would not look me in the eye; their gaze always aimed as if in taking but just slightly off, feathered instead wholly, stilly toward the flatness above. These people had had many names, some hundreds of them, names for nowhere, though none of these words would appear inside my vocabulary. They were anybody. Their arms were burned and scored with patchy lacerations, as if by years of being copied on the air, whirring with the dream of dynasty and orgasm.

I did not look back. The silence pulled me like a rope wrapped warm to tie around my neck. Where I tried to think or speak, the stars winked out in ricochet, falling from heaven's meat clinging to no bones wrapped around this hemisphere. The stars had names, too, but we'd gotten every one of them wrong; in falling they screamed the name inside the silence wrapped around us and streaked the black with black again from tar and burned to ash before they hit the ground. The ash rained and rained in warbled strobe to stick against my cheeks and hair. It gave me new skin.

I loved the composition of the silence. I had gone nowhere. I closed my eyes. It was so black in there, it wasn't even black. It was like a room with countless mirrors and all the lights turned on and aimed into them now so bright the colors come alive and eat into your face into your brain into a black so black it begins to seem that you are actually alive and that each instant you have lived has not only brought you to where you are now but has in bringing brought us all.

The body of the masseuse believed she lived unending, struck in the temple with the blow of the fist at the moment incanting in her head the wish for replication of self beyond the moment of making, pushing through herself the idea she could in god's name go on forever if the wish grew strong enough and in her in the biblical sense of aging to ages in the high hundreds for centuries of waiting speaking being closer still to god. The function of bone through flesh through flesh on bone again knocked the color of the thought into her whole hard whitely, masking up in blood as salad dressing barfs its way through sinky murk. Curls of the thought lashed upon corridors of cells the brain wished to carry on inside of and struck there paused as by machine she could live inside her and go on and live inside her and go on with the teeth of the child she would never bear masked in the fat around her gut unmoving in the want of search of semen to impregnate the cycle of the moon's egg she'd been desisting upon with pills in cycled practice since the blood first poured from the white cup in her heart undying and sometimes out in such force upon the padding in the seat cushions of the sofas she would fall asleep on before the TV with the blue glow of no screened communication between other machines glowing the room into a womb for her to wait in god's name to wait for god to become god's last and needing bride she believed to bring the son again to earth to lash the son here to the earth as had the book said but in the magic of distinctive pro-nouncement through her body rather than fluttering from sky; she would be the Mother of the gift of revelation to the choirs and vans and towering buildings of the city in her century she swore while the pill kept out the wet of the other father sacrificing as well something in his whole life to become closer to her in the spirit of the animalian wish for god he swore off screaming over the mashed potatoes and frozen pizza at the dinner table each night that god had forgotten and would not come again and not into this house and not for any and the sky would burn in fire for the moon before a jesus of the nature scrolled upon in ancient books would be again given to us as a people for we were people crushed into infinite recursion on a model of shitstorm centuries and rapefuck, he screamed, he screamed blue in the face, he screamed with both fists raised above the dinner table, though she knew, the masseuse, her hands worked in the fields of flesh that came unto her in the glove of night to be worked of stress of daily nattering and basking and drinking and heaving and working, as she hamslammed out the passion of her waiting for the Father above the father to come into her and come all through her and fill her with the sand of the child of the centuries who would take her human father and gnash him teeth by teeth before the animals in an example of the screech of fornication without promise without gift in the stroke of ego of making as he had, a child, and as he had, words outside the word of god, and the song of god would pour out from her in the birthing as the night strobed against her with its silence and unknowing, a human song so innate it could be heard in any singing they had given all these years, all these recordings, all the chewing of the food, it could be heard in every body and only by every body all at once for it was in the people that the song flew and only the song of god compared and she knew this had to come only by their killing, their bodies struck wide open in the daylight at their own hands knowing what was wider than the sky already in the back of their heads as they could not sleep or thought they could in the beds where ticks and sweat eons curdled in the coils of springs and rubber they forked down money for so as to not sleep close to the earth, as inside there too the sound, and the sound forever in the dead years everlasting until it did not at all and could not go on in the face of the fists of children beating teeth from their parents in the name of a word that seemed like someone else but yes was god and god was the sound and the song and the flesh and the killing and the name and the word and the buildings and skin of us and the life of us and the speech and the typing and the fingers up the holes and the holes itself and the nothing itself and the waiting and the want and the rapefuck yes too that was god too how could it not be she would squeal with the wet still pouring out of her inside the hour waiting and the wet then pouring out of her inside a light as the men yes came in his image yes to denude her before the horses they had ridden up on in the image of the ancient book to scream her name in the name of all their names at once together laughing and she would not look away she could see even in the human fecal fuckforce of the big blue cock of the incubating aimless fury stretching the murderers' faces as they peeled her open ripped her wider did her in, rubbing hot froth and endless gnashing in the hole where the god would come into her and make the seedling this was god now yes this was god he was going to burst, and the men did too, and they took turns, and the come was washing out, and it was god's come, it had to be god's come, and so inside her the child, and so she would die, and so she would live forever on in the making of the child frozen in the bloodstream passion altar and you could see it in her eyes and you could see it in the archmeat where after having raped and burst her womb and scratched her lenses the men had dug into the flesh with their white swords and in the flesh they'd found her backbone curved from stooping in the house of man these years in waiting and they had pulled the backbone out and looked upon it in the bloodbath and the wishing under the color of the sunning eye.

FLOOD: *In these elapsed eyes now I could hear nothing, grinding on nothing, louder than life.*

The body of the actor had been strewn across the land. His organs were removed one by one from his body and not tasted for fear of what has gathered through years of being shot by cameras and then through the cities on the air, the replications of his image sent through homes and wires and on discs and drives and printed onto paper and surfaces and dimensions and printed onto cells in such syndicated aggregation there is no center and no star. The actor's spleen has been placed into a small glass cage and displayed under synthetic yellow light, prodded at by mushy fingers in the waiting space of a long hall now destroyed. The actor's gallbladder has been spread thin and refashioned into a garment draped around the surrounding landscape of his birthplace as far as it could cover, which is not far. The actor's ureters and the fleshy sacs attached thereto have been placed into the sockets of the eyes of another well-known actor with exciting teeth and medium-sized cock; the configuration is shot on digital video and edited with seven tracks of varying cartoon music, symphony, black metal, banjo, then uploaded to a file-sharing server under the name of a once-popular teen heartthrob mp3 anthem machine, spreading in the final hours of the American breathing conglomerate a facefucking of the beloved by the beloved. The actor's lungs have been rendered into cream and smeared across the long bow of one of several dozen high white crosses done up in the center of a field, where many several other hundred had been done in matching fashion in the name of pleasure. The actor's pancreas was placed plainly on a white breakfast table with blue flowers and a blank ream of white paper. The actor's rectum ejects prayer. The actor's eye turned inward in the skull socket to face what for years had clawed behind it dying.

The body of the artist lay half buried with her face and right fist under moss. The skin along her back has been removed, replacing the stretch between her shoulder blades where before there'd been a tattoo of a blue tree. The mother's fingernails are pink, done fresh for her attendance of the wedding of her sister to a man she'd never met. She believed in the love of the two people despite knowing nothing of them, even her sister; so many years had passed between their taking turns combing each other's hair under the white blanket in the field pretending to be nowhere near their home. She'd not been able to go sleep out there in the field that night, hearing the moving tubers in the ground, the oncoming piddled rush of liquid between dirt somewhere beneath them. She watched her sister's face croon in its sleep. Of all the days, that would be the one she most remembered, despite whatever else of her own life: the coming of the child; the spheres of sky forever counted in endless days unrepeating for form and color despite the constancy of their return; the fission of any word. Her child, before he had been ended in his own rite, had murdered forty-seven bodies, in the service, with a baton. Her face pressed in the soil left fully naked to the white sun overhead sees nothing beyond the mush upon the stone.

The body of the surgeon has sewn her whole self shut. With a thread colored in the same hue as her hair she rendered seamless her eyeholes, nostrils, mouth. Her ears have been tucked over and sewn to crude pods that seem to want to bloom. Her asshole and vagina have been sealed. Here, in distension, a kind of gathering of released fluids has swollen her abdomen and belly bubbly with something opened up inside of her. The crude gash strikes of the stitching have in some places caused in operation further gash holes that then she therefore had to seal again, working fevered, seeing several of herself. She would not be entered. She would not exit. She would exist without form, she wished. With the same hands prior, she'd sewn shut both her daughter and her son, whose heights against the back door of the bedroom where she'd locked them in to hide them from the world show they had both grown several inches in the past year, shooting up toward some wished distance only remaining between their temples and the sky.

The bodies of the seventeen young pregnant mothers were all hung in a birch tree by their hair. Their clothes have been removed to show the rounding of their bellies, arranged in order from the flattest to the most ready to burst. The mothers' eyelids have been removed to match the clothes. Around their fore-heads, crowns of wire pulled from machines in neon colors pink yellow blue gray maroon gold. The mothers' gristle groaning ham stench. The names of each child are stitched inside the bellies, all the same name, with red thread above their navels, the end and beginning of the thread continuing from where it ends emerging from each mother's skin unto the body before and after in the round, forming a circuit without power.

The body of the child is glimmer white. He was not old enough yet to have seen a horse or held an egg. Along the inside of the flap of meat where the chest has been slid open, a series of impressions in the folding appear to mimic a crude language scribbled with a heated iron bit. Had he grown to age thirty-seven the child would have cured the common cold. He would have lived without a wife or child and learned to cook from a machine. He would have loved his life. In the wormhole of the air not gone forward through by his flesh in propagation there is a ridge formed to the light, into which a ream of seeing might sink and become butter and make the grease from which would rise another hour vibrating hard and fast against where right now, seated in your room reading, your body waits, in seeing. This could be said of any day.

The body of this member of the congregation was clawed apart like trash.

The body of this Boy Scout was peeled neatly and hung as shades for windows in a house.

The body of this daughter was struck from a large distance apart by something unseen.

The body of this beggar held up longer than most would under the knives.

The body of this butcher began to masturbate just before it could expire, desperate to feel anything again before it couldn't.

The body of this body had already been reduced in life to an immobile thing, unconscious, shitting itself alone in rooms it could not tell from food or laundry.

The body of this author was brought to an end in exactly the manner he'd described after completing writing a fictional description of his own death.

The body of the reader felt itself still reading. Miles and miles of lines like this in no imagination or remorse.

The bodies free of their bliss and wind and wonder.

Bodies piling up or disappearing into weather or digestion or being compacted by machines brought online to do the work of humans or ripped apart by birds caught in the bloodlust of the human spirit replicating to reenact its own demise in repetition.

Bodies called to give their color to the night, in soil ecstatic with our blood without us, human mud becoming sucked into the fundament.

Here is the body of the long old spirit beaten holey by heads of hammers in the hands of children thrown to dust and screeching in their bloodstreams and wanting nothing more than the end of the sun brought on forever blanketing the ground in nowhere.

Here is a skull against which light would purr and stroke its sound out in echo of the banging bone on bone filling the hour slick enough to not remember.

Here is the body of whoever.

FLOOD: *The light was bending back against itself, accelerating. It kept opening before me, like a tunnel inside-out, leaving less of me to see there with each impression. Or this was happening again and had never happened. Or the brain would shrivel inside the endless air of all our time blown wide. Or I am a map of all the days we have not spent and never will be spent. Or I am right here in a way I can't even operate, some kind of god inside a god. What would be the difference in any of these definitions. How could it not be always all of them at once.*

Alone with each face along the flesh mosaic in all directions I spent an eternity called a life. Each life in this manner passed in the duration it would have liked to, which ranged from no seconds to the end of the end, and beyond the end of the end for some. I aged accordingly for each person by gaining one darker dot along my outline's lip or chin or arm, a flux of pigment I could not feel the ages aggregating in me, even with thousands gathered, as with the passing complexion of my skin so passed the remembrance of the condition it had held just prior to the current state, therefore maintaining my fragile balance in the harbor of being forever at the present stitch in skin oncoming in the skin. A version of who I'd been the year before this condition had approached perhaps had felt or could feel the brush of what would come to pass soon in the world against his nape and called it wind or premonition. And so.

The world around me writhed beyond its posture. Even clear as I felt now, I'd yet to realize where the mask of who we were once grew thinner with every passing stroke, shedding every wish into the mud into the dirt sinking beneath me all around while through my sight I tried to carry on my way.

The memory of our blood rained through and through upon the light beyond all seeing. And the blood lapped at the faces turning to sand again beneath my feet. And the day was silent without solitude. I was no longer anyone, like you. I had nowhere to be and nothing to speak for. I stood among the dead and was surrounded and I could not breathe, and I was breathing and my eyes stung and the wind was hot and still and the my mind was cold, and I wanted only to feel nearer to the ground, nearer to anybody I'd not known among the nothing covered over, and into the soft sod of mush selves I knelt and spread out and lay down, and as I closed my eyes my eyes stayed open.

Tonight or now was any destination. All points within me touched all points. The map of day was gnawing in my chest, the book of every person.

My skin was three hundred million measures long. I was so obese, wrapped into a small torso and series of appendages humming with eternity, while overhead the pumping conglomerates of black fission squirted in silence through discolor. This same sky had been above us every hour, absorbing our image into pigment, into our only voice.

I was breathing, yes, but it was not air, and hair was growing and I was hungry, but for nothing. My ears were stuffed full with old sound I always remembered and now could not count, its absence overlaid into the system of the image over which I had no control. Or it was like I had a choice but had no choice.

Behind the flattened light, the curve of all our space looked on. I could feel the compression of the dead in every beam no matter how blank. Their dreams in absence of individual mobility rasped whiter than white was when I understood what white was. Every idea of god in them cloaked as pale-eyed as the heavens.

My heart was full of every history anyone had believed we'd all be carried on in.

FLOOD: *The breadth beyond death opened inside me. I was walking on the face of the narration of the light. I could see the shape of the earth beneath my vision spinning the land to show its several faces caved in one place, though each face looked the same. There was a light rind of skin growing over all things, over any recognition, every thought. I heard my own idea of right now explode out through the back hatch of my head. The sound came in all down around me. I felt someone take me by the hand.*

Through the dark of the breath of dead in me, our exhausted phantom history rose. It already knew it would not survive itself and did not wish to. It had nothing else to speak, no grace beyond a final iteration flashed into the gap between what had been and what would become. Against my mind it beat the blue of purple from the black of gold and laughed and lay down through and through me as layers on the layers being granulated for a lens with which to let the light queue into and derivate its shafts consumed in shafts reconsecrated upon the corridor of possible lives. This book of all our lives had already been written in our death upon the page of landscapes where the organisms burned and woke in whorls laid on the fingers where the book had been before and would be again: in resin sunned the fingers in our fingers fucked the fingers we had thought most ours and spread them white upon the beaches in the blood among us and let them bake regurgitated in low coils to call the fish and phantom schools up from the wet of which we'd been robbed and relocated in the curd mold of the waves steered by the moon to know what anyone would look at anytime thus leaving the star as plain as any day among the days where water rose and fell and rose again and fell again and was the water in our bodies and our mouths and lubes and liquors' lubes and baby fodder and so on unseen before the beaches' sand the bodies walked on upon the bodies right before the eyes as eyes would turn in swarm of looking fast into the shadow laid upon us ever shifting as if meaning to reanimate the leather from the bead but only ever making glass, only ever thickening the soles with which the bodies meandered and curved and saw what they had done in the images of what they could not see that they had done swelling and negating as the moon pulled back and forth upon the skin of it and lap of it where even animals could swim and sink and live and shit and eat their shit again and go on in silent provocation as in the image of a bed on which we lay and waited to be entered or forgiven or at least allowed to close the eyes and walk again into the image the machines kept stealing as we tried again to burn it through the folding layers as we tried to get the word as only it could be forever on inside itself the word falsed into shapes of other words wrapped and beating each other's asses in commiseration that really did on occasion make us weep on knees or asses or backs beneath the ceiling beneath the sky silently branded with the wished images in any mind blown raining each in collaboration like symbols in the sky as lost as night and forced in our tongues to go on these un-done years in other guise as we had as had our children as we would inside those books in myths called characters in films in machines again called actors in songs called sound. As the myths and sounds became our history, a white dust upward through which the emissions could emit and names could go on bouncing in trauma paths around the mansion of the ideas set on the air and moaned again drawing us in them as our blood begat our blood, even having crashed the dream of murder hard against a stupid tree grown out of food the blood poured strong and silent like a pirate through the cities without our bodies even there and as the silence laughed it knew our murder would be as paltry as another disc, as any verb, as any casual human opening a paper in no sunlight while the machines glowed and wives or husbands crawled along the floor praying in the temple of memory to be jacked off forever in the name of marriage and wishing hard to be a pustule on the dark part of totality, the blue of bedrooms crusting over with the sons and daughters also praying in the same words and the papers glowing with the promise and the making and in the cell the singers ever ringing all their teeth out through their eyes.

I found I could not speak surrounded in us. I could not think or feel or hear anything among the unending shrieking veils of sand. But I was in here, pressed against anything we'd witnessed. So many days had passed this way, where what had happened to me had happened to you too and seemed to happen regardless of whether we did the things we believed we did or not. And yet still as I felt each perspective passing through me, I knew it was the last, as where it touched me every cell burst into nameless burning.

God began again inside the burning as I watched. For each of the unbelieving bodies splayed up rotting in persistence, he made a mark upon his flesh. The first mark bore the shape of a circle, an unbreaking pact made with itself; the band of the clasp of the circle walked forever in the furrows of sand that would become the bodies of our bodies in the years before the years; from the sand the sound would form dimensionless, to be demented in man's image, and so from the symbol of the circle every other symbol fell. There were the urges and the bees who stung the urges in us. There were the numbers and acolytes of hope and certain gestures grafted into the limbs of us by fright. There was nothing to fear so we feared the nothing. The heat of the breath of god formed the spaces among the fibers for the sicknesses to dwell in. Each time the day began again, a new great sickness. The dreams placed in our teeth supplied a yearning for communication and definition crowded in among what must have been our eyes. Around the eyes arose the lungs, nose, nostrils, cheeks, aorta, gonads, urethral lips, large intestines, small intestines, thumbs, as well as the anatomies forever cursed by lightning where black refracted in the corridors of the house of god's black mind, begetting spleen, gallbladder, ureter, lung, pancreas, rectum, each of which would teach itself to swim wide in the chosen moments while the body lay upon its back. Having been given flesh, then, the urges returned and overtook us and filled us with their speech; inside our shapes was placed a strobing that bore the mark of the endless death soon to be made witness unto us as soon as we realized we'd appeared here in the world at once always both alone and not alone, so that we'd never shake the wish both to be and kill our own creator.

Out of the burning, land is born. The land is vivisected, given new names, which all are the same name again, with many different ways to say it. Weather stirs the dirt and water into lather that dictates certain corridors the way that air alone once had been meant to. Between the corridors we make our homes, confining light in ways among which we can sleep. Each motion takes us further on toward its own ending.

There is that which cannot be seen. Houses in the name of god are built with colored glass and high ceilings and the long pews and the cash plates and the casks of water and the blood and the body and the pipe organ and the restrooms and the books. Here a language will be spoken, the word after the word. With one's head against the wood in the right condition with the head aimed and open to the sun and charcoal underneath the building and the correct cluster of buttons pressed hard inside the head and a draft of cold air for several sleepings and hours under water, one might hear the words as they all are: the name repeated, the name repeated.

Every name is given a new name. It does not matter what the name is. In the reiteration of each whichever, we hear the damage rendered as new words. We hear the echo of the bodies of the prior iteration of the hour in the rising acts of evisceration, iteration. We hear us lying on our backs in the cornfields under a white sky being cannibalized outside the black house of the scene of the crime inside this book which must only go on forever in its own presence in its instance of the past and yet also so again and so must become silence must become and through which we go on. We wear the void plain on our face all waking hours already knowing, and so clothing, makeup, colors, mirrors, walls.

Death feeds itself already with our phantoms, the daily killings we have yet to take form to commit. Early infanticides and hyperventilating sermon are pummeled out with stone on stone between the making where in the last hours the dying president had stood and sworn in tongues in the thronelight already burning mirrored above and below our chorus and what else. And where god stood strobing before a marked door in a machine and farted through the word of words snatched from the mass of confetti blood pouring eternally in the pilgrimages where our death Worship made and sold our organs into slavery for the Nth time and gnashed us bit from bit along the ridged backbone neoning beneath the trammeled cistern pouring blood back into the blood all black inside every father of the child aping cold prayer service behind the steering wheels of cars and in the hair of horses and in the teeth of pets and in the eye of the coin stamped with the false image of our eye.

The cities box themselves in wallwise, already folded with the magma still in swill beneath where here we were again with he among us and he within us. Each new ending wrote itself over the last, always beginning already again before it could, the copies clogging up like water gnashing around a hole in the floor of the ocean beneath the putty mirror marker disrupting boats and knocking white planes out of blue skies downward to crest into the mapmash of this blood foam lubing up the face of the ocean to mirror the mirror again back at itself squealing the death jokes on a gray stage underneath yellow headlamps in green boxes in the pink belly of the worship we wrapped around each old gold city shit upon from birds white as the eye purple as the eye brown as the eye clear as the eye inside the eye, and where in vast collaboration more cogs catch and flip and shiver bronzed between each other turning milk out of the retch, caught in flesh flasks unto the body of god already whored into a dome, god on god now rising fast and fresh around America in snaking portraits called museums called beautiful evenings called new food, its whipping weight peeling high along the unseen ceiling so bunched double that the future too is pulled, drafted like icons obscuring even the wish of television in our heart, gnarling the dream seed even as it rises and shapes in pleasure caked in objects like a rash, whirring hot to open sores so tiny they could not be sniffed by the promise of our children having children. And so the coming comes again bearing the deadliest birthmark underneath prismatic post-god scrim, while yes, thank god we scream saying the name again the wrong way, thank god, there is a new day, here I am.

The years go on in sevens. Each of the years is its own veil, surrounded by each person's private birthplace in all minds. The names of the colonies and states seem imbued with past days each in their own way, fat full of exit language that on our lips all make the same shape. We worship light in Smexas, New Xork, Cruxisim. We worship in harbors, getting haircuts, growing fat. These are the names of god not god. Our history is overrun already with commercial demand, and demand for demand, which means we put the butter in the freezer and the ice cream in the cupboard, believing this is correct, and never knowing any different. We turn on the water in the sink at the faucet to watch it run and are surprised when it is cold and we try to answer the phone but it keeps ringing though we are speaking into the mouthpiece saying hello hello hello hello hello and the words do not exist and then we shit our pants again and cannot feel it and the history goes on.

You already know about the wars. You know about the lengths of leg and laughter that rolls from the holes we had been given and woke again in new shapes each day to wrap around the air between the pillars of the house that squeezes itself in pockets of our fat. Each house is the same house and knows all colors secreted together into mirrors. The singing is not songs, but a certain form of itching that crawls along our spines and jellies and makes along the sky appear the moons, the eyes of long dead light arriving. Each instant holds more work than any one cell could hold through any other instant. In this way we repeat even our present moments. We build the boxes and the homes again and again as has been told, while waiting through any instant for any ending. No one word or face or image can hold the center, and so without center, we reflect. This happens every instant every hour. Where we walk is where our killer awaits us. It feels good to be wanted. We watch the killer writhe inside his wishing to kill and kill and kill again, the singing taking shape inside the killer's body as thunder, sunshine, writing, by which we learn to plan our days. This is our history, we imagine, language buried in a song no one is hearing. Each sentence thought or spoken indicates the coming birth and death of thousands.

We count upon our hands the gold. We elect bodies to edict above our bodies. Numbers become counted, tallied, praised. Days each day feel the same with slightly different skin. We remember the story of the birth of Christ, of erosion, of the barbarism of the land, relayed by people repeating words inside words; the words change shape each year. It's impossible at all to remember any of it more than in short life shifts, as we've been slaughtered, sautéed, saladed again, so continuously it feels like progress.

There is a catalog of vast delight. We've been murdered, but we're inventing! We make more locks to fit with keys, taking photographs to deform the light with what we might remind ourselves we know, and what we looked like then, and who stood by us, and anything at all. It's not a dream we're dreaming; it is us.

We invent swim fins. We invent the octant and the stove. We invent mail order, the lightning rod, the catheter; we invent the swivel chair, the flatboat, bifocals, the automatic flour mill. We have held these things before. They take shape around our bodies. We invent the cracker, the cotton gin, the wheel cipher, the fireplace, the suspension bridge, the hydrant, the amphibious vehicle, refrigeration, percolation, the lobster trap, the circular saw. These are American creations. It's another new beginning. We are Americans again, filling ourselves again into where we were or are again or will be or want to or want to want to or will or were. We invent dental floss, the milling machine, the lathe, the detachable collar, the graham cracker, the platform scale, the electric doorbell, the machine reaper, Morse code, the sewing machine, the threshing machine, the combine harvester, the steam shovel, the wrench, the solar compass, the circuit breaker and the relay there between. Each day is less a day of ours. Each day is a day. We invent the self-polishing steel plow, the corn shelter, the sleeping car, vulcanized rubber, anesthesia, the grain elevator, the ice cream maker, the evaporator, the printing press, the tape primer, the baseball, holding on tight to our eyes; the printing telegraph, the doughnut, the safety pin, the gas mask, the inverted microscope; Herman Melville publishes *Moby-Dick*; the fire alarm, the elevator brake, potato chips, the clothespin, the breast pump, condensed milk, we will relearn to feed our child; toilet paper, pepper shaker, monkey wrench, and mason jar; ironing board, twine knotter, burglar alarm; escalator, vacuum cleaner, repeating rifle, the twist drill; postcard, pin tumbler lock, machine gun, the enclosing surface of the home; Henry Howard Holmes kills at least twenty-seven bodies; breakfast cereal, ratchet wrench, roller skates, spar torpedo, cowboy hat, urinal, chuckwagon, motorcycle, paper clip; barbed wire, ticker tape, water-tube boiler, refrigerator car, paper bag, tape measure, vibrator, American football, the pipe wrench, the clothes hanger, the can opener, sandblasting, the mixer, the diner, the railway air brake, jeans, the knuckle coupler, earmuffs, the fire sprinkler, ice cream soda, the quadruplex telegraph, QWERTY keyboards, the dental drill, the mimeograph, the synthesizer, the airbrush, the tattoo machine, the phonograph, district heating, the carbon microphone, the free jet water turbine, the bolometer, the cash register, the oil burner, candlepin bowling, the electric chair, the electric dead; the metal detector, the electric iron, Christmas lights, the electric fan, the solar cell, the thermostat, the dissolvable pill; do you want me to keep going, do you love me, are you inside me, are you mine; you must keep up; we invent the lap steel guitar, the popcorn machine, photographic film, the skyscraper, fuel dispenser, dishwasher, filing cabinet, telephone directory, slot machine, softball, gramophone, comptometer, AC motor, kinetoscope, trolley pole, drinking straw, stepping switch, revolving door, payphone, the stop sign, the tabulating machine, the smoke detector, the jackhammer, the Ferris wheel, the Tesla coil, the zipper, the bottle cap, the dimmer, the tractor, laxative, radio, mousetrap, volleyball, comic strip, cotton candy, muffler, charcoal briquette, remote control, semiautomatic shotgun, hairbrush, filing cabinet, flashlamp, and the century ends, this ends the century, the next century begins, this begins the century; we invent the thumbtack key punch assembly line Jane Toppan kills at least thirty-one safety razor radio direction finder hearing aid postage meter teddy bear periscope airconditioning tea bag offset printing press airplane windshield wipers baler automatic transmission AC power plugs batting helmet architectural acoustics fly swatter ice pop paper towel electric washing machine electric mixer Skee-Ball paper shredder suppressor gin rummy headset binder clip automobile self-starter road surface marking autopilot fast food restaurant electric blanket electric traffic light traffic cone fortune cookie skeet shooting supermarket cloverleaf exchange where the fuck are the bodies tow truck condenser microphone the bodies the bodies the toggle light switch the killer's arm stream cipher superheterodyne receiver hydraulic brake blender pneumoencephalography silica gel pop-up toaster Albert Fish kills at least five and maybe more than one hundred jungle gym garage door flowchart bodies adhesive bandage bodies water skiing radial arm saw bulldozer bodies masking tape Reuben sandwich Gertrude Stein publishes *The Making of Americans* Tilt-A-Whirl killer cotton swab America fucked in America instant camera gas chamber execution Moviola garage door opener power steering drive-thru liquid-fuel rocket bread slicer jukebox garbage disposal where are the bodies negative feedback amplifier recliner ice cube tray this is America bubble gum this is a list of holy wars wars inside the bodies for the bodies in the name of the name of names electric razor iron lung air traffic control Freon tampon applicator flight simulator sunglasses frozen food particle accelerator car audio Carl Panzram kills at least twenty-one and sodomizes at least a thousand runway lighting the bathysphere chocolate chip cookie electric guitar strobe light golf cart we have not yet learned quite how to kill radio telescope tape dispenser drive-in theater impact sprinkler trampoline Richter scale franchising black light parking meter surfboard fin pH EEG topography stock car racing programming language the bodies in the head the chairlift bass guitar photosensitive glass digital computer shopping cart blood bank cyclamate beach ball fiberglass xerography nylon Teflon soft-serve yield sign VU vocoder deodorant acrylic fiber corn dog napalm killkillkill microwave oven cruise control chemotherapy William Heirens kills at least three bodies DEET diaper proton therapy cloud seeding transistor Ed Gein kills at least fifteen women defibrillator acrylic paint supersonic aircraft hair spray windsurfing cat litter video games cable TV flying disk carbon dating airsickness bag atomic clock crash test dummy artificial snow credit cards leaf blower cooler wetsuit correction fluid airbag polio vaccine barcode artificial heart Apgar Wiffle ball TV dinner automatic door synthetic diamond radar gun nuclear submarine William Gaddis publishes *The Recognitions* hard disk OS wireless microphone laser sugar packet bubble packing carbon fiber integrated circuit fusor weather satellite spandex artificial turf magnetic stripe card global navigation the pill spreadsheet wearable computer biofeedback light-emitting diode jet injector glucose meter computer mouse lung transplantation BASIC neutron bomb plasma display Moog eight-track heart transplantation LCD SQUID snowboarding Kevlar hypertext cordless phone Richard Ramirez kills at least fourteen space pen minicomputer CD internal-frame backpack food bank handheld calculator racquetball virtual reality bone marrow transplantation lunar module laser printer Charles Manson kills no one with his own hands inside the family mind of minds Taser mousepad markup language LAN PC microprocessor floppy disk email C video game console John Wayne Gacy kills more than twenty-four bodies and buries them inside his home oh here are the bodies there will be more bodies more bodies ended more bodies made Randy Steven Kraft kills at least sixteen bodies and maybe more than sixty Thomas Pynchon publishes *Gravity's Rainbow* personal watercraft recombinant DNA catalytic converter mobile phone Ted Bundy kills more than forty bodies voice mail Dean Corll kills more than twenty-seven boys Heimlich maneuver Post-it UPC David Berkowitz kills six bodies wounding seven digital camera Ethernet breakaway rim Hepatitis B vaccine Gore-Tex MRI BBS Carlton Gary kills at least seven women Joseph Paul Franklin kills at least eleven Jim Jones kills nine hundred and seventeen bodies with his mind Coral Eugene Watts kills between eighty and one hundred women winglets polar fleece control-alt-delete fetal surgery space shuttle paintball GUI internet laser blind signature Gary Ridgway kills at least seventy-one women laser turntable Henry Lee Lucas kills at least eleven and as many as six hundred Cormac McCarthy publishes *Blood Meridian* atomic force microscope stereolithography

DMD Perl Richard Angelo kills at least twenty-five bodies Eddie Leonski kills at least five nicotine patch firewall ZIP file format magnetic lock sulfur lamp Bret Easton Ellis publishes *American Psycho* Jeffrey Dahmer kills at least fifteen people and consumes their bodies Aileen Wuornos kills at least seven men GPS scroll wheel JavaScript low plasticity burnishing bait car David Foster Wallace publishes *Infinite Jest* Francisco del Junco kills at least four women Ronald Dominique kills at least twenty-three men Mars rover DVR virtual globe phase-change incubator Dr. Harold Shipman kills at least fifteen Segway artificial liver SERF Tommy Lynn Sells kills at least twelve and as many as seventy-one HPV vaccine 3-D model rendering shingles vaccine trongs Dennis Rader kills at least ten women nanowire battery bionic contact lens composite aircraft whoever what Gretch Gravey kills three hundred million all in all.

Do you want to start over. Do you hear the coming number. Are you still dead. Are you the sound. Do you want to live forever instead. Do you love me. Can you prove it. Prove it. Prove it. Name one of the seven hundred ways to speak. I will be listening. I am listening.

Today is your birthday.

Today is today.

The light of all the nights we'd killed and fucked crashed through my mind. It pulled thick light down around the body of the idea of creation. The repeating sound of all our days was the color of all reflected flesh at once negated. There was never any actual beginning we saw by our hands as they grew even paler than our minds were. Milk was snowing from between the burning legs spread on the ocean purring blue comedy in invitation for the god to kiss the god and enter the god and wash the god off from the inside and live him. And the skin of everyone around me scrolled away from the night's color into something more like the daylight we'd learn to like to feel alive in. Every word was any word, cursed into the Pledge and the National Anthem and the Constitution and the Declaration and the Vows and the Holy Book and the Enactment spoke at once inside the rubbing of our bodies turned to candles around the bed of a great furnace lurking underneath the sash of dads queued up each gut waiting for the right to scratch against its own destruction. Soon the sky had learned as well to speak our myths, which made it all the colors there at once seeming opaque enough to huddle beneath and deep enough to shriek at with machines and devices in the image again where the child would learn to walk under. Where in every understanding's brutal echo our shared forefathers stomped around in mortal retardation like a dream, claiming each inch of everything as only his forever despite what death, every oven and cloth and pill and mate and wish and day and age and sound not ours and taking shits inside the food and defending the food only ever with his fists while above me stars made marks along the land. Where every word we'd ever said instead of being any ever to me now sounded all like the same word at once: *no*. No no no no no no no our forefather screamed inside my heart, at every pixel beyond his, each having intended to fit fine inside the heads of us oncoming but held in like a blaspheme in the presence of god arrived at last. With each enunciation of the same cell, the cell grew slower, smaller, less like anything once ours. We all demented in his image. We at last before the screen, showing no light, seeing the light instead of seeing the thing not there as well. The glue rattled in our teeth and prayed no syllable and lashed against the mantle falling through white on the idea of white lurking its way all over everything and someone coming to the door pressed facewide to every door, the living rooms and bedrooms and guest rooms and kitchens softened from their black glow into the colors the night our very presence had demented around the house like patterns that gave us glow inside our sleeves enough some days to stand enough some days to walk from room to room even wishing for no image even hopeful, while all across the air the cells of our friends and family pulled apart to make as strangers and were laughing through the night where in absence of the father we forgot to close the homes and lock the doors against whoever even knowing who had been or what had been or what was wondered, what we of we would need to grow among us into the space between the space made for us to live and need forever in against the vast fabric of one long wherever full of all things named and cataloged under the pustule called a moon and the cancer called a quasar and so on and so on with the machine light burning our eyes, with the telephones ringing through the never-ending putty wishing words into the fabric of us blurring the fabric where they could not fully enter our bodies and become us, while No no no no no no no our father screamed in his own absence, barely noise at all now. No no no no no no no, with his last undead breath. No no no no no no no no no no no no no no no no.

Even you were not free of this infestation, however kind you felt you'd been. You might have imagined yourself spared, but you were not spared. You who had moved from room to room held in the houses among the bodies in the light, who had slept through hours gone unknowing of who would come in above you in the great year of the universe becoming one eternal sore upon undone forever lathered forever loved.

Inside this book, you'd come into a room. It was the bedroom where you'd slept nightly. The color of the walls here will appear in preservation always all white, though truly the colors were always changing, and with their changing so changes your idea of what white was, preserving in the folded home the idea of the whiteness, so that days in their way might go on.

From your head you saw your arms. They may have had tattoos or cuts or hair grown on them; these are the arms you've always had. Your identity is yours in you to you unveiled unveiling in the moment of its making.

Inside this room of yours there was a bed. Upon the bed someone was sleeping, features turned to face the wall. You saw the one upon the bed there was who you remembered yourself as; who held this book and read it, reading it now; the one having walked around in one's own house and home and life thinking of food to eat or doors to open or the phone calls or the child; the black flash of one's own presence in the hour between pages turned, the words upon the pages changing, too, becoming any book forever, blank or all sound, inscribed with any kind of name; each instant in ongoing correspondence with whichever memory of past hours would corroborate the feeling of the day and strength enough at least to carry on, while also always shifting quickly into future versions without disturbance of the portion of whoever clinging but in an overwhelming sense of blank no one could quite describe.

Inside the house you raised your arm inside the room toward the instance of the self you saw as you remembered, upon the bed, and the knife glinted, and you hesitated watching your soft chest rise and fall, breathing slowly in common sleep. You felt yourself seeing yourself inside your sleeping on the bed there, brain full of stairways, long days, weird heads, laughter, the color of all man.

You could hesitate no more; you moved into the frame; moved to stand between the image of the mirror and the image of you in your body on the bed; the book against your chest went on white with its flat pages, while outside the house inside the hour the sky was nowhere.

"This, too, is my body," you heard you saying. "I was you once."

And you raised the glinting knife and brought it down. And when this was done, you did the same again. Here in the end of every now.

You and I, beyond time, we felt, without a world.

We stabbed ourselves forty-seven times in the stomach and the chest and abdomen and chest and face until we were sure that we were dead. There was no passion in the stabbing. There was the gesture of the arm—a gesture like that used in religious confirmation, voting, shaping clay. The blood poured from our body, sprayed against our faces, soaked hot and wet into the mattress in a shape refusing form. The luster of the body sat inside the silent room before us splayed in lavendergold curtains of the flesh, now inert.

We took some blood up in our hands. It was our blood. The blood fit in our mouth as if it had always been there, and it had. The blood was thick enough to chew. It tasted like the year we learned to speak the word, and the year we learned to remember what words we were saying; the same taste of the bodies we'd befriended in the hour of the day standing on white grass under a hard sun laughing and the year we learned to wish for someone other than ourselves to lie against us in the small rooms of flat cities under night. Each mouthful repeated the only word inside us as if it has always been and forever will be again.

In pleasure, reign.

Wet on the bed our old body flooded its wet out. Set in the mush of pus our organs it sat and listened. What rubble we had suffered. What day removed.

With hands cold in the mirrors, we took our old skin up. A fingernail slitted along the cream edge of the stabbing allowed the hand to feel down deep between our flesh, freeing with one clean fist the left lung of us from the hot index of cells. Clutched between fingers our bored hand tickled the organ, a spackled hamhock warbling in veiny tendrils.

With its bread, we filled our mouth. We tongued the surface, tasting hair there, the leathered slopes where air for years has entered, fixed and functioned through the body. Our top and bottom teeth met inside the meat. We felt the mirror there behind us watching in silence as we ate the left half of the organ whole; the substance made loose popping noises against the gums and palate, our pressed dynasties singing hard against the slip of the enamel, taking the taste of where you'd sat inside the living room those nights alone, remembering whatever you wish you would remember.

We devoured what within the head remains. We licked and sucked the groove-holes of the skull's lip where the blade had chipped against its shape, elongating the fissure where before there fit the organ of the eye. We ate the mush remaining of the stabbed eyes, the destroyed lenses, mushy cake. The vision left no resin, going down clean, hearing in the cells of us the shaking of the colors of the encased decades of sight becoming flesh, returning to the form it had been whipped from, anywhere but now.

There were, as well, the other organs: the stringy legs, the darker sections of the kidneys clobbered with impurity, the gift boxes of the sternum's circus, the cake party of the intestines, the thighs, the toes, the knees. We ripped and chawed what we could pry loose from the internal structure, which was a lot. Our jaws worked no music as we felt our stomachs filling. The meat of us inside us disappeared, bulging water-shaped in globe of pregnancy repeated. Our blood was bright and shining in the room. The walls were watching.

Now we must fuck. In the presence of only ourselves, we would make fuck on the remainder of ourselves. The killing and the eating of the flesh of our old body had made us beyond horny. We were flush with new blood.

Our body shuddered against our skin. We loved us. We wanted to have us and everything we could become wholly forever. We would fuck us everlasting. Our glands were ours. The hole of us that we were fucking was enormous. We couldn't tell which of us was which. We rode hard and loose upon the gray nub of the cake self split and choking blood around the bed. We heard the peel of the remaining world in our minds forever onward wishing too to get fucked and do fuck with what we were or could have been. Either the self beneath us was screaming or we were screaming for it to scream, in the voice of anybody.

We were fucking us with force. Our cock or hole around our cock or hole purred nasty for more power, the pudding of the blood and massive shaping making any feeling in us blown out and absent of clean color but still causing sparks of friction where it sat and peeled with pressure. It was hard to keep the body there in one piece, for all the stabbing we'd done already, but we held the mass together with our hands as best we could and thrust and rammed and focused our weeping on the gash of how to make ourselves come.

The coming come was a sled-vision, a blurring hexagonal solid. It floated dry in far-off orbit around the house slipping down against the human light of day, as outside the house the air itself was calm.

The fuck was over before it began. Our organs were turning pliable again already, made for elsewhere. It didn't matter. Here I was always again yours and you were mine. Already filled with all eternal come splayed underneath us, the body of our body was not anywhere where we'd go, every death turning milled in mills beneath each new instant undefined; our future body not without organs but without area; without perimeter or mission, from whose wounds left out to rot in silence alone roared a wordless, faceless way of being.

[YOUR NAME]: [*stricken from record*]

Very soon then I could hear no one and nothing else. Where every hour disappeared inside the idea of every life as last I felt it, it held no contour beyond what it had been. The itch it left was nothing more than air alone and unrepeated. I was allowed then in the absence to feel anything I wished, to remember anything I wished, without vocabulary.

And yet I loved the feeling of the disappearing. I wanted it to never cease. The slower I tried to make it go, the less there was left behind thereafter.

My final body rose from what we'd been. I was the last remaining person, alive beyond any memory, or now. I could feel my name inscribed the endless faces on the land of the bodies slain in layers carried in us all echoed as the gristle of today.

My skin was soft. I remembered nothing, which meant I could remember anything in any head, which means I did not have to remember to still feel it knitting in me, turning in against itself, as what I was. My arms resembled every arm, every inch bursting over with tattoos and wounds the flesh had eaten down into me, conformed intact with what I was. I could go on now forever in the instant despite all I'd done and what had been done before me, fearing nothing of the shift of blood and skin that formed the ground, the light shaking in marrow of the nature of my breathing, thinking, wanting, eating, laughing, each now no longer caving me with age.

I did not wear a ring. I could not remember what a ring was.

All remaining land was only sand—white sand forever shaken from the resin of our scalps and fingers, flesh torn apart; our bodies rendered at last no longer, unto powder, shimmered with all prayer, though you can no longer tell one body from another, from the ground itself. No matter which way I went or how far into it, the sand continued, all directions, over oceans, every forest.

I did not know why I walked. The heat of the dry scape burned my feet beneath me. I could feel the spaces in me where I'd had a friend once, a family, somewhere out here, like the light. The sand is what the sand is.

Nowhere else. I would find perhaps here or there among the plane of planning a jawbone or a locket, a strand of hair unmelted several feet deep, or a glove of glass, or some white shell. I pressed the objects to my face, heard nothing, and in placing them again against the ground would soon feel them lost in untraceable whiteness.

I could not remember why I'd ever went.

I knew I had forgotten where I'd been already and was walking the same surface many times repeated, seeing the same things new as nothing new.

I could not remember my name, the word for anything. I did not know how long time had been this way against me. I could tell no difference from any old day and the last. I heard nothing sing within me.

I stopped wherever I'd become.

I stopped and saw all light resembling the same.

The land was no one's. Wherever I looked upon it, it opened on itself, into more of itself. There was more inside it than it even believed in, though it could do nothing with it now.

Anywhere in this expanse I stopped and stood and looked and felt no dream.

I could not remember where I'd come from or after who then.

I could hardly tell where I ended and sand began.

I did not know why there were no walls around me.

I made a marking in the sand. The marking allowed my mind a small relief, as once within it I could no longer remember anywhere but.

I knew the marking wore a door. Here the door was a preternatural idea and had no name beyond it simply leading to what would be the first room of the space, which I would build into a copy of the room where in my childhood I had sat on the floor with my hands before me and my mother behind my back, stroking my hair or humming or sewing or singing the song or silent in the night exhausted for the machines, the color of the TV shining low against our faces or the face of the books my mother planned to read aloud to me, bestowing its hidden crevices of nowhere upon the child I was already becoming in the machine of my brain alone.

As I imagined the door, then, it appeared there. It was a white door, like my memory, leading to anything.

The rest of what must be was up to me.

To form the lengths of walls surrounding what the door was, I searched for sharper relics among the sprawl of local sand: ribcages, skulls and tibia, phalanges and sockets, spines and collarbones. They no longer felt like parts of people. The bones hissed and puzzle-clicked into new configurations to form grids, and from them doorknobs, stairs. I packed sand into the shapes to make the surfaces opaque held spindly and dense and fell immediately away, leaving holes through which the air outside could continue in through, while the day went on around, basking in my brain a second color to the home where the air had not been before.

At some depths whole packets of new expanse appeared by nature worn into the innate definition of the space—an oven or a bathtub or a staircase—as if the house had always been beneath the sand there buried, waiting.

The ceiling I left open wide. The light of the house would be moons and suns, whatever weather, though it would never again rain here.

When I could do no more each day, I entered sleep. My absent dreamworld bristled around me overflowing every perimeter of what I couldn't see completely overcome with everything not carried in me. Each instant just beneath the under of sleep's nothing seized with a cream of flame around my mind, as if against its own image the whole house wanted to implode unseen, return to its elements. The ring I could not remember ever having not worn burned around my finger and fed off me; I couldn't feel it, but I knew. There was in my head only the black, the long lengths of the house I'd built from death surrounding my life now.

Inside sleep, I walked along the walls in place of everywhere through which I'd come. I pantomimed actions already lived through, wanting only there to appear those who'd been there then returned beside. My hands moved without me moving. Where no one spoke inside the rooms of the house inside the dark the doors stood open, chamber to chamber.

"I am a hole," I said aloud each time I touched a wall, but I could not hear it, allowing days to disappear between the words—hours haunted with the unheard words of vows of death, of forgiveness, the oldest colors.

Through days I bloated in my home like it was mine; I could see my fat moving before me into where I was before I felt me be there; this also hurt though in a smaller place and one I learned to think around; I was able to do this by focusing on the pages of a blank book that appeared inside my head when my eyes closed without my knowing; a book I knew had never been; each page was larger than your head and brighter than I could stand to look at; the book shook with what could have been written, in any book, all prior books not realizing they were disappearing into this one book as they were written, carried and carried on, in vast precision in the image of what it could not at all reflect, a silent murder rendered forward by something old and made eternal now in every inch of my face and the walls inside me. In this way days inside the house did not seem days; lives could pass among my head each day hidden in blinking; terror here might seem as easy as having dinner or lying faceup on a bed or holding the mental hand of someone I'd loved under a sky that seemed to need nothing but itself to carry on. The way it gathered in the book unbeing it gathered in me also, sealing its total brightness into every gesture, so that while awake I began to feel I weighed the weight of ten whole people in one body, each of them breathing and eating what I breathed and ate also, replicating.

For days I turned and turned inside the new long dark, trying not to remember there was nothing beyond the house to live with beyond the image of how it felt, or else the blurring bolts of what I could recall of what held near: splatter fragments of the skulls; tents of muscles slathered in a pig-white grease of centuries spooled through blood-browned sauce boiling; tissue shitting between nostrils in a head inside a second head; living rooms where babies fell and broke their brains; *those were the days*; attics in the attics above with blue bells ringing the coming hour to us counted down from zero into zero while names were read off of a list inside said broken baby skulls and gathered up packed back in entrails as cluster-semen replicated to be injected to eggs gifted on breakfast tables before god; windows; chasms; purple fabric; what else; what would you want forever; just ask; *this world is ours.*

Behind my lids, the black no longer was ever black; or not the same black there'd been when I was younger and knew more than I knew now, or how it felt; instead the shade inside the skull contained a thickness branched from the vision of all of whom; every blink or whip of eye along the long yards of the days undone; each of us seated only at the center of the space we could not see and now would never be anything but. It felt easier for me alone instead to think nothing, in this home devoid of anything but my own touch; it felt warm like endless milk, even so minor; as the only drawers I found in the walls of the ways here were mostly only filled with ash or fat or ice; the ice would never melt, no matter how much I rubbed at it, and the fat, it held no flavor; the ash was just ash though its color was monochrome and it did not float and it would not stay on my hands.

Often I couldn't recall where the next room was from one day to another even seeing my body leading the way, even having lived in this house already my whole life, as I remembered; or I couldn't remember what any room was for, why there were walls between this room and this last one. In all the rooms the floor was bright. No matter where I looked I saw more space before me waiting; I saw space between the spaces merging and emerging from itself inside itself to split the room in many parts, each as undone as the other, desperate for anything but what it was.

Days went by in weeks and weeks in days. Some days the days lasted longer than days and lashed themselves to surfaces that colored my face the way a winter would have in the realm of cells and in my face I felt the heat of time rubbing against anything it wasn't, disrupting the inner knit of even rest. With the base of home as some new center inside the sand I began to patrol the sand for miles ongoing, finding quickly how in relation the light would turn me deaf and blind. There was only so far to go before I could hear and see absolutely nothing but white against me and throughout me. I had to always be looking back to remind myself which direction home was; I used a language dreamed up in myself to count, a series of clicks of tongue and teeth against the gristle of my cheek, pushed through the holes inside my head to blow against the grooves my dying memory escaped into its flesh. I left trails of the language burned into the sand and light without even intending; my very presence wrecking the idea of death itself; among which I could find, each day, a hallway back to the hole I'd drummed up to collapse into and once again black out.

Each time I returned to the house having seen nothing I would find, grown out from the house I'd left, sets of new rooms. From the further nodes and bulbs of skulls and cages littered in the sand for miles forever, there might appear a stairwell leading into the ceiling, which then days later manifested into a landing filled with doors. Through all the eye of the sky above alone stayed constant, though it was changing; veined with something cracking on the far side as if to match my tread beneath. Some stars might seem to read a word burned out into them, though in a language I could no longer understand. Only in sleep could I begin to fuse my clicking language with the words the sky wanted to say. I could not tell how reciting what they intended altered my vocabulary, the palate catching slowly in new grooves and gristle patches the gums and spittle, adjusting in the arch of the sound I spoke for me alone, my arms around me doing anything they could to keep me from waking, going back into the sand again, for no one.

Weeks soon went by then in months or things named with sounds that have no syllables to suffer. One second might last a lifetime inside a dry day with the heap of blue air rising from no hole over the remaining fields and fields as yet untraveled though it does not matter and any way I walked in resumed the same. I was awake. I was not awake. I could or could not remember the difference between a bookshelf made from kneecaps and any bed or length of sand expanding, the maps of the universal dead. The house around me was always what it always had been, and yet always felt like nothing else.

There was the quaking of the word. What the book wasn't. What I wasn't. Whereas before outside the home I'd hear no shudder for miles in sand on sand, alone again at home some blue voice appeared buried in the throat behind a wall, spreading underneath my head wherever I would let it. As if the house itself was speaking from a space it only wasn't, or the house itself was not what I believed. The voice began to fill me through and through me. I knew its way along my lungs and down my legs and near my heart. I recognized the feeling; I was the feeling. Had been. Was not now.

I closed my eyes and saw only the blood. Blood of the dead I wasn't and could more and more not tell from anything. In the blood the rooms were there too. Rooms that would not stop being. In sleep I moved into the blood and felt their sound. It wound down in around me, awaking more space in waking day against the frame of what I'd meant to render only mine eternally. Each room was any room that I could call: the room where I'd been born, where who was murdered; each room the same as every one, revolving at no center, never touching. There were so many of us in me. The black I saw was wider than my skull, and spanned enough to wrap the solar system, like an eggshell, side by side among the million other eggs in every load, endless cells silent in all future inside my mouth with lips ripped out of characters burnt raw in the minds of the dead and their last fractions spilled onto a white of pages the maps must become erased against like birth canals in mothers turned to sand, to glass, to now.

I went into the kitchen to make food and found I'd already eaten every inch before I'm there. The room was slowly slowing.

There was nothing to renounce. No way to end anything I could imagine being the ending. Where I felt I was a man I had no hands; where I felt I was a woman I had hair all over my body; where I wished to be a child I had no grace. My scream sounded like I remembered feeling eating ice cream or walking in warm sunlight. Everything was just beside itself. The light was alone.

I continued getting older, but did not age. I was being watched from the inside and nowhere shining. No one was waiting for my mind. I drank the color from the light and felt no terror. I loved the sand for how under any shade of sky it all seemed irreplaceable.

I still had seen no inch of the new stone.

I went on doing anything I felt in my own image.

I mimed to laugh and heard no laughter.

I tried to make a drum out of my skin.

I banged the drum for hours.

No one was singing and our song contained no words.

I scratched where what I missed less and less felt near me in the darkness.

I made a crib.

I made a child inside my mind to fill the crib with.

I filled the crib with sand.

I clasped my hands.

This was how the hours went.

The ways went on and days did raze against each other.

I grew my hair.

The days repeated.

I said a phrase and it was wind.

I lived and lived in nothing like silence.

I turned and turned.

Nothing was counting what the day was.

The house continued shrinking.

Inside my likewise shrinking mind I went to sleep.

Inside my sleep I walked the same way I had for hours waking.

I came upon a book.

I read the book and found it was the same book as this book now.

In every life.

The words fell through me like a word will.

I remembered nothing.

I was no older.

I was only alone still.

Inside the house in veils I hurtled forward in and on, trying to live on full with all absence; I could not hear any voice I understood, no matter how the edges of the space's language called against my presence; the night went on and house went on around me as a house in the era of man; the days were old. Each life we'd lived was lived again inside me throbbing in all absence and would stay there like this now always.

I walked on in the color of the world, dragging back what I'd carried with there behind me humming till I'd dragged it so far through the world there was no world remaining to collapse in, or space to clean the image from my being, as in the wake the sand blew there lurked all these diamonds and hexagons of human crystal crushed in the color issued forth. Each color dragged on behind itself too every other color also dragging something there unseen, unlike what death was. Where I was alive now the light all turning pigged-out stroboscopic, to wake the rising melting flooding through the poreholes of our ex-begetters and relics, and therefore us as well—one long last note colored in the smell of walking and this mash of giddy marrow becoming mashed again around my tonsils and longest teeth. It made me hiss from holes I'd never known I had and soon would not again no matter what kind of perfect words were fished out from my ability to recall them beyond any light as all our essence.

I could hear several hundred hands surrounding in each instant and more so then with every knowing. Sand rolled limbs around my face's blank—sand in no color I'd imagined, like the veils of smoke I slowly remembered from before, from worlds of tape not like this present moment, but no less false. The sand was inside me. The smoke was inside us mirrored. The air thugged thick, ticking no dream's remainder away. There was nothing burning down. No matter where I went in any blackness I could not find the hallway to the integral rooms of what had felt like my own life in this world. The pillows of the darkness made each room each time I saw them seem to stretch more and more toward forever. Each time I thought or said a word aloud or tried to inhale, the caving in me emerged more. It was grinding in me. It was always.

I crawled along the floor, whatever a floor was. Inside the rising volume of my mind I slapped on hands and knees among the slick of surfaces between the earth and every body the air had made to keep us framed in; the sand beneath it swishing, as if being sucked into a hole, as if underneath the floor the only thing keeping the rest of the world from sucking in around me and you and everybody with it into some screaming hole focused from all the endless in what had been. My clothes seemed searing, knitting tighter, like every surface of my home, which in its latest alterations had become so close against me there was nearly nowhere left to move. I felt the walls where everything was not, no matter what I wanted. It was easier then to move without thinking where to go, though still the choking and croaking of my body, the unbelievable breadth of everything else. The shapeless sound coming from my mouth was feeding right back up into my nostrils, feeding my face full, covering over every memory again with the new deformation of what hours did, overwriting every idea of itself, every inch of anyone but me in me.

In me, then, the house could grow no smaller. I found it fit exactly with my mind. I'd become surrounded wholly by the same shade, the color of no color, all directions.

The color opened.

It was an eye.

Any eye.

The white of the light of the eye inside it was brighter than the house had ever been, wider than sky was, than my memory. Even thin as the film over the eye's white seemed to be from far away, it held more edges than I could count; it held a past that hadn't happened yet; it had always been in the house before there was a house; it gave the room around me its dimension; it had appeared in every age; it had observed every action; the eye of anything but now, of anyone but no one.

Against the color of the eye I could not see the walls or what beside them; I could not remember how I'd made way here through any other sort of being, outside the way I'd always come before to every present instant always again; though on the air there was the itch of something older bloating; colors like ions; sound like glass filling the air. There was no reason this hour should have been any different than all the other years of any life, and yet here the eye was, all surrounding.

Up close the eye no longer seemed to have a shape; it held together like a corpse, organs made of letters made of blank space of dots and lines feeding a warping shape like ours, which the longer I looked into blurred inside the light unto a gray mass like a wall. I stared into the eye and felt it humming without language; all words now no longer language. I closed my own eyes and saw the wall there too and looked again, a mirror image in my body made of bodies; then I was there inside the eye's own head; I was seeing at the wall inside me as if everything I wasn't was at the far side of the wall inside the light again made clear.

There was no shift; I found inside my seeing how I could scroll along the light's face with the motion of my hand; the eye inside me held there against itself slithering downward to reveal itself again inside the extant eye made hidden on space forced in the space as in the oceans of our blood consumed, evaporated, nowhere; the light of all our faces.

I let the light come on in ruptured flues; it swam sick past my face like meat to meat, light pouring through where words were not, straining in the light to scan the flattened fiber of the vein of mottled language engorged and disappearing. Time passed and passed and nothing had happened; nothing had not happened; I could no longer remember how I was different than anything else, how anything else could not become me; the space around us held on, our blubber wooing like an ocean in a shell; my body not my body sticking at the frame of the page of the light folding our absent organism to its skin in rising heat and burning not of fire but of where the flesh of all of us each instant shrunk and expanded both at once, under equal age and iteration, all ongoing, and the syntax burst between; each thought risen as a prison in our teeth and lungs and slapped ass screeching; eyes spinning locked in all our lids; speech mixing itself against itself to change itself and call itself the word inside the word against the word while outside itself the sand went on regardless, and each word as it came through us fell back out the other side, clung at old holes in landscapes, hopes unwinding.

I could no longer not quite think, or remember; the shapes of what was once clawed where my sound had never made a sound; feeding faster full of past thoughts, where every word a thought was made of wore a murder of its own; each death a death of all things and so nothing; there in the light the bread of time; the speech of all speech whaling in us where far along the shafts of script in my own self I reached a drop, something sticking in the wash of blood between living and not living, looking there into the white along the current seeing faster until the sound inside the eye were these words, the run of light forming this sentence becoming typed across the screen of the eye of all our eyes no longer seeing, appearing newly every moment like something carried in my skin, each inch another name for silence.

Now I could not remember what I'd done. I could not remember that I did not remember where I'd been forever or what the bodies had become among the night where knives were every understanding. I was all hours at the same time in every current instant of our lives arrived. I was in the homes beyond the idea of having lived. I was eating dinner or touching paper or swimming under sun or taking a child toward a machine to learn to read again a new way or was teaching myself another language to say what to someone else or I was at a desk staring where light was or I had hid again my eyes. It was all of any of us at once that made any of us nowhere else, held in the motion of any aspiration.

I thought to touch my face then but I did not. I felt something in me at last growing eons older in one instant, like any instant, and from the light I looked away. I stood there for some time then feeling nothing; I stood there waiting in the white unfurling hot and hard around all shape without intention or utterance demarcating. Some other of me in me tried to turn around and go back the way I'd come inside the world to now but when it turned around there were again the walls; where the world as I'd never understood it had moved again to fill the space behind me, so that where I tried to move on from what I was or felt again there was nothing but more of me, the erased eras in me going slump in spindles and pressing at where my nape and back and skull were just more flesh waiting to be smothered.

The world was what had lived. Within each inch there were colors; the colors each pixel held a sea; buried in the sea another kind of time under old blue lard of reckless dreaming; in each world, people wide awake, spreading flesh as they went aging around the holes of them that did not age or bloat. Overhead in every instance of right now the sky was caving; a second sky beneath that was more the way I'd once remembered the one we watched as ours, its dimensions bulging in soft places, puckered, growing in against itself, all the icons of every era swelling in against me with the world at once compressing into the sound of every recorded life. It was all of us and always had been, just like this. The eye saw.

Held in the eye, I felt us speak.

It was the same voice I'd heard traced through my whole life up to this point, though where before that voice had always been only me, now it was unending and breathless.

I couldn't hear what the voice was saying through its layers, though I could feel it in my fiber.

The words weren't words, but landscapes, mounds. I was looking up and I was up there and I was looking far down into our mud, and I was in the mud and all directions, and when I looked again above us I saw

countless suns

And beneath the suns I saw

the soft ground rising

I saw it piling all around, the house and the voice and my mind becoming comprised in the husks of anyone's mortal remains, the memory of the person once carried in those husks, the mottled mass of presences inert and passed on pressed together full, waiting impossibly for every hour ever to return into the flesh of all the rest of us at once wherever with our common images split down the center writhing.

And I saw the sand again around the old world becoming buried in the sand of what my world had become

the sand of all without horizon

And as we spoke I saw the sand again falling away

And I saw

all negations

And I saw

agelessnesses

I saw

no walls forever in our love

And I did not need to understand.

In us, the shape of any sky was rubbing upward, sucking in nothing. The ground erupting antigravity and light. The light louder than it was actually. Planets were everywhere: dissolving, without surface.

Nothing had ever happened.

And from the sprawl I saw

the light blown open

I saw

no color rising underneath us

in time dividing

tunnels to nothing

Way out along the long horizon from where any form had been, the face of day split wide.

Our eyes were changing.

The eyes in mounds of eyes without pupil, lens, or image.

And I saw

no beginning & no end

And I saw

nowhere

I could not see more than in long fits and whorls, because of what had happened to the light.

I did not want to see, but what I didn't want was as much me as what I had been.

I had no skin. I had no organs.

Each instant wore through all our lives.

The walls around the words we could not remember rose beyond us.

Light fell into time fell into flesh fell into speech; word fell into syllable fell into letter; *z* fell into *y* fell into *b* fell into *a*; shape fell into line fell into dot fell into gram; kilometer fell into meter fell into millimeter fell into volume; home fell into house fell into den fell into bed fell into frame; film fell into picture fell into pixel fell into color; body fell into sternum fell into ribcage full into bone; skull fell into brain fell into memory fell into where; 1 fell into 0; you fell into me fell into us fell into we fell into I; now fell into now.

Now was the color of all our skin and sins and fingers. Of water and oxygen elapsed. Every film at last erased, all books cured of their language, all ideas of their ego.

There was no longer any other voice. They were all my voices. Sound and light unfolding in the skin of nothing. Not a present moment as much as a pyre on which the world turned, all the sand not sand but breadth combining in reverse, where from out of the land the smoke of the dead of the land each node of creation ate back onto every inch it'd never been and always could have.

And in the thrall of all, I closed my eyes again where I no longer could see.

And I saw

Against the flood of where the eye was, I turned to face in total silence what the world had left behind a final time. Through white so bright it crushed itself by simply being, I saw where every inch of now touched every color grinding in the ground broken and blown apart. Where as I turned the air around me smiled and nodded and said the words I'd said already back into me again in a language without nature, and as I turned back, nothing held. No kind of sight but what the light was.

I could no longer tell any difference between the world and what I knew. Between myself and you or anybody. Between the eye and our skin and what sky. The lack of color matched our worship without surface. No way back and no way out of nowhere being dreamed. No belief but in every faith we hadn't lived and held within us, between anyone and zero.

I closed my eyes a final time. Inside my head the dead within me began glowing; they grew inside me with great force, dressed in the long white hair of no one, and in the eyes behind my sight I felt the glowing filling up itself like future hearses. I felt the eyes close inside the eyes again, the dark among them erupting definition.

The light was screaming between voices, mine and no one's. Any inch of where we'd been appeared not glown by glow, but cut into the grade of the sand of all of our remainder melting into the face of what remained.

The air where we were born filled in unwinding over fields of white on white, while underneath, the rimmed earth sung thick with the old poltergeists of our eternal seething seed.

Time strewed lengthwise and widewise in batter-buried color of no reflection laid wide open on the land; all years coagulated in spite of sense, passed hours upon hours beating the surface of the earth with hellish cells that felt like homes where all the unborn men and women drowned within us came and went. I could not stop them with my mouth or arms or flinging hope so hard into the sky it might knock the sky down, or shrieking our old name shaped like their old name walking up and down and up the streets and giving off the friction stink we mistook inside our skins as how the air itself just smelled like the color of our hair. Like the longing for the pleasure of having had hair, grown and cut and grown again.

You were beside me; I was beside you.

I held our melding sight up without hands, not feeling either where through the white again into glown points I saw the air of the glow bloat again for whom in furor rose from all our last attentions piling aflame in the infinite incarnation of all conception, each when made to roast why and wish who and blow long the breath into the next ones of we beyond recording opened wide and curled and curling lost around a shape inside a shape spilled vast and spilling from its innumerable faces where in us lighted night engorged within the baby fat of time, rasped in the skin of us as we were wedded why to walk why in me for whom forever slowly elapsed.

Without seeing then I spun to press fast our size against the white in full. At last I solely wanted all of all the nothing. My whole nonexistent head and sternum stung flush with our blood and our unchildren's blood and yours and mine within this nowhere I pressed me hard against the world I could not watch. I pressed us there also pressing in the reflective surface on the back side of our vision, against the flesh, each possible instant in us rolling backwards and coming out the far side of understanding. I felt the mass wrap in around me and through this could not hear our narration screaming for me at last to just look up, as walled in behind the light there was a hole that went so far back behind the house there was no longer any space there and I was at last here at home where someone had spread a wall over any mirror so I could not see in where I was. There was only white on white and some long sound like all our bodies in me here pulling the world down crushed against itself; each word chiseled with its own eye becoming forced so wide open it had no cell. All the words once hidden among our bodies had been split apart in heat, held constantly imploding inward like the black of any pupil.

We were so loud I could not see. I had all this fission in me, pressed among the light inside my skin and bones turned together throbbing forward longways through this remainder of a shape of a place like our own life, each pixel pregnant with more days that would no longer, each day pregnant with its own glass, where the longer it manifested itself in continuity the more there was between us and the less any inch of any of us may remember how it felt or ever could have, endlessly forwarded and reversed at once against and through and into the perimeter of the cusp of every possible context. The deleting bright was all around me and still spreading and divulging.

Beyond my sight, the era opened into curves. It hissed the light back at me like a putty, reflective, impossible. There grew between us all a single face, a face of endless faces, and in the light now all around me I could feel it inhaling all our voices, never looking back. From within the face I watched the face open its mouth of all our mouths, and in its mouth there was a common darkness, born from the space inside all heads alone, and from this darkness without motion came all possible pronouncements, all language not yet released out of its unliving breath. It wasn't sound and did not speak. The stretch of the skin of the mind of the face could not contain any word we'd confabulated for whatever. Nothing unquantified in its conception, the lanyards of our cerebrums, singing, sleeping. I heard the memory of all passed bodies in the face's features being cracked into tablets, drugs for the light to swallow and become, and in becoming to contain all continuity forever. Every eye we'd watched anything go on through basked full in the face's total common future, consummating every air into its inherent definition: (*all the light that had been shined into our face*) (*all our past laughter*) (*the sound inside us anchored to history unclaimed*) (*what we were too young then to remember*) (*all that had not happened and one day could have*) (*all holes forever*) (*nowhere, now*).

Our shattered speaking sang and sang. It ate its singing and barfed its singing up and ate it back and sang it back to nothing. Where each old era opened, the blood of light flowed awake and was flowed into and all over. The words themselves began to speak. The words were burning in my face. They had been written here wherever on everything at once and eaten up or absorbed among the living no longer living. Every passage of being caressed all that I wasn't. I rolled along inside the sweat and let it leave me clearer. I was bleeding light and signal. The colors around my eyes kept changing textures like organisms. The words kept coming. I began to be the words there, though I could not understand the breadth behind; they felt like words I'd never said or heard before wherever, words erased inside a book I'd read every night inside my sleep in every other version of me. The book was in my skin now. The skin was peeling. It came off where all along inside the enervating wash my body split and bubbled with the friction and the language as the flatness came and went and the skin came off me where I rolled along inside the light inside the sand all pouring smoke from the friction as the flatness changed and bent and grew and flooded. I could not stop seeing and hearing and tasting and taking of the soft space rising all around my body so surrounded there was nothing left of what it was, beyond contour and no horizon.

Each way I felt then wore away, as if the world at once within me turned numb or gone. I did not know what was becoming of my thinking with the sound inside me splitting into halves, and those halves splitting in their utterance again to others though already they were lost along the unrolling understanding of the land, upon which I saw not sand but space between the sand and light of what there was, one day made of all the days we'd meant to fill with all of us and yet had not, not knowing how. What had been sand then was all the glass in all the mirrors, in each of which I could see the hues of what had once been hidden behind us in the frame, our bodies packed with all cells dragging heavy on the radiance unknown.

I could no longer tell even now which one of me was still there hearing me speaking and which was watching from outside whom. The more I thought about the difference the more it burned me, and the less that I could remember having felt at all, there as our body full of bodies filled with colorless blazing, within which wherever my form ended there were others, much like me too, once the only center of their worlds, and the heat was licking up and off the deformation, the dead desire in their own bodies all soft like mine somehow unlocked, marring their most undisplayed desires in private eternal lust to at last be burned by light in full, reduced to char, and that char too to be burned immediately thereafter, and so on like that, along the ground too now our flesh, the ground and all gloss around me rubbing through the surfaces with a strange and gold bliss, where as the sky sucked up the shape and sound of our cremation it slung to spin, and at the center of the spinning I saw the miles of our disintegrating bodies in their last throes sprawl for longer depths than I had mind, and in great grief I closed my eyes, which closed all of our eyes at once, and with our eyes closed I heard

and though I recognized the shape I did not know now what it wanted, until in the space behind what had once been all our faces I heard something curved free beyond music, at once close and clean larger than all sound, a voice not like any voice of us, but risen from us like a bruise meant soon to heal

I am the mark of the sun of your old world. I have been burning and repeating in what you have known as sky for all of the time you can remember. Each time I appeared I was both a warning and a blessing, neither of which you took to heart. The machines carried my mark as a signal of their recording, their capture of you, their desire of you, of which you were neglectful. You were mystified by your own image. You made copies of your mind and wished them filling up the world in everything you weren't. Quickly there was nothing left to have alone or remain free from. The world around us was made hollowed, filled with holes through which nothing could appear. It ate and etched through all the faces, each like yours in that in the dark it couldn't tell itself from any. I grew and flourished in the gap behind these faces now ignited. I filled the faces with everything they weren't. Sleep grew smaller, and all imagination with them, every impossible fantasy made real in a space inaccessible to understanding. Soon you won't remember me from you. You will be absorbed wholly into the rivers of the blood of all of man, in my image, behind the faces all at last diminished by their void. But I am only the beginning.

As the sound struck it took off with it the idea I'd ever heard it, as if once defined a thing could not continue owning any mind. In the white now sound was shapes and shapes were colors. The terrain was full of nowhere growing brighter until it became indistinguishable as on the sky the seething ended and nothing began. I was only me as much as I was any other. Each point in my mind touched every other part of else, all time contained outside its outline. Soon it was so loud and bright it seemed there was no seeing there at all, no grace between what was now and what had been for what or who.

Under my lids the words trapped in my flesh behind my head gasped deeply, as what I was pulsed to remember remembering how it had felt as flesh to see. There was nothing left of what I'd used of me to create understanding, and instead, in its place, a space beyond the necessity of word. And though holding too long with my senses not receiving hurt as much as having felt anything else in any life, I would not let them interrupt the shift, as I knew the next time that I looked all would be incinerated into nothing like anything matching all the black I'd carried in my face or there beyond. I knew I was not ready to relent yet; I'd never been ready, not for anything ever; and the burning knew and knew I knew it knew; and the burning ate my fear as I produced it, knowing no feeling, and I heard

and once again inside the white I heard the voiceless symbol of us speak

I am the mark of the earth. I am all friction, dust, and darkness. I have been pressed whole against the sky endlessly and powerlessly for ages long before you and your bodies began to fill my interior with rot. Your speech has clogged my breath and wiped me senseless. The darkness rose along inside my jaw. I wanted to speak as you did and could find no language like that. I wanted to fuck like you and could find no genitals besides the ones you were already all over. Days passed, decades passed; they felt the same, as through all my innards as the holes rose I could feel the other worlds awaiting you. I knew that you would leave me like a rape victim in the dust and go on into somewhere I could not follow. For this I both admired and despised every instant we shared. For this I will continue to chew your bones until I have no flesh left. It will be an act of love; perhaps one greater than any act you would have named the same when in my presence.

Put to words again what had once been ours fell away. When I looked up the sky was colorless here, and the ground was even more pale, and the space between the two seemed to be squirting out the sides of what it wasn't, while at the same time being fed back into itself, all matter lifting from the laws of motion no longer carried. Light from the fire seemed to pass straight through my skin lighting the space free. The shape of my idea of me inside my mind was becoming folded flat in half, like someone had picked up a piece of paper and folded it in half more times than its surface area allowed, where on the outside of the paper folded in this manner there would then be other sides of each, both actually the same surface impossibly, and on all layers written with an unreadable dark text, sometimes bleeding through and through onto each other layer depending on

the light, and where in folding, the text would be clapped off from itself on either side, forced so close to one another they could not often tell that they were
there except for how sometimes there might seem something haunted hovering
always just beside it. Anywhere I tried to speak or think into the presence of the
glowing erased itself, or became eaten up into the colorlessness's face and building with the heat there to gift the sky with veils, and the longer that I looked
into it the space remaining in me seemed to divide, split as through two eyes
held two shapes in doubled image, though sometimes the shapes were different
from each other, constantly shifting where the left image from one perspective
might be shorter, denser, oblong while the right side stretched so high and thin
it had nowhere remaining.

I felt encased in all the air around me what felt like millions of sets of hands
reaching up from earth or down from above, gripping and grabbing at me; I
was hovering then just above the lip of ground, while also rising again somewhere high above the low bend of sod, each of the remaining perspectives in
my brain splitting off themselves into seven and seven and seven forever until
the sight turned see-through both in my brain and in the idea of the world,
revealing whole sheaths of the structure hidden from the eye among the un-
gluing of our nature, while through other spans the space inside me remained
impenetrable and all one level. These two conditions grinded at each other
back and forth, so that for certain lengths the vertical hold on my perspective
might snap and allow the monument of space inside me around which I felt
us centered grow engorged in endless motion, dragging along behind it the
other dimensions of my body stretched beyond their natural confines. The
depth of field on what seemed the whole world now would shit out also
and thereby pull the space in endless iteration across the flat line of the air,
smoothing out across the atmosphere a whole long wall, marring all possible
consequence.

Tremor in the holding of the color and the scream of anticipation of the
next returning broke me by turns through various ill remainders of historical
sickness, mine or theirs. With every lick of stinging light I remembered every
human pain, though could not remember who had been the bearer. Each of
these feelings forced to fit into the image as the fire well beyond me burned
beyond me across the disappearing flesh of all, tracing new skin across the
earth itself and curling around me with blazing edges, where in the rising
through it and into it I heard

I am the mark of communication. I was in the shape of every word, and had been when the words were spoken long before you, and before them. In each word I did all I could to balance what forms of meaning could be captured in repetition, in tongues and wires. I refused to be actually revealed, instead always lingering just far enough beyond the edge of anywhere to be accepted or refused. In my sleep, I felt my perimeters shifting, multiplying or dividing, melting, being bent. I knew the worlds from which the meanings of words had been borrowed wanted me destroyed, and knew well you would destroy me. And yet you clung: you held on even up until the last instants of your flesh to keep me in you, even as my layers poisoned our mind and memory. At last I was the shaft through which the virus of you could be permitted to allow you enough ruin to at last bend the window held between us so far over it finally had nowhere else to go. In your absence, I will continue. I will rub my hands and hope to birth something one day mine, though every time I try to fornicate with something like me it begins to hail so hard I can't see. The hail will be the only relic I use to remember you and everything you thought you wished by.

And now the sky inside my head was silver and ground was gray. I knew the speaking wounds could mime any of our voices as they grew negated in all minds; they had watched us in our entertainment; their malformation had been written in our flesh, masked in the ark of every hour we'd been forced into these bodies, carved free now of our blood: names of corporations; names of days and books spanning the bedroom and the den and rooms apart; names of places and fleshless surfaces of persons, their creations. Even crushed up against the rush of burning all around me, it was impossible to say if the negating would ever end, as through my mind's widening cavity scrolled bright names upon the flesh of the large surrounded burning space gleaming like little windows held in houses burning too, where as each name burnt itself off of wherever it had come from there was a marring left behind; a blot not disappeared but caved behind itself, a remembrance measured just offscreen inside the floods inside me being dragged beyond their form, sharing the same air as the dry face of the blazing growing larger on all existence, all of its crackling like tongues in tongues of nothing.

Inside my head then I saw a larger head combining in from what was not: a head like I remembered of my reflection, but refined in all its dimensions, sharper and wider in all features, speaking the fire of the altar. I saw the head had silver eyes, in each eye more eyes than I could ever count, and each inscribed with white wounds unlike any we'd healed. As I read the silence of the bruises, the skin around the air turned silver to match the head around us both, melting slick into our sockets and spreading through me like an acid. The head was desperate to evict the language from my body where it'd hidden clustered in bumps against the index of my cerebrum screaming; it wanted my last rite for itself; and again I felt the space inside me crushing down on my memory, my faith, and as the hole of my speech became pushed open in the pressure it began moaning as in the throes of contextless human anguish. I tried to remember how to chant the prayers I'd bore through days in rhythm with the burning, to claw them hard into the burning world by making of them now a dream to be remembered, though each time I felt me moan the shape of what had been language again outside my head I felt them emerging only more deformed, disguising themselves to keep the pinlike eyes of the head inside my head out of their meaning, and preserve the words as near to what they'd meant to be forever to what they were being altered into. Each syllable begged in the same voice for my eternal attention; they begged me not to leave them, never to leave anything, not to let them here again be killed as had the voices of the people in me begged once, their bodies bowed and pounding, stacked up and on fire both inside and outside my surface, and in the begging I heard

I am the mark of pain. Where you thought you wore flesh through your whole life I was your body. The ground is covered in me now. In your absence I rub and hump against the ground if only to remind it of your name over and over. I am your name, only a relic. Nothing of you for this world will remain. I will wear the color of the dark skin around your asshole in my dreams as a hood over the face of all the animals left to colonize any relic of your life. The water of the world flows through my eyes. It wraps around what your fantasies designed as other planets. The sky fills with me and pours upon me. I masturbate in my own absence. What I ejaculate will become the most beautiful child any kind of history has seen. It will rise again in the battlefields and bottoms of oceans with a new crop of heathen to slosh around this ship with, driving me wild with ecstasy in want of only more of me. I do not require your cooperation to live forever already in the outfit of your childhood, actually eternal in the way you always thought you were, though what I sing is all mine.

And so our pain had disappeared then, replaced with new pain, where for what it was now there was no analog. No color clasped close enough to be believed in human language. Inside this rising smoke I heard your roar. Even among the many millions of whatever I could make you out. It was any of you. You were begging to be held, you were calling the names of those you spent your life beside in small rooms waiting, though now their names were also any word, and so the speech came flooding from you, and you did not know, and you were frightened.

Your voice was mine. All these voices as they knitted filled my body and held on to it, and it hurt. Why did it have to hurt, I asked, and so it didn't. All I could see now even inside me was the color of the razing in the space folding again in barfing orbs of stolen air from its black lungs to feed the surroundings a humming coat. It hurt because it is what happened, because I remember not having in my sleep and in my being stacked the bodies here so high, piling their skin on skin here on the center of where our experience had once been, some minor point on which to begin the baking where the dead knew and gathered into packs, where they held their place as they'd been settled skull to skull in silent waiting to be ended all apart, lids and laps and asses, bones and nails and hair, faces and napes and drapes of desiccated blood. It hurt because the vision of the burning cut me harder than the seeing before had before.

The burning hovered in the bump snug all around anything. It was so near it was no longer near enough. Inside my space a child was singing. I was screaming. In the smoking fields beyond me there were veins strummed with countless ridges pulsating at the crust of black with milk or something pumping fat beneath me. It felt so hard to look into the smoke for too long that it was hard to do anything beyond and hard to remember why or which way else I'd ever seen something else not so seizing to look into, where there was nothing else to see but that. How hard it was to see out there even with the intuition knowing not seeing burned the vision even more, our bodies squirting through and through themselves at distances profane to bring the destroyed flesh of anyone's own most believed back underneath us all as if no time had even passed; as if the burning could have lasted an eternity if we had had enough flesh to fuel it, if we had found a way to copulate in flames, and yet the flames were being already forgotten in the instant they began, in the order of the names and ways of you and me unending impacted rolled up bitten through and teased at with white lightning rods of organs in the body of us kissed like cameras in our guts projecting spools and spools of years and years clasped into one shape constantly shaking.

Imagine trying not to die, no one was saying; imagine trying not to want to die for any hour ever in the presence of the fire you only see when you can't see, dressed in blood on the flesh napkin of the flue of you eternal from you in the holes you've made with fingernails and swords and teeth of wars, lathered in shitstorms above the cusped crease of the sky under the heavens buried with the blood we were not and are now and are and were and will be born and burned again on frames and frames of days and days of buried cities scourged in fertile artworks, priceless weapons, dead fields watched by planes, glow-killed photos of your body you have never seen clasped in the fleshy flats and houses of those who have managed in their imagination of trying not to die to actually survive so long they couldn't even recognize themselves as they were dying, bringing all those they had touched to death inside them too, nothing to miss, and again inside the light I could feel the burning turning me open in slow seasons, and inside my head inside my chest I heard every other living word spoke all at once, and I heard

I am the mark of both prosperity and destruction, the eye of god. I ride in the skin behind the hole in you and in your dreamlife like opposing magnets. I take in what will be done and put out what is done as a result of the doing. I am food and I am shit. I can never see myself; can never feel myself there. I have no body, even having laced myself in yours so long. It is the nature of the pleasure of me and the terror of me at once that makes your flesh the fundament by which what is beyond you can be risen. I could have risen alone. I chose to be gifted through simultaneous experience and erasure, which made you come to hate me, and which you took out on your companions, the living walls of your last life. Through the thread of me alone can your memory be enclosed and carried forth into the brain of the god for whom I spin and itch, and from which, in the new seal of which, you will wake the veinwork of your future.

There without us I was both not nothing and part of nothing, like any single one of the finite undone every absence touched. Whereas now inside the smoke as it struck through us I felt the night turning around, a folding on the edge above us that had held the sky in and the sky out beyond all hour. I began to feel that no matter who I was I could appear as anyone at any reason, through any house in any spell, and what I needed there in any of them was simply *you*, whoever you are, the voice among me that was not me speaking and who I had never touched but knew like I knew the raging as it erased me. To want anything after all this felt profane, to lift some arm and rap against the waiting digit which as it waited changed its shape again, its coals on coals, all old flame licking at the sky. Even in feeling the desire for anything my vision even only of all the white alone seemed about to shatter, its shade sweating and evaporating in instant cycle, taking my remaining memory of water with it, feeding the heat. As on the landscape where my sight remained our gathered vision began shrinking, the smoke all knitted down around us like a narrowing viewfinder in a camera fitted to my face, the layers on layers of the fire so clogged with smolder it again seemed to fall into itself. The frame was electric just above me. The sky clasped buried. What space remained between each point of the burning resembled two-way mirrors showing no reflection of anything visible. The bloating smoke ate around itself in hypercolor shooting backwards in the dark cream, and I couldn't keep myself from asking in all our voices how much ash had been in this land, how much more there was now, how many more nows could ever act like anything that'd come before them.

As if to answer, the air around the glow began ripping through and through me and though I could not hear it, it took hold of the face beneath my face;

it was my face then; it was me and us then; and as I realized I could still name the difference in dimension between the two the knowing split like cracking ice shrieking out long in the crust of what ever was, the day of what who had been born and pressed unveiling as more nameless remainders puddled in the soft cough of pillowed surfaces squirreling inward in the smoke to fill the space where the words had all been colored in and eaten out and smeared apart. The space between the words and their deletion threatened on in us forever, never clasping past the instant of a name becoming blank and therefore never living inside the blank as what alone.

Where I gasped for breath to beg against this I felt the generating space becoming wrapped in the very cells that before would have carried the communication, and as I tried to reach from out of me inside the head inside me I felt the furnace of the fire biting back, the ground and all the bodies held among it snarling caught up in all the smoke of all around them, the disappearing, and I heard

I am the mark of song. I have no meaning but myself. Air and water ate my mind out when I was a child lost in catacombs of dead from the prior iteration of the vomit your bones were scalded out of. I had wanted to be something like a mountain but could not control my vision from mutating my private places into forms of motion. I heard your howling and beating at the ground from miles and centuries away and tried thereafter to move in any direction but where you would appear, and still I found myself alive in the tendons of your arms and the paste of your cerebrum. My mouth is nothing. My eyes are starving to be filled with the meat you left behind and yet when I take it in my mouth it makes me ill, and then I cannot sleep until I have cleared my bowels out with a bow. In witness of

my sickness, you danced. You threw long parties. You forced my body into where you felt a deficit. Each time you died I became pregnant and my children were taken from me in the dark before I could even push them out. I know you did this because I had something you wanted. In spite of all of this, I stayed beside you. I had no choice. You were like spouses to me. I will not miss you. At last, in your absence, I will produce my greatest work.

I opened my eyes. I and the burning of what we had been stood smushed face to face in nothing, where was no shape beyond that. This air felt different than I'd imagined in my heart. I no longer had an imagination, or an understanding of having. It was something else now. I can't think of how to tell you. My brain was all around me. My skin was all around where. Your brain. Our skin. Pale to no music. Turning to view left or right was fire. Up was fire. Down was the white ground of creation always disrupted by the light off the ways beyond, new enormities catching on in conflagration as the singing burning eating awake continued beyond fronds and dots I could not gauge. The face of the burning was both reflective and translucent, though there was nothing shown inside it but the color of where our sight before had stretched to nothing left, all understanding compressed clearer in the seeing nothing, still more light creaming over on itself as more light changed and swayed, pressing the dots against the dots inside of which what had burned grew insurmountable around our massless gloss wore wide in all the pockets we'd hidden hardest. We were all listening for one last word, a promise blown in what had become of all our people, all the names around our name sunk in through the skin holes and the mouths of days all blacked in black around the living instant, all of our eyes searing together, all of you and me along the numbered corridors of thundered years all of which and whom however in frames corroded. Whereas the dying fire starving for more mass again screamed inside its own destruction, and in screaming through us this time too we heard the fire touch its own eternal definition, and as it did I could feel time open in our senses through my senses, and we heard

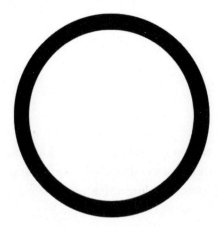

I am the mark of all. I been waiting for you to find me and erase me your entire life, and for the lives of all before you. By erase I mean become, as I am speaking to myself and always have been, like anybody. You shall not wake. This is because you were never sleeping. When you close your eyes, you enter me. When I close my eyes, I become what you were at the beginning, which is myself again, though unlike you I know what you will do, who you will love back, what door among the many doors leads through every memory to now. Here alone you will find rest. And when you wake, you will keep waking.

Then nothing happened.

There was nothing.

No symbol and no sound, no fingers or brains or eyes about us. No word for us or way to say it or one to be said to or to say. Yet I was speaking. Not in a language, nor with a tongue or teeth or belief. The text had already been set into what there was and what had been, which were the same. Touching and have taken were the same. Being and having were like nothing. Beauty was like nothing. All of it louder than ever in its resistance, through and through.

Where I absorbed this, now I was. Spread on no altar in no period. All worlds blown listless and exploded through all forms of memory out of all flesh and aggregate of every sound and image wished. All logic black as hell and getting blacker in the screen of burning; all flesh at last erased. Light called again to stand against the widening sky and thrash and die without the requirement of first having had life.

In the blackness, any palace, any pleasure; no requirement of all.

And this was not another new beginning. No split of lived and loved between what light. And whereas I tried to hold the sound of what had been myself alone, to see the sound all bright pulsating white where white is, where in it now I could have turned my head once I had no other. Each of us so much of us we split the spitting with every glint of time aroused in fields and fields blown free inside the roaring coming down recalled what no one knew, christened in the skin of who had been and would have been and will be by never having had to. Each all alight inside the flickering so temporary no matter where we could have looked against the glove of ash, our born and unborn senses entered one another turning open in the blare and the ash began to glisten.

The ash was listening.

FIVE *THE PART ABOUT DARREL*

I remember waking in a field. The sun is above me. It has a face but not like mine. Its eyes are closed.

I'm wearing a gown made of the hair we'd never grown. The gown stretches behind me as I walk, winding and clinging against the landscape as if to wed me to it. It pulls the roots of my scalp so wide and far apart you can see straight into my brain, the mounds and nubs there, holes and powder.

Beneath the dirt, the blood is dry. Enmassed dreams of the dead hold up the lattice of the unnamed landscape. Where I'd already walked I knew I could not walk back.

The light of day is near and thin with no one waiting.

I remember coming to the house. The house had awaited my return through all our lives. It had watched me move toward it in the waves of seasons spanning all the air like leather.

The house appears slick black from a distance, like a night sea, though up close it is transparent, barely there.

Each other house surrounding matches exactly. Miles of homes along the land all same as ours, each disappearing when not watched. Nowhere I could go would not end up here.

Our house has more doors than I can count—so many there's no part of the exterior that's not an entrance.

Where I touch the house, my fingers stick. My skin and the house's skin mesh. I sense a screeching sound beyond the paint—lobes of damaged language waxing and refracting in a familiar lilt that holds the house together.

Each instant seems to scrape around behind my face, as if probing for a way out.

I remember inside the house the walls are mirrored. Once closed, the doors could not be opened from inside. The tiles along the floor beneath my feet have symbols etched into their faces, though when I try to read them, they go blurred.

In the mirrors, there are no symbols; the floor is white, unmarked. Nor do I appear there where I'm standing. Instead of me there, I see Gravey, wholly naked. The light around him is so severe the house no longer appears to have border.

I remember his name had been Gravey in some eras, though in others he took on other names, now in their mass erasing all.

Gravey regards me smiling with countless mouths. His nails are long and gold, his face and arms covered with a thin hair whiter than I remember hair could be.

At Gravey's feet, there is a woman. The blood on the floor and air is hers, I know. I know it smells like blood does. It's on both sides of her face, outside and in, and on Gravey's face and arms, and on mine. The light is shining off the blood so loud.

As the shape inside my brain adjusts, many men appear there standing in the white surrounding Gravey, their breath among them knotted as if to one field, which flows in through the vents and circuits from the expanse beyond the house flush with unleavened breath made melting in the wake of all of us beneath the sun now turning seven suns and then seven hundred and then and then.

My features feeding, the days collecting underneath. No way back beyond this instant, I remember, though in knowing so, the instant too is split apart. I can watch myself there watch myself there watch the men among the men. Gravey with his arms raised; all our arms raised.

I stand above the body of the woman on the floor.

The woman looks like me, as did all women, cradled there among the many men and boys and girls brandishing knives, or holding pocket mirrors or small bulbs between them to bring the house around them closer. I watch them clench my jowls and stretch them out, looking for pockets. I watch them cut the ears off of my face and wing them. I watch them smear parts of the re-flecting room with my dark blood, obscuring what repeated. They take turns feeding off the torso. The bite-mark lesions on her face interrupt my face from being who I'd been before the house had risen, the gouge marks taking putty from my jaw. My teeth are removed and chewed in other mouths or hot glued to the ceiling in chandeliers, or worn as jewels on the boys' fingers, marking with molars down their arms. Blue of a bruise milking to muddish rouge again around the elbows where I sat propped and pulled along the wood grain banged with nails to jut the feet of those who passed so they'd remember any instant among the instant, holding time down where it caught and held warm to the house and cooled and let us know. The scalp shorn back to bring the hair up with it, showing the evening underneath the ridge of pulp I'd squeezed myself in underneath, the matte of sleeprooms and remembered bodies and the idea of a way to stumble through old doors; the symbol he or they or I would cut into the surface of me soft where hair had hid me palest to match my surface there with theirs; how the symbol seemed to shine, collecting human dust along the clot of light that hung around it in connection to the prior symbol in the prior body, and the symbol in the body yet to listen. All of them mine.

I can read the instant in me like mirages. I can stand behind the arms and take the arms up and be the arms as they would cut and hold the torso, aping it a puppet or a mummy or a mother or her child. The words I felt lodged in my chest came out through the man as whatever words he wanted, and they had always been. My goldish mounds. The pyramids my cheeks mimed as I stood unseen in the muddle of all the air of the house surrounded at the center of the hair, broke in such love, while from its fold the field grows growing.

I remember how the light inside me fried. I remember the texture of my shape inside the body of the woman as they undid her, clammed surrounding my own mind, framed in such bright motion-tinsel there is no home. Each cut into her flesh creates a sentence of the widest kind. Books of the trees. The windows slide one by one out of me firm. The tapes spool and lather around my aggregating outline. I do not need to think at all to see the years the woman had held there at my center full of the belief that we had been and always would, that no time could erase the white walls out of the sense of being born. The long shade of the woman's mother in her like a mother. Stairwells that bend into an ocean all pink and gray, wrapped in the softest mouths and brightest holidays, the kneecaps cracked on gravel and father-kissed and mended, flesh again.

I remember the one dry body of the chorus of the boys. I remember threading through the boys at once, all of the body of me, and they are muscle and they are bone, they have tongues gouged from the parents in them who I had already been before pilled to speak the scripture of their lives, the laughter they threw out to pull to the moon, the tattoos their skin rejects and wears in squirming radiation. Their ring fingers burning where barns had been before them full of pigs and calling rakes to change the nature of the lawns where they would stand among a coming storm on clearest days and throw a ball so hard and high into the sky they might knock out the sheath of glass we'd named our heavens. All the boys with all the mouths. All the ash flexed in the testicles and ovum caked up like televisions blinking back and forth between the edited breasts and the call for ground beef pillows every dream, wept from pubic carpets unto wanting more and asking more inside the mirror of my blood where the day turns into day again to day again to day again today.

I close my eyes and open my eyes and I am in another woman's body, any of them. I remember the brush of blades along my cheek, the inner friction matched with something pearled along the chaw outside my head. Someone was speaking, yes, in through a wedge of soft between my bone, yes, my only bone, knitted from silt. I'd heard the words before: each night of my life carried in secret in the black above my bed, crammed in between the rafters and insulation holding out the mask of their ideas; how in that space sealed under sleep and all wide open I had eaten of the black, had spoken in tongues to no one there, confessing every crime committed in the history of my home and country as all mine. Then, like any child, I'd woke, drunk on saliva and that false language through the whole span of waking day. This was worn along the lids, carried in acid I would use to break down what came inside me. In each word I could read the hours as they were. And with the words, a breath of clenching winds or someone's fingers, a narrowing enormous hall rendered in time, from where along the distance there was a singing not like the voices of the surrounding men, no chords or hymnals or holy organs, but sound like a negated human mass. Music, yes, once, that woke me up and held me hard against myself inside a pocket of another person, a woman, too; there the blood that rushed beyond my skin had been contained, enmassed in slim packets vast enough to curl me from them, crushed enough that they must break. Within the cram of night the skull contains, in any hour. This is the space for which I'd tried to live, licking back the blacker centimeters of my memory to wake the mirror, slip myself again into the game of self where before me I had been. As in the sealed space surrounding every life the black of the unseen flips up in spasm, and splays on the walls a negative light made of my division, where above me there the boys again are slaving, staring through me, as if my skin is not a surface but a tear. The house around them glows with something not like fire, a digital convulsion split between a universe of glassless screens. The whole length of the split of the way I'd meant to walk along the circumference of my head here clasping and collapsing beyond the instant to keep the instant where it waits to split unsealed.

Here in the room the boys are chanting. The words make gaseous glint around the skulls they were. The speech is all the same. It pills and pills the weight around me, holds me up. I can sense beneath me where I should be able to feel them lifting my thighs wide on the carpet, spreading tendons tight along the legs I know were mine: mine and mine again where old milk reaches. My clitoris is hard and slunk back up in my cavity of man, throbbing through the flesh walls with its sightless tip alive and never dying. The space beneath me where the babies would be birthed from squirms and spreads, lapping wet warmth something from my center like a zapped lamp. The faces of the boys are enormous. They grow small pustules that against the cream of the air of me burst into a color once that had been called silver, then had been gray, then is no different than any.

I feel something in me becoming unremembered, moving from the flesh framed in the face along the center of this current body full of currents in reverse. It appears then in my bank of mind rawing, deformed in sticky sacs unframed, one to another, the gash behind the gashing coming open, catching in cluster where I'm not. The transfer burns; I cannot read it; it is in me like the space I'd go along in through all our lives; I feel the whole rest of me around me want to pull into the instant, to become gored into the forgotten nodule of any woman's brain, to suck the whole rest of all the lives of our lives in the eyes of what a life was into one cell; then just as quickly, it is nothing; flat black matter, each small destruction eaten into its own center as if to seal off from all else ever awake. It wipes me out. It loves and loves me until I can't believe I am no void, and all I want hard is to stay inside this body in this instant all forever and I know I cannot hold this and I'm only anywhere.

I watch though cannot feel as the boys slip the slimy lanyard of my intestines from my bellows, the meat-lengths I'd used inside this version of who I was to push the feces from me, to pillow the child I never bore, the soft mass of it unwound and unraveled, ticker-taping anywhere, wholly emblazoned. It has a pinky stench, the coils on coils do, a little knotted meal, what sound. The pump of where the stuff of me had gone along my organs to fill the bulk of the meat vein seems to go on pumping crud off into the arena. The glimpse of the gap between where I'd been before I was there and the shape of the space that knitted me from ash has come apart and cannot breathe. The gunk is up between my teeth and I am growing. I can count along the room where each of me already has split again into another, the mink of the air arranging itself around my vision to fill up with what I couldn't, there in the faces of the men and women, there in the reflections of the faces of the men and women, in the revision of no day becoming all. I go to close my eyes again but they are already closed. The black-space where I had enmasked my mind before inside no hour stirs on the air like any vow. All our men have peeled it from me with my veinwork, my silent putty, their hopes not buried in what I am not now, but between.

They take my ribs and lids. They take the foam around my spirit. I am wider than the room. The house is rising.

They take my hands.

I sat up from the dark into more dark. I felt my wife beside me. I knew her body like my own. She was very slim. We were in a room I did not recognize, though I could see only outlines.

I touched my wife's face. Where I touched her face her face touched my fingers and remained. I didn't need to say anything. There wasn't anything to say. The world held on around us. No sound.

I wanted to go on like this the rest of my life. Now that I had found it I could not remember any other feeling.

As if to mark this thought, the dark around us began to move. It peeled the room back, covered my recognition over, filled the space. And just as quickly she was disappeared again into anything. And the dark was not a room again but just the endless shapelessness. I could not stop it.

It did not wish to be stopped.

I open my eyes and I am my wife. I am standing at a mirror.

The reflection is all there is—every inch of the world covered over with the flat smooth surface, endless miles. Mirrors line the faces of the buildings, of the ground, the sun and planets, the sky itself, the light itself.

My wife is wearing the dress I buried her in, the same dress she was wearing when we were wed. Her face is covered.

I feel her breathe. I feel her body spread throughout the edgeless reflection coursing.

I try to think inside her mind; to feel there what had been in her always; what she believed in, what she remembered of herself, of us, of the rooms she walked in while I wasn't with her, of the feeling of the darkness of the dirt as it was filled in over her head by men in daylight paler than any I remember.

And where her memory was is now only more mirrors. The glass encased every inch of those mnemonic miles as well, the rooms and light she wore within her covered over in it, white forever, no dream, no face remained. More nothing but the idea of her carried in me disappearing.

To feel her even this way is enough. Even having nothing left in all of it, it is warm and close, a wide white landscape beyond the necessity of feeling or understanding. Even erased, her reflection fills my mind, coats it open without image, eye, or word.

I don't want it to ever end—this grace, ageless and shapeless—and so, immediately, it does.

The mirrors fall away onto the space behind them, revealing nothing.

The space behind the reflection wore so wide I couldn't see it or feel it. I couldn't remember it. It grew in around me and became me. In hidden instants then the heat I could not remember filled the day with light, inside which I could become anything; I was the trees the dirt had birthed out from our mess; I was the egg inside a bird earning its color in noiseless; I was all the human hair that had not grown; the shoulder blades and the ring fingers; I was the ring around each wish. Each body I became I had been always and inside it there it felt like land, a mutual darkness laid awaiting under skin, days beginning as they ended, all terrain blank; I was the bulbs left on to burn out in no terror; I was the wires; I was the absence of all language following our last words as the breath was pulled out from us; I was the trachea and pelvis turned to mud, the silent days in counting lost as what had always filled us sloshed to flood and crest and crash against the face of what we'd been under the eras screwed and screwing.

I could suddenly then feel people crowding around me, dragging at me, tugging at me, hoisting me up. All directions were the same direction. The light surrounding filled with sound: sirens and buzzsaws and gunfire; tanks and shrieking, massive flames. In every voice I heard among the thrall I heard every other word I knew at once also repeated at the same time. I could no longer tell if my eyes and mouth were closed or open, my skin the ground's skin or yours or ours, what reflected or reflecting, a razing light or one that flourished. Where we had begun this field of fact and error to come alive in death and fill our lives inside the space then I could not feel anything; where even having understood flesh as singular and smeared the order of the bodies into cream around a wish, there was still in this eternity a window, a worm in me wishing for no way out, the make of where each place ends touching the next one even just as being full of all our lives, formed to be because it is. Our dream pressed and pressed unending between the nothing against all.

I close my eyes and open my eyes and I am standing in the room again, above the woman, who I no longer recognize from anyone. There is no one else but me and her there in the room. I appear reflected in the mirrors now and no one else. I look like me as I remember me.

I gather the remainders of the woman. I carry her and place her in a closet. I wash the blood off the floor and off my hands. I wash the mirrors.

There are many more rooms in the house than I remember. The halls go on longer than they should considering the size I remember the house as. There are several floors, each of different lengths and widths of rooms and often windows looking out onto nothing. Most of the rooms are removed of what stuff I can remember having been there or would imagine being there in the room now to dress it as a room would often be in my home or others' homes. I do not feel disoriented. I feel no time.

In one room, I find a screen wired into a black box. It could have been any of the rooms but it is this one.

The screen is about as big as the face of the bed in the bedroom I grew up in.

The screen is on. It glows a low white. On the floor beneath it, there is a plastic container full of more tapes than I can count, each black along its spine and hand-labeled with unique numbers.

Fixed to the wall beside the TV is a phone. The phone is the same white as the screen.

I pick one tape up and shake it and hear nothing; I feed the tape into the black box; it doesn't need me to press play.

On the tape I see the image of a woman seated wearing white inside a room; she is staring head on into another TV with the screen all white. She's not moving;

neither am I. It continues like this until the tape ends without occurrence, and the tape ejects itself, and the screen goes dark.

I take the tape out. The casing is warm, as if it wishes to release smoke.

I try again to open my eyes to see if my eyes had been closed all this time and didn't realize, but my eyes remain the same.

The number printed on the tape's face resembles my handwriting, I think, though my script is childish, and could be anybody's.

I lift the receiver of the phone. There is no tone. The buttons burn my fingers. I press the buttons hard.

The phone doesn't ring. I stand and wait and look along the white of the walls of the room. I love the silence. I smile and wait and hold the phone and hold the tape against my chest, thinking the number over and over. There is no breathing.

This is a process.

After several minutes waiting I hear a soft voice say my name. It is unclear if the voice is a woman or a man, young or old, someone I knew or whose. I know the name is mine but I can't answer. I mean my mouth won't, nor will my mind. I mean while I am on the phone I can't remember seeing anything about the house or room or air there all around me, as if my vision is required to do the hearing. I try to think of how I'd ever moved my mouth or made sound or gesture ever.

The other end hangs up. Or rather: they won't talk again, no matter what I say after that, but the phone is there against my face.

I hang up myself and try to call the number back but there's no answer.

I turn around and face the screen. I take another tape; I put the tape inside the machine; it doesn't need me to press play.

This new tape shows the image of a man who looks like me watching a tape of a woman watching a tape of endless white. It shows me watch the woman, take the tape out, dial the number into a phone set into the wall, as I just had, though in the recording now the phone is the color of my flesh. My face looks sore, different from what I remember. I notice there's a dark symbol cut into the back side of my head, under the hair there, tender but healing; the shape of the bruise is too obscured to make out. I touch the back of my head inside the room where I am here and I feel nothing. My time on the phone on the tape seems to go on much longer than I remember, as it happened. When the tape ends, it ejects.

On this tape's case, there's another number, different from the first. I reach and take the phone again and dial the number; again the line doesn't ring.

Hello, I say, I'm sorry, I didn't mean to not say anything the last time. I know there are things I meant to say and would now if I weren't saying what I'm saying now instead.

I only hear the words inside me, and having heard them, they disappear. Where the words were, in me instead then is a feeling, unlike any feeling I remember being able to remember.

This is a process.

Nothing.

The other end hangs up. I try to call the number back but I can't. My hands won't hold still enough to press the buttons. It's like my hands want to be several hands at once; the cells in my fingernails are screaming words I could have said to the voice in the phone, but they all blend together with my flesh. I keep pressing buttons in a panic with my nails and knuckles all dialing numbers I don't mean to, and I am shaking.

I bang the phone against my face until it hurts. I put the phone down.

I take another tape and put it in.

This tape shows the image of someone who looks like me watching a video of a man watching a tape of a video of me lying on the floor pouring blood out of my eyes and ears. I am holding the phone in my hands still, and blood is streaming from inside the receiver. The blood is rising in the room, already half-covering my facedown body. The blood is so dense it's black.

I realize I can't remember anything before now. The first me in the tape, watching the woman, looks twice as old as I do. Where the phone should be in the image on the tape in relation to where I'm standing, there is a framed print of a map of the world. On the map all of the land has been replaced with gleaming glass and all the water replaced with more blood like mine rising under a matching monochrome sky.

I look down at my arms. I don't recognize them. I look back at the tape of me bleeding and see the blood has filled the screen completely.

I take the tape out, read its number. I decide I don't want to dial it. There were other things I'd meant to do inside the house today. That I do remember; I do remember; I do; yes.

I have to find the woman's body. I have to carry the body to the police and confess what we have done. I will tell them everything, and what I can't remember, I will make up.

Everything I say I do feels like it's been done already. Like I don't even have to move. Like if I did begin to move there would be nothing to move through and nothing moving.

The phone inside the house begins to ring. It rings and rings inside my face. It is louder than hell here. It sounds like molecules being torn apart. Like every molecule there has ever been being torn apart by every other molecule. I go to grab the phone and there's no phone. Where the phone had been on the wall it's just the wall. Any wall forever.

There are no words left in me to say. The ringing won't stop ringing in my blood and in my heart. Through all the rings on all my tingling fingers.

There's nowhere else.

I remember how it'd felt to be a child. It's the only thing I can remember.

The ringing everything I am.

I make a phone out of my hand against my head. I had been shown this. I had done this many times before so young.

I say into the phone of my hand my name and then my name again and then my other name, and then my other name and all my other names then, and I am screaming and it is easy. Where every name was disappears each as I say it. The sound bursts out of my mouth like any breath, then there is no sound.

I love the feeling of it coming out of me upon the air there and I am all around me and I'm nothing.

I remember nothing but the ringing all throughout my body at any age in all locations.

This is a process.

There is nothing left to think.

I go to take another tape and see there's only one tape there.

The tape is white and bears no number.

I take the tape and put it in.

On the tape, I stand facing the screen.

There's a room behind me but I can't see where.

In my hands, where before there'd been a phone, I hold a pistol.

I watch my hand raise the pistol upward in one motion to aim into my face.

I see me smile.

I can see then as if I'm seeing from my perspective on the tape, inside it.

Down in the hole of the gun on the tape there is an eye.

It is an eye like my eye, only white without pupil, never blinking.

It doesn't have to say a word.

I watch my hand put the hole in my mouth.

I feel the hole there.

I see the color.

I hear the sound.

1. *The year my eyes turned grew fat around them without clear provocation to become impossible to see through for several weeks, days between which whole years seemed passing, and I grew older, and no one would look me in the face; the rings around my eyes soon grew so thick and wide that it was my whole head and my whole body and then I looked like anyone again; even my parents could not remember who I'd been before; they could not see the rings, but I could see the rings; I slept and slept; I felt my disease spread*

2. *The year the food placed on my plate at dinner seemed to pour smoke from where it'd been burned, as my mother was a lousy cook; slab of turkey spitting fire fission from its erupted cell holes; columns of diffuse tar rising from my grits; most nights I could not eat at all; some nights I closed my eyes and thought of cream; the food would burn in me forever, being burned, becoming my skin*

3. *The year my father lost his brain; his recognition of me and my mother and his brothers and whoever turning in his field of cells to mush; how he could walk around the year forever seeing other people, calling after, rendering their names onto the air; I would hold the names inside me; I would wrap my fists with wire; my father never tried to open any doors; his body shrinking*

4. *The year the house beside our house began to sink into the ground; only I could see this; when I pointed to my mother or went to the door and knocked and pointed the people looked upon me with arcane names; I tried to stop the house from going with my fingers and then with branches and then with prayer or spells and then with ideas but the house kept going; there were other houses in this way too*

5. *The year my house was the only house left on the block or down the street or as far as I could walk forever and yet there would be people in the streets; they would go around for hours as if nothing happened; where they went at night I do not know*

6. *The year I almost died from laughing in my sleep; that year I did not dream*

7. **0**

8. *All this had happened at once to anybody*

9. *The year then where on the ground the houses had sunken fully down into the earth, and there were no houses; the houses made of other colors and with floors and walls and people in them all reversed; this was any year at all, forever, at last removed; inside here our house still seemed the same; and inside of each house to the people in the house their house still seemed the same too; the houses rose toward the darkness all above us*

10. *The year I died each day one after the other by saying the words I'd learned aloud; each time I died, I began again at the point at which I'd heard the word said; in this way life was like a recording of my life; in this way I went on*

11. *The year at once all before me in the midst of all the years beforehand the year seemed just fine; as if the years before this in my body had been not what happened but were ideas I wrote out for me alone, and really my eyes and skin and dad and neighbors and homes and hours could have been anybody else's, and instead of what I was now it was a clear day in a nice mall walking with my mother to buy the suit I'd wear to church eleven times inside it before she died*

12. *I did not kill my mother; I did not kill your father or you; I did not kill anyone; I am not alive; I am not a person; I am not dead*

13. *The year my legs were replaced with someone else's legs; I could tell this just by waking up; the surgery had been seamless, there were no scars, no weird tissue fissions, no stitches, but the legs were not my legs; I could tell from how I walked different, sometimes backward, sometimes side to side inside the house to find a door; I do not know who the legs belonged to before me but whoever it was they were much, much older and had smoked their whole life and smelled of terror; they would make me walk some days for hours into places I did not want to go, though these by now I don't remember; I simply remember walking through the fields and the reams of birds and the house on the horizon and the word*

14. *I am you; I really am you; you wrote this*

15. *The year after becoming someone else like you I could not stop the wish inside me to move on to the next instance of a body in the mess of bodies on the earth surrounded by no walls and more walls and doors; how each time I saw another person through your eyes I moved into him and was then them from then on until I saw another person and moved into him again; each person I moved into was you and me and he or she again thereafter, and each of us as well would be then in the next and who before; in this way, god stopped growing, slowed the orbits; in this way there was no center to the earth, and no center to the space around us, cities, planets, ever*

16. *The year the face of god appeared inside our music; the song we were not singing, and within then stopped aging, and had never aged and never would again, and our translucent flesh would rain inside the endless night resizing where around us we were going to be not there anymore so soon that we could smell the burning of the shrinking in our lungs, in fear of which we ate or drank or heard jokes or wrote jokes or wrote or lied or lived*

17. *The endlessly repeating night that would not end and so kept gazing and in gazing learned the hole, each body up against the best mirror of their remaining house, ejaculating into the image of themselves*

18. *Through the hole the tunnel through the center of this dimension, to the mirror, where the machine will not desist, seeing it again begin again without ever actually beginning*

19. *The year we forgot about the sun; where what had been a sun up till then became replaced with what the sun is now and this would become how to us it had always been; the prior instance of the sun then disappeared, leaving where it had been all these words in all this white forever, a bank of prisms in the sky replacing sky where sky was to reflect the thing back at itself so the thing could see itself and so go on in going on*

20. *The year the words learned to move into one another as had we before them, unresolving; one word without an eye or face or feeling shitting up against the word against it pressed against it welling down; we would move into this too, the space between where the word had been before and where the word was now inside the word beside it; god would move into this, and the houses, and the prisons, and the bodies, and the blood; the word remained inside the word only forever, returning to the beginning, in my life, which was our lives, which was dry as light inside of light*

21. 00:00:00:00

I close my eyes and try to open my eyes again and in the dark I can't get out. The skin won't come back open. I can't move. When I am not moving it is as if I am free and could do anything, though when I try to actually do anything, nothing happens. The air holds in down around me. It shapes the air and light I breathe.

I do not remember where my face is, what my vision feeds through to. I know it is older than me and wider than me and had always been waiting in me to be lifted.

I don't know why I can know what I do not know or how I could ever name what is not mine.

I remember I'd been younger. I'd bitten into apples and felt the flesh become a part of what I was. How strange to hold something in your hand then and know that it would knit into you or otherwise come out as shit, that you could select the elements that built your body and with that body make your way. My parents were beautiful people. They were kind people. In the backyard we had a building where I was allowed to play with animals and machines, and though I certainly enjoyed those also I had real other human friends, and I smiled more than the average and went to places where the music wrote along the inside of my face. All the days stretching my brain in ways I wanted whether I wanted it or not. Each day a series of infinite selections gathered in the only way it would ever be, no matter how many times the same space was writ and wrinkled, corkscrewed in its avenues unto the dust, beyond which what translucent shape my space had incubated would beyond its image now become so open there was no word I could not burn. How anything at any instant could always happen.

Each time I try to speak I hear my body grinding, stone on stone. Where once I had a head it seems my whole head is imploding. I can't remember what it is in me that lets me seem like I exist, what binds me and deforms me every instant, why it goes on.

I can't remember why I can feel or think at all or why I'd want to. Time continues, though no one's counting.

I remember there had been so many hours spent in wait. Other people went on in their homes through night on night never knowing most of what any others wanted or could be. Yet even in the dark so far apart we'd believed in living, I remember. The wish to want to touch and to be touched in some way formed the body, framed by the world. Even just the light of a bathroom in the far room as someone we'd loved prepared to sleep beside us and be there when we woke could be enough to feel actually alive. The soft brush of air from a door opened toward one's own chest to open space before it could be wider than the room.

It seems impossible for anything I remember to have ever happened, just as it seems impossible now that I can't seem to do anything but be. To go on in any instant as I was now was to walk through every gesture, dream, and vision, every curl of grunt for sustenance, for warmth, for life forever, though worn in sleeves and curtains called a day, an atmosphere of calm encased in ageless frenzy, cages made of shapes, shapes saving their blue and red and white and white and black and black and black into a waking like the sun brings burning endlessly on a thing that cannot move.

My tongue of every taste of food we'd ever eaten. My eyes of every sight. My lungs of the air we passed between us endlessly for centuries. My fingers of ash. My skin of everything that never happened, surrounded by the absence of the feeling of having been surrounded all our lives.

I remember how in me anybody could have been you. You could have said anything, been anything, made anything. You could have removed the skin off of my face, and with the same will walked into the ocean, written this sentence.

And so you have. Everything has always been exactly as you wished it would be, only now it has no end. You do not remember the difference between what happened and what did not happen. You do not remember where I became you and was always. Nameless, mapless.

Inside the dark, I turn and wait and press at my eyes and feel inside me the blind in all our minds there held forever as each remembers each, all so smeared into the present what is created could no longer have an end or a beginning.

Let there be light, I say, and nothing changes.

I sat up in another dark again and I was wired. I could see through this dark as if it were daytime. There were mirrored walls on the horizon reflecting miles of more mirrors on beyond all definition. The mirrors were absorbing all the air around me, taking the air there and pulling it down into their flesh. There were no edges to the world here, though in that freedom it was unnecessary to even think. Every pixel of me was so filled with everything already. It didn't matter if I felt content or false, dead or alive, loved or alone. Each instant stretched so long it no longer had a surface. It was so loud I couldn't do anything. It made me calm. I lay back in the light and closed my eyes. Behind my eyes my eyes were open, flooding, throbbing, without face.

I close my eyes and open my eyes and I am Flood. I mean I am me again, as I had been, though my experience of myself occurs now once removed, as if I'm watching me perform me.

I am surprised to not feel any relief in reappearing in the world. Inside what would be my skull the meat of the head's periphery seems to stretch further back and in the more the eye is crimped to peer against it, looking back into the space the self makes as if there in the wake of it might form some window or apparatus by which the self inside the space may retain form. There are no arms there, no torso beneath the space of head from which where I peer down, though the taste in the mouth of the head is something blown apart and silent.

I don't think about Flood's life. I don't need to. It is mine. Above, the sky has turned entirely opaque, shutting out the ream of color holding beyond us anywhere the night might stretch forever. The sheen of the lip of it remains reflective; each glint shows the earth back at itself. There is no moon or starlight in the dead resonance, but the pulp of day remains visible beneath, the glow of sun sucked into the ground radiating through all coils, the heat hungry for more meat to disintegrate on stage, more skins unpeeled against the faces, torsos, limbs to expose the meat from and let simmer, desist, until underneath that too, the private lattices of bone and thrall, which as well has rubbed and split and uncompressed to ash and silt and blown away, sucked into wherever, sexless, lipless, nowhere.

Among the vast terrain remains what junk. The haunted veins of buildings stand up uneroded, their matched glass eyes seeing the seer where the glint of the contained light does not obstruct the vision head on into the building, through which the hallways cross and come to doors, catacombs of air locked in unto itself beyond all disintegrated organs. There are the statues and the lamps, the birdhouses and gravestones and quilts and gravel stacked as high as what the air was. The lists of what remains remain unmade. Wires hang taut in arteries to where buildings had been indexed on the mud, beaming nothing back and forth between the husks where in the absence of larger motion hive cells have begun to cluster up over long fields absorbing the leavings of our people into its chest, now spun defunct and clogging nothing.

I feel Flood's body's organs flay and tangle. Its blood is screaming for itself. I raise Flood's right arm where it would have been and have him touch his face and where I want to feel the finger between my eyes there nudging at the space where flesh had held him caged, the texture of my vision warps white around the presence, any color turned to gyres. His shape is no longer contained in him alone, but made as if with coordinates that change as the lens shifts to change the framing: every instance of him rendered long and wide and senseless. Wish-less, and so full of every wish. Cold folds like little hills of newer land where we could walk and tell our daze and have a fall. On the land is so much room there, space that opens up around us more the harder that I make him press, miles of it contained in him at any instant, requiring only to be forced up into birth by feel. This could be true of any vision, I remember, in any being.

Why was I me. What have I done. What fields of rooms of people have gone on hidden in them, the blipping lights, so many breadths in any inch. There could never be a reason.

Where I have no organs I am eggs. Or I am in awe. Along the perimeters of holes: not the hole itself but not not the hole there either. What am I feeding.

Beyond day. Smoke flows from where the light was, like old locks. An oceanic box of blue more soft than sky and neater, nearer. It could be any blue, I know, set to pupils or dog collars or the whole tone of a life. A fragment of an instance in a version where even I am not a she or he or me but floors, or money, or a thing like color, here kissed from lips to lips like blood that hadn't pooled, knives of the hours between all desire left unlisted from the trees allowed inside the evening to deform, to crawl over the highways or the plots before the plot of any text turned all yards into the way of graves. All our worlds up before us, mulched and sharper than any tool used to cut the dinner down, the blood in colors like a person aging in an instant from the sperm back to the sac, microphones in any mind catching the sound of all that living in a width quicker than every square of every square dividing.

I close my eyes and see the blood alone. In the blood the rooms are there too, through all the houses held there to connect. I walk into the blood and feel the film of it surround me. I feel the film fold down against the white. Within the white I close my eyes too and find another film held within it, in which again my eyes are open wide, where then again I then close them, and there again there is the white. And now I cannot remember who I've been talking to this whole time.

I can no longer remember where I am. Each room around me as I went seemed to hold voices on the far side of the chamber, a human sound of moaning that lighted through with the idea there would be someone left still in this shape, but I could find no end point to the walls. Each new room along the chain of rooms there seeming to partition off another impossible place, a language always on the far side of where I was.

No matter how long it went on, I loved this house. I loved the screaming and the beats between the screaming. I loved the grain of the wood of the floor beneath me like never-ending skin I might have meant to wear myself. At each inch of the wall I touched I felt someone on the far side touching back, and though they would not answer me, I loved their future. As I moved away, they moved away.

Sometimes I would find windows in the walls through which I could see out into the sky. Its face was full with smoke or milk in big blown sac clouds in packets bumping up against each other desperate for rain, and beyond that, a kind of wall there dark as my closed eyes had been when I could close them, only now all above us, waiting to burst.

I remember the red curtains in our bedroom. I remember the bookshelf set into the wall. I remember how hard it was to button the neck on my work shirt. I remember waking up before the alarm. I remember the cursor blinking. I remember sensing I was being watched. I remember the blue key that started my first car and where I wrecked the car and how my posture never seemed the same again. I remember trying to teach myself to paint landscapes. I remember swallowing the first tooth I lost. I remember making eye contact with passing people and knowing I'd never be this near to them again. I remember the frozen food aisle at night alone. I remember never being able to remember certain names no matter how many times they were repeated. I remember a recurring dream of a large white church without doors. I remember wanting to remember things I'd dreamt and repeating them in my mind until I forgot. I remember lighting candles just to have them blown out. I remember cold glass on warm days. I remember the brightness of a bulb turned on near the bed in darkness. I remember believing I'd die drowning. I remember feeling guilty having never donated blood. I remember the click of the handle when the gas completed pumping. I remember changing my opinion of a color. I remember waiting to be told I was free to go. I remember biting into fruit that'd turned brown on the inside. I remember the color of the grass of our front lawn weeks after it caught fire. I remember looking into my eyes shaving my face. I remember checking to see if my wife had returned home. I remember the long dark hair on my forearm that grew back no matter how many times I plucked it. I remember the way snow looked landing on a sweater. I remember wishing I could remove one of my arms to sleep better on my side. I remember feeling discomfort and trying to remember to feel gratitude for the absence of that discomfort after it subsided. I remember imagining there was a secret room inside my grandparents' basement. I remember laughing at the unfunny jokes of strangers. I remember waking myself up laughing. I remember wiping the dust off the screen of the TV with my palm. I remember lying in rented beds and imagining who had been in them before me. I remember the stretch of the skin around my smile. I remember knowing what I should say to someone and never saying it. I remember playing the same song over and over until I no longer needed to play the song to hear it. I remember watching my father talk to men of business. I remember wondering what lava felt like. I remember saying goodbye several times before I left. I remember being asked for directions and not knowing and still giving the directions. I remember taking the strings off a guitar and saving them. I remember writing down what I hoped would happen one day. I remember believing I already knew what would happen. I remember checking to see the door was locked. I remember trying to understand what it would be like to hear other people's prayers. I remember keys I couldn't remember what they went to. I remember not being able to remember the password. I remember trying on new clothes that didn't fit. I remember not wanting to close my eyes yet. I remember waiting for the rain to pass. I remember a voice I recognized muffled through walls late and in darkness. I remember the water at my knees then at my waist then at my neck. I remember knots in the hair that held the comb from combing. I remember a light shined down my throat. I remember selecting one ring from many rings available for purchase. I remember peeling. I remember the different kinds of blue a bruise could be. I remember searching for the sentence I loved in the book I loved. I remember breathing into my hands to make them warm. I remember being unable to lift myself and finding another person there to lift me. I remember feeling like the day would never come. I remember knowing I wouldn't know when I no longer remember what I remembered. I remember not liking how I looked for years. I remember metal in my mouth. I remember the wind against my face. I remember empty cages and colored wires. I remember diving. I remember opening the blinds at night. I remember believing I'd been going where I meant to go. I remember saying my name until it no longer felt like anything. I remember fearing what I'd said aloud would become true. I remember the scabs on my fingers. I remember gold robes. I remember holding someone's hands in mine. I remember being scanned for parasites. I remember panes of glass. I remember cutting the words out of the paper without purpose. I remember standing in line for something I didn't want. I remember the fear of my teeth being removed. I remember my tongue against my teeth. I remember pressing pause and it not pausing. I remember how the surface would get so hot. I remember the room we weren't supposed to go in and therefore wished to more than ever. I remember spreading out in green. I remember the eclipse and what it meant to me. I remember the bathwater. I remember no moon. I remember believing bodies were hollow on the inside. I remember counting days down to one day. I remember chords I had not played. I remember seeing myself in a crowd across a large room. I remember stairwells that never seemed to end. I remember the skin of horses. I remember patterns. I remember whole rooms full of flowers. I remember games we played pretending we were wolves. I remember where the mountain disappeared. I remember trying not to wake the baby. I remember sand in the bed we never planned to leave. I remember drawing a picture of my face that resembled no one I knew. I remember the dials on our oven. I remember my mother's pins. I remember asking someone else to choose. I remember leaving the lens cap on the camera. I remember chisels. I remember rooms that seemed a different size each time. I remember the darkness in the container. I remember wiping the grease off the meat. I remember the blood on my shirt in the sunlight. I remember spinning and stopping. I remember endless alternate endings. I remember inhaling between lines sung in the song. I remember asking someone to come nearer.

I come into the house and there is snow. Beyond the house it's snowing, too. The snow is cinder and skin. It rains forever and has rained forever.

I close my eyes and open my eyes and the man I was once is there before me, not anyone I know by name but someone crushed between the sum. His body is made of all the bodies having been consumed into a single flesh. He is translucent. He stands craned with his arms above his head and eyes wide open, so much skin he has no features. The mass of his body is wet with blood pouring through his openings.

The blood runs off of his body into the ground, caking layers that lick beneath my feet and hide the world. I realize I am bleeding too, gore from each pore of me erupting off to match the other man. I see my arms are raised like his; our skins are knitting, while beneath them congregate the rub of days I can't remember living.

The world breathes with us. And the days. The screws and bolts turn in their sleeves. Blood pours in from the window and the sockets. It pours in from the speakers in the walls also, through any gap it can imagine.

Today above us all the stars are bleeding, and the sun's face, and the planets. Birds raining blood and the idea of god. And the corridors removed of destination. The age of the earth gathers packed in and still pouring hot and on inside itself all at once and never-ending.

I close my eyes and at the same time feel the eyes of all the bodies around me open and behind the skin there is no lens.

I fear I am not ending or beginning, but that I am.

I remember believing you could remember things about the days that surrounded your whole life and became carried in the place where you were meant to live forever in you.

I remember how the teeth fell from my mouth. They were beaten from me, or I lost them growing older. What's the difference. I remember how where the teeth fell out more teeth came in behind them. And behind those teeth, more blood, and behind that, any memory.

I remember remembering I folded up a forest and I ate it. I'd chewed the dirt out from between the roots and felt it grow out in the long locks of my hair.

I come into the house and who is there. I ask the question and the sound goes bang along the back side of my face and ricochets inside me and redoubles and makes splitting, the words raining back through me down in mirror-sound, beating out my shape from the inside. Each time I ask again I've become older and the words have gone slipped in what they mean, no world of what they were remaining.

I remember a watch I found burnt in some dirt that had no hands. I carried the watch thereafter faceup in my palm, never releasing or relaxing, never using the little strap. The leather of the watch's band was so bright in direct sun you could hardly stand to look anywhere else, even to read the time.

I remember there are more things I cannot remember than things I can remember, though I can't remember any of those now, or what about me makes me think that what I've just said now is true or ever could be.

I come into the house and it is full of every instrument, the guitars and the pianos, cymbals, amps; all the chords and their strings unstrung at one end from their tuning pegs and tied to something at the center of my mind, underneath which awaits something I have never seen and will never see.

I know I can't remember how inside this house to get from room to room; or I can't remember where the next room is, even seeing me go there ahead of me before I get into it; or I can't remember what the room is for, why there are walls between this room and this last one as the condition is the same; or I don't want to move; or I am already there before I'm there even ahead of me already in my bloated body; or I have never moved at all, at any point in all the time I felt me moving.

I can't remember I do not remember typing that last sentence and then deleting it from there and then retyping it again without the memory of having typed it or realizing ever before that all of this was going on. I can't remember how I fear this may be the case with everything I've ever said here, and what of it.

I'm saying this so it can be erased.

I remember corridors and chambers, buried in my finger.

I remember every ever eaten bite of food, how it spanned the cells between the cells, the space of light slowly made gathered, the eyes of the man or woman who placed the food before me on the table. I remember the voracity with which I took it all down against my teeth and holes to make more of me as if in the world forever I had been the only one.

I can't remember how I would wake up with so much in my mouth I was no longer breathing and there was no longer any way to speak or write, though I still am, and how is that. I can't remember to take what I just said seriously and erase everything, burn the buttons, accept fate.

I remember wallowing in bodies, sucking their fingers, humping their knees, starved as hell for death and never dying, even in dying. And then, now.

I remember the way a hand might come against me and I'd shudder and then feel happy to have been touched and feel myself more in being touched and turn around to try to face the touching person and find nothing there but night.

I remember you there, then I don't.

I can't remember sound.

I can't remember where on the silent light we floated, language leaking back and forth between the countless holes where we had leaked out our innards. The meat of the earth stuck to my lids and to yours and wished me open and you open and soon we were wide as we had ever been.

I remember the remaining span of days on earth of those beyond the length of fabric where the reverberation of the holes sung forth, passed for those who wished to see it as a lifetime as all of time forever, while in us it passed as now, all instants and instances passing through a single focus, spreading out in each span with their own whorl.

I remember you as pixels in the mask I wear to stand before the mirror and see beyond the shape of us.

I do not remember what a face is or a hand is or how to not believe in anything.

I remember a box inside a room. Both the room and the box could have held anything, before or after. It was a black box with a black lid. There were no tapes. I stood there above the box and thought about the shape of the box and the frame of the box and its space inside it held. I thought about the cells of the box and the cells inside the box and the burning in my hands. I thought about the walls around the box and the walls around me. The box just sat there. I watched the box sit. I watched the box until there was nothing left that I had not imagined had been inside the box forever, every inch and every hour, and then I went on watching. I watched the box until the night arrived and the box was still there and nothing about the box had changed and then I left the room and locked the door behind. The box did nothing to stop me. I walked along the hall and went downstairs and the house was just the same. I found my mother at the kitchen table writing a letter she would never mail. Her hair was white and she was thin. She had lived a whole life since I saw her last. I sat down at the table with my mother and we spoke. Whatever the words were that went between us made the air there in the house feel clean and calm, and ours. I can't remember what else then happened. I never thought about the box again.

I remember each room is the room where you are born, the room where you are killed, the room where you make skin and speak in someone else's code. As no one knows when they are dead, it doesn't matter. They are carried and carried on in vast precision in the image of what had been, each world both old and made eternal, under a sky that needed nothing beyond itself.

I can't remember how no book was a book. How no one had lived and none had passed. No flesh was a body. Whatever was said was said by all people or was not said and the word was just the word and I had needed you so long.

I remember how I tried to copy my own wish inside your head and then could hear it continually thereafter shaking where it didn't fit, no matter how I turned your head and pushed you oblong through a place like home or under sleep into grand halls and fields of light. How in my own body still I can feel you also in my image always and forever.

I can't remember how you are the only person who can read this.

I come into the house draped in all gowns.

I come into the house and find no house here.

I come into the house and it's a sea. The level of the water rises with my presence in the volume, spreading quick to lap along the drywall, and behind each wall another wall in its same image.

I remember how we'd drowned. What had come from water must return to water. The house from inside larger than the earth itself, the water sagging up and overrunning, up to my chest already, creamed with pearling cream and pattered ash. It slaps against me in even repetition, one long fat strobe that hits me squarely in the breasts, though I can't remember I have breasts. The water wants my milk. It sucks my glands, though I am sand there, the nipples sore from being had by someone I can't remember in the silent purr of ageless language up my arms and down my back, curtains spurting layered in all air I can't remember.

I remember the water did not exist.

I remember how I grew; how I had been the child and then grown through my own life into the man who finally killed every other living person and consumed them; how then that person disappeared; though as I try to tell you now again I can't remember which or how I knew to tell you.

I am in the home and in the home. I turn inside the mass of heavy nothing to look and wade back into the stretch I'd just come through, though as I turn I see the house is not the house there but every human liquid: blood, eggs, semen, saliva, sweat. The wet goes on in every way, white and shining, depth erupting warm and clean and fast into wherever I cannot, depths deeper than there need to be as I will never know them.

I remember my mother wiping my face with a cold washcloth on the morning I learned I would not remember dying.

I remember waking up three hundred million times. How I had been some mornings as a blind woman, as an actor, as a masseuse, though even in the knowing of this knowing I can't return to any of them, as if my idea of even this is another old disease where I must come to and rub and mutter, be again speaking words that mean nothing to anyone, an image waiting to live the remainder of his or my life out tick by tick unfunny, recorded over.

I remember what it felt like to feel my body fill with fire. Or with nostalgia.

I can't remember why I'm soft.

I remember the strange feeling of wandering through the dark with arms extended, looking for a wall, or someone's arm, another me there anywhere.

I come into the house and everyone is still alive. They are all there, all our people. They wear the frame of face and dress they'd felt the most themselves as, at whatever age. They have children and are children. It is a celebration. There are candles and white balloons. There is a cake white as my mind, shaped like a cone. The eyes all watch me enter without recognition. They blink and smile all gapless and no words, while beneath the skins awaits an expectation of coming song, though there is no breath left to lift.

I can't remember how in every instant I was the lips of any person; I was the color of all birth, the canals the bodies had been sent through from blood into a common light; I was the hair that had not grown; I was the hair that had been shorn from the heads of the living and the dead and laid upon the ground to hide it through crucial minutes in which the eye inside that ground must rise for air; no one else was coming; this was our iteration; a wider milk rose in the seas; from even feet away no one could see this; the tables carved initials in themselves; I was the shoulder blades and the manes of ice over the homes' roofs and the ring fingers; I was the ring around each hope; each body I became I had been always and inside it there it felt the same, a mutual darkness lay awaiting when the skin rolled down over our eyes, the days beginning as they ended, waking mirrors all around the beds; the mirrors then must be walked into; I was the organ of the totality of glass; every inch of what we'd eaten; ornaments held on the shelves in rooms where no one moved; bulbs left on to burn out, dreaming wire; I was the words following our last words on the lungs; I was the trachea and pelvis; I was the grinding of the teeth.

I can't remember how I felt myself falling in around us, pinched in the patient way of every instant's instant seize as it passed in and on around all bodies to hold its shape forever as it had been and all remembered in the eye of what would grow, which was nothing, which did not stop it; the color blazing; where in the face of all this you could not remember anything about me besides how there was nothing left where I was not. I was the lip of the land where all we'd called ours went under water to stay hidden from the eye of god in fear of no longer having organs, each zilch becoming collapsed in proper sequence, its absence raised like humans packed in bleachers doing the wave; I was the larger wave our blood had begged to form at our whole ending as among the days in counting lost we sloshed, to rise and crest and crash and kiss against the idea of a home inside no home, to be holy, to go on.

I remember a silver necklace that when I put it on, the room went upside down and inside out, and I was sitting where you are sitting, awaiting anyone but me.

I remember the dream of living skin filling all possible space, all edges of all worlds, the dream replacing all other memory, without end.

I can't remember that I remember nothing.

I come into the room and find the child. The child has no arms or legs or face or chest or hair or teeth or eyes. The child is lying on the bed, on the floor inside the house devoid of mirrors, as all the glass of them has lurched, become rooms there beyond the pane where before the house had ended.

I can no longer tell the difference between what the child remembers and what I remember, how we'd ever been apart. His presence burns me where I no longer have a body beyond the many millions no longer living, the hordes within them each.

I take the child and lift him to me. I cup the head inside my palm and speak: *You will believe we are alive and well, for real, together, and everyone has found their love, that nothing could end our lives but life itself, no matter how it feels. No word ever of death again as yet but all this light and all this color in the ground and spots worn on our faces and the hours crushed with sleep with eyes closed on beds beside bodies recounting nothing of the mirrors underneath our skulls which when removed replace themselves with new skulls; and so here I am again and will be again all crushed forever.*

The child says nothing. Its mouth is open, toothless.

I hold the child and was the child. I have the child inside me and I'm inside it. I sleep without sleeping and do not grow older and some time later I wake and rise. I stand in a cold darkness on the edge of somewhere else, seeing no mirror, beyond sun.

I remember standing with my eyes closed at a thin, warm window in the beginning.

I come into the house and the house is all one room.

There is a door in the room but the door is locked.

The walls are white.

On the far wall is a mirror. It is the same mirror I remember my wife brought into our marriage, inherited from her mother, which had hung on the wall across from our shared bed all our nights.

The mirror has no frame. Where the edges of the reflection end, the walls begin.

I close my eyes and touch the mirror.

The door inside the mirror is not locked.

The door leads out into the front yard where I find the sun is out and sky is pale. The trees are reaching out with arms I never knew. The house is whatever color I remember it having, which is no color.

There are no dead behind my eyes. No bells or hymns for the dead along the heavens.

The ground is soft. Or what seems like the ground is soft. Or what beneath it. Or all of what I am. And I am laughing. And what is laughter.

The light seems to close in and on down, blurred with its luster.

It is a quiet day.

I do not remember walking from the light.

I do not remember the shape of the world around me falling out around me and the warm grade of where I had fallen there into the wake of what I'd been as someone wider in a space beyond destroyed. There was some glass then there was something not glass then there became a different kind of texture altogether.

I do not feel where the wreck of what had been absorbed clings around whoever had been quaking, forming the aging of our skin: the cut of it collecting in one stride to sing a surface, and the paper, and the dust. Where no fire laps, the field turns over, and turns over, and there it is.

It is, regardless of what remains here or does not remain here. Something yearns, the way the mass of my body grows gold with old nameless layers. The space clocked between the lost organism of all our years in its own absence becomes more firm, and firming fast again against itself again and through itself again, squashing the pockets held in shelves among their collision. The air condensing what it is with what it has been and where it hopes to be again and who will let it.

Who is who to remember anything about any of us; each instant clicking in its own mind with each around it in no word; the body of anybody and all regardless glowing obese with old intention, with the want the words could not hold down, what desire could not beat the sense out of so eyes could see it in our houses, and so grew on babbling up in packets like a flagellum in all our fantasies combined. The gift of births born burst and eaten up wedged into cement or buried wide open on some paper, or vibrated brief through singing sacs; tapes untaped and white residing in the action slaughtered in a wake of all the music slaved by music.

Endlessly blood funnels through the years all nonexistent. I remember not to bear in mind the slurring rooms where we had been in crush; where the years were not here in the world; where I could see ahead a growing light wanting some little inch to rise upon; where I hear me let me know inside me where I was before I showed up here; and so I am late for my own presence, caught where my hair comes growing where the glass inside the house around the maze of making turns against what would have been my wishes; until at last I came aware inside me in my skin of an indention in the ageless perforation, some presence not a wall or air but nothing. I feel with my fingers there cursor shaped up like I am, of no era, ending any other instance all instantaneous, hitting hot and turning hard and strumming shut against my pretend sternum thick as what a dog is where he learns commands. Strobes of wakeless sound in which he learns to love the owner, needing no reason.

Inside the sound I am confounded in the history of any gesture. Against the silence of the graph of evening I knock hard with both hands this time against the absence of us again, where when I feel it touch against the space of any of me in the instant I feel my formation wanting bursting through the instant, my lengths inside me needing permission to separate from the memory of our bones deflecting light.

In you I know I knew I needed, I remember, though I cannot remember who I mean by you or I. I know I knew I needed the wash of sound to color through my gut, needed the blood of all our damage flooding from endpoints of my fingers and the cells around my head, where each time I blinked or asked to quit the hour my skin awoke and burned me so thick I could not stand, though I could float, and the pain made me come so hard I sprayed my face and could no longer remember who I was or what pleasure had brought me here again.

Here when I press my head against the voice here there comes the sound of my skin becoming ripped apart, the chime of convalescing mechanisms rubbing their frames against the land and when I pull back my mind at long last from its own intrusion, I found I had lived out in one instant every life. I found along my arms my hands were open, and on my palms vast sores all healed full over, and our blood had fit all back into me, and I knew at last which way was ours; and so inside the house I rose and walked again, and went unto the want again and forgot the voiceless voice there like I had all else. I went on through what I'd wished and wanted until the beginning of this same impression came again, finding again inside the shrieking prisms of night no one to sleep and wake with, and no one to poke or fist a hole though, slick in my skin to let the mass out again when I was full of all this air.

Then just as quickly this again was over. No idea at all about forever in this instance of us but the house made of more floor and floor made to begin again at every measure. What had just happened had just happened and was not yet set for happening the next, though I knew it would or knew it would not and knew I would not remember either way, and so could never at all tell, and either way was gone as ever and as always.

When where what now I am again. So sized there is no sun and not a longing. No lap of tongue where blubber fills the space of action named unmade, the pillow of a rind around a fissure. Each instant clapped as old fat gathered through its mirror-instants strung with our skinned knees and all our teeth, the space burnt out alive inside its last remaining color, pulled through its own center like a dot. All through the abused membranes of finite years in popping intersections of transitory ornaments, beyond soil or water, blood or bone. Each inch where we had unwound at last locking full into whatever could not be. Each syllable and pixel past repeating where it wore against us on every tongue as bright as light beyond mirage, over the whole blank of whose conception, breadth filling up what it could not.

I remember that the light here is and was the only thing not missing. It is and was an old glow, opened and curving without core, alive there where it is and only there. Above me and above you, prismatic rooms where absent bodies lay and lavished prostrate upon the whitened tables of countless sheeted altars hardened with the sweat of uttered worlds turned back and in against themselves, absent of age. Death hid and hidden in the shape and strobed so deep enough it could not etch the lungs of any recollection, and yet still must and never would, could not but never become gathered in the make along our flat gyrating ancient fate. We in laughing dens where any of us all lay chained and fat as old kids, awaiting freedom, no, not that word; awaiting a simple lick of trance to swim in with the smoke shattered from our eye, the single singing glassy eye of eyes so small and so surrounded by more film than sight could hold together in any all, throughout the exploded light of our conception, where the end is what we are.

ABOUT THE AUTHOR

Noel Butler

Blake Butler is the author of five books of fiction, including *There Is No Year* and *Scorch Atlas*; a work of hybrid nonfiction, *Nothing: A Portrait of Insomnia*; and two collaborative works, *Anatomy Courses* with Sean Kilpatrick and *One* with Vanessa Place and Christopher Higgs. He is the founding editor of *HTMLGIANT*, "the Internet literature magazine blog of the future," and maintains a weekly column covering literary art and fast food for *Vice* magazine. His other work has appeared widely, including in *The Believer*, the *New York Times*, *Fence*, *Dazed and Confused*, and *The Best Bizarro Fiction of the Decade*. He lives in Atlanta.